chef

LYNDA THROSBY

DEDICATION

This one is for my Mum and Dad.
Love you to bits.
Thank you for always supporting and believing in me.

chef

Macen

I'M SITTING, LOOKING AT THE cell in my hand. I can't believe the call I just received from NYCS —the New York Culinary School — regarding a job opportunity. It's always been my dream to work in one of the top restaurants in New York City, and I think from the conversation I just had, my aspiration could be about to become a reality. However, first, I have to go tomorrow and meet Caspian Kade for an informal interview. I did four weeks of work experience at Casper's, his Michelin star restaurant, during the first year of my course.

He won't remember me, of that I'm sure, he hardly said a word to me when I was there, and, in my opinion, he was right up his own ass. Very cocky and arrogant when he did speak to me, which like I say, wasn't much — I got the feeling he didn't like me much. The fact that he looked like a God, with his brooding dark looks, made it even harder for me, and I used to blush every time he said something or even looked at me. I only really had to deal with the sous chef, Francois Hutterall. He was such a nice guy. I wonder if he still works there?

But, this could be it finally: my chance. My first step.

I've wanted to be a chef for so long. I'd bake with Grandma all the time. She made the best cookies, muffins, and cakes. I learned a lot from her. Then I used to help Mama cook meals. She was sick and needed help, and she wanted me to be independent and to be able to cook and clean.

It was just the two of us at home — my poppa left when I was a few months old, and I was only eight when she started to teach me. I loved it because we did it together. She would show me how to do a roast dinner, pot roasts, casserole dishes, mac & cheese, meatloaf, and all kinds of pasta. By the time I was eleven, I could cook almost anything, bake the best brownies and muffins, and do the laundry and clean the house.

My Mama got really sick.

She couldn't breathe properly, but she still insisted on smoking. She smoked a lot. My clothes always smelt of nicotine. She got so bad that she was coughing up blood. She never told me what was wrong with her. I loved my Mama, and I got sadder, the sicker she got. My grandma spent a lot of time at our house when Mama was in bed for a few days. She was so out of breath some days she couldn't even get up. She ended up having oxygen to help her breath. When I was twelve, she died. I found out from Grandma she had Chronic Obstructive Pulmonary Disease, COPD: a disease of the lungs. I was there when she took her last breath, and she whispered to me to look after myself, be good, and go to school to learn, but most of all, to do what I wanted to do in my life, and always be happy. She stroked my cheek and told me she loved me. Then she died as I sat crying, telling her I loved her so much. It broke my heart, and it's something I will never forget.

Grandma moved out of her small one-bedroom apartment into my house to look after me. She was all the family I had left.

I never knew my poppa, although he sent Mama money every month.

Mama told me they were never in love, not really. They were young and fooled around, and she got pregnant with me, and his parents made him stop seeing my Mama. He didn't fight them. I think they were rich, important people, but she never told me who he was. With Mama gone, I could find out, but I didn't want to. Not yet anyway.

I'd missed a lot of school because I cared for Mama a lot towards the end, so Grandma made sure I started to go regularly. I promised Mama I would go and behave and get a good job.

I started to have extra lessons. I found I was a quick learner and it didn't take me long to catch up and become top of my class. I excelled in academic studies, and as I got to fourteen, I enrolled in cooking school to be a chef. I excelled there too, always finishing top of my class.

My grandma was so proud of me, and she said Mama would have been too. At sixteen, I had the opportunity to go to culinary school, but it was in New York City. That meant leaving Grandma alone because we lived in Atlanta, in a small town called Senoia, so moving to NYC was going to be a drastic change. Grandma was worried because I was so young, and NYC was a huge and overpopulated place. I didn't want to leave Grandma, but she told me it was the best thing for me to do if I wanted to follow the career path I was taking. The school secured me a bedroom in a shared house with other students. At sixteen, I would be the youngest student in the school.

I CAN'T WAIT to phone Grandma and tell her about my interview. She's going to be so pleased for me.

chapter 2

Caspian

I'M THE OWNER AND HEAD chef at the world-famous Michelin star restaurant, Casper's in New York City, and I'm in the process of opening one in LA, with London and Paris to follow. I'm twenty-nine, and one of the youngest Michelin star chefs in the world with 3 stars — the highest awarded by Michelin, and I'm proud of it.

My New York restaurant is running like clockwork, and we are booked solid every night for the next six months. I have an amazing team behind me, but my current commis chef is leaving us soon. He's just got a new job as the station chef at a new restaurant opening in Washington. That's the next step up his career ladder, but it leaves me up shit creek.

I could do without this right now. I have too much other shit going on. The LA restaurant is opening in four months, so I need to find a new reliable commis chef. I usually get my staff from recommendations or the New York Culinary School. That school is the best in the US. It's where I trained and was one of the youngest to get full honors on my course. One good thing about the school is they not only teach you everything from knife skills and food prep to nutritional information, but they put you into top restaurants to learn skills from real life chefs. That's what we do here. Each year, I take on two students for four weeks, and I teach them what I can in that time about the kitchen. I make them start right at the bottom, as dishwashers and gofers, progressing upwards to letting them be sous chef and station managers for a day.

I remembered a few years back that I had a girl in for the four weeks of training. She was amazing. She reminded me of myself. She was enthusiastic and eager to learn anything. I was told she was the best the school had ever had, which put my nose out a bit. She was only four years younger than me, and she was stunning, I mean stiffy-causing stunning. She used to blush when I spoke to her, which did all kinds of things to me, including making me rock hard.

I had to let Francois take control during those weeks and teach her most of the goings-on in the kitchen because I found it difficult being around her too long. I wanted to teach her more than what went on in the kitchen if you know what I mean. But I always keep it professional where the kitchen is concerned only she stuck in my mind, as she was so talented. I contacted the school to see if they could get in touch with her and ask her to come in to see me. It was a long shot as I was sure she would have been snapped up by now being that good.

The NYCS knew exactly who I was talking about, and they contacted her and arranged for her to come and see me tomorrow for an informal interview. I already knew she was good at what she did, and Mrs. Webster from NYCS confirmed it, so the interview is just a formality. I have no doubts that I will hire her if she's available. I only want the best.

Mrs. Webster has just phoned me back to let me know that Ms. Macen Donald would be here to see me at 10.00 a.m. She told me I had the best student that she had ever seen and that included me. Well, that's saying something and being as competitive as I am, it had my hackles up a bit. Maybe this wasn't such a good idea after all.

There are two things going against her before she even steps foot in the door. One: she is beautiful, and I can't imagine she has changed too much in the last couple of years, at least I hope not, and number two: she's being described as better than me. However, I desperately need a great commis chef.

I'm supposed to be on a close tonight, but now I want to finish early and get ready for tomorrow and by that, I mean I need to call one of the many women that I have on speed dial for a quick fuck. I have a few that are no-nonsense, no frills — just sex — that I can count on. I'm sure some hang around hoping I will have a relationship with them, but that's not me. My business comes first. I don't do the whole relationship bullshit — why would I? I can have almost anyone I choose. Yes, I'm that arrogant, but I know who I am, and in the culinary world, I'm at the top: a God, a star, an A-lister.

Last year, I had my own slot on Good Morning America. Every Monday and Thursday I demonstrated a different meal, and it made me even more popular and now, my restaurant is booked six months in advance. I'm in talks at the moment to have my own TV show, which will air sometime early next year when my LA, London, and Paris restaurants are up and running smoothly. But first I need to get me a new commis chef to make sure Casper's runs like the well-oiled machine it is today. I will not have any glitches or chinks in my armor. We will remain the top restaurant in New York City, of that I have no doubts.

Macen

I GET DIXON, MY FIVE-YEAR-OLD, to bed as soon as I can, then I can concentrate on getting his things ready for the sitter tomorrow before I get my stuff sorted. I will not be late for my interview. I'm smelly from working at the diner, so I take a long soak in the bath.

Since finishing NYCS three months ago, I took a waitressing position, working five hours a day while Dixon's was at Kindergarten.

Tomorrow, I will need Becky to take him for me, so that I can get ready and get to my informal interview on time. I phoned the diner to let them know I wouldn't be in work, which they weren't pleased about, but this is far more important. This is the opportunity I've been holding out for since finishing NYCS. I could have taken jobs in restaurants, just not the ones I wanted to work in.

I know working in a top restaurant will be long hours, and I will need someone to help look after Dixon with me, which will then take most of my earnings, but it will be worth it to get my foot on the career ladder. I want to own my own restaurant someday, just like Mr. Kade. I really look up to him and admire what he's achieved at such a young age. I know he didn't have a five-year-old to bring up, but I will make this work, no matter what it takes, as long as Dixon is not suffering or missing out in any way because he is, and will always be, my priority.

Do I tell Mr. Kade I have a son, or should I wait to see if I get the job first? I'm worried if I tell him, he might think that I won't put 110% into my work, but he would be wrong. I can still bring Dixon up and be committed to my job. I will just have to prove it.

All I can do if I get the job is to try and juggle my work life with my home life and see how it goes. If I think it's affecting Dixon too much, then I will have to reassess.

I'm thinking of asking Grandma to come out and stay with us for a while if I get the job, just while I find my feet. I'm sure she would love to come and help out. I know she misses us both like crazy. We talk to her every night and Dixon keeps asking when she's coming to see us. If Grandma agrees, that helps me financially as well.

I phone Grandma to sound her out and tell her about the interview, and she's really excited for me. "Oh, Macen, love, this could be the break you need, the opportunities are endless if you get this job. I'm so proud of you."

I laugh at her. "Grandma, I haven't gotten the job yet. It's just an interview."

"I have no doubt you will get the job, love. No doubt at all."

I take a deep breath. "Grandma, if I do get the job, do you think you could come to New York and stay with us for a little while? Just until I get myself into a routine and make sure Dixon isn't affected by the job." I hold my breath.

"Macen, of course I will, you have no worries there. I miss you both so much, and I miss out on so much of Dixon's growing up. How is my little boy?"

I tell her he got star pupil of the day today and has made another new friend at Kindergarten, but he misses her. We finish talking, and it makes me happy to hear her voice but sad when we say goodbye. She said she would come for a month or two and then decide what to do after that. She's a country girl, not a city girl, which is one of the reasons she didn't come to New York with us in the first place. I love Grandma, and she has helped me so much since Mama died. If it weren't for her, I dread to think where I would be in my life right now. She has supported me right from the get-go, and when I moved back and had Dixon, she was there for me. She was in my corner throughout the ordeal I endured.

Moving into the shared house at sixteen was daunting for me. All the other students were older, all eighteen plus, and they all got on well and hung out together. I was kind of a loner. I talked when one of them talked to me, but I never struck up a conversation. I mostly kept myself to myself. If I wasn't in my room studying or making up new recipes, I was in one of the kitchens cooking and trying things out. Most of the time, I let one of the other housemates eat my offerings, which was good because I got opinions on my cooking from them.

The house was big, with six bedrooms, a communal room with a TV, and three kitchens, because it was owned by the NYCS for the purpose of helping us cook at home as well as in the classrooms. There were four males and two females, including me: Mark, Julian, Sefton, Toby, and Lesley. Lesley was a flirt, and I'm sure she had slept with all four of the boys. I could walk past the communal room, and she would be with a different one each time.

My room was right at the top of the house towards the back. It was quite secluded from the rest of the house. There were four floors in all, with two kitchens on the ground floor next to the communal room, one kitchen on the first floor with two bedrooms, three bedrooms on the second floor and then the one at the top of the house on the 3rd floor, which was mine. It was a converted attic, but I didn't mind, as I got my own bathroom. I think the school put me up there because I was so young.

My housemates hosted a lot of parties, but I didn't bother going to most of them. I just stayed in my room. The first year was the worst. So many couples would wander up to my room expecting it to be empty so they could have sex. I asked the school to replace the broken lock on my door, but it was taking forever. I ended up making a paper notice and sticking it on the door whenever they had a party, saying: room occupied.

As the course progressed, I became more confident with the others in the house. We were all doing the same course, which helped, and the second year wasn't too bad. Most of the partygoers knew my room was out of bounds, and I did wander down to one or two of the parties. It was full of students, mostly making out, loud music and consequently, loud voices trying to be heard over the music, lots of raucous boys and very flirty girls. A few times, I walked in on couples having sex. That was an eye-opener for me, as I had never even been kissed. Sefton and Mark used to tease me for getting embarrassed and blushing.

I was nearly eighteen and in my second year of school, when the others were having another party just before the Christmas break, and it was getting very rowdy. I could hear it all the way up in my room and only managed to fall asleep at about 1.30 a.m.

My door creaking disturbed me, then I heard a rush of loud music, before it went quiet again, apart from a rustling, which slowly brought me around. At first, I thought I'd forgotten to put the notice on my door, and a couple had come in for sex, but suddenly the covers were pulled off me. I froze, not sure what was going on. There were no voices, which I would have expected if it were a couple, but there was nothing.

It was so dark in my room that I couldn't see a thing. I started to sit up but felt a hand pushing at my chest, forcing me back. I was just about to scream to get the hell out of my room when something was shoved into my mouth and then something else was tied around my face over my mouth to secure it. It smelled terrible, and it felt woolly like a sock. I couldn't say anything or scream, I started to shake with panic.

Whoever it was then climbed on top of me, pinning my arms to my sides with their knees so I couldn't fight them off. Hands started to pull at my tank top, ripping the thin spaghetti straps and tearing it off me, exposing my chest. I was trying to wriggle and buck free, but the person was much too heavy for me, and I wasn't strong enough. It was so dark that I couldn't make out who it was, and they never spoke. I did notice the smell though. It was a cologne I had smelt before — a man's scent mixed with cigarette smoke. He was grabbing my breasts hard, pulling on them. The pain as he twisted my nipples was excruciating. Then his mouth was on one of my nipples, and he was biting hard and drawing blood, I could feel it trickle between my breasts. I was getting exhausted and weaker trying to fight him off.

He started ripping my night shorts and panties down, and I went into a panic, my throat was sore with trying to scream. I tried with all my might to wriggle and buck, but I was no match for him. He still never spoke.

I then had something tied around my eyes. At this point, I was naked. He must have been too, which explains the rustling when he entered my room — he was undressing. I could feel his thing pressing into my tummy. It was hard and felt wet.

I was hysterical and trying to plead with him through the gag. I knew what was about to happen. He was going to rape me. My first time would be forever tainted by this pathetic ass who was going to force himself on me. And I couldn't do a thing about it. I felt so helpless — the covering over my eyes was getting wet from my tears. I wanted to just die. After trying to buck him off me and shaking my head no and trying to scream, I was physically worn out. I felt him shuffle further down my thighs before he parted my legs and started rubbing his thing on me. I froze. He'd moved my hands, and they were now being held very tightly in one of his huge hands by the wrists, and I couldn't get free of him no matter how hard I tried.

I started to choke on the gag in my mouth. I felt suffocated, and I was sure I was about to pass out. I was sweating, but I was cold, and I started to shake and convulse.

No one was going to come and save me.

No one ever came to my room.

No one could hear me: he'd made sure of that.

I was defenseless — pinned down now by his bulk while he found where he wanted to be.

Without warning, he rammed into me so hard that the pain was excruciating. I tried to scream through the gag. I must have passed out, and when I came too, he was still shoving into me vigorously, grunting as he leaned over me. It was brutal. He wasn't being gentle. He was being a savage. He didn't care what he was doing or how much he was hurting me. I just laid there as stiff as a board with the tears soaking whatever was over my eyes and running down to my ears. I prayed he would just finish soon and leave, I was exhausted and I had no fight left in me. It seemed to go on forever, thrust after brutal thrust, as I lay paralyzed.

Eventually, he stilled. I was relieved when he got off me. I felt like I was on fire down below, and I was so sore, but he then tied my hands to the headboard of my bed, so I was still trapped. I started kicking and kicking, breaking through the pain threshold, hoping I'd strike him, but I didn't. I only wore myself out more. Then I felt something between my legs. It wasn't his thing. It was cold and hard. I started to buck, and kick and wriggle trying to get my hands free, but it was no use, I couldn't do anything. I felt his breath on my cheek, then in my ear, as he gritted out, "Leave, bitch," as he moved whatever he had in his hand onto my private parts towards where he had invaded me. I was terrified. I had no idea what it was or what he was doing until he slammed it into me hard. I screamed, and screamed into my gag, and my eyes rolled back into my head. I felt like I was going to die. I wanted to die. My body started to convulse, it went into spasms as he kept shoving whatever it was in and out hard, and I passed out.

Later, when I woke, there was light in my room. The things had been removed from my eyes and mouth. My hands were free, and my cover was thrown over me. I lifted my head slightly, trying to look around the room to make sure whoever it was had gone. My head was banging. My wrists were sore from being tied up and me struggling to get free. I slowly peeled the cover off and very gingerly sat up, swinging my legs over the side of the bed. I was in so much pain that I screamed out. I clutched my tummy, hugging myself, the pain so horrendous. I couldn't stand up. I looked at the bed — there was so much blood. I was completely naked, I could see blood between my legs and bruises on my chest, with dried blood all over one of my nipples and between my breasts. I sat like that for ages, not daring to move. I had so much pain everywhere, I just wanted to curl up and die.

I sat crying with my head in my hands. I had been violated, sadistically. Who would do this? It was Sunday, so no one would even think to look in on me. I had three more days left of school before Christmas break. I didn't have lessons on Thursday or Friday and was going back to Grandma's for Christmas on Wednesday straight after finishing school. I couldn't go back to school. Not now, not knowing that who did this could be watching me.

Sometime much later, I managed to gingerly get off the bed. I pulled the sheets from the bed, throwing the comforter over the stained mattress. I needed to get in the shower. I needed to get clean, to get rid of him, to wash every trace of him from me. I tried to clean in between my legs, but the pain was so intense when I went near my private parts that I almost fainted from it. I had to push through the pain. He had been in me, and I needed him out. I started to clean there, and I tried to scrub inside. There was a lot of blood flushing down the drain, but I didn't care, I needed to get clean. After a lot of scrubbing I collapsed onto the floor of the shower, curled up in a ball, crying and rocking. I stayed like that for a long time. The water ran cold, but I didn't care. I wanted to sleep and never wake up.

There was a knock on my bathroom door. I didn't hear it at first, but then they knocked again louder before the door opened slightly, and Lesley peeped her head around the door, calling my name. I looked up just in time to see the look of horror on her face. She ran to me, turned the water off as she got the bath towel, and threw it over me to stop me from shivering. She helped me up off the floor. I wasn't crying now. I was just a zombie. No feelings. This just felt like existing to me.

I wasn't going to tell anyone about this. No one could know. I was so ashamed and embarrassed that I could let this happen. How could I let this happen? In my own bed as well? I just told Lesley I didn't feel well, and I must have passed out in the shower. She didn't really believe me. I didn't let her help me dry because she would see the mess I was in, so I did it quickly and got into my sweats and baggy hoodie. She noticed my wrists and held them up and asked me what the marks were. I pulled my arms away from her and pulled my sleeves over my hands and told her it was nothing. She looked at me skeptically, but I told her I felt better and thanked her for helping. I don't even know why she came to my room. She very rarely came to see me.

I only left my room when I thought they were all out, and that was to just get some soup. I called the school on Monday and told them I had a bug and wouldn't be in until after Christmas break. Monday night, I flew home to Grandma's with no intention of ever returning to school again.

Caspian

I PREPARED MYSELF LAST NIGHT BY burying deep in Darcy. God, the things that woman can do with her tongue. It drives me nuts, and I love it. Darcy is my number one go-to girl. She doesn't want anything from me, and she doesn't need my money, she's a trust fund brat, and socialite, so doesn't need the fame either. We're just good for each other in the bedroom, and once we are done, we leave. She was at my midtown apartment last night and left straight after she sucked me dry. I thought I was already sated from our mammoth session where I made her cum with not only my cock and my tongue, but she loves my fingers up her ass as well. Then she got me all riled up again just so she could suck me. I wasn't going to complain about it, no, ma'am.

This morning, I feel quite relaxed and ready for the informal interview with Ms. Donald. God, I hope I can cope with being in the same room as her. What if she's hotter than I remember? I won't stand a chance. Maybe I shouldn't hire her. I might not be able to keep it professional, but then again, I need her to work for me. She's the best, and only the best is good enough for my restaurant. I may just have to leave her to Francois to train up and stay out of her way. Yes, that's the best idea because I do need her here.

I arrive at the restaurant at 9.a.m. She's coming in at 10.a.m., so I have enough time to see how all the prep is coming along. I don't have to be here for the prep, they know what they're doing, which is why I don't normally come in until 11.45 a.m. Just in time to check everything is ready for doors opening at noon. Then we take last orders at 10.30 p.m., and we are usually out of here by 12.30.a.m. I've got a great shift rotation that works well for us.

I've gone through all the set up with the team, and everyone knows what they are doing for today's menus. I'm just finishing my espresso coffee in front of house when I spot her walking past the window towards the main doors. Fuck, I'm screwed. She's fucking stunning. I watch her as she stands, straightening herself out before coming to the main door. She's in a trouser suit, and she's curvy in all the right places. She has fantastic, childbearing hips. Fuck, did I just think that? Children? Oh no, not even going there. But, god, I could hold on to those hips really good while plowing into her from behind. Fuck. I'm getting hard just thinking about it. Shit, fuck, shit, I need to think of something else, but I can't. Looking at her, she hasn't changed and is maybe even more beautiful in an understated type of way.

She's not my usual type at all, but there is something about her that just gets me right in the chest — and in the trousers. Her long red hair is tied back in a ponytail held up with one of those claw clip things so the end dangles down, and she has bangs, which I fucking love. She reaches out for the door, but I haven't unlocked it yet, so I have to move over to unlock it. I hope to fuck she doesn't notice my fucking traitor of a cock.

I unlock the door just as she is about to knock, and she looks up, startled as I swing it open. She has a shocked expression on her face, probably because it's me opening it. She flushes, and my cock is granite now. Those fucking eyes of hers mesmerize me. I'd forgotten how stunningly beautiful and unusual in color they were — like the aqua green of the Indian Ocean. I stand behind the door slightly and motion her inside.

"Good morning, Ms. Donald, lovely to see you again."

"Oh, huh, good morning, Mr. Kade." She's embarrassed. Maybe she's noticed my cock. "Please come in and take a seat at the bar there." I point towards the bar. I need to stand behind it so she can't see how hard I am.

She walks towards the bar, and I close the door and lock it again. I don't want anyone wandering in before we're open. I follow behind her, and as she sits on a bar stool, I move behind the bar. "Can I get you a coffee, Ms. Donald?"

She looks around as if expecting someone to come in and bring the coffee, but the espresso machine is here.

"Hmm, yes, please, Mr. Kade, that would be lovely. Can I have it white with one sweetener please?"

"Coming right up." I turn to make the coffee for her and one for me, even though I have only just finished the last one. In truth, I could use a whiskey, but it's a bit too early for that, and I have a long shift ahead of me. I turn back and slide the coffees onto the counter between us. My cock is starting to deflate a bit now, thank fuck for that.

"Thank you, Mr. Kade."

I nod at her. Time to get this interview going.

"So, Ms. Donald. I spoke to Mrs. Webster the Dean at NYCS and she tells me you passed your course with full honors, top of the school. Congratulations on that."

She blushes and hangs her head down. I suspect she's playing with her hands in her lap, but I can't see them from behind the counter. "Yes, and thank you," she says quietly.

"If you passed with full honors, why is it that you've not been snapped up by one of my rivals as yet?"

She lifts her head and smiles. "I was waiting for the right opportunity. I've had offers, but I didn't think working for them would help my career but, rather hinder it, so I've not taken any of them up."

"How so?"

"Well, my dream is to work for the top restaurant in New York City and work my way up to the top. Once you're in the top restaurant and reach the top, then the only progression from there is to run your own restaurant, just like you've done Mr. Kade. I've followed your career." Wow, I'm mesmerized by her and the enthusiasm she has. "The way I see it is, if I take a job in one of the lower ranking restaurants, then it would take me twice as long to get to running my own. I would have to work my way up there, then work for the top restaurant and then onto my own."

Ok, wow, at least she's honest and knows what she wants. I don't have a problem with that. It's inevitable that employees want to work here, to learn from the best, me of course, to then open their own restaurant, and I can't stop it no matter what. So one of the clauses in my contract is that an employee can't open a restaurant within twenty miles of one of mine and that they cannot use any of my dishes. That way, they will not be my direct competition.

"Well, thank you for being honest, Ms. Donald. If I do hire you, I do have clauses in my contracts to stop my employees opening up a restaurant within twenty miles of one of mine?"

"One of yours, Mr. Kade? I thought this was your only restaurant?"

"I'm in the process of opening one in LA, closely followed by London and Paris and maybe more around the US."

"Oh, that's wonderful, Mr. Kade, congratulations and how exciting."

Well, fuck me, she's happy for me. I can see it on her face that she means it.

I need to stop staring into those eyes. I can't help it. I'm just drawn in by the color. Ah, fuck she has freckles on her nose and a few on her cheeks. I never noticed before but up close, standing opposite her, there is something so pure about her. Shit, what were we saying? Oh, restaurants. "Will, that be a problem for you, Ms. Donald? Will it interfere with your plans to open a restaurant?"

"I don't think it would be a problem, Mr. Kade. I would never disrespect anyone that showed me respect." This woman is something else.

"Do you have your own recipe ideas, Ms. Donald?" This is my trick question to see if a potential employee will share any ideas they have or keep them for themselves.

"I do, Mr. Kade. I have so many ideas. But I would never tread on anyone's toes here and would always seek advice from the head chef. I have a complete book of recipes. My specialty is trying out new ideas and new ways to cook. I would love to run some of my ideas past you to see if you thought they were up to standard for Casper's if you would like to see some?" She lights up when she talks about cooking. It's a pleasure to see, and one of the reasons she reminds me of myself. She has the raw passion for cooking that I can relate to. I see it written all over her face. It's the passion I have always had, even when things were tough for me. It was my way to escape, to immerse myself in something other than what was happening around me, to get lost in my head with recipes and ingredients.

"Yes, I would like that — to see some of your ideas. I can see how passionate you are about cooking. I have to say from the glowing report that Mrs. Webster gave you and seeing the passion for myself, I would be a fool not to hire you."

I would also love to see if that passion transfers to the bedroom as well.

She looks shocked and takes a sip of her coffee, keeping her eyes on me all the time. I can feel the spark. I'm sure she can feel it as well. I need to put a stop to this before it even gets off the ground. She lowers her cup and puts it on the bar "Are you offering me a job, Mr. Kade?"

I pick up my coffee and take a sip, this time keeping my eyes on hers as she puts me under some kind of spell with them. I take my time and see her swallow a few times in anticipation of me speaking. "Yes, Ms. Donald,

I would like to hire you. I remember you from your work experience with us, although I was not a big part of your training, Francois gave glowing reports on you. If you want to think about it th…"

"No, I don't need to think about it. Yes, I would love to work for you, Mr. Kade."

I laugh a little "Well, okay then, when can you start? My current commis chef leaves in four weeks, and I would like you to work alongside him for as long as you can, to see how the team works. So the sooner you can start, the better. I do need you to think about this, Ms. Donald, it's a very stressful work environment, especially if things go wrong, which they do quite often in a kitchen. I need to know you will be dedicated to the job and give it 110% of your commitment. Can you do that?" She goes to speak, but I hold my hand up to stop her and shake my head. "Let me finish. Go and think about this and if you can commit and give me 110% then I will make sure you take the steps needed to further your career. It will be early starts and late finishes on rotation. I need to know you can manage that?" She's sitting, nodding her head at me.

"I can, Mr. Kade. I don't need to think about it. This is my dream job. It's what I've been holding out for. You have no idea how excited I was when I received the call from Mrs. Webster. I can commit and give 110% if you're willing to give me the chance to prove myself. You won't be sorry, Mr. Kade, I can assure you."

She's beaming at me, and I can't help but feel her joy, and I know she's telling me the truth. She has that passion. This girl is going to go far. I know she is, and it's my job to keep her on her toes and put her through the paces of a highly intense kitchen.

"Okay, welcome to Casper's," I say and hold out my hand for her to shake. She reaches across, and as soon as our hands touch, I feel the electric spark between us — all the way to my groin and my fucking cock that has been at half-mast for the last twenty minutes and is now at full mast like a steel rod. She feels it too. She gasps and takes a sharp intake of breath then quickly releases my hand as though I have just electrocuted her. I eye her warily, but she doesn't look at me. She's turned away to get down off the barstool.

Just then Francois comes into the bar area.

"Casp, we need you in the kitchen. Slight emergency." Thank fuck for that he just saved my embarrassment. I nod. "Francois, do you remember Ms. Donald? She has agreed to join the team at Casper's and will be our new commis chef. She is starting with us on…?" I look at her, and she turns back to me.

"Is Monday okay with you? Hello, Francois, nice to see you again."

"Yes, Monday is perfect. Thank you for your time, Ms. Donald, now, Francois will see you out while I go and see what the emergency in the kitchen is." With that, I walk out of the bar towards the kitchen, but I need to stop off in the bathroom first. I can't walk into the kitchen with a rock-hard cock, and I need him to deflate. God, it's going to be fucking torture working with her if this is how I react by being in her company. I can't remember ever responding like this to a girl ever. I've never felt anything like that with anyone in my life. Fuck, I truly am screwed.

chapter

5

Macen

I WALK OUT OF CASPER'S WITH THE biggest grin on my face. I feel like I'm floating on air as I glide down the street. But what the hell was that all about when I shook Caspian's hand? It felt like he'd burnt me. It traveled all through my body, all tingly like thousands of little pinpricks all over me. Wow. I've never felt anything like it. I have never been attracted to anyone. I thought Caspian was hot back when I did my work experience, but that was it.

After my attack, I just wasn't interested, yet here I am, with all these fuzzy feelings running around my body because of one touch. He is one stunning man, but he knows it too — those brooding looks he gives with his chocolate brown eyes and long eyelashes. He's arrogant; I know that from working there before, and he always seems to be in a bad mood, unless that's just around me. I bet he can have anyone he wants. I felt a fool gasping when he shook my hand, and he gave me a confused look like he didn't understand something.

This is my dream job, and I must keep it professional no matter what. There is no way I'm screwing this up for anyone. He's up his own ass anyway. He wouldn't look twice at me. I mean: I'm no Kendall Jenner. I won't stand a chance when he finds out about Dixon — he'll probably fire me.

I can't wait to phone Grandma and tell her the good news. I know she will be excited for me. I would love for her to move here and be with Dixon and me. He misses her so much. I get my cell out to call her, and as soon as she answers, I just spit out, "Grandma, I got it. I got the job at Casper's. Can you believe it? My dream job. I'm going to be a commis chef in the best restaurant in New York City?" I haven't even given her the chance to speak.

"Oh, Macen. I knew you would get it as soon as you told me you had an interview. Congratulations, my love. Now I guess I need to pack."

"Grandma, that would be wonderful. I start on Monday, but you don't have to come that quickly. I can sort out care for Dixon."

"Nonsense, I want to be there for your first day, and I can't wait to see my little cherub. I've missed you both so much."

"We've both missed you too, Grandma. I can't wait to see you. When are you thinking of getting here?"

"How about Saturday?"

"The sooner the better. Wait until I tell Dixon you're coming. He will be so excited. Wait, no, I think I will leave it, and you can surprise him."

"Yes, let's do that. I love you, Macen and I'm so proud of you. You know that, don't you?"

"I do, Grandma, and I love you. See you on Saturday." We hang up, and I make my way to the diner to let them know I won't be working there anymore. I'll finish my shifts this week for them, but after Friday, that's it for me.

On my way home, the doubt starts to set in about working at Casper's. It's my dream, but can I do it? He didn't ask any personal questions, so I didn't mention Dixon. I'm sure when Caspian finds out I have a son he will fire me. I'm in a dilemma now. Do I tell him or not? Do I hope he doesn't find out for a while, and by then, I'll be so settled in my job that he won't fire me? He may accuse me of lying even though I haven't lied — he hasn't asked, and I just never gave the information.

I don't tell people about Dixon freely unless asked. I hate the typical stereotype image I get for being a single momma — all the comments about being knocked up so young, wanting to trap a man by getting pregnant or being a silly girl throwing away her life. It's a stigma most single mommas have to live with. However, my circumstances couldn't be further from that. They don't know that, but still they tarnish us all with the same brush, they don't know if the Poppa just left as my own Poppa did, or if he died, or in fact if it was an attack like me. I work hard for my son, and I love him more than life. He is my life, but I still want to follow my dreams.

After the attack, I thought my life was over.

GRANDMA KNEW THERE was something wrong with me when I got home for Christmas after I was attacked. I didn't tell her what had happened. I just said I wasn't well and would be fine in a few days. The truth was, I didn't know how I was functioning or even how I was acting normally. I felt my life was over — I wanted it to be over.

Grandma asked me a few times what was wrong. She said I could talk to her about anything, which I knew I could, but I just couldn't bring myself to tell her. I didn't want her being disappointed with me. I was so ashamed of what happened, so embarrassed that it happened, and so angry I let it happen. I was back home for Christmas break. Home for four weeks.

Four weeks to decide if I was going back to school.

Four weeks to try and pull myself together.

Four weeks to stop the self-loathing for letting this happen to me.

Four weeks to stop the guilt I felt.

Four weeks to work out if I wanted to live.

Four weeks to try and carry on with a normal life.

Four weeks — not long enough, but too long at the same time.

Four weeks, or twenty-eight days, or six hundred and seventy-two hours. That long to decide, it wasn't long at all, but I knew it would drag and the attack would just play over and over in my head, like a record on repeat and I wouldn't be able to stop it. I knew it was going to kill me. I wanted it to.

I kept myself to myself while home with Grandma. She had her routines, meeting with her friends for book club, coloring sessions, or bingo, and she carried on with them just like we used to before I left for school in New York.

She didn't see me curled up in a ball all night.

She didn't see me crying.

She didn't see me wince every time I went to the toilet with the stinging down below.

She didn't see me trying to walk with my legs closed because the pain was so severe.

She didn't see the painkillers I had in my bedside table that I was taking like sweets.

She didn't see the times I had poured all the painkillers into my hand to swallow all at once.

She didn't see how I cried from pain in the shower trying to scrub myself down below hard.

She didn't see the razors I held in my hand in the bathroom, wondering if I could do it.

She didn't see the turmoil I was living in — thinking I would be better off dead.

She didn't see me soaked with sweat and having night terrors.

She didn't see I wasn't sleeping much.

She didn't see I was barely eating.

She didn't see I was barely living.

She was the only reason I was still living.

I did manage to leave the house once but only to get a present and a card for Grandma for Christmas and stock up on more pain meds. It was torture. The pain was excruciating from walking. I was wearing sanitary pads because when I walked, I would bleed. I knew I needed medical help but that would mean me telling them what happened, and I couldn't do that. The shame alone would kill me.

I was trying to be as normal as I could, and I thought I was doing a good job — until Christmas Day.

It was just the two of us like it always was, but we always went full out with the Christmas Dinner and all the trimmings and exchanging presents. I helped Grandma in the kitchen, cooking the small turkey and the vegetables she bought for us, but I was quiet.

Usually, when we did this, we had Christmas tunes on, and we would both sing as we cooked, but I didn't put the songs on this year. Grandma put them on, and she started singing, but I didn't join in. She was cutting up the potatoes when she suddenly put the knife down on the counter top and turned to look at me. I could see her out of the corner of my eye, and I knew she was going to question me, but I just carried on cutting up the carrots.

"Okay, Macen, out with it. Please tell me what's wrong, love. Please don't shut me out. I can see you're hurting. You haven't been the same since you came home. The fact that you came home before school finished told me something was wrong.

"I can see the dark rings around your eyes, which tells me you're not sleeping."

"I can see your eyes are bloodshot, which tells me you've been crying."

"I can see your clothes getting looser on you, which tells me you're not eating properly."

"I can see you wince sometimes as though you're in pain."

"I've left it long enough now. I have eyes Macen, and I can see all this, love."

Ok, I was wrong. She did see me.

She came to me and pulled me into her and hugged me. And, I broke. Right there in Grandma's arms. I just broke. It's lucky she had me in her arms to keep me upright.

"Oh, Macen, love, tell me what's wrong. I can't help you if you don't tell me. Is it a boy? Have you had problems with a boy?" I couldn't speak. I was heaving as I tried to take in air as I sobbed. She moved me to the couch in the living room and sat me down very gently —hugging me. I put my legs up on the couch and curled up into her side, sobbing. She kept rubbing my back, telling me it would all be okay. Eventually, the crying subsided, and I hugged her back. She kissed the top of my head.

"Macen, love, nothing is ever as bad as it seems. I can see you're hurting both mentally and physically, and I know you will tell me, but just know, love, that no matter what it is, we can get through this together. You have me, Macen. I'm here for you, no matter what, my sweet girl. I love you so much and will do anything to help you. Please just let me know what's happened." I knew I needed to tell her, but I found it hard saying it out loud, as if saying it made it real, which was stupid because I knew it was real.

"Oh, Grandma, I'm so ashamed. I can't say it."

"Yes, you can, Macen, why are you ashamed? Did you do something to someone?" I shook my head. "No. Someone, someone…" I tried to get it out. I tried to tell her, but I had an enormous lump in my throat. I looked at her. "Someone hurt me."

I felt her take in a sharp breath. She's a very wise woman, and I think she guessed what had happened immediately.

"Macen, love? Was this a boy that hurt you? Did he physically hurt you?" I nodded yes into her. I felt her shake a little, and when I looked up at her again, I could see the silent tears falling down her cheeks just like mine.

"Oh, god, love." She hugged me tighter — I think to help her to compose herself for what was to come. After a while, she asked me to tell her, and with great difficulty, I did. I told her everything that happened that night.

She was crying hard when I finished. We both sat there, hugging and crying on the couch. It was the timer on the oven that broke us up, letting us know the turkey was ready. It was the only thing that was ready, and neither of us wanted to eat. When she returned to the couch after taking the turkey out of the oven, she sat and faced me, holding my hands.

"Macen, we need to take you to the hospital." I shook my head, no, vigorously. She grabbed my cheeks in her hands to still my head and looked me in the eyes. "You have to go, Macen. You need to get checked out, love. You have no idea the damage that has been done to you. They will need to thoroughly examine you. I know it's the last thing you want, but we have to report this to the police. They need to know."

I started to rock backward and forward on the couch, pulling away from her grasp and putting my head in my hands. "No, no, Grandma. NO, I can't do it. I can't let anyone go down there. I can't do it." She stopped me rocking and hugged me. "Yes, you can, love. You have to do this. You must be brave and strong. There might be some sperm left inside you if he didn't use a condom. We must try to stop him doing this again to anyone else. Macen, look at me. We have to do this for your sake, my sweet girl." I knew she was right, and I let it sink in as we comforted each other.

A little later, Christmas day, she drove me to the hospital where a sexual assault nurse examined me and asked me all about the attack. The damage down below was severe. They said whatever he used on me afterward really damaged my cervix and one of my fallopian tubes, which is why I had excruciating pain in my stomach as well as down below. They did a blood test on me also to see if I might pregnant, it was still early days for that but they wanted to try anyway, they said if it came back negative to try a urine test in a weeks time.

I prayed to God I wasn't.
The test came back positive, and I broke all over again.

Caspian

I HAVE TO FLY TO LA OVER THE weekend, and I won't be back until Wednesday. Fuck, I'm going to miss Macen starting on Monday. I wanted to be there to welcome her to the team on her first day. I know it's not usual for me to do that when someone new starts, but I just felt like I wanted to do it this time.

I haven't been able to get her out of my mind. I even phoned Darcy for another round, but then I canceled at the last minute. I didn't want her. How fucked up is that? Me, only wanting one woman! And one that is out of bounds, too! Where does that leave me? Fucking celibate that's where because I can't touch Macen. Fuck that. But it leaves me fucked or fuckless as the case may be.

I'm not looking forward to my trip to LA. I know there are problems that I need to sort out with the equipment I've ordered. The electrician was due to start but didn't turn up. Why the fuck do I pay a project manager to oversee everything, yet I have to go and sort shit out? And also, I want to see Macen.

The days have dragged. I've been jerking myself off to images of her in my head: in that pantsuit, bent over, with me ripping the pants from her, tugging those hips of hers right onto my cock, and plowing hard into her. I need to stop; I know I do, but I can't help it.

I have the LA restaurant to get sorted, but it's her I keep thinking about. I have never been like this over a woman.

A part of me hopes she is shit at the job so that I can fire her, or get Francoise to fire her, then I can get her where I want her, but while she is an employee, I can't go there. I need another distraction. Maybe I can call one of the models in LA… They are hot, especially Janella, yeah, I can phone her. We've hooked up a time or two or three — I've lost count. I might even go to Soho House on West Sunset. I pay thousands to be a member there, so I may as well use it. You just never know what action I may see in there.

I head to Soho House and catch up with people I haven't seen for ages, and I hook up with a new model, fresh on the scene with long chestnut brown hair which reminds me of a certain someone. Her name is Kacey-Jay, and she's fucking stunning. We have a bit too much to drink and decide to leave, getting to the exit of the club, clinging to each other for support before she trips and falls, taking me down with her, landing on top of her.

There are fucking paparazzi hanging around places like Soho House, just waiting for its exclusive clientele to fall out of the club and make fools of themselves just like we have, so they can get all the best pictures to sell to TMZ, and all the other tabloid's.

We make front-page news on those other tabloids: "Celebrity Chef caught playing with his food in public." Is the headline this morning on TMZ and no doubt plastered all over the Internet. Those bastards knew she had tripped, and we were not doing anything sleazy, but what do they care when they get the picture they need to net them a pretty paycheck?

I think I best stay in the hotel for the rest of my time in LA. I don't want any more sleazy headlines written about me that aren't true. I wouldn't mind, but after that, I just made sure she got to her hotel safely and left, so I never even got my rocks off. Fuck my life.

Macen

I'm so excited when Grandma arrives. I take Dixon to the airport and say we are meeting a friend. We get off the bus at the terminal and make our way towards arrivals, but I stop suddenly, frozen on the spot when I see him, Caspian, walking towards departures. Oh, god. I haven't been able to stop thinking about him and trying to analyze what those feelings I had were, since my interview.

I wonder where he is off to, even though it's none of my business. He doesn't see me, thankfully, although for one moment I think he has when he stops and turns around suddenly as though looking for someone. Luckily, Caspian's view of Dixon is obscured by people, even if he did spot me. I quickly crouch down and talk to Dixon, knowing Caspian can't see either of us. That was a close call.

We make our way up to arrivals just as Grandma is coming through the doors. Dixon spots her, and he leaves me, making a beeline for her, running, and shouting, "Granny, Granny," before leaping into her arms.

He nearly knocks her flying; he's getting so big. We all hug and cry, just standing there in the middle, so everyone has to walk around us.

"I missed you so much, Grandma," I tell her.

"I missed you both very much. I can't wait to spend some real time with you," she replies into his neck.

I take her bags, and she holds Dixon's hand as we head out to the bus terminal. I don't drive and to be honest, you would have to be mad to drive in New York City.

"Let's get a cab?" Grandma says to us. "My treat."

"I'm not gonna argue with that, Grandma. It will be quicker than the bus."

We get back to my apartment, which is quite big for New York. I had money left from my dad's fund. I have never even met the man, but he has always looked after me financially, which has been a godsend to me since I came back to live in New York.

AFTER I FOUND out I was pregnant, they wanted me to stay in hospital while they did a hysteroscopy, inserting a very small camera called a hysteroscope into me, to see the extent of the damage I had sustained. They explained that it takes pictures of my insides and sends them to a monitor so they could have a visual of what internal trauma I had. They said it was best to do it now rather than wait, because of the pregnancy, in case the trauma I had could affect the fetus. I consented and let them do what they had to. At that point, I didn't care about anything or what anyone did to me.

I was numb.

I had no feelings at all.

It was a quick procedure. I didn't try to look at the monitor because I didn't care. The doctor doing the procedure then started telling me what she saw, but I didn't take any of it in. The doctor must have seen I was not listening, and she asked if they could bring Grandma into the room, and I just nodded, yes. All I heard was: torn, severe damage, serrated edge, cervix cut, one tube severely damaged. Too soon to see the baby growing, but not sure it will survive with the amount of damage.

I turned my head, still not caring what they were talking about. They said I could go home and that the police would be coming to take a statement once they had all the facts of the rape. I remember wishing they wouldn't use that word. It grated on me, and I bit the inside of my cheek, grinding my teeth. They gave Grandma some leaflets that she took and said she would read. They wanted me to make an appointment with my own doctor to have regular check-ups every week. We left.

When we got home, Grandma saw me to bed, bringing me some soup as neither of us had eaten anything that day. I just curled up in a ball. She sat with me the rest of the night, hugging me to her. I knew she was devastated about what had happened, and I also knew she would be on the phone to the school as soon as term started again. I knew Grandma, and I knew she would give them hell, especially about the lock on my room not being fixed.

I was supposed to go to the doctors. Grandma made me an appointment, but I refused to leave. She still didn't see me completely. I mean really see me.

The me that still took painkillers even though I was pregnant.

The me that still poured the bottle into my hands trying to take them all.

The me still standing in the shower scrubbing myself to rid him from me.

The me in my bathroom with the razor blades in my hands.

She pulled the leaflets out and sat with me on my bed to read them. One was on abortion, and one was on adoption. I think she wanted me to decide what I was going to do. I still didn't believe I was pregnant, so I didn't care.

She made me go to the doctors the next day. She dragged me out of my bed, and she dressed me. I reluctantly went with her. I was still in denial. At the doctors they took blood, and I did a urine test. It confirmed I was pregnant. They also had the results from the hysteroscopy.

The doctor told me that if I did want to proceed with the pregnancy, there was a very strong possibility I would not carry it full term due to the internal trauma. That it was questionable I would be able to have the baby, and it was also likely I wouldn't be able to get pregnant again, even if I did carry this one full term. This could be my only chance at becoming a mother. At that, I looked up at her. I actually registered what she said. I might never have children because of some selfish bastard who not only took my virginity but also ruined my life. I either attempt to have his baby, or I never have a chance at being a mother again. The tears just streamed down my face. Grandma took me into her side, and we left the office. She told the doctor we would be back.

The police had tried to come and see me a few times, but I wouldn't speak to them. I wasn't ready. It was bad enough telling the nurse and doctors at the hospital. It was New Year's Eve, and I had already ruined Christmas for us. I was eighteen years old and should have been out celebrating, yet I was stuck in my bedroom wallowing in self-pity, blaming myself for everything that happened. Grandma wanted me to see a counselor — to speak to someone. I just nodded when she said it, and I think she took that as yes, I would.

I just didn't want to do anything. I was just existing — going through the motions. The police came, and Grandma made me go into the living room and speak to them. She sat with me, holding my hand as I told them everything. I felt drained going through it all, having to live it all again as though it was happening all over again. I couldn't control myself, and I broke down. They recorded my interview with them, as well as taking notes. It meant I would not need to attend the court and face whoever it was. I couldn't tell them anything about the bastard who did it. They asked me questions, trying to trigger my memory. They asked me about smells and if he'd spoken at all. I had forgotten about that. I told them the smell was a cologne I had smelt before but didn't know where or what type and also it was mixed with cigarette smoke, and then I remember what he said to me. 'Leave Bitch'. I didn't know what it meant, but I remembered his voice — how angry and bitter he sounded. I remember feeling spittle on the side of my face when he leaned in to say it next to my ear — quietly but with so much venom in his words. Oh god, what if I heard him again?

The day after New Year's Day, Grandma drove me to see a counselor. I didn't protest because I didn't care. I sat in the room of Dr. Elizabeth Donnar. She was a nice lady, and although I didn't speak much during the session, she actually vilified how I was feeling: the guilt, the anger and rage, the loss, the not caring if I lived or not, and she was spot on. I looked up at her quizzically. How did she know how I was feeling? She told me she too was raped in college, and she felt everything I was feeling. She thought her life was over, and she wanted to die. She went to counseling and from there decided that was the path she wanted to take — to help others like her in the same situation.

I left the session still not feeling anything, but considering that something good had happened from something so horrific to Dr. Elizabeth. Was that going to happen for me? What good was going to come from the brutal attack I went through? While thinking all this walking to the car with Grandma, I didn't realize my hand was on my tummy until I saw my reflection in the glass window. I looked down. I was being protective of what was growing inside me. But, I still didn't know how I felt about the baby. I had no feelings.

I went to see Dr. Elizabeth a few more times, and I started to open up to her. I told her what had happened. The smells and noises I remembered. It was like re-living it all over again, and I cried telling her everything. She understood me though. She knew everything I was feeling. It wasn't just sympathy — she knew. When I told her I was pregnant, she smiled and asked me how I felt about that.

Was I angry?

Did I want it out of me because it was conceived from such a bad situation?

Did I think about it at all?

Had I decided to keep it or terminate it?

How did I actually feel about it?

I told her I hadn't thought about it, but if I didn't have the baby, then I may never have the chance to be a momma, and that scared me more than anything. I wanted to be someone's momma someday. I just never envisaged it being so soon.

I knew it was too soon — I would only be nineteen when I had it. Could I do that? Have the baby? Would I hate it because of the circumstances? I said these things out loud, which made me really think about my situation. I think at that moment, in Dr. Elizabeth's office, that was when I decided I wanted to keep the baby. It wasn't the baby's fault, and it would be my baby — not his. I didn't know if I would always look at the baby, and it would remind me of that night, but it was a chance I wanted to take. I would be a momma if I had the chance to be.

Grandma phoned the school to tell them what happened and that I was not going back to finish my course. I couldn't walk around the school not knowing if whoever attacked me was watching me, waiting to do it again. There was no way I was going back to that house. Grandma had the school ship my belongings back to me. She told them she was going to file a lawsuit against them, but I stopped that. The school offered me a place whenever I was ready, and there would be no fees to pay. They said it was the least they could do. I don't think I will be going back after the baby though. I thought my dreams of becoming a top chef were just that now — dreams.

The police kept Grandma informed on how the investigation was going. They had interviewed all my housemates and also got a list of everyone who was at the party. They didn't have any DNA from my attack, so until the baby was born, they wouldn't be able to do anything. They did take DNA samples from all the males who were at the party that my housemates knew of, including my housemates, so they had them all on file for when the baby was born.

Lesley tried to contact me a couple of times, but I wouldn't take her calls. I didn't want anything to do with any of them. I don't know if she'd found out who attacked me or if she knew anything, but I just stayed with Grandma and buried my head in the sand. I preferred it that way. At least I had a purpose to survive, and if anything, I think it made me stronger.

Caspian

I'M BACK IN NEW YORK, AND I can't wait to get to the restaurant and see Macen. She's all I can think about. Those spectacular eyes haunt my dreams — those freckles on the bridge of her nose that I never noticed before and those fucking hips of hers. The fantasies I have of wrapping her long red hair around my wrist and pulling her head back while I ram into her. Oh fuck.

I sorted the shit out with the LA restaurant, and it's all back on track. Sometimes I wonder why I put myself through all this, but I know it will be worth it in the end. My dream has always been to have a chain of successful restaurants, and that's what I'm going to have. I will have four before I'm thirty, five if I'm lucky. I want to go global. Who knows where it will take me?

I head straight to my penthouse — a prime spot with the most amazing view over Central Park. I even have my own rooftop garden, which I love to relax in — when I have the time to relax, that is, which isn't very often with my business.

In the cab on the way, I decide I'm going to nip to the restaurant and grab myself something to eat. If Macen is working, then I will stay and eat. If not, I will go home with the food.

Fuck, everything is revolving around her. When did that start to happen? The cab drops me at home, so I pop in and ask the concierge to take my bags to my apartment then head straight to the restaurant. It's on the corner of 5th and W 57th Street, opposite Tiffany's. In the early days, I relied on footfall and passing trade, and being on 5th made sense. It cost me an arm and a leg to get it up and running, but now it's a huge success. I'm billed as the top celebrity chef in the USA and probably most of Europe too. I've traveled a lot.

I do the three-minute walk to Casper's. It's busy tonight in NYC, and as I get nearer to Casper's, I can see the line outside. There's a line most nights. Although I'm fully booked for six months in advance, I have six tables a night that I always leave open for walk-ins. It helps keep our reputation; it's just they do end up in line for a long time. I figure if they are prepared to wait, then they should be able to eat at Casper's.

You never know what celebrities are going to drop in, so I have a special room on the mezzanine especially for A-listers who want privacy. It has floor-to-ceiling bi-folding doors that at the flick of a switch become frosted glass if the celebrities want complete privacy. It seats sixteen people — that way they can bring family and friends and not get disturbed. I have a few regular celebrities that like that room and who use it a lot.

I pass the line, greeting people and saying hi, even allowing one or two selfies. I can't say no, even though I want to tell them to fuck off because it wouldn't be good for business. More people seem to be stopping me tonight, and I just want to get in there to see if Macen is there and get some food.

Once I manage to get inside, my Maître d', Tobias, greets me. He is calm and collected, just what we need front of house. I nod and say hello, then move past him to the kitchen. If I were eating in, I would let him seat me and get me something to eat and drink because he knows what I like. I reach the kitchen and hold my breath before opening the in-door. I step inside to the hustle and bustle of a working kitchen. I love it, this relaxes me, and this is where I feel at home.

My expeditor, Simon, is calling out orders while putting garnishes on the dishes ready for the servers to take out, my sous chef, Jean-Paul is shouting out orders to the pastry chef and my salad cook. There is so much going on, but it works, and it runs like clockwork. One of my servers passes me, and I check a couple of the dishes on his tray. Spot on, they look fucking perfect, just how they should be. I pat him on the back and nod, sending him out with the tray as I scan the kitchen. No new commis chef. Fuck. I thought she might be here, but no, it's David on tonight. Macen is shadowing Louis until he leaves, and I guess it's not his shift tonight. That's just put a dampener on my evening.

"Simon, can you get me a Portobello mushroom salad to go, please, and I wouldn't mind a buttermilk panna cotta and honeycombed sandwich too."

"Sure, thing, Casp, will be about five minutes, is that okay?"

"Yeah, sure, I'll just be in my office. Can you bring it through when it's done?" He nods at me as I head into my office. My main chefs and staff call me Casp when I'm not working but as soon as I put my whites on its 'chef' to everyone.

I don't bother turning my computer on. I look through the papers on my desk that have piled up since I've been gone, and I come across Macen's file. I look over it. I already know she's twenty-five, but I have her address now and her cell number. It would be inappropriate of me to message her, but I put her number in my cell anyway. Just in case, I tell myself. I've been staring at her paperwork for a while when Simon comes in with my food. I'm going to look up her address on my laptop when I get home. I slide the paperwork into my draw because I don't want anyone coming in and seeing it lying around. I take my food and head for home, leaving out of the back entrance so I don't get stopped in front of house again.

Once home, I grab a beer, plate my food, and go up onto my rooftop. It's a lovely evening, although getting a bit cooler. I put the garden heater on just to take the chill off and start to eat my food. I fire up my laptop and search for her address. I see she lives in Yorkville on the Upper East Side on 78th Street. Fuck, that's not that far from me, and quite upmarket, rent is quite a bit around there. I wonder how she can afford to live there. Maybe she has parents that help with the rent, or she lives with a boyfriend. Fuck, I never thought of that. She did mention she was working part-time in a diner until the right job offer came along. You get minimum wage in diners, and I don't expect the tips are huge. I never asked her where she lived in the interview. My mind was blank half the time and the other half I was just thinking about what I wanted to do to her. Not exactly the best way to conduct an interview, but I already knew I was going to offer her the job, how could I not with her glowing report from NYCS.

I eat my food and drink my beer. It's a perfect evening to just sit here and think, and I decide to do some research on other locations where I can open a new restaurant. I bought the properties in London, Paris, and LA, and I want to buy one in Canada. I search for the best areas in Canada, and I send an email to a realtor there with a brief on what I'm looking for and ask them to look for me. LA will be open first, closely followed by London; the interior structures are all being worked on there, but it will be sometime before it's ready for fittings. That one will probably open in about ten months, then Paris, and then hopefully Canada.

I think back to Macen coming into the restaurant and what I was thinking about her childbearing hips. I want to find someone special eventually, but I don't see me settling down anytime soon, with all the new openings I have going on over the next few years. I do think about it. I do want a family. I have always wanted a family. When I was younger, all I wanted was to be loved. I was told I lived with my dad for a little while, but I only remember being brought up in the foster system in Florida. I lived in a few different homes. I wasn't a bad kid. I never got into trouble until I was a teenager and even then, it wasn't too bad. I was bullied throughout my life, and I guess that's why I'm the way I am now. I won't let anyone walk over me or give me shit.

WHEN I WAS in group homes, the other boys would pick on me because I was quiet, timid, and small for my age. I remember once, the older boys all came and dragged me out of bed late one night. They took me to the bathroom and made me smoke something funny. I was choking on the smoke as it went down my throat, burning me, and I ran to the toilet to throw up. They were all laughing at me, telling me what a wuss I was. Then the biggest one grabbed me by the neck, calling me a chicken shit. He shoved me to my knees, and then two others got hold of my arms, and the big guy pushed my head into the toilet bowl. The same toilet bowl I had just thrown up in.

My face and head were full of puke, and of course, I threw up again, only for them to repeat dunking me. They left me soaked in puke, and through fright, I had peed myself. They all thought it was hysterical and never let me live it down.

They did that a lot, dragging me out of bed to bully me. Once they had a bucket of pee and tipped it over my head. I couldn't tell anyone, mainly because there was no one to tell. No one ever listened to you and thought you were just telling lies.

I have a slight recollection of living with my dad. I remember he was either asleep or he was shouting at me — I do remember the shouting. I used to cover my ears up when he bellowed. It became instinct, and it was something I continued to do growing up. I was told he was a drunk. I was also told my mum left us and that he didn't want me, so he just drunk himself into a coma each night and neglected me. I was apparently very scrawny for a five-year-old, and when welfare came to collect me, they thought I was only three years old until they found my birth certificate. From then I went from home to home. Apart from the bullying, I was neglected throughout my life. I just tried to shrink into the background so no one would bother me — only it didn't work.

I remember the older I got, all I wanted was a family and for someone to love me. I used to dream about a long-lost family, or my momma coming for me, but they never did. I have never tried to find my parents. I figured they never wanted me then, so they couldn't have me now, even if they were alive.

All the bullying has made me stronger and made me the person I am today. Yes, I'm an arrogant ass, but it's my survival mechanism. I have never had a chance to show anyone the nice side of me. I have never had a relationship with anyone. I've been too wrapped up in getting to where I am today, being successful and the youngest Michelin star chef. I hope I will have time to settle if I find the right woman, but I don't see that happening, and I'm okay with that.

I've just played around all these years. I've never found anyone that I thought 'yes I want to spend my life with her'. I've fooled around since I was twelve when I lost my virginity to a girl in one of the foster homes. We became good friends and looked out for each other. She was older than me by three years, but we didn't care, and she wanted me to be her first. We fumbled, but we did it. It was okay, but from then, I just had sex whenever I could. It was my way of getting the affection I craved. I got it the only way I knew I could, and I became a whore. I would screw anything and the older I got, the more attention I got.

It's getting late, and I've had a long day. I finish my Internet searching and decide to call it a night. I can't wait to get into work tomorrow and see Macen.

Macen

I HAD A GREAT WEEKEND WITH Grandma and Dixon. We went out and did a bit of shopping, and then had a picnic in Central Park. We went up the tower in Belvedere Castle, and we walked around the Jackie Onassis Reservoir. It was a lovely day, and she was worn out with all the walking. Dixon was tired too, so they both had an early night.

I had butterflies in my tummy this morning.

I got up earlier than usual, as I had all of Dixon's stuff ready for school. I packed his lunch bag so he was ready, and I did myself one.

I kissed Grandma and Dixon goodbye, as they were leaving later than I was. I wanted to walk to Casper's. I knew it would take me a good thirty minutes to walk there, but it was a nice day, and it would calm my nerves, or at least I hoped it would. I wasn't sure if it was just first-day nerves or if it was the thought of seeing Caspian again. I haven't stopped thinking about him since my interview: his jet-black hair, striking brown eyes, chiseled cheekbones and, oh my God, the dimples. Those dimples make him even more stunning if that's possible. I need to control all these alien feelings I have for him. It won't be good, working for him and feeling this way. Nothing can ever happen, no matter what, and I will not screw up my one chance at making it and getting to the top.

As I near Casper's, the butterflies are fluttering harder in my tummy. I was told to go around the back of the restaurant and knock on the back door. Francoise said he would be there first thing to start on my paperwork and go over the kitchen with me before it got too busy. The team doesn't arrive to start prepping until 9.a.m., which will be my usual start time, but for today, Francoise wants me there at 8.a.m. He has a lot to show me.

I knock and wait but there's no answer. I knock louder and listen. I can hear footsteps, then the door being unlocked as Francoise opens it. He smiles at me, seeing I'm slightly early. Francoise is an older man. I would guess at about forty to forty-five, with dark hair that's peppered with grey, he's clean-shaven, as most chefs and cooks are. It's a bit of a taboo subject, but they say you are not to have any facial hair while working in the kitchen. That applies to everyone — someone needs to tell Caspian that fact. Francoise has green eyes, and he always looks quite stern except when he smiles.

"Good morning, Ms. Donald. Nice and early. I like that — shows you're eager. Come on in."

"Thank you, Francoise, and good morning to you. Yes, there is no way I would be late, especially not on my first day. Please call me Macen."

"Ok, Macen, let's show you where everything is, then get us a coffee and you can fill in your details on the paperwork Mr. Kade left for you." My face drops. He left paperwork for me. Does that mean he isn't going to be around today? I daren't ask Francoise because it's none of my business and to be honest, it might be better if he weren't around today for my first shift. I think he will just make me nervous. Funny how my butterflies have disappeared now that I don't think he will be around.

Francoise shows me around the restaurant — everything from the bathrooms to the employee room, the storeroom, and the gigantic fridge, then all the different workstations, finally finishing up at the workstation that I will be sharing with Louis until he leaves and it becomes mine. Once we finish the tour, we head into an office, which I think is Caspian's. I start to fill in the paperwork while he gets us coffee. It's mainly my personal details, nothing unusual, and he gives me the staff handbook and the contract of employment to look over, sign, and return to him or Mr. Kade within the week.

This all takes us to 11 a.m. I assume the team arrived a while ago and are in the kitchen, prepping for the lunchtime rush. Apparently, it's busy right through from opening at noon to last orders at 10.30 p.m., and doors close at midnight. Thankfully there is a specialized cleaning crew that comes in at midnight each night to thoroughly deep clean the entire kitchen. Caspian does not want anything to jeopardize his Michelin stars, and I can't say I blame him. I think I will do the same when I have my own restaurant. That's something new I learned today that I hadn't even thought of. In the diner I was working at, it was up to us, the employees to clean the kitchens and the front of the diner.

Francoise takes me back out to the kitchen to introduce me to the team, and Louis, who I will be shadowing for the next few weeks. He goes through them all, but there are so many. How am I supposed to remember all these names? Most of them just quickly say hi or welcome, then get on with whatever they are prepping.

"Macen, can you shadow Louis for the next hour or so while I get on with my prepping, then once the customers are in, I want you to try some of the dishes. Mr. Kade said not to show you the menu, just let you sample a three-course meal and write down exactly what you think of each dish. He said he wants your honest opinion and for you to note down if you would change anything about the dishes? If so what?"

"Oh, okay, yes, of course. Will you let me know what time to take a break to do that?"

"No, that would be up to you. Part of running a kitchen is time management, getting the dishes out to customers in a timely manner, which means being at your station, getting your dishes completed. Do you think you could do that today?" I nod yes at him.

Noon arrives, the doors open, and its non-stop for almost three hours. As it's my first day, I obviously have no idea of the flow of customers. The best way to find out if we have a lull is to check the reservations list at the Maître d's station.

When he enters, I quickly head to him, see his name is Tobias, and ask him for a copy each day. He doesn't seem happy but nods his head. Not long after, he comes back with today's reservations. I see we have a lull between 3.45 p.m. and 5.15 p.m., which will give me time to make sure I have some of my dishes prepped ready and then try some of the other dishes like Francoise asked me to. I'm so relieved that Caspian hasn't shown his face today. I feel I can breathe a bit better knowing he isn't watching me and assessing me.

At 3.50 p.m., after making sure I have enough sauces prepped, Louis says I can have my break, but not to be too long. I ask Francois to select the three dishes for me to try. He brings them to me in the employee room. For the appetizer, he picks a soup, which I guess is cream leek and pea soup with croutons, drizzled with sage and a floating bruschetta in the middle. It tastes as good as it looks.

For my entrée, he brings me poached salmon with dill and lemon zest, the flavors are so good, and then for dessert, it's apple and cheese granola cake with some vanilla ice cream.

I'm looking forward to trying the dishes, as I'm starving, not having stopped since setting foot in the place first thing this morning. Francoise joins me in the employee room, which has a small kitchen, a couch, and two tables with four chairs on each table. I've finished my entrée and am making notes, just about to start my dessert.

Francoise asks if he can look at my notes while I tried the dessert. I'm not ashamed, so I let him read them.

"Ah, you liked the soup, but you think it should have a hint of mint added to the sage drizzle, interesting. You also liked the hint of garlic and thyme. Very good, Macen."

I'm eating the dessert and smile at him. "May I?" I say asking for my notebook back so I can make notes on the dessert. He passes it to me and lets me write down my thoughts. I pass it back to him to read while I finish the dessert. It's so good that I eat it all.

"The poached salmon you thought it was slightly over poached making it a little dry, but the lemon and orange zest added a nice touch making it a little tangy, but in all, the flavors were good." He looks at me, and I look down to my plate.

"Then dessert, ah ha, you really liked that except you would have liked some apple pieces layered into the apple puree. I see the ice cream was to your liking using vanilla pods and it was really creamy."

I look up at him. "They are just my opinions on the three dishes I tried. I don't mean to criticize the chefs. That's the last thing I would want to do."

"This is perfect, Macen. This is exactly what we need to hear. I will have a word with the fish chef and make sure the poached salmon is not dry. I don't want customers saying we are not up to standard. Thank you." I hope he doesn't tell the fish chef it was me that said it.

"It was really tasty. I liked the dill, couscous, and herb dressing inside the salmon, which took away from it being a little dry. Maybe customers wouldn't notice. It's my job to know these things."

"No, I will make sure it is not too dry as it goes out. It must have been left out too long for it to dry up, in which case it should have been thrown out."

With that, he leaves me to finish my drink. I manage to call my grandma and speak to Dixon just to let them know it's going well, and I don't know what time my shift will finish today. I head back to take my dishes to the kitchen, and I see Francoise talking to the fish chef and checking one of the plated-up salmon. Francoise glances at me and just nods. I feel bad. I hope he doesn't tell the fish chef that I said it was dry. I don't want to be in the bad books on my first day. I notice the pastry chef looking at me. He's plating up some desserts but keeps glancing at me. I can't remember his name, and I wonder he knows me or if we've met.

It's just coming up to 5 p.m., and Louis, the commis chef I'm shadowing, tells me our shift is finished now and once I have cleaned up the station ready for David, the other commis chef to arrive, I can leave. He tells me our shift tomorrow is 5 p.m., and that we usually alternate early and late shifts with David, but I can sort this out with David once he's left.

I head to the employee room to collect my things ready to leave, and the pastry chef I saw earlier is there, sitting on the couch. I smile and say hi, but he doesn't acknowledge me, just stares at me. He unnerves me. The look on his face is mean, he has a sneer on his face, and his eyes are dark and piercing. I start to grab my stuff, and I can feel him watching me when I have my back to him. The hairs on the back of my neck stand up in fright.

"How was your first day in the mecca of all restaurants?" he asks me with anger and venom in his question, while I rummage through my bag trying to find my phone. I turn to look at him, and he's still staring at me as though he hasn't spoken.

"It was great, thank you. I'm exhausted though. It's been a while since I worked a full day like this."

He doesn't speak again just stares at me with that sneer. It's as though he didn't ask me a question. It's weird and freaking me out. He really makes me nervous and scared. I don't like the way he looks at me, or how he spoke to me. I want to get out of here.

"You going home now or going out?" I can't tell if he's just trying to be friendly or creepy.

"I don't have the energy to go out. I'm going home to put my aching feet up. Good night," I say as I reach the door. I turn as I open it and he doesn't speak again, he's just watching me, squinting at me with a frown on his face. I leave the room as quickly as I can, and I go to find Francoise to make sure he is fine with me going home.

I find him in the office and knock on the door. "Louis said it was okay to head out now, but I just wanted to make sure that was alright with you?"

"Yes, yes, but sit for a minute, please." He points to the chair in front of him.

I sit. "Tell me, Macen, what did you think of your first day? Was it what you expected?"

"I loved it. I didn't stop, but that's what I loved. I was so busy and shadowing Louis has been great. I'm learning so much. I don't want to let you or Mr. Kade down."

"Oh, I doubt you will do that, Macen. From what I see, you are a natural. I know Mr. Kade thinks the same or he wouldn't have hired you on the spot. He knows a good thing when he sees it. So, are you coming back? You haven't been scared off?"

I laugh at that. "Never, I will be back tomorrow. Louis said we are on the late shift, starting at 5 p.m. Do you need me to come in early for anything?"

"No, no, you are fine just coming in when Louis tells you what the shifts are. If I need to talk to you, I will do it during your shift. I'm just about to speak to Mr. Kade to let him know how your day went. He called earlier to check you were okay and probably to make sure you were still here." He says this with a big smile on his face. I flush with embarrassment and look at my hands on my lap. I want to ask where Caspian is, and if he will be in tomorrow, but I daren't, and I don't want Francoise to think anything of it.

"Do you have any questions or concerns about your first day? If there is anything at all, let me know. I suspect you will be honest about things like you were on the food you sampled today. I would like you to sample each meal we have on the menu and write your review in your notebook for me. I like your honesty, Macen."

"I'm always honest where food and recipes are concerned, maybe to a fault. But no, I don't have any questions or concerns. Thank you for today."

He nods at me, and with that, I get up from my chair and leave. I can't wait to get home.

I leave Casper's out of the back entrance and start to walk round to 5th Avenue. I'm going to get a cab home. I'm so tired — it's been a long day. I move away from the line of customers at Casper's so the taxi drivers can see me, and I hail one down. Just as I shut the door, I feel someone watching me, so I turn to look out of the side window across the street. As the cars move past, I see him, standing there, leaning against the wall between the shops — the pastry chef. He's standing with one foot up resting on the wall behind him, smoking a cigarette, and he's looking straight at me. Almost like he was waiting for me to leave.

It's my second day, and I'm excited to get to work again. Being on the late shift means I can take Dixon to school and pick him up, then leave him with Grandma to put to bed. We all eat dinner together before I leave for work. I get the subway today, but I will get a cab home because it will be midnight and much safer. I have a busy day at work, and I love every minute of it. I have another three-course meal and give Francoise my reviews. Caspian isn't in again, but I don't ask anyone where he is. I do find out the name of the pastry chef though, as I hear someone shout out the name Reid and he answers. I didn't look at him and didn't have to speak to him during the day, but I can feel him watching me at times. The hairs on my neck stand up. He is really starting to freak me out. I still don't know if I know him from anywhere, but he seems to have a problem with me, and I don't know why. I now want to get home and away from here because of him. He is making me so uncomfortable. All through the shift, I felt him watching me.

chapter

10

Caspian

I HEADED INTO THE RESTAURANT EARLY. I had a pile of paperwork to do, and I wanted to see Francoise before everyone else got in. I wanted to know what he thought of Macen — strictly on a business level of course. He'd phoned to let me know she enjoyed her first day and was definitely coming back. I hope he didn't hear the relief in my voice and the sigh I let out. To say I wasn't bothered about seeing Macen again would be an outright lie. She is all I have thought about since last week. It's killing me. I don't even want to sink into anyone else, and I can't fathom out why in the world she's having this effect on me. She's not my type.

There's no one around when I get there, so I head straight to my office to sort through the paperwork piled on my desk. I get stuck in, and it feels like no time at all when I hear the back door go and Francoise comes strolling in.

"Hey, Casp, how's it going?" I look at my watch. I've been here for nearly two hours!

"Hey, Francoise, good, thanks. Sorted out all the stuff in LA, so hopefully, that's all back on track. Shall we have a coffee? I'm parched. Been here two hours sorting through all this stuff. I didn't realize it was that long till just now."

"Yeah, let me get the coffee. You finish off, and then I can give you the rundown on everything." He heads out to get us coffees. I pick up Macen's paperwork and read it yet again until Francoise comes back in and sits down. The rest of the team will be arriving in the next half hour, so we need to get on with this. He looks at what I have in my hand.

"Great call with Macen. She's damn good at what she does, Casp. She's a natural, honest as well. I've had her tasting the dishes on the menu and writing a review on each one. Here, look." He passes me a notebook, which I take and flick open. On each page is the name of the dish, the date and time she tried it, then underneath is her opinion on that dish and what she thinks of the way it's cooked — if it needed something adding or taking away from it. Fucking hell, this girl is like me in so many ways. This is exactly what I did when I got my first job in a restaurant, and I do this with all my employee's when they start, but she's the first one to do this methodically and give her opinion on the actual ingredients. She's going to be an excellent chef, and I have no doubts that one day she will own a successful restaurant like me. I want her so badly the more I find out about her, but I know I can't go there. I'm royally screwed. Actually, I need to go out and get royally screwed to get her out of my head.

I finish with Francoise as the team starts arriving, he's told me all about Macen and how she has taken to the job quickly. Shadowing Louis is not a problem, but she seems to know as much as him anyway. She is due in any minute, and I need to avoid her for a bit, but I know I have to get her in here to welcome her and ask her how she's finding the job. Shit, I hope the feeling isn't mutual on her side. I don't know if I can resist her if she feels the same way. If it is, I'll have to put her off, and that means being an ass to her. After all, I am her boss.

I put on my chef whites and head into the kitchens to see what's going on and to make sure everything is up to scratch. That way, I get the respect of the team as chef and not just Casp. As I walk around, tasting each item, I acknowledge every one of my team by name. It's one thing I have always insisted on, getting to know who works for me and make them part of the team, which is why I need to speak to Macen. I finish my rounds, except the one station, which I have left until the end for a reason.

Macen.

It's almost opening time. I can't drag her away because the lunch rush will start very soon, and they're still prepping, so I head to her station

"Louis, Macen, everything good here?" I say looking from Louis to Macen. Fuck, why did I do that? She's stunning in her chef's whites and hat. I don't know why but her hair in a net and her hat is a real turn on for me. She looks at me shyly or is that my imagination and wishful thinking?

"Yes, Chef," they both say in unison. I nod at them. I then taste the sauces they have been preparing. The first one I taste is perfect. It's a lemon cream sauce that goes with the sautéed sole, and it is the best I've tasted.

"This sauce is perfect, well done, Louis. I have never tasted it this good before."

"Not me, Chef, that's all Macen's doing. She made it all herself from scratch." I turn and look at Macen, who is not looking at me but is chopping up some herbs for the next sauce.

"Macen?" She looks at me — her face is red.

"Yes, Chef?"

"Well done. This is the best lemon cream sauce I have tasted. Did you follow my recipe?"

"Yes, Chef. I just made sure the cream was thick to make it rich and creamy, then slowly added the crushed garlic and lemon to the cream."

"Well, it tastes as good as my sauce, Macen."

"Thank you, Chef." She carries on with her chopping.

"Macen, when it gets quiet after the lunch rush, can you come to my office, please?"

She looks at me wide-eyed and flushes. "Er, Yes, Chef."

I leave the kitchen and head back to my office to take my whites off, and then I head to front of house to see the waiting staff and my maître d', Tobias. I need a coffee — a strong black one. Being in the same space as Macen kills me. I can feel my cock starting to stir, and that's the last thing I need in front of my staff. I speak to Tobias for a little bit while I drink my coffee. He tells me Macen is the only chef that has asked for the reservations list to be given to her at the start of each shift so she can see and plan the day. That doesn't really surprise me. That's what I do all the time.

The restaurant is all set up, and there is a line outside waiting for lunch. Tobias goes to open the doors, and I stay and greet the first clients. I like to show my face in front of house. It makes the clients feel special when I greet them.

I'm back in my office, going through more paperwork and answering an e-mail from my Canadian realtor when there is a knock on the door.

"Come in," I say but don't look up.

"Mr. Kade, you wanted to see me?" Fuck. That voice. I look up at her

"Yes, Macen, please come in and sit." I motion for her to take the seat in front of my desk.

"I wanted to welcome you to the team at Casper's officially. I'm sorry I wasn't here for your first day to welcome you?"

"It's okay, Mr. Kade. Thank you."

"Casp or Caspian is fine when we are in here, but it's chef in the kitchen."

"Sorry, Caspian. Francoise was great, thank you. He showed me everything, and Louis has been wonderful with me. I'm really settling in now, and everyone is very friendly."

"From what I have been told you really know your stuff, Macen. Francoise is very pleased with you and your honesty when trying the dishes. You know you're the first one to actually take that bit seriously and give honest answers with suggestions. That tells me a lot."

"Just doing what I was asked, Caspian." Fuck I love her saying my name in full and not shortening it. No one ever calls me Caspian — it's always been Casp or Chef. My cock is hard just from that. Fuck, how am I going to work with her?

"Well, carry on with the good work. I have no doubt you will be running this place before fulfilling your dream of owning your own restaurant."

"Thank you. I will. I promise. This is my dream, Caspian. I have waited a long time for the opportunity." She flushes again and then looks at her hands, which are in her lap, playing with a button on her chef whites.

"So, how are you finding working in the kitchen? I know you said everyone is friendly but are you enjoying it so far?" She's now looking at me, just staring. She doesn't look like she's heard what I just asked her, and the way she's looking at me right now, I could just kiss her, and I would have no problem bending her over my desk. I smile at her. I find it amusing that she's gone into her own little world. I put my elbows on my desk and lean on my hands with my fingers on my mouth, waiting for her to answer me. This goes on for a good minute, so I repeat my question to her.

"I am, yes, thank you," she replies.

"Good. You best head back and get your own lunch before the next rush." She gets up and heads out of the door without looking back. As she closes the door behind her, I breathe out a sigh of relief. Fuck, what am I going to do?

Macen

I SEE CASPIAN WALK INTO THE kitchen. He doesn't look this way as he goes around each station, but I keep my eye on where he is. My heart is beating fast, nearly coming out of my chest, and I have butterflies in my tummy. Why is he having this effect on me? I have never had these feelings for anyone.

I catch Reid looking at me when I glance to see where Caspian is. What is it with him? He gives me the creeps. Everyone else is really nice but not him. I'm definitely steering clear of him. He watched me get in a cab on Monday night, then he kept watching me yesterday, and it's making me paranoid. Is it in my mind or is he just minding his own business and I'm making something out of it?

Oh, god, Caspian's coming over here. Oh no, I can feel my cheeks getting hot, and I feel a bit nauseous. I don't look, I just concentrate on the chopping, but I can feel him near. The hairs on my neck stand up, and I have funny tingles down my spine. I can feel him look at me.

"Louis, Macen, everything good here?" Oh, God, he's speaking to me.

"Yes, Chef," I say at the same time as Louis. He tastes the sauce and speaks to Louis, but I don't listen until he speaks to me directly, and I have to answer him. I turn and look at him, feeling my face burn because I don't know what he said.

"Yes, Chef?" He congratulates me on my sauce and then asks me to go and see him after the lunch rush has finished. Oh no. I don't think I can be in the same room as him. I can't seem to control all these strange feelings. I have to keep it strictly businesslike. This is my dream job, and the chance I needed to get where I want to be. There is no way I'm blowing this.

I head to Caspian's office after the lunchtime rush, but the conversation is all a bit of a blur. I am mesmerized by his bright eyes, his smooth voice, and his messy black hair. I wish I could run my fingers through it. Holy shit, where did that come from? He smiles at me at one point, and the dimples in his cheeks just floor me. He's taken off his chef's whites and has on a white shirt, which is rolled up to above the elbow. I can see both arms covered in tattoo's, his shirt is tight on his biceps, and I can make out the muscle definition when he brings his elbows onto the desk and clasps his big hands together, pointing his two index fingers and resting them on his lips.

He says my name, he must have asked me a question, but I have no idea what it was. Thankfully, he repeats the question so I can answer him, which I do.

The entire time, I'm clenching my legs together, trying to get rid of the feelings I'm having down below. I'm sure I'm bright red the whole time I'm in his office, and my butterflies are fluttering away. I'm struggling, and I honestly don't know how I'm going to continue to work for him.

I grab my lunch in the employee room, and I'm eating my wrap when the door opens. I know without looking that Reid has walked in. The hairs on the back of my neck stand up, with fear and I have tingles running down my spine, but not in a good way like I did in Caspian's office, these are chilling, scared tingles. It feels like a warning for me to be careful.

I'm on my own in the room, and I don't look up at him straight away. I don't want to acknowledge him, but then I don't want to be ignorant either. He goes to the left side of the room and opens the fridge. I glance at him and find his attention is on me, not what is in the fridge.

I smile a small smile, not too friendly, and say, "Hi," but he doesn't respond. Shit, what is his problem? I need to get out of here and quickly. I put the rest of the wrap in its bag, and close the magazine I'm reading, then get up and start for the door, but before I know what's happening, Reid's blocking my way to the door. I jolt to a halt. He's so close to me — invading my space.

"Excuse me, please," I say to him, trying to be friendly, but he doesn't move. He just looks at me, tilting his head to the side. Shit, he looks like he hates me. He's scowling, causing all the lines on his forehead and round his eyes to wrinkle, but it's the look in his eyes that unsettles me most, so dark and sinister. There is a look of hate on his face, and something else… resentment. For what, I don't know. I don't know him, and he looks a lot older than me, and he's really not attractive. His eyes have wrinkles around them, and his hair is a funny color, not brown and not black it's somewhere in between, but it doesn't look natural, it looks like he's used a bad hair coloring. His eyes are so dark and evil, why would he just stand blocking my way out? What did he want?

"Excuse me, please, may I get past you?"

"Do you recognize me?"

I look at him quizzically because I don't.

"Sorry, no, I don't. Have we met before?" I say this with a shake to my voice. I hate how pathetic I sound, but he's scaring me. I just want to run and get out of here.

"You have no idea who I am?"

I shake my head, no. I'm getting worried and pray someone will come into the room.

"N-no sorry, should I? Have we met before?" I ask again.

Just then the door opens behind him and nudges him in the back, which makes him move right into my space. He reaches out to stop himself from falling and puts his hands on my shoulders. I try to step back out of his reach, and I manage to shrug him off and step back, away from his hold on me. It's Caspian entering the room, and the look on his face is one of confusion, morphing into something unreadable.

"Excuse me," I say moving around Reid and past Caspian and rushing out of the door, not looking at either of them.

I hurry into the ladies bathroom to try and calm down. My heart is beating out of my chest. I'm scared. Could things get any worse? I have Reid who is scaring the shit out of me, then Caspian making me nervous as hell.

I take a couple of minutes to calm myself before facing any of them out there. I don't want Louis to pick up on how I'm feeling. I wash up, then head back to my station. As I enter the kitchen, I see Caspian talking to Louis. They both look up as I approach and stop talking. Caspian gives Louis a grave look, then he stares at me for a beat.

"Macen, I think you should get back to prepping your sauces for the afternoon, don't you? The employee room is not to be used for anything other than to have a drink, rest, or eat. Do you understand me?"

"Yes, Chef."

"Work." With that, he storms off in the direction of the front of house. I'm confused about his attitude. I was only on my break.

"Don't know what you did, Mace, but you sure rattled his cage. Never seen him like that before. I could see the veins in his neck popping when he was asking me about you?"

"Sorry, Louis, I didn't do anything wrong. What was he asking?"

"If you and Reid are a relationship. I told him I had no idea. I haven't even seen you look at Reid, let alone speak to him. I didn't know you knew him, and I told Casp that."

I drop my head and sigh, unsure whether to tell Louis how Reid is intimidating me.

"I don't know him," I say quietly.

When Louis goes for his lunch, I see Reid at his station, and he's staring at me again. I have only been here for three days, and now I'm uncomfortable at work. If this carries on, I will have to tell Francoise or Caspian that I have a problem.

The dinner rush is immense, and I'm glad when my shift is over. I'm worn out and stressed about the Reid situation. All afternoon and evening he was watching me. Louis even commented on it, saying that he thinks Reid must have a thing for me if we're not an item because he kept watching me. Chef even shouted at Reid at one point for messing up the dish he had just put out.

I head for the employee room to get my things. I'll get a cab again. I'm too exhausted to walk home or fight on the subway even though it's only three stops. I get in a cab on 5th and have the same feeling of being watched again. Sure enough, I glance over the road, and there he is, in the same spot, leaning against the wall, watching me. I'm worried. I have the job I dreamed of, but I have this guy who has taken a dislike to me, making it difficult for me to enjoy my work. I don't know what to do. Maybe I should speak to Francoise or Caspian and ask if our shifts could be changed because he always seems to be on the same shift as Louis and me. I feel sick just thinking about it. I can't wait to get home. Dixon will be in bed, so I will talk this through with Grandma and see what she suggests I do.

FUCK, WHAT HAVE I JUST WALKED in on? Is she in a relationship with this dipshit? I would never have pegged the two of them to be together. However, the way she jumped back out of his arms, and he dropped his hands from her, I would say that's a sure sign something's going on with them. Fuck, why am I seething about it? Admittedly, it's for the best — I certainly can't pursue her. But why him? He's the biggest ass I employ. He's had several warnings in the time he's been with me. I need to fire his ass. Maybe this gives me the reason to do just that. I stand, glaring at them both, waiting for one of them to say something, but neither of them does. She storms past us both, not even looking my way. Well, fuck her, and him. "Reid, my office, twenty minutes," I rage at him. The dipshit doesn't say a thing, just smirks at me and nods his head. I turn and leave the room angrily. I'm fucking livid, and I know I shouldn't be. I can pretend it's about the no fraternizing rule in their contracts that's made me like this, but it's not, it's her, this is all about her. I feel… fuck, dare I say it, jealous! She's really rattled my fucking cage.

I need to find out if there is anything in this, so I storm into the kitchen to ask Louis, but he tells me that he doesn't even think Macen knows Reid. That strikes me as a bit odd. Macen works closely with Louis, and if anyone knows I thought he would. "I find that hard to believe," I snarl at him, "I just caught them in a compromising position in the employee room, and I'm not fucking happy about it." Just then, I notice her heading this way. Both Louis and I look at her, she looks down, but continues toward us, "I'll speak to you later," I say to Louis as she approaches. I storm off to front of house after snapping at her to work. I need a large brandy to calm me down.

I'm sitting in my office when there's a knock at my door. I know it's Reid, and shout for him to come in, but I don't look up as he enters. To be honest, I would prefer not to see him right now. I'm too angry, and god knows what I will say. I make him wait for a minute while I pretend to carry on reading the papers on my desk. I can't read the words, but it gives me an extra minute to calm and be the professional I am. I raise my head and look him in the eye, but I don't ask him to sit. The fucker can stay standing. "Do you mind telling me what I just walked in on between you and Ms. Donald?"

He doesn't speak, just looks at me. I raise my eyebrow, letting him know not to fuck with me. "Nothing, Casp, that was nothing."

"Don't bullshit me, Reid. That wasn't nothing. She jumped back out of your arms as though being caught doing something she shouldn't." He doesn't say anything. He just looks at me, the cocky shit.

"I will not tolerate any kind of intimate relationships while on my premises. Do you know there is a no fraternizing clause in your contract?"

"No, to be honest, I didn't read it all. Guess I skipped over that part."

The fucker is sneering at me. Keep calm, Casp, don't let him rile you. You don't want a lawsuit against you, I tell myself in my head before I speak. I take a breath. "Well, there is, and I can fire either one or both of you. I caught you in a compromising position, so you can't bullshit me.

How long have you two been together? Ms. Donald never mentioned knowing anyone that worked here in her interview?"

He has his hands in his houndstooth trouser pockets, and he looks down as though he's thinking what to say, before looking back at me. "We've known each other on and off. Just casual, you know? But if anyone has to go then it should be her. She's only been here a couple of days."

Well, fuck me, he's throwing her under the bus. That pisses me off even more. "She may have only been here a couple of days, but I can tell already that she is a far better chef than you. How many warnings are we on now, Reid? Four, isn't it? This will be your fifth. I should have let you go on your third warning, but I gave you the benefit of the doubt. Tell me why I shouldn't just fire your ass now? Give me one good reason to keep you around. You don't seem to have any regard or respect for the job?"

He takes his hands out of his pockets and folds his arms across his chest defiantly. "Look, I'm sorry. It won't happen again, Casp. I promise you won't even know that Macen and I know each other. I promise to do my best with my meal prep and presentation. I have improved. I haven't had a warning for a couple of months now."

Now the fucker's changed his attitude. Still doesn't excuse him trying to get Macen fired though. "Get back to your station, Reid. You've been away long enough. I'll let you know my decision when I've spoken to Ms. Donald. Until then, keep your nose clean and work your ass off."

He doesn't say another word. He just turns and leaves.

I need to go and see how the kitchen is going, but my head isn't in it. For the first time I can ever remember I'm distracted from my passion, and it's all because of Macen. My restaurant is my passion, my baby, my life, but right now I don't want to be here. I need to speak to her, but I can't right now.

It's 5 p.m. She'll be leaving anytime now. I suppose it's now or never. I open my office door, head for the kitchen, and I just see her leaving through the back door. "Macen," I call, but the door shuts. I walk towards it, expecting it to open again, but it doesn't. I open it and look outside, but she's nowhere to been seen. I guess she didn't hear me call her. I'll check what shift she's on tomorrow, and I will speak to her about what happened today. I need to hear what she has to say — to see if she is trustworthy or if she's going to bullshit me as well. I thought she was dependable; she's been honest about the menu and her recipes, but when her dream job is on the line who knows what she will say? Fuck, now I need a distraction for the night.

chapter
13

Macen

I'M SO RELIEVED TO GET HOME. I NEED to see Dixon for a cuddle. He's in bed, but I lay with him for a few minutes. Grandma has some good old mac 'n' cheese on the table for me with a glass of wine. I'm hungry. I didn't eat all my lunch with Reid coming into the room.

Grandma sits with me at the table with a glass of wine in hand like she always did when I was living with her. She tells me about Dixon and the drawings he did at preschool and how he helped a girl out because a boy was being mean to her. "How was your day at the restaurant?"

I hesitate and inhale a breath. How do I tell her I'm not enjoying my dream job? I put my fork down, take a sip of my wine, and look at her. "I'm not enjoying it." I hang my head in shame. It's the job I've always wanted, and I absolutely love being there.

"What do you mean you're not enjoying it? You were full of beans over the last couple of days. What's changed, Macen?"

I look up at her and sip my wine again. "Macen, what is it, love? What's happened? I know you, and I know there is something wrong."

I take another sip. "I love the job. I love learning, and I fit right in." I look down again. "However, there's this one chef who works there, Reid, and he scares me." I tell her all about the things he's done to intimidate me, including blocking my exit from the employee room and watching me get in my cabs.

"Do you know who he is?"

I shake my head, no. "That's just it. I don't think I've ever seen him before. I certainly don't recognize him from anywhere. Maybe he has confused me with someone else? Maybe I look like someone he knows or knew?"

I take another sip of my wine and tell her what happened when Caspian came into the room today. "Caspian was really annoyed with me. I hope I still have a job."

She takes my hand. "I'm sure you will, Macen."

"Do you think I need to tell Caspian about this Reid? The venom in his voice when he asked if I recognized him terrified me, Grandma. The hairs on the back of my neck stood up with fright. I don't know what to do. I don't want to lose my job just because one chef has taken a dislike to me." I shrug my shoulders and hang my head.

Grandma gets up and comes around to my side and hugs me to her. "I think you need to make Caspian aware of the situation. Don't throw this opportunity away because of one man. You have come so far and gone through so much to get here. You need to speak to Caspian tomorrow."

I know she's right. I give her a hug. "Thank you for always having my back no matter what. I'll speak to Caspian tomorrow if he's in, and I will avoid Reid as much as possible. I don't have anything to do with him in the kitchen, thankfully." I clear the dishes away and head to bed. It's been a long day, and I'm shattered.

I've been lying awake for what feels like hours. This Reid situation is really playing on my mind, and I'm not looking forward to tomorrow. I've been racking my brain trying to see if I can remember him at all, and

I've just come up blank. I don't remember him from any of my schools or anywhere that I've worked. I'll speak to Francoise about it if Caspian isn't in. I need to let them know what's going on.

chapter 14

Caspian

I KNOW I ENJOY MY CELEBRITY CHEF persona, but even I have to have a vice. Usually, it's burying myself in women, but that seems to be off the table because all I can think of is fucking Macen, literally, so I decide the next option is to watch. I don't care that voyeurism has a stigma attached to it. I love to watch, and I'm not talking about watching porn on the TV; I like to watch it live.

Luckily, there's a very exclusive club I'm a member off on the Upper West side of Manhattan on W65th Street, called Arthur's. It's very private and exclusive — to become a member you have to be someone famous or have deep pockets. That way, not just anyone can join, and members don't risk it hitting the tabloids that they are a member, although, I don't give a shit. I'm young, free and single and can do what the fuck I like in my private time.

The club has very strict rules: no cell phones allowed on the premises, and you have to produce a clean medical certificate regularly to prevent STI's from being passed on.

Sexually, almost anything goes.

There's a communal room for participants and a viewing area for the voyeurs like me, and private rooms, some with viewing areas.

There are also fetish and bondage rooms for Dom's and Subs, but they don't do anything for me. I like watching vanilla sex, and I like some gadgets and toys, just nothing too heavy.

With the day I've had today, walking in on Macen and Reid and then dealing with Reid, I need a distraction. I need to try to get Macen out of my head, but that's easier said than done. When I saw her leave Casper's, I was so fucking annoyed. I wanted to speak to her because I'm not in for the next few days. I'm flying to Vegas to look at a potential restaurant there. There is only Francoise that knows anything about this one.

I enter the club and notice it's been refurbished since I was last here. It's like a five-star hotel — very luxurious and very modern. I like it. It's more my style. I get a brandy from the bar, and I scope the place to see if there is anyone I know. I see a few familiar faces: some I've fucked and some I'd like to fuck. Macen flashes into my head at that thought. It's like I can't think of fucking anyone else, only her.

As I wander around. I notice a few celebs. There's an arrogant young singer who has recently hit the big time and a female anchorwoman who is stunning. I wouldn't mind giving her a fuck at some point. Macen pops up in my head again, shit.

I head up the long sweeping staircase to where the private rooms are allocated and enter a private room with a small voyeur gallery. There are three chairs, separated by a small table beside each one, complete with a box of tissues and a set of state of the art Bose headphones for listening in. The chairs are facing the wall of the room, which has one-way glass right along it for viewing. I pull the curtain across the entranceway, hoping no one else joins me. I like to be alone whenever possible while watching. I sit down, drink in hand, and see what's going on.

There's a woman and a man. I can't make out her face. I can only see her side profile. She's on her knees on the bed facing the headboard. She has short black hair and is wearing a red lacy basque but nothing else. Him, I recognize. He's an English chat show host, with a number one rated show. He's very good. I thought he was happily married. Oh well, each to their own.

He's standing completely naked, looking toward the glass. He can't see me, but he probably knows he has an audience. "You ready for this, Mol?" he asks the woman as he turns and heads for the bed. "Yes, Tommy. Please hurry, I've waited long enough, and I want you." With that, he gets on the bed behind her. He runs his hands over her ass, squeezing and pinching, he then bends his head and bites each ass cheek. "Ohh, Tommy, please hurry." "Shhh, Mol. I'm getting there. I'm going to make you cum so hard you will be screaming."

His hands wander around her front, where he grips her nipples. The basque is so tight that her tits are being squeezed out of the top. One hand slips back to her backside, where he runs a finger down the crack of her ass, then his hand disappears between her legs where it looks like he's finger fucking her. "Oh, Tommy, more, please more." He nips and sucks her shoulder, his hand moving between her legs. She's gyrating on his hand up and down, round and round. "More!" she screams.

He stops and shuffles backward away from her. "Don't stop here are you going, Tommy?" "Nowhere, Mol, just going to change position. I want to taste you. I want to stick my tongue inside you, and I want you to cum all over my face." He turns and lays on his back, shuffling back up towards her. "Spread those legs wide for me, love," he tells her. I can't take my eyes off them. I have my glass held as though going to take a sip, but it doesn't reach my lips. I'm hard as fuck watching these two. They are hot together — they have chemistry.

He edges between her legs, then grabs her hips and lowers her pussy onto his face. She grabs hold of the iron rods on the headboard to steady herself as he slips his tongue inside her. He's pulling her down onto his face as hard as he can, trying to get in there deeper. She starts moving around and round, and I can hear the noises from how wet she is. These headphones are amazing — they pick up everything. She starts moaning for more, and he moves a hand from her hip and slips two fingers into her ass. She's getting louder and louder. She looks down to watch what he's doing and let's go of the headboard. She leans back with her hands on his torso, trying to find his cock. She grabs it with one hand and starts pulling. The more he sucks and penetrates her with his fingers and tongue, the louder she gets and the rougher she gets with his cock. She is close, very close.

I don't even realize I've put my drink on the table next to me until I'm yanking the zip down on my jeans and pulling out my cock. It's like fucking steel. I start pulling, replicating what she's doing to him, yanking hard, moving up and down. She's now practically jumping up and down on his face. He has fingers in her ass with the one hand and is rubbing her clit with the other, as well as his tongue in her pussy. That's it, she explodes; and gyrates harder and faster as she climaxes, screaming his name. "Tomeeeee, fuck, Tommy, fuck, Tommy." I explode straight after watching her cum, but although I'm watching her, it's Macen's face that I see as I close my eyes and let my cum spurt out. It's Macen I see gyrating and screaming with her tits hanging out and her pussy so fucking wet. I'm squeezing and milking my cock. It just won't stop with the images of Macen In my head. "Fuck," I shout out, not realizing how loud I am. I finish off and then clean myself with the tissues.

"Fuck, Mol, I love it when you cum all over my face, doll. Turn around, so you can suck my cock while I go for seconds." She starts to turn so she can do as he asked and looks toward the mirror, licking her lips seductively as though she can see me. I wonder if she heard me shout out. She has a slight grin on her face as she moves her pussy back on his face, then, still looking into the mirror, she licks her lips again before lowering her mouth to his cock. She licks it like a popsicle, grabbing it by the base. She's putting on a show for me, and I'm fucking hard again already.

He must have inserted his tongue into her pussy again because she gasps and starts gyrating on his face. Fuck, that's hot. She keeps pulling him out of her mouth and licking him, then putting him back in all the way. She grabs his balls and starts playing with them, and then her other hand disappears, and I know the moment she's stuck a finger in his ass because he starts bucking like a bronco. He has hold of her hips, pulling them down hard as she tries to gyrate. Her head is slightly turned towards the mirror, giving me a show at the same time, and it's fucking hot. He is close, she is close, and so am I. I'm yanking on my cock so hard, and I play with my balls with my other hand, replicating what she's doing. I'm about to explode. Just as I do, they both follow suit, and it's fucking amazing. I screw my eyes shut, pumping away to images of Macen again. Fucking, Macen, why can't I get her out of my head? I'm here to forget her, but it's just made it worse. I want her even more.

"I fucking love you, Mol. Come here, baby. I'm going to fuck you so hard." He pulls her wig off and it's then I realize this is his wife. She has long blonde hair under the wig. He lowers into her and starts to fuck her nice and slowly at first until they both become like rampant animals, going as hard as they can against each other. I clean myself up and head out, leaving them to it. As I pull back the curtain to leave the corridor, the anchorwoman I saw earlier passes me. She's holding the hand of the arrogant young singer, leading him to a room at the end of the hallway. I contemplate following to watch them. She's about fifteen years older than him, but I suppose a young kid like him he will take whatever is offered. I know I used to. If I go and watch them, I will still only see Macen, and I need to head back and pack.

I leave the club and decide to walk back to my place. I need a breather and to try to think about what I'm going to do about Macen. This obsession is getting a bit much. I can't fuck anyone else, and even when I watch, all I see is her. I have to decide if I should fire her after what happened today or if I will keep her.

Macen

I'M ON THE DAY SHIFT TODAY. I SAID goodbye to Dixon and Grandma, and I'm currently on the subway to the restaurant. I have a very heavy heart this morning. Last night I couldn't sleep much, and I even thought about quitting, but then, why should I when I haven't done anything wrong? Why should I suffer yet again for a man I don't even know?

After my attack, I got so angry because I had to leave school and that wasn't my fault either. Life can be so cruel sometimes, but this time, I'm not quitting. If Caspian wants to fire me, then that's his decision to make.

I have my ear pods in with Linkin Park's *Hybrid Theory* blaring away in my ears, so I don't hear the announcement for my station, and being lost in thought, I miss my stop. My day is officially shitty, and it's only just begun. I get off at the next stop and walk back towards the restaurant. It's early, but already busy. New York is always busy. I'm just minding my own business, listening to my music when the hairs on the back of my neck stand up, sending a chill down my spine. I stop suddenly and look around.

He's there. He's behind me. Is he following me, or is this just his usual way to work? He looks me straight in the eyes as he carries on walking straight towards me. Shit, what do I do? Do I let him walk past me, so he is ahead of me, or do I turn and continue walking to work, ignoring him? I'm not waiting for him. I don't know him, and we certainly are not friends.

I turn back and carry on walking to work but startle a few minutes later as he suddenly appears right at my side, touching my arm with his. I jump at the contact and take a pod out of my ear. "What the hell!" I say, annoyed. He doesn't speak, just looks down at me with a sneer. We're not that far from the restaurant now, and I don't want to walk in with him, so I stop. He realizes and turns back to look at me. We just stare at each other. He doesn't speak, so neither do I. I turn and head for a pharmacy I just passed, and I don't look back, but I know he's watching me. What is his problem? Why can't he leave me alone? He's freaking me out. If we were proper work colleagues, then he would have said good morning or something like that, and he certainly wouldn't have gotten into my space again.

I'm in the shop just wasting a few minutes really, hoping Reid has gone on before I start back for the restaurant. I get some headache tablets, as I have no doubt I will need them before the day is over. I cautiously step out of the pharmacy doors, looking around to see if he has gone, and I let out the breath I'm holding when I don't see him anywhere. I put my pods back in and head to the restaurant, but as I head for the rear door, I stop dead again. He's there, leaning against the wall as he does across the street when watching me, with one foot up on the wall, smoking a cigarette. What the hell? Is he waiting for me, or is he just having a smoke? I choose the latter and head for the door.

His hand flies out and grabs me by the elbow as I pass him. He grips me tightly. I try to yank him off me to get loose, but he grips harder. "What the hell is your problem? Get your fucking hand off me," I snarl. He doesn't speak, but he drops my elbow. He takes a drag on his cigarette then drops it to the floor and makes a show of stamping on it and grinding it into the ground. Then he walks to the door, opens it, looks back at me with that horrible sneer before disappearing through it, leaving me standing here, dumbstruck. I don't move for a few minutes. In fact, it's only Louis coming around the corner that shakes me out of the trance I'm in. "Good morning, Macen. Hey, you okay? You look a bit pale."

I put a brave smile on my face and nod my head "Morning, Louis, yes, I'm good, thank you. Just daydreaming. Guess I'm still tired."

"Well come on, girl, let's get in and get our sauces prepped for a busy day ahead."

I head to the employee room with Louis to get my whites on. I know before I enter the room that Reid is in there, but I'm with Louis, so I feel safe. I open the door, and sure enough, he's there, but not getting changed or anything, just leaning against the table opposite the door with his arms folded and one ankle over the other.

His face takes on a look of frustration when he notices Louis right behind me.

"Hey, Reid, how's it going?" Louis greets him. I don't say a word. I walk over to the lockers and start to get changed. I only have to take my coat and sweatshirt off because I have a white tank top on that I wear under my chef's white jacket. I put on my jacket and start on my hair.

"Hey, Louis. I'm good thanks, or at least I will be when Macen stops screwing me around like she is."

I freeze, but then slowly turn and face them. They are both looking at me. "What the hell are you talking about?"

Reid shrugs, gets up off the table, then heads out of the door. Louis looks at me quizzically. "I have no idea what he's talking about, Louis. I barely know the guy. In fact, I can count on one hand the number of times he's actually spoken to me."

"Hey, Macen, not my business, but I told you yesterday that Casp was pissed about it. A bit of friendly advice though between you and me. I don't trust that guy. He's a bit of an oddball. Doesn't really fit in. If I were you, I would steer clear. You know your contract also has a no fraternizing clause in it right?"

"Believe me, Louis, I have every intention of staying away from him. He creeps me out — he's there at every turn. I don't even know the guy, but he seems to be making out we know each other. He terrifies me." I turn back to my locker, put on my hair net and chef's hat, and we head out to our station and start to prep.

"Macen, this doesn't taste quite right."

I turn to look at Louis who is standing over my lemongrass sauce. "There's something missing. Here, have a taste." He passes me a spoon, and I try the sauce. He's right. It's missing the kaffir lime leaves, which I'm sure I added. I look around my station, but there is no sign of them. Shit.

"Macen, you need to get your head in the game or Casp will have your ass."

"I'm sorry, Louis. I know you're right. I'm a little distracted because of Reid. He's been watching me all morning. I can feel his eyes boring into me." Louis turns to look in Reid's direction, and it just so happens he's watching us.

"Do you want me to have a word with him for you? If he's freaking you out, I don't mind. Hey, I'm leaving in a few weeks anyway, so no skin off my nose."

Oh no, I can't have Louis getting into trouble for me or have Reid do anything to Louis. I could never live with myself. "No, thanks, Louis, I don't want any trouble, and I certainly don't want you in the middle of it. I spoke to my grandma about it last night, and we both decided that I need to speak to Caspian about it today."

"Okay, if you're sure, Macen. You need to do a new batch of sauce though. Doors open soon, so you don't have much time. We can't send this one out. If Casp or anyone else tries it, we will both be in for it."

I redo the sauce just in time for the doors opening. Louis has saved me from a potential disaster today, and I'm grateful for that. I need to keep my head on my work and ignore Reid as much as I can. I haven't seen Caspian yet this morning. He must be on the late shift. He always comes and checks on the kitchen when he's in. I'll have a word with Francoise and see when he's due.

The time flies as it always does. I still haven't seen Caspian. He would have been in by now, even if he were on the late shift. "Louis, do you mind if I take a break while there is a slight lull. I need to find Francoise?" "Sure, you go and find him, we have enough sauce prepped." I head out to the offices to find Francoise. He isn't around, so I head for a quick drink of water in the employee room. Big mistake. There are a couple of other chefs taking a break, and just as I close the fridge after grabbing my water, he's there, leaning against the worktop with his arms folded. He wasn't in here when I came in, so he must have followed me. He doesn't speak but moves to stand right next to me, with his arm touching me like he did this morning. I step back away from him, and he scowls down at me, but I scowl back at him. Anyone watching us would think we knew each other— it actually seems like that's the image he's trying to portray. Neither of us speaks, so I move away from him and head out of the door.

I stand in the hallway for a few seconds, trying to calm down. I let out my breath, then I realize he's followed me out of the room. I don't look back at him or acknowledge he's here, but head for the office hoping Caspian or Francoise is in there. I knock on the door, hearing, "Come in." I open the door and rush in, shutting it firmly behind me, without a second glance. I don't know if Reid is still there watching me or if he's gone back to the kitchen.

I let out another breath and relax slightly, looking up to see the puzzled look on Francois's face. "Are you okay, Macen? You look a bit flustered."

I must look like a complete idiot, and I feel embarrassed. I didn't plan this out properly. What do I tell him? "Yes, sorry, Francoise. I, erm, I have a little bit of a problem."

He puts the pen down he has hold of and motions for me to sit in the chair opposite him. "What's the problem, Macen? Are you not enjoying working at Casper's?"

"Oh, Francoise," I say rushing to sit in the chair. "No, I love working here. I'm enjoying the job so much, and everyone's really friendly and helpful. Everyone, that is, except one person." I look down at my hands in my lap. What do I say, that I'm paranoid? That I think Reid is stalking me or has got a vendetta against me?

"Macen, if you're having a problem with someone, then please let me know so we can find the best way to handle this."

I look up at him. He's sincere and not angry with me, which is a good sign. Maybe telling Francoise is better than telling Caspian. Caspian intimidates me, and I'm not sure what he would say or do. "Macen, do you want to tell me, or do you want to wait and tell Caspian?"

"I feel kind of stupid now. Maybe this was a bad idea. I just got a bit spooked. Maybe it's me — maybe I'm imagining it, maybe he's okay, maybe…"

"Macen, you're babbling. Do you want to tell me who you are talking about and what has happened?"

I look back at him. "It's Reid, Francoise."

He smiles at me as if he knows. "Ah, yes, Caspian did tell me about the fraternizing he walked in on yesterday. I have to say, Macen, we are both surprised and disappointed that you never mentioned being in a relationship with one of our chefs when Caspian offered you the job. The contract states no fraternizing between employees, which I'm sure you read when you signed it. Then he walks in on you both in a compromising position, and it's only your first week. Caspian wanted to speak with you about it today, but he's away on business for a few days and was going to speak with you on his return."

I'm horrified. First that they are disappointed in me already, second, that they think I'm actually in a relationship with Reid and third that Caspian is away and won't be around for a few days. It's the latter that really gets me more than anything, and it shouldn't be. "Francoise, I'm sorry you are both disappointed in me, but there is nothing between Reid and me. I'd never even met him until my first day on Monday."

He looks puzzled again. "That's not what it looked like to Caspian and Reid seemed to back up his suspicions when he spoke to him yesterday. He seemed to imply you two were together and have been on and off for a while?"

I gasp, shocked that he would say something like that. Now they're going to think I'm lying to them. They will surely believe him. They've known him longer than me.

"No, no, Francoise, I have never seen him before working here. To be honest, he's scaring me. It feels like he's watching me all the time. He's there at every turn, and when I get a cab on 5th after my shifts, he's been across the street leaning against the wall, staring at me. This morning, he suddenly appeared at my side while I was walking to work. He always comes into the employee room when I'm in there. He came in just now as I went to grab some water, and he stood right next to me, touching my arm. To others, it must look like we are together."

"What did Caspian walk in on yesterday?"

"Reid came into the employee room, as I was eating my lunch, and he made me uncomfortable by standing and staring at me. I got up to leave, but he blocked my exit, that's when Caspian came into the room. He knocked Reid with the door, and as he jerked forward into me, he grabbed my shoulders. I jumped back out of his reach to stop him touching me, and then I left. I know what it must have looked like to Caspian, but it couldn't be further from the truth."

He steeples his fingers and rests his chin on them. He's thinking about what I just told him.

"I'm so sorry, Francoise. I feel like I'm telling tales on someone, and I've only been here a few days."

"No, Macen. Don't be sorry. If this is true, then we can't have you feeling uncomfortable in work by another member of the team. Have you spoken to Reid or him to you at all?"

I think about what Reid said to me, and the venom with which he said it. Do I tell him that or leave it? Am I making too much of this? Surely if I speak to Reid myself, we could sort out what his problem is with me.

"Macen?"

He's waiting for me to answer. I decide to go with the truth. "He's only spoken to me a couple of times since being here, the last time was asking if I recognized him, and he said it with so much venom and hate in his voice that it froze me on the spot. That's when Caspian walked in."

He looks at me again for a few seconds. "So do you know him from somewhere else?"

I shake my head, no. "I've been trying to remember if I know him from anywhere like school or previous jobs, but I have nothing. I don't recognize him at all. I wondered if maybe he had me confused with someone else. I have no idea, Francoise, and I'm scared because he's making me feel like I should know him." I put my head down again and pick at my fingernails. "I need to get back to my station, Francoise, it will be getting busy again, and I need to prep some more sauces. I just felt I needed to tell Caspian or yourself. I needed you to know there is nothing going on, and that I love my job, but I know I'm the new girl, and Reid has been here longer…"

I don't finish, and I feel a tear slide down my cheek.

I feel terrible. Terrible for being in this situation in the first place, but also the fact I've only been here a few days, and I've caused trouble. "If you want me to leave, then I understand, Francoise. I know Caspian it set on having a happy team in the kitchen, and I've caused trouble already. I truly am sorry." I get up to leave.

"Wait, Macen. I believe you. I'll discuss this with Caspian and see how he wants to proceed. I don't want you to leave. I think the best thing to do right now is to see if we can re-organize your shifts, so you and Louis are on opposite shifts to Reid. That way there won't be as much contact between you until we sort out what to do. How does that sound?"

I wipe at my face, and I nod my head, "Oh, thank you so much, Francoise. That would be amazing if that can be done. Thank you. I will get back to my station now." He nods at me. I turn and leave.

I head to the bathroom first to make sure everything is in place with my hair and to clean my face before heading back. I feel so relieved that he believes me. But then, it's Caspian that matters and what he believes and what he wants to do. He may think differently after walking in on us in the employee room and thinking he saw something going on.

Walking into the kitchen, I feel Reid's eyes on me. I feel them follow me to my station, but I refuse to look at him or give him the satisfaction of knowing how much he un-nerves me. Louis looks at me, and I smile. He looks to where Reid is and glares at him, letting him know he's onto him. I slightly squeeze his arm, thanking him for being on my side. I prep the sauces ready for the rush.

Caspian

I THROW MY PHONE ACROSS THE hotel room. What is going on? Is she pulling the wool over my eyes to cover her ass, or is he bullshitting me? I hardly know her, but oddly, I do trust her. Him, well, he's an ass. I don't trust him at all. Fuck. Francoise said she was really upset and uncomfortable at work because she loves her job, but Reid is making it difficult for her. I never want any of my team to feel like that. We should be like a family. Francoise's idea of making sure they are not on the same shifts is a good one until I can get to the bottom of this. I feel so protective of her already, and I need to curb my feelings. My restaurants are my priority. I need to get back there to speak with her and sort this shit out.

I've had a productive day, and I have to say, being here and seeing where my restaurant would be is thrilling. This is what I thrive on. The current restaurant occupying the space will be closing in less than a month. They grew too quickly and are now facing financial ruin. The hotel said if I want it, then it's mine, once we go through all the finer details, of course.

I have to say though, I want it, but I have LA opening up in a few months — can do this as well? Am I running before I can walk? Am I doing what the current restaurant owners have done, opening up too many in a short space of time? Can I even afford to do this with the others in the pipeline? I need to think about it all and consider my options. I could put Canada on hold and open up here instead. There's no doubt Vegas is a hot spot, with millions visiting each year from all over the world. I just have a gut feeling about it.

I head back to the restaurant to have something to eat and to speak with the manager. He knows I'm interested in buying the space and has offered up any info I need. I can pick his brain and see where he's gone wrong, then scope out the area and see what else there is around — what the competition is like. There are a few celebrity restaurants popping up in the big hotels: Gordon Ramsey, Bobby Flay, and Wolfgang Puck to name a few.

I'm sitting here waiting for my meal to arrive when a woman heads my way. Why is it, wherever I go, I attract attention? She looks quite a bit older than me — a bit mutton dressed as lamb — and she's staggering on her feet as though she's off her head on something. "Hey, handshome, do you fancy shome comp'ny?"

Here we go with this shit. I plaster my fake smile on to be nice. "Sorry, no, I'm actually meeting someone."

She either doesn't believe me or doesn't care, and she sits on the chair opposite me. "I'm shure I would be much better company. How about it? You could buy me a meal and a drink, and I could repay you later." She winks at me, batting her fake lashes that are so long and thick that I don't know how she keeps her eyes open.

Time to get stern. "No, look, I'm waiting for someone. I'm about to have a meal and a meeting, so if you wouldn't mind leaving my table, I would appreciate that."

She looks at me indignantly — like, how dare I turn her down? What is it with some of these women?

Just then, Tirone, the manager comes over. "Hey, Caspian, sorry I got delayed."

I look at the woman. "If you don't mind, please leave my table now."

Tirone looks at her, realizing she's not with me and saves my ass.

"Excuse me, ma'am, do you have a reservation?" She looks at him like he's crazy. As if she doesn't need one. "No, why? Do I need one?" "Yes ma'am, you need a reservation to be in the restaurant. I must ask you to leave unless you are a guest of another diner."

She huffs and puffs as she gets up. "I didn't fucking want to eat here with you anyway, you ass," she aims at me, as she storms off. Thank fuck for that.

I sit talking with Tirone for a while, finding out the details of the restaurant. I still think I want it. I'm going to head back home tomorrow, so I'll see where I am financially and speak to my lawyer about it. I need to sort out this business with Macen and Reid, which is the real reason I want to head back sooner rather than later.

I head out onto the strip and wander into some of the other hotels to take in their restaurants and see how busy they are. They all seem as busy as each other really, just like the one I'm considering. As I walk into one of the casinos, I'm passing by a craps table, when I hear a voice I never thought I'd hear again. I stop dead, and my hands fly to my ears instinctively, covering them up until I realize what I've done and quickly put them down.

I look at the table, scanning each face to see if I recognize anyone. My eyes stop on him, and I know instantly it's my poppa. Fuck. I thought he might have died years ago because he never came looking for me. I stare straight at him. He must sense someone looking at him, and he looks straight into my eyes. His brow furrows slightly as if trying to register what he's seeing. He looks like a much older version of me. Very wrinkled, and leathery from this distance. His hair is different shades of yellow and white, and he has a cigarette hanging from his lips. He looks like someone who lives in a dingy trailer park.

Shit, I don't want to speak to him. I don't know the man, and I have no intention of getting to know him. When he picks up the few chips he has and walks towards me, I turn and start heading out of the casino the way I came in. "Casper, Casper, wait up, son," he shouts out to me. Then keeps shouting my name. Fuck. I stop and wait for him to catch up to me. I don't turn to face him, and he has to come around the front of me. This close, he looks worse than I thought. The years have not been good to him. "Casp, son, is that really you? Fuck, fancy running into you after all these years."

The fucking cheek of him. Running into me like some old lost pal of his. He neglected me. He didn't give a shit about me. How dare he call me son. He doesn't deserve to call me that. "Yeah, fancy, long time no see?" I say this with so much venom and sarcasm, he recoils slightly.

He runs his hand through his horrible yellowy hair. "Look, son, I know I should have come back for you, but I wasn't in a good place. I couldn't look after myself, never mind a kid." "Yeah, well, it's all good. No worries there. Nice seeing you, but I got to run."

I start to move around him to leave, but he reaches out and grabs my arm to stop me. "Look, can we talk, go for a coffee over in Starbucks?"

A coffee — is he for real? I shrug his hand off my arm. "You being serious, old man? You want to what? Catch up on old times or something? See how good life has been? What, a coffee and no liquor?" He reaches for his cigarettes in his pocket, looking nervous. I can see his hands shaking as he tries to take one out of the packet. "I don't drink, Casp, haven't done for fifteen years now. Been clean of drink and drugs, this is my only vice now," he says holding up his packet of cigarettes. "Well, this, and I like a little flutter every now and then, but only when I'm in town, which isn't often."

I take another good look at him. Although he has aged badly, he's smartly dressed, in a suit. My first instinct was that he was trailer trash, but now, I wouldn't say that. "Can we grab a coffee? I would love to speak to you, son."

I run my hand over my face. Do I want to do this right now? Do I want to have a coffee with a complete stranger? A loser who let his kid be taken away from him —and who didn't give a fuck about his kid to begin with?

"Please, son."

Fuck, I squeeze my eyes shut and rub the bridge of my nose. I'm at war with myself. On one hand, I want to hear his pathetic excuse for leaving me in the system, and on the other, I want to just walk away and never see him again. I mentally do the math. If he's been sober for fifteen years, that means I was twelve. The fucker could have come looking for me and taken me out of the system. That pisses me off no end. "No, fuck off." I march away from him.

He's following me. I can sense him. Before I reach the exit, I turn abruptly, and he's right on my heels and almost slams into me. "Leave. Me. The. Fuck. Alone. Old man," I grit out at him through clenched teeth. I don't want to cause a scene by shouting at him, that would draw attention to me, and god forbid this gets into the tabloids or on TMZ.

"Son, I just want to talk to you. Please let me just say what I need to say then the ball is in your court if you want me to leave."

Is this the only way I'm going to shake him off me? He no doubt knows I'm a celebrity chef — does he want money? Is that what all this is about? But then it can't be. He has never contacted me for money, and he didn't know I would be here in this casino, in Vegas, at this exact time. What a fuck up this is. "Right you can have ten minutes, then we're through. If this is the only way to get rid of you." That hurt him, and I see the pain in his eyes. He looks down for a second, then back up to me. "That's great, son, shall we go over to Starbucks?"

"Don't call me that."

I storm off in the direction of Starbucks. I don't wait for him. I just want this over and done with. I want his explanation for my own sanity and for no other reason. Maybe it will curb the feelings of abandonment that I have? There's only one way to find out, then I'm getting the next flight back to New York. I need to sort out the shit with Macen, but most of all I can't wait to see her. Fuck, I'm screwed in all directions.

Macen

AFTER MY TALK WITH FRANCOISE TODAY, I went back to work, and I felt Reid's eyes on me all the time. He really loathes me. I asked Louis if Reid had wanted my job, but he didn't think so. I'm out of ideas.

I finish my shift, but this time, I hang back and wait for Louis to finish so I can head to the employee room with him, hoping to put Reid off. It doesn't work. As soon as the door shuts behind Louis and me, it opens again. Reid just stands by the door, looking at me, with his arms folded over his chest. I turn back to my locker to get my coat and bag.

"What the fuck is your problem, Reid? You've been a moody shit all week and what's with all the glares at Macen?"

Oh no, I didn't want Louis to say anything to him. I don't want any trouble.

Reid doesn't speak. I don't turn to see what he's doing, but I turn to look at Louis and shake my head slightly, trying to let him know not to do this. "Come on, you ready, Macen?" I nod my head.

Louis heads for the door, bumping Reid out of the way, "Watch it dipshit," Reid grits out angrily.

"No, Reid, you watch it. Leave Macen alone and stop intimidating her. She's done nothing to you."

Reid glares at him for a beat, then turns his head very slowly in my direction and glares at me, "Hasn't she?" he spits out with venom.

"Come on, Macen, let's get out of here." Louis grabs hold of my elbow to get me past Reid. I avoid looking at Reid and rush out.

We walk out of the back door in silence. "I'm sorry, Louis. I didn't want you involved in all this. I know you're leaving, but I don't want you in trouble before you leave."

He stops walking and looks down at me. "Hey, I'm not having him treat you like that for no reason. You're with me in work, while I train you, so that makes you my responsibility." He shrugs. "I don't know what his problem is, Macen, but I strongly recommend staying as far away from his as you can. He's bad news, and he has it in for you."

I hang my head. "I know."

We walk round to 5th Avenue. "Will you be okay now? I go the other way, but I can walk with you to the subway if you want?" Louis asks.

I'm going to walk home. I need to clear my head a bit. I'm exhausted, not just from work but from all this Reid business. A nice brisk walk will do me good. "No, that's fine, Louis, thank you. I'm going to walk home. You get going, and I'll see you tomorrow."

He looks at me for a minute. "You sure you should be walking home? I'm not sure which direction Reid goes in?"

"I'll be fine, honestly. There are a lot of people around, and I don't think Reid is out to hurt me." If only I believed that myself. I hope Louis doesn't see through me. "Okay then, see you tomorrow, Macen."

I start toward home. I have my ear pods in, listening to my latest audiobook, it's the new one by E.L James called The Mister, and I've been waiting to start it. I walk fast, so I should be home pretty quickly. I'm engrossed in the book, but suddenly I get an eerie feeling. I turn suddenly, expecting someone to be behind me, there's no one there. I swear I felt someone really close behind me — now I'm freaking myself out. Maybe it's all this Reid stuff making me jumpy. There aren't many people around this far up 5th Avenue, and I'm walking along the road that's parallel with Central Park. I carry on walking but quicken my pace. I'm going to cross the street at the next crossing.

I feel like someone is following me, the feeling is making me jittery, but when I turn again, there isn't anyone there. I turn down a couple of streets doing a bit of a zigzag but still heading in the direction of home. I turn to look behind me a few times, but see no one, at least no one that looks suspicious. I can't shake the feeling though. The nearer I get to home, the better I feel. I can't get into the building and shut the door behind me quickly enough. I stand, with my back against the door, my eyes closed, just breathing.

"Shit!" I shout and jump out of my skin, banging the back of my head on the door, when I feel someone touch my arm,. "Sorry, Macen love, you seemed miles away. I called your name, but you didn't hear me. I didn't mean to startle you."

It's Mrs. Klamenski from across the hallway. "Oh, Mrs. Klamenski. I'm so sorry. I didn't mean to offend you. I didn't hear you. I was miles away."

"Are you okay, Macen, you look a little pasty?"

Do I? I'm not surprised the way I'm scaring myself. "Yes, I'm fine. It was just a long day at work. Good night, Mrs. Klamenski." I say smiling at her and head to my apartment.

As I enter my apartment, Dixon comes running to me, almost sending me flying. "Whoa there, Dix, where's the fire?" I crouch down to his level and give him a big hug. I miss my boy so much. "Mommy, I've been waiting for you to get home. I wanted to tell you that I had an invite to a party. It's my friend from school, Rory. His poppa is very rich, Rory says. I don't know his job, but he has a lot of money and Rory is having the best party, and he invited me. Can I go, mommy? Please? Grandma said I had to wait and ask you first. Can I, mommy?"

I pull back to look at his face, wondering why Grandma said he had to ask me first because how can I deny my little man anything? "Well, as long as we don't have anything else on at the same time, I don't see why not." I see his face light up as I move the hair on his forehead away from his eyes. I get up and hold Dixon's hand as we walk into the kitchen where Grandma is.

I walk over and give her a kiss on the cheek. "Hey, Grandma, how was your day today? Dixon is very excited about a party invite. Do you know when the party is so I can check my schedule?" I bring up the diary on my phone then look at Grandma because she hasn't spoken yet. She's looking at me funnily, then grabs the invite. "It's a week this Sunday. But you need to…"

I interrupt her. "Yes, Dixon, you can go to that, we don't have any plans. I will see if I can get a late shift so I can take you."

He jumps up and down "Yay, thank you, mommy, you're the best. It will be so much fun." He's hugging my lower half again.

I look at Grandma because she's staring at me with a strange look on her face. "You might want to read the invitation," she says handing it to me.

Before I have a chance to read it, Dixon takes it from me, trying to read what it says. He's good at reading, but I can see him struggle. He starts jumping about again, making T-Rex roaring noises. "You sound really excited about this party, Dixon. Where is it? Can Mommy read the invitation, please?"

He walks over to me. "We are going somewhere to eat first, for burgers and milkshake, and then we are going to a dinosaur park where the dinosaurs are alive."

He hands me the invitation, and I gasp at where they are all going to eat. Casper's. Oh no. How and why? I didn't realize we did children's parties, but then I haven't even been there a week yet. I look at Grandma, who is giving me a knowing look because I've already said Dixon can go.

I read the rest of the invitation, which sounds great. It's just the Casper's bit. I'm done for. If I'm not working, or on a late shift, then Dixon will want me to take him, and if I'm on an early shift I will be working while he's there. How am I going to get out of this? Caspian or Francois will be there, and there is no way I can pretend that Dixon isn't mine. Shit.

I mouth, "What do I do?" to Grandma.

"Right, Dixon, let's get you ready for bed while your mommy eats her dinner, then she can read you a story." She gives me the look to say we will talk about it when Dixon's in bed.

Dixon falls asleep while I'm reading to him. I head into the kitchen, where Grandma's making some coffee. "What do I do about the party? I had no idea Casper's did children's parties. I'm going to have to come clean with Caspian and Francois. There is no way they won't find out now." I'm deflated. "Well, Macen, I would say it's for the best. They should know you have a son. You shouldn't hide it."

I feel terrible now. "I know, I just wanted Caspian to know that even with a son I can work hard and give 100% commitment."

I have one more week to prove myself to him, and he will still want to address the Reid situation. I guess I will cross the party bridge when we come to it.

chapter 18

Caspian

I'M SITTING AT A TABLE IN STARBUCKS. My poppa is being served at the counter — if you can call him that. How did this happen — of all the places in the USA, we came to be in the same place at exactly the same time? You couldn't write about this shit.

Do I even want to hear his pathetic excuses for leaving me in the system? Leaving me to be bullied, and to fend for myself most of the time. All I ever dreamt about was he or my mother coming to find me and us being a family. It was all I ever wanted.

It never happened.

I watch him amble over to the condiments counter and grab some sugars and a couple of stirrers, then head in my direction with two coffees on a tray. He lays the tray on the table and hands me a coffee. "I wasn't sure how you took it, so I got it black with a pot of half-and-half and some sugars."

Yeah well, fucker, if you had been around you would know how I take my coffee. "Thanks," is all I say as I take some sugar from him. I have my coffee black but sweet. He finishes faffing about, then he sits opposite me. He messes with the sugars and cream for a bit, neither of us speaking. I'm not going to speak. He wanted to come in here for a chat and coffee.

He looks at me straight in the eyes. "I'm sorry I didn't come to find you, son."

I put the mug down a little too hard and coffee spills on the table. He takes some of the napkins and starts wiping it. "Leave it," I grit out.

He stops and looks up at me. I just glare at him.

"Look, son, I know you don't want to hear this, but I need to tell you." Here we go with some pathetic excuses. "When you were with me, it was hard. Your momma had died and…" What did he just say? "Died, what do you mean my momma died? She left us?"

He looks at me quizzically, "Yes, she did leave us. She died, son. She was taken from us, killed by an intruder, a home invasion while you were both asleep, and I was working nights. I thought you knew that?"

No! How the fuck would I know that? I was five years old.

"No, I didn't know she was killed. I remember I was a bit older and, in a home, and they told me there that my momma left me. That she didn't want me, and neither did you. It destroyed me, growing up thinking no one wanted me, I…"

"No, wait, God we wanted you, son. We were both elated when you came along. I ended up working more because we didn't have a lot, but we wanted to make our home nice for us as a family." I can't believe what he's telling me.

"I took more shifts at night so I could spend a bit of time with you both in the daytime. It was one night while I was working that it happened. You were nearly four. I wasn't sure if you'd remembered any of it. You were taken from your bed, son. They took you, and they killed your momma, it…" He hangs his head and rubs at his eyes. I'm not sure if he's crying or if it's just tension and him remembering what happened.

"I was taken? Who took me?" He looks back up at me, and he looks broken — like he is at war with himself if he should tell me or not. "I came home and found your momma de…" He chokes up, composes himself then carries on. "She was dead on our bed. There was blood everywhere. They slit her throat, son. I won't and can't go into the details. You can find out on your own if you want to. I just… I still struggle talking about it. Anyway, I ran to your room, screaming for you, but you weren't there. I ran around frantically looking for you. I phoned 911 and then searched everywhere for you. I couldn't find you. I was screaming, and running all over the place — inside and outside. It was only 5 a.m., so I woke the neighborhood up that morning. The sheriff arrived, then, when they realized it was a homicide and child abduction, they called in the FBI. The place was swarming with law enforcement and soon, the media. I was numb, son; I was in a daze, not sure what was happening or why it was happening." He takes his coffee and starts sipping it, giving himself a break. He looks up at me, and I can see the turmoil on his face. I can see how hard this is for him.

I mirror him by sipping my coffee. I don't know what to think. I can see he's hurting talking about this, but this is my life. This is something that happened to me, and I had no idea about any of it. I feel my life has just been one complete lying fuck up. This man is sitting here, talking to me, this stranger telling me shit I knew nothing about — about things that happened to me. "Son, did you hear me?"

I shake my head "No, what did you say?"

"I just said that I was in your bedroom. I was sitting on your bed when a female police officer walked in with you. She was holding your hand. You were still in your PJ's, and you didn't have anything on your feet, which were all black from dirt. I remember running to you and kneeling down in front of you. I grabbed you gently, looking you over, making sure you weren't hurt anywhere. You looked okay, but you were crying, I asked if you were okay and you said you that you hurt, and you were scared. I looked at the officer for answers, wondering why you hurt, but she shrugged, shaking her head, saying she didn't know. Just then, the paramedics came in to take you so they could check you out. I wouldn't let you leave my side, so I went with you. They examined you, and…"

Fuck, he can't speak. I can see the lump in his throat and tears sliding down his cheeks. What the fuck happened to me? He's scaring the shit out of me now.

He shakes his head. "I can't, son. I just can't."

"Can't what? Tell me? You can't what? Don't stop now."

He shakes his head again. "No, I can't go there, son. Let's just say, you were in the hospital for a little while. You had sustained some injuries."

I stare at him for a while, trying to comprehend what he's saying. "You can't just leave it at that. This is my life you're talking about. You're the only person who can fit the pieces together. Tell me what happened," I grit out at him, spittle flying out of my mouth. I look around, as I realize I'm raising my voice and the last thing I want is someone spotting me and filming any of this to put on social media. "Fuck, we need to get out of here. I can't have this conversation where people can hear or film me. Where are you staying?"

He looks around and sees a couple of people looking our way. "I have a room here. Why would people be filming you?"

"Let's go," is all I say as I get up and start heading for the door.

As I leave Starbucks, I stand just outside the entrance looking around at the casino. All these people look like they don't have a care in the world, and I feel like my world is just about to shatter. I feel him approach me. "Let's go to my room, son, then we don't have to worry about people filming you, although I don't understand why they would."

Could it be he doesn't know what I do for a living? I'm arrogant enough to think everyone knows me and what I do, so I find it hard to believe. "Lead the way, old man."

He shakes his head at that term. I take it he doesn't like it.

We reach his room, which has a small seating area. I sit on the chair so he can't sit next to me, and so I can look at him as he speaks. "You gonna tell me the truth about what happened now? How they found me? Did they catch who took me and killed Momma?"

He sits opposite me as I get up and go to the fridge. I need a drink. It's empty when I open it apart from some sodas. Great. I need the hard stuff, and this is all he's got — the recovering alcoholic. I take a soda and grab one for him, passing it to him as I take my seat again. "Well?" I say.

"No, I can't tell you everything. It kills me just thinking about it — the shame of it and the guilt I've carried for all these years."

Wait, guilt, why? "What have you got to feel guilty about if you didn't do anything?"

"That's just it. I couldn't help. I couldn't do anything. It's my fault because I was working. If I hadn't been at work, it wouldn't have happened. It's all my fault," he shouts at me — the tears streaking down his face.

"That's why I turned to drink. I just took solace in the bottom of the bottle. I drank myself to oblivion, day and night afterward. That was the worst kind of neglect on you. Leaving you to fend for yourself at such a young age. I hated myself, and I didn't want to be there. I didn't want to live. I tried to overdose on a few occasions, but like the failure I am, I failed at that too. I can never apologize enough to you, son. No apology would ever take away what you went through."

He still hasn't answered my questions. "Who took me? Do you know?" He nods his head, yes, then looks at me. "It was a couple who had moved into our neighborhood about ten months before. They were an odd pair. I remember them well. The house they lived in was a dump, and they had newspapers up on the windows that were all yellowed and starting to peel off, the garden was a mess, full of rubbish. They were scruffy. I would have said in their mid-fifties at the time, but I found out later they were both forty-three. They didn't have any kids, but they used to sit, watching all the kids play in the street. It was a cul-de-sac we lived in, so it felt safe for kids to play out. Steff, your momma would let you out sometimes, but she was always watching you making sure you were okay. I remember when the three of us would go out walking to the park this couple were always watching us like hawks. It unnerved your momma. She always had a bad feeling about them. She told me how they scared her. They never spoke to us, just watched all the time. I remembered her one time saying she found them outside our house just stood staring into the window. I told her to call the police, but she didn't want any trouble. The silly woman."

"Fuck, so they knew the people who took me! Did they kill her as well? Where are they now? Locked up, I hope."

He looks at me. "No, son, they're dead."

I get up from the chair. "How long are you in town?" I ask him.

I need to leave this room to sort my head out and get something harder to drink.

He looks at me as though shocked that I'm just going to leave. "You're going? Now?"

"Yeah, can't take anymore. I need to sort my head out. Can we meet tomorrow? I was going to head back home tonight, but I will keep my departure slot for tomorrow as originally planned. I leave at noon. Will you be around in the morning?"

He nods at me. "Yes, I leave tomorrow too. My flight is at 10.45 a.m. We can meet early for breakfast if you want? I'd like that."

Fuck, he thinks I want to get close to him when it's the furthest thing from my mind. I don't want to start a father-son relationship with him. Not yet anyway. I need to sort my head out and maybe do some research on what he's been telling me. It could all be bullshit for all I know. "I'll be here at 7 a.m. Be ready." With that, I storm out of his room. I would slam the door if it weren't on one of those fucking soft-close pressure things. I head back to my hotel.

Macen

I'M ON THE LATE SHIFT TODAY, SO I get to take Dixon to preschool this morning. We're ambling along the street — he's talking about the party, not because of Casper's, but because of the live dinosaurs. He loves his dinosaurs. He has many dinosaur toys, and he can name them all. One of our routines is him going through each one and telling me what they eat — he lines them up in order of who eats who.

"Momma, do you think they will have a diplodocus? He's my favorite."

I look down at him to see his big smiling face looking up at me "Well, I hope they do, and a T-Rex as well, that's your second favorite, isn't it?" He nods his head. "Yes, the diplodocus is my favorite plant eater, and tyrannosaurus rex is my favorite meat eater, closely followed by the velociraptor. How do you think they stop them from escaping? How do they stop the pterodactyl from flying away?"

I stop walking for a minute, and I crouch down in front of him. He needs to know they're not real. "Dixon, you do know dinosaurs are not alive, don't you? Remember we went to the museum to see them and how they used to be, with all the skeletons? They lived about a million years ago. For this party, you're going to see robot dinosaurs. They are not alive, just robots, so they can't really escape or fly away."

He looks a little puzzled, then shrugs. "I knew that really, Momma."

We carry on walking to school.

We're not far from school, and I have this feeling of being watched again, just like last night. I might be getting paranoid, but the hairs on the back of my neck are sticking up. There are a lot of people around, dropping off their kids, and I scan all the faces but don't see anyone out of the ordinary, apart from one man, whose face I can't see as he's walking away from the school. His jacket collar is around his neck, and he has a beanie hat on his head. He's probably a dad just dropping off his kid. I can't shake the eerie feeling though. I kiss Dixon and give him a big hug then watch as he runs into the school with his friends.

I'm walking back home when the feeling comes over me again. I stop and look all around me because this is getting ridiculous now. I don't see anyone again. I quicken my pace, rushing to get back home.

"Grandma!" I shout as I get inside.

She comes out of her bedroom. "Macen. Goodness, are you okay? You look flustered."

I let out a breath and steady myself because I can feel my hands shaking. "No, I think someone's following me."

She looks at me with a frown. "What do you mean? Have you seen someone following you?"

I shake my head, no. "I know I sound stupid, but last night, walking home, I felt someone watching me, and I swear someone was close behind me, but when I turned around, there was no one there. Then just now, at the school, it was the same feeling. I looked around but didn't see anyone. I know it sounds silly, but honestly, Grandma, the hairs on the back of my neck were standing up. I felt it. I felt someone watching me. It's not the first time the hairs have stood up on my neck this week either. I was thinking about it on my way home. This is exactly how I feel when Reid is near me at work. Grandma, I'm scared of him, and I don't know what I've done to him to make him hate me like this."

She gives me a hug. "Let's have a coffee, shall we?"

We sit in the kitchen, and I fill her in on the conversation with Francoise yesterday and the confrontation between Louis and Reid. "What if Reid goes mad because they change his shift and he takes it out on me? I think I should quit, Grandma. The last thing I want is to be causing trouble at the restaurant. I know I will never get this opportunity again, but, I can't work in an environment where there is hostility." I have both hands around my mug, and I hang my head.

"You listen to me, Macen. You will not quit this opportunity because someone has a problem with you. If Francoise changes the shift so that you very rarely work together, then that will be better, and you will be able to relax more and concentrate on your job. Let's see how it works out first. If there's still a problem, then you speak to Francoise or Caspian about it. Do you hear me?"

I nod at her, but I don't feel very optimistic about the situation at all.

We decide to go and do some shopping in the city — a girly afternoon. I take my chef whites with me so I can just head straight to work afterward. I will be in work early because Grandma will have to leave to pick Dixon up, but I don't mind. I'll sample some more of the dishes.

I'm in work an hour before I need to be, so I head to Francoise to see if he is okay with me sampling some dishes. I knock on the office door. "Come in," I hear a voice shout. I open the door and freeze. It's not Francoise behind the desk, but Caspian. "Oh, sorry, Mr. Kade, er Caspian, I didn't know you were in. I was looking for Francoise."

"Hello, Macen, please come in and take a seat. You saved me the bother of looking for you later. I wanted to speak with you the other day, but you left before I got the chance." He motions for me to sit. He doesn't look pleased to see me, in fact, he looks annoyed, and the tone he's using is serious. Oh no, is this it? Is he going to fire me because he thinks Reid and I are seeing each other? I sit down hesitantly, not looking at him but rather looking at the chair and then the floor. He makes me so nervous and being in his company turns me into a shrinking violet. Why does he have that effect on me?

He doesn't speak for what feels like an age, so I look up at him sheepishly. He's weighing me up, leaning back in his chair and rubbing the stubble on his chin. I feel like shriveling away on the spot from the intense look he's giving me. "So, Macen, before I get to the point, I want to say Francoise is extremely happy with you. He says you're a great addition to the team." I feel confused. I thought he was going to fire me. "Now, tell me, how do you feel about working here?"

I gulp but decide to tell him the truth. "I'm so grateful for the opportunity you have given me Mr. Ka… Caspian. I love working in such a thriving environment. It is so busy all the time, and I'm learning so much. I thank you for that."

He's looking at me strangely, and he leans forward putting his forearms on the desk. "I feel there's a 'but' at the end of that?"

I nod. "Yes, it's the situation with Reid."

His face changes. I see a flash of anger across it. "Yes, well, that is my next topic to discuss. I know what I saw in the employee room, Macen, and I had a word with Reid. He tells me you and he are an item: on and off."

I'm stunned, and I go to speak, but he holds up his hand. "No, let me finish. What happens outside of here is nothing I can control, but I will not tolerate any of my team fraternizing on the premises."

I hang my head. Why would Reid say that? "Mr. Kad…"

"I said, let me finish."

The tone in his voice is harsh and he's rude. Maybe I should just leave now. I frown at him and decide, no, I need to tell him the truth before I leave.

"Now I spoke with Francoise yesterday after he spoke with you and he told me about the conversation you've had. If you're saying you don't know Reid and have never met him before then we have a problem — not with you, Macen, but with him. I will not have a member of my team intimidating and lying about another member of the team. That is not how I operate. I want my team to feel comfortable with each other. It's stressful enough working a busy kitchen without the added pressure of friction between members."

I look at him. He's gone from being harsh and angry to a little pitiful and dare I say it, concerned. But is this his way of saying I'm being fired? I'm confused, but I don't want his pity or his anger. That riles me up, and I sit up straight and look him in the eye. "I understand, Mr. Kade. I will leave now. Don't worry about paying me for today. If you just pay me for the days I've worked, I'll be out of your hair and your harmonious kitchen," I say this with sarcasm because now I'm angry. I start to get up.

"Sit," he says very assertively, and I stand, glaring at him. "I won't ask you again, Macen." His tone is harsh. "You are not going anywhere." I lower myself back to the seat as he scowls at me — back to being angry again. Well, screw him! I don't care who he is. He shouldn't be angry with me. I haven't done anything wrong. I get up off the chair and head toward the door, but as I reach it, his deep voice says, very calmly, "Macen, if you walk out of that door you will not set foot in my restaurant again. We need to discuss this — now sit." I consider this and walk back to the chair, trying not to look like a spoilt kid.

"I agree with Francoise's suggestion, and the first thing we will do is change the shifts so you're not on at the same time as Reid. Unfortunately, we can't do that until Monday, which just leaves today's shift. He leans back in his chair again and steeples his finger to his lips. He's thinking but he also still looks annoyed. He leans forward again, looking me straight in the eyes. "I need to know the truth from you, Macen. Do you know Reid?"

I shake my head. "No, I've been trying to think where I could know him from, but I have no idea. He asked me if I recognized him, and he was very intimidating, and he invaded my personal space. That was when you walked into the room. I was trying to leave, but he blocked the door. You knocked him forward with the door, and he grabbed my shoulder, which made me jump back from his touch. I know what it must have looked like, Caspian, but I can honestly say, I have never met him until I started working here. I think he must have me confused with someone else."

I don't look at Caspian because I feel stray tears flowing down my cheeks. I wipe them away. I don't want him to see me upset. I'm stronger than this, but I feel so intimidated both by Reid and Caspian although for completely different reasons.

He hands me a tissue. "I'm sorry if I upset you. I don't want you to leave, Macen. If what Mrs. Webster says about you is correct, then I would be a fool to let you go. I want you to feel comfortable and safe at work and if sorting out Reid is what I have to do, then so be it."

What does he mean by sorting out? "I don't want to cause any trouble, Mr. Kade, please just change our shifts, and everything should be okay."

He leans forward, resting his elbows on the desk and steepling his fingers in front of his face. I can't help but stare at his mouth. "One problem is that he lied to me, Macen. He said you were an item and had been for some time. I can't have liars working for me. I will discuss this with Reid, and in the meantime, please let me know if anything else is said or anything happens."

I nod at him, hanging my head, but relieved he wants me to stay.

"Okay, what did you want to see Francoise about? Is it anything I can help you with?"

"I was just going to see if he wanted to pick some dishes for me to sample. I'm early for my shift and thought I could try them now rather than try fit them in later. I take it we will be really busy with it being a Friday night?"

He laughs a little. "We're busy every night, Macen, the weekends are no different. Do you have your journal with you? I'll see what dishes you've tried so I don't repeat any. I'll get Don to bring them to you in the employee room." I hand him my journal. "Great, thank you, Mr. Kade."

"Caspian, Macen, it's Caspian." I smile and leave his office. I'm shaking like a leaf again; he does that to me every time.

Don brings me three dishes along with my journal. I taste each one and write my notes. I'm just finishing the notes on the dessert, a dark chocolate cylinder with smoked praline and salted milk ice cream topped with a ball of caramelized puffed rice — the best one yet —before getting ready for my shift. I need to go to the fridge to get some ingredients for my sauces so I head there on the way to the kitchen. I'm in the huge, walk-in fridge when I get the prickles on the back of my neck. It's him. I can also smell him. It smells familiar but maybe just because he's been hanging around me all week. I don't turn around. I close my eyes and take a few deep breaths. I have my arms full of all the ingredients I need now, so I turn to head out, but he's blocking the doorway, sneering at me. I move towards him, I need to get past. "Excuse me, please," I say as nicely as I can. He doesn't move, so I start to squeeze past him at the side. He suddenly grabs my forearm, and I jump, dropping all the items from my hands. "Shit" I shout.

"Macen, you okay?" It's Caspian. Great, that's all I need.

Reid turns and leaves, not saying a word to Caspian as he passes him. Caspian crouches down to me, helping me gather the fallen items "Hey, are you okay? What happened? Did he do this to you?" I look at him, "I'm really sorry about this, these will all have to be thrown away now, Caspian. What a waste."

He looks angry. "I don't give a shit about these things, Macen. Now, did he do this to you? Did he hurt you?"

I've caused enough trouble. "No, he didn't hurt me. He startled my grabbing my arm as I was trying to get past him. He blocked my way, Caspian. But I don't want to cause any more trouble."

"Fuck," he says. "Are you okay to start work, or do you want to go home? I'll still pay you if you want to leave your shift today."

I shake my head. "No, I'm fine to work. I'll just get what I need and get to my station. Can you do me a favor and throw these out for me?" I smile at him, and he shakes his head then gets up and waits for me.

At my workstation, I tell Louis about what just happened. I can feel Reid watching us. Is it hate he has for me? Or does he just like intimidating me? Or is he somehow fixated on me, and he doesn't like me talking to anyone else? I find the last scenario hard to believe. I also tell Louis about the shifts being changed so we don't work the same ones. He agrees it's a good idea for now.

"I still don't trust him, Macen. You keep an eye on him, and if he steps a foot wrong, you tell me, and I'll sort him, do you hear me?" I don't want Louis getting in trouble for me. I just nod.

The day goes by without incident. I see Caspian quite a few times as he's head chef today. Every time he looks at me, my heart skips a beat, and I get butterflies. The thing is, every time he looks at me, I feel it, and I look at him, then I have to quickly look away, embarrassed that he's seen me looking at him. I don't look Reid's way once. I'm saying goodbye to Louis and some of the team and just heading out the back when Caspian catches up with me. "Macen, thanks for the notes on the dishes you tried. I'm going to try your recommendation of using cilantro and see how it turns out. I appreciate your suggestions and your comments." I blush because he's taking me seriously. "How has your shift been? Any problems? Any more incidents with Reid? I've tried to keep an eye on him today." I start to walk towards the back door to leave. "Macen," he says very assertively.

I stop and turn to face him. I notice Reid behind him, watching us. Caspian notices me looking past him and turns to see what I'm looking at. "Goodnight Mr. Kade," I say walking off, rushing to get in a cab as quick as I can and get away from here.

I hail a cab in my usual spot and sigh with relief as I lean back in the seat. I automatically look across the street just to make sure Reid isn't there watching me. Caspian must be talking to him while I get away. I need my bed and to and spend quality time this weekend with Dixon and Grandma.

Caspian

O NCE I GET BACK TO MY HOTEL IN VEGAS, I head straight to one of the bars for some whiskey — neat. I'm in bed, in my suite, with my laptop and more whiskey, and I decide to search what happened to me when I was four. If my poppa can't tell me, then, I will find out for myself. I need to know if it's true, but I'm also terrified to find out the truth. I do a quick search: Home invasion, Florida, Kade, and fuck me, there is article after article on homicide, home invasion, child abduction, sexual assault, although not for Kade, but for Kaden. I click on a piece to read anyway.

Maybe this is a bad idea — maybe I should just leave it and not find out. Isn't ignorance bliss? Isn't it better to just leave it that way if I've come this far in my life without knowing? I wonder if not remembering is my way of coping — blocking all the bad things out.

I take a big gulp of whiskey for courage, then start to read.

HOMICIDE AND CHILD ABDUCTION IN A SLEEPY TOWN IN POLK COUNTY

A mother, Steffanie Kaden, and her four-year-old son were disturbed in a home invasion in Polk County in the early hours of Monday morning. Steffanie was brutally attacked in her bed while she slept: sexually assaulted, then murdered. The intruders cut her throat after stabbing her multiple times in the chest in what the police are saying was a frenzied attack. Her son, Casper, was taken from his bed while he slept. Steffanie's husband, Charles Kaden, was working a night shift at the water utility compound and found his wife dead when he returned home at five a.m. after his shift. His son was missing.

Eyewitnesses say that Mr. Kade ran around the neighborhood screaming for Casper and it was this act that saved Casper's life. The young boy started screaming for his poppa when he heard him shouting his name, and one of the neighbors heard it.

The neighbor alerted the attending police, and they entered the house, where they found Casper on the floor crying. The couple, who have been named as Dana and Rexford Sotton, both aged forty-three, were both on the premises. Eyewitnesses say there were three gunshots fired. Both Dana and Rexford Sotton were shot by law enforcement. One officer suffered a gunshot wound to his arm and was taken away in an ambulance. We were told he was released from the hospital yesterday.

Eyewitnesses say a female officer took Casper to his house to wait for another ambulance to arrive. He was then taken, along with Mr. Kaden, to The Heart of Florida Regional Medical Centre in Davenport. Casper has not been released from the hospital yet.

The Sheriff's department released a statement confirming two people had been shot and killed by armed officers in their home after officers entered on suspicion of abduction, murder, and sexual assault. The officers were shot at and had no choice but to open fire. Casper Kaden was unharmed in the shooting, but it's been confirmed he was sexually assaulted and has sustained internal damage from his attackers. Mr. and Mrs. Sotton's blood-soaked clothes were tested, and the results confirmed it was the blood of Mrs. Steffanie Kaden. They confirmed that on entering the house, Mr. Rexford Sotton was on the floor with Casper, and Mrs. Dana Sotton was standing over them. She had a gun in her hand, and she turned and fired at the officer's when they entered. One officer did sustain a gunshot injury but is now resting at home. He also confirmed that the other officer did shoot both Mr. and Mrs. Sotton.

Fucking hell. I can't breathe. This is me they are talking about — this was my momma and me. I can't believe I have no idea about any of this. I don't remember anything. It doesn't compute that it's me I'm reading about. It just feels like a story or a news article about someone else. Why did they keep referring to me as Casper, not Caspian and the surname as Kaden? Come to think of it, my poppa shouted Casper when he tried to catch up with me. I'm so confused — is this definitely about me — my family? The picture in the article is me — I don't remember my momma, but that's definitely my poppa, and you can't mistake I'm his son. I'm the spit from his mouth as they say. Why has no one ever asked me about this? The media and TMZ usually dig up anything they can on celebrities. Why has this never been brought up? Is it because of the different names? But the names are so close: Casper Kaden and Caspian Kade.

I drink more from my whiskey bottle, and read a few more articles, which all back up the original one. I get to an article, written two months after the tragedy, which I'm sorry I start. It says Rexford Sotton sexually abused me — they caught him with his dick in me. I feel sick — I run to the bathroom and throw up. He sodomized me. I was four fucking years old. He fucking did that to me, and he killed my momma, and then my poppa just threw me away after all that. No wonder I don't remember anything. I must have shut it all out — my way of coping with it.

I get back into bed, take another gulp of whiskey, then sit, trying to rack my brain.

I wake up with a bit of a start at my six a.m. alarm. The whiskey had obviously helped me sleep because I went out like a light and didn't wake once.

It all comes flooding back to me: meeting my poppa, and then all the stuff about my past. I feel sick. I rush into the bathroom, and I heave, but nothing comes up.

It's so hard to process any of this or believe what I read was all about my Momma and me. I get ready and pack my stuff. There's one thing about all this shit in my head — I haven't thought of Macen once since running into the old man last night.

I stand at his door, contemplating if I want to do this. I've found out everything I needed to know — all except why he didn't come back for me. That's the only reason I'm standing here. I'm just about to knock when the door opens. He's dressed and ready for breakfast.

"I was thinking, maybe we just eat in here and order room service. I don't know if we will get any privacy downstairs and the last thing I need is to lose my rag over anything and end up in the tabloids."

He cocks his head to the side slightly. Fuck, that's exactly what I do when I'm trying to comprehend something. He looks puzzled. "Yes, yes, of course, come in. Let's order in; but why would you end up in the tabloids? You said something like that last night, and I didn't understand then. Casper, are you in trouble or something?"

He has no clue who I am. Asswipe, doesn't know he has a famous son. That's why he never came looking for me. If he'd known, I bet he would have come knocking sooner, looking for handouts.

"Why do you keep calling me Casper? I read a news article last night about what happened to us, and they kept calling me Casper?"

He looks at me again, cocking his head again. "It's your name, son. You're confusing me now."

He's confused? Try being in my shoes, old man. "No, my name is Caspian, and do you honestly not know who I am? You have never heard my name mentioned anywhere?"

"I'm so lost with this conversation. You are Casper Kaden, and you are my son. Of course, I know who you are!"

I run my hand over my face, up to my hair, then over my head, as I sigh out. "Let's order breakfast then sort this shit out, or we won't have enough time."

We position ourselves in his room, in the same seats as last night. "Right, my name is Caspian Kade. I own a famous restaurant in New York City, on 5th Avenue, called Casper's. I live in New York City, where I have done for some years now. I also had a slot on Good Morning America for a while, cooking dishes. I'm what they call a celebrity chef. I'm the youngest, 3-star Michelin chef in the world."

He looks at me, bewildered, and runs his hand over his face up to his head. "Oh," is all he says. Surely there's no way he didn't know who I am. I mean, come on, we're so alike it's unreal. "That's it? Oh? Are you telling me you didn't know who I am?"

"No, son, I'm not one for TV and especially not in the mornings. Yes, I've been to New York a lot of times, but I have never seen your restaurant. Maybe the Child Protection Services changed your name when they took you away from me? Maybe they didn't want me to find you or for your past to come back to you in any way? I don't know, son. I didn't know it had been changed, but it does explain why they couldn't find you when I went to the CPS to look for you."

"Wait, what? You looked for me? You tried to find me?"

He nods his head, yes. "Not for a few years, son. I was a drunk, and I took drugs, I ended up on the streets for a couple of years. I couldn't look after myself, never mind a little boy. I almost died and ended up in the hospital. That's where I met this amazing woman who helped me. She took me in and helped me get sober. I got straight and clean eventually, but it took a long time. You would have been about twelve by then. I needed to find you. You were my son, and I loved you so much, so, I went to the CPS to try and find you. To see if I could see you and try to get you back living with me. Each time I went, they said they couldn't find a Casper Kaden on their records, and there was nothing they could do to help. I didn't know what to do or where to go. I've never forgotten you, son. I've thought about you everyday since my life turn around. I wish I could have found you." He hangs his head just as there's a knock at the door — room service with our breakfast.

Neither of us speaks as we eat our breakfast. I'm trying to process what he's just told me. He tried to find me. He didn't forget about me. Fuck me. Do I believe him? I think I do. I don't know him, but he seems so remorseful and genuine.

I need to leave. I need some time to think before I jump on the plane, and I know he has a flight to catch. I don't even know where he lives, what he does or anything really — fuck I know nothing about this stranger in front of me. Do I want to know him? Do I want to know who he is and all his personal shit? Do I want to know if he has a new family? If I have any siblings? Fuck I'm so mixed up. I need to get out of here. I stand suddenly, turning on the spot, looking at the door, to my escape, ready to walk out without a word.

"Look, son, I know it's a lot to take in, and one part of me wishes we hadn't met so you would never have known what had happened. The other part, in here," he says tapping over his heart, "it says yesterday was one of the best days of my life. Seeing you all grown up and successful fills my heart with so much pride. I'm so proud of you, son. I know you will think I don't have a right to be proud, but you're my son, and I love you more than life itself, and I always have. The tragedy that happened that night has impacted all our lives for so long. It kills me when I think about your momma and what happened to you and how it tore us apart. I can't take it all back, but I can try to make some amends if you'll let me."

He takes a drink of his coffee, gets up, and starts to grab his bags. I face him. "Look, I'm not making any promises here, old man. I don't know you — you're a stranger to me. I don't remember anything from back then except you shouting at me all the time. For some reason, that is the only memory I have, and it's going to take me some time to process all this shit. If you give me your details, then maybe I'll contact you, but I'm not promising anything. Maybe I'll want to keep things as they were — maybe we will both be better as it was."

He looks pained at what I'm saying, which makes me feel like a fucking ass. "Look, I don't know, okay, but I need time to process."

We both walk out together and ride the elevator to the lobby, where he checks out. I stand watching him. I can see so many of my mannerisms in him. He comes over and gives me a piece of paper with his details on. I take it from him without looking at it and put it into my back pocket. "You will never know what meeting you has meant to me, son. I really hope you call me." I don't say a word. I let him walk out of the hotel to catch his flight. I feel numb and confused about everything. I need to try and digest it all and decide where to go from here.

FUCKING REID. I wanted to talk to Macen. I wanted to make sure she was okay. I just wanted to talk to her. My feelings are so strong for her. Every time I see her I fall harder. Coming back from Vegas, I thought about her and how I would love nothing more than to tell her what had happened — to have her comfort me and tell me what to do.

When she walked into my office earlier, I melted like a fucking wuss. I was elated, but I had to control myself. I had to be an ass to her. She nearly walked out, and I panicked because there is no way she could leave. Not yet. I wasn't ready to let her go.

Then this, just now with fucking Reid. He's going for sure. I saw the horror on Macen's face as she looked past me over my shoulder, and I knew he was there, I knew it was him that made her look terrified. I need to sort this out now. With this on top of what I just learned in Vegas; my life is going to shit. Fuck why is my life suddenly so complicated?

chapter 21

Macen

LYING AWAKE IN BED, ALL I CAN THINK about is Caspian. He was a bit of an ass to me today, and his tone was very forceful but also supportive in allowing the shift change and giving me the benefit of the doubt.

I wake up to Dixon pouncing on me. "Oh, Dixon, Momma's tired please let me sleep." He gets into bed next to me. I turn towards him, and we lay face to face. I can just see the clock over his head, and it's 9.27 a.m. I thought it was earlier than that. "Guess it's time to get up, hey, monkey? Where's Grandma?"

He nods. "She's in the kitchen, finishing her breakfast. I ate all mine up, Momma. What are we doing today?"

"Let me get up and showered then we can sit and decide what to do. How about that, monkey?"

I tickle him, and he rolls around in fits of giggles. "Stop, Momma, stop." He gets off the bed and heads out of my room.

We're all sitting in the kitchen while I eat my toast and have coffee and Dixon is trying to decide what he would like to do today. "How about we go to the Museum of Natural History so you can get a refresher on all the dinosaurs ready for your party next week? I'm going to be working next weekend so now would be a good time. What do you say?" He loves the museum, and we go a few times a year.

"Oh, I would love to do that, Dixon. I have never been to the museum, and you can tell me all about the dinosaurs we see."

He grins at Grandma. "Yes, let's go there, Momma, then I can teach Grandma all about the dinosaurs."

We walk straight through Central Park to the museum. In the park, I get the feeling of being watched again, and I turn around, scanning everyone I can see, but again, there's nothing out of the ordinary.

"You okay, Macen?" Grandma has stopped ahead of me.

I walk to her. "Yeah, just getting that feeling again." I give her the look, hoping she knows what I'm talking about without saying it in front of Dixon. She nods at me, and she also looks around us before we continue to the museum.

We spend almost all day in the museum. Dixon and Grandma love it. He tells her all about each dinosaur, and she is really impressed with his knowledge. Grandma wants to treat us to dinner out, and Dixon decides he wants pizza, so we try the new Gotham Pizza place on 1st Avenue, which isn't too far from home. I get the same feeling as before, that I'm being watched, and it's really starting to freak me out. Grandma notices me picking up the pace and looking around again because I have hold of Dixon's hand, and he has hold of Grandma's hand.

"Hey, slow down a little, Macen, you're almost sprinting, and nearly pulling Dixon's arm off there."

I stop, not realizing I've picked up the pace. Grandma must see the panic on my face. "Come on, let's get that pizza," she says.

"Yay," Dixon shouts.

Dixon is exhausted, so as soon as we get home, I get him bathed and put to bed early. I go to sit with Grandma in the living room where she has some wine poured out for me. "Macen love, twice today you were on pins, is it just a feeling you get?"

I take a sip of wine and rest my head back on the couch. "Yes, I can't explain it, but I'm almost sure someone is watching me, Grandma. It happened in the park, then again on our way to the pizza place. I feel like I'm going crazy." I turn my head towards her. "Do you think I'm going crazy? It's only started this week. Is it all this Reid stuff that's making me paranoid do you think?"

She looks at me. "No, I don't think you're paranoid, but I am worried if someone is following you."

Yeah, I'm worried too.

Sunday, we stay in. It's raining, so Dixon and I do some dinosaur drawings and play some games. I'm actually looking forward to work again tomorrow, knowing I won't be on the same shift as Reid. In my room, getting ready for bed, and as I close my blinds, I have that feeling again. I look out of the window, and I see a figure across the street, leaning on the railings of one of the houses. It's too far away and too dark to make out who it is, but he has a cigarette in his mouth. I can see the glow from it. He's standing with one leg crossed over the other. It's definitely a male, and I can make out a beanie on his head. Oh god, just like the man I saw walking away from the school. Is it the same man? Why is he following me? The way he's standing and the cigarette reminds me of Reid. No, it couldn't be, could it?

Caspian

THAT STUPID PRICK, REID, STOPPED me from speaking to Macen. I wanted to walk with her and make sure the day had gone without any other incidents. Louis informed me that Reid had been intimidating her most of the day, just by watching her, so I wanted to see if she'd tell me about it. Then, he was there, behind me, watching us — the fucking ass.

He's defiantly going, after what I witnessed today at the fridge.

There is no way I'm having him treating her like this. I asked him what he was doing, standing there, and he just held his cigarette up to show me that's what he was doing. I told him I wanted to see him on Monday before his shift started. By the time I got onto 5th Avenue, she was long gone. I'm so conflicted with my feelings for her. I can't stop thinking about her, but my business head is telling me to leave well alone when my heart knows I can't do that.

I wake up with a start. I'm soaking wet from sweating. I look at my watch, and it's 5.30 a.m. I was dreaming about being younger — someone had me and was hurting me. Fuck my pops for coming back into my life and stirring all this shit up. I've never dreamed anything like this before. There is no way I can sleep now. I may as well go for a run then hit the gym as I'm all sweaty anyway. I wish I were sweaty from being with Macen. Shit, where did that come from?

After my run and gym session, I get dressed and go into Casper's. The team won't be arriving for a while yet, but I've got lots of paperwork to do, and I want to see if I can get hold of my lawyer about the Vegas restaurant and get the checks done on it. I know it's Saturday, but when you pay them big bucks like I do, they work when you need them. I put the call into Patrick, my lawyer, and ask him to get his team onto it. I set up a meeting with him for next Friday when he should have all the information together.

The morning goes slowly. Macen isn't in this weekend so I'm not going to stick around for long. I don't want to see that dipshit, Reid. I'll see him on Monday and fire his ass then.

I leave the office and decide to go for a walk in Central Park before I head home. I want to think things through, and a walk in the fresh air helps. I'm going to do some research on my younger life and try to find out who changed my name and why it was changed. Maybe if I check with the Florida state courts and see if I can get a copy of the petition to change my name, it may shed some light on it.

I'm just about to head home when I spot Macen. I'm 99.9% sure it's her although she's wrapped up well with it being so cold out. She's with a kid and an older lady. The kid's holding the older lady's hand, not Macen's, so maybe it's a nephew? She never said anything about a kid, but then again, I never asked her. All she said was she would give 110% commitment to Casper's, which was good enough for me, and to be honest, she's done that this week.

I stand and watch them walking when suddenly she stops and turns around. She's looking for someone, scouring the faces of everyone around her. I'm standing next to a tree, and I duck behind it so she can't see me. I pop my head around, and I see the older lady looking around too. Maybe they're waiting for someone else to join them — the kid's parents or someone? I watch, still hidden behind the tree, and they carry on walking. One thing, I know for sure it's her. I couldn't mistake her beautiful face. I'm wondering if the kid is hers. Is it lying to me if she didn't disclose it? Fuck, something else to ponder on.

I've been going through article after article on my younger years, and I think the dream last night must stem from that. I can't believe all this is about my family and me, and I don't remember anything. I've had enough, and I need a break. I would love nothing more than to bury myself in Macen to help me forget all this stuff, but that's not going to happen. I need to do something though. Maybe if I visit Arthur's again, that will give me what I need and help me forget for a while?

The communal room at Arthur's is not doing it for me, so I go up to a private room area and see if there is anything up there that will help. I enter the viewing area of a room, which is occupied by two women and one man. This is better, and it looks like they have only just started, as the women are both still in their bras and panties, although the man is on the edge of the bed, naked. He pulls one girl to him by the waist, who has long dark hair with purple streaks in it and a stunning curvy figure. He starts to lick her tummy and slowly slips his hand into her barely-their panties down the front. He starts stroking her pussy and inserts a finger or two, and she starts to gyrate on his hand. With his other hand, he pulls the other woman, who has shorter blond hair, to his side, stops licking the dark-haired woman but keeps finger-fucking her.

"Take her bra off," he demands the blonde, and she does. "Now yours," he says, and she takes that off too. His other hand then disappears down the front of her panties, and he finger fucks them both. "Suck her tits" he commands the blonde, and she turns to the dark-haired woman and takes a tit into her mouth. He then takes one of the blonde woman's tits into his mouth. The dark-haired woman then grabs his cock and starts wanking him at the same time.

They are all moaning, and the dark-haired woman explodes on his hand. She stops pulling on his cock, and once she comes down from her orgasm, she drops to her knees in front of him and takes his cock into her mouth. He's still finger-fucking the blonde, who by the looks of it is getting close to her own orgasm. This is hot, and I'm rock hard, but I'm not ready to rub one out just yet. I want to see the penetration first.

The blonde explodes. She moves away, lowering her panties, so she's standing naked in front of him. He pulls the dark-haired woman's head off his cock. "No, I want to be inside to cum." She gets up, and she too takes off her panties — they are both now naked.

The dark-haired one pushes him backward on the bed, so he is lying down. She crawls on top of him and edges up his body towards his face, then manages to turn so she's facing the other woman, edging back slightly until she is kneeling up over his head and he is looking straight into her pussy. He licks his lips, then blows gently onto her pussy. The blonde woman then straddles his legs, positioning herself above his cock. She puts her hands on the waist of the dark-haired one, then together they both lower themselves: the dark-haired one on his face and the blonde on his cock. Fuck, I take my cock out, and I start to rub gently over the tip, spreading the pre-cum over my cock, up and down. I want to try to wait and cum when they do.

They are all going at it. The blonde is bouncing up and down hard on his cock, and the women have their tongues in each other's mouths. The dark-haired one is gyrating on the guy's face, grinding down on it, and I'm surprised he can breathe. She is flicking the clit of the other woman while he is pushing up as hard as he can each time she slams back down on his cock. He is now putting a finger into the ass of the dark-haired woman and pumping in and out as she gyrates on his face. She screams with the release of her orgasm, panting hard and has slowed down the gyrating while he milks her for every drop she has, sucking her dry. He is still pushing up hard into the blonde as she slams down on him. She's getting frantic now, and the dark-haired one leans her head down and starts licking his cock and her pussy as they slam into each other. She's trying to flick the other woman's clit with her tongue and suck the juices from them both, and he has spread her butt cheeks and is using his tongue on there as well as his fingers. The blonde screams out over and over. She's now grinding down hard on his cock, milking him as he explodes inside her. The dark-haired woman is lapping it all up from them both. He is quiet as he lets his release take him away.

I explode the same time as the blonde woman. I try to be quiet, but it's all too much. It's fucking bliss. I'm cleaning up when the curtain suddenly pulls back, and a woman comes in. Fuck, she is hot. She sits next to me. She watches the three in the room as they come down from their orgasms, still licking each other and caressing each other. Suddenly, the woman next to me edges her chair a bit close to me and takes my semi-hard cock into her hand. She starts to pump. Fuck, I come to watch, not participate, but I'm too far gone to stop her.

The three in the room move around, and the dark-haired one lies on her back on the bed. The man moves above her, and the blonde gets behind him. They are going at it again. He enters the dark-haired one as the blonde inserts her fingers into his ass and starts pumping away. The woman next to me moves faster and harder, and in no time, I cum all over her hand. I breathe out and close my eyes tightly, hoping she's gone before I open them again. The only image I have in my head is Macen. How I wish it were her here with me, but it's not, and I feel guilt and anger. I grab a handful of tissues and wipe myself clean. I shoot up from my chair, fasten my zip, and storm out as she's still sitting there. I don't even look at her. I didn't want that.

I leave Arthur's. It's late now and dark, so I don't go through the park. I use the main streets to get home. Any New Yorker will tell you to steer clear of Central Park once it's dark. I can't shake the anger and guilt I feel as I get near home. Why do I feel guilty? I feel as though I've just cheated on Macen, which is fucking insane because we will never be an item. I hate this feeling. I feel drained, sad, and angry all at once, and I shouldn't.

In my apartment, I pour myself a drink then head to the shower. I stand under the hot showerhead for ages, just letting the water wash away the guilt and anger that's built up. Everything comes flowing through my head: Reid, my poppa, my momma and me when I was young and what happened to me, Macen — what am I going to do about Macen? Should I get rid of her too? Because, in all honesty, I don't see how I am going to keep my hands off her if she sticks around. Every day is torture when she's near, and every night is torture because she isn't near. I head to bed, hoping I can sleep.

Again, I wake with a start, and this time, in my dream, I remembered seeing my momma lying on the bed covered in blood. I remembered someone grabbing me and running with me. I remembered being hurt and crying. I'm going to throw up. I run to the bathroom and collapse on the floor by the toilet bowl. I heave and heave, but all that comes out is bile. I curl up into a ball. Fucking dick, why did I have to run into my poppa? I'd obviously shut all the trauma out, and reading all about it must have triggered my memories. Now, not only do I have to put up with remembering the bullying trauma in the homes, but this shit as well. I feel sick and violated. I think that's why I was so angry yesterday at Arthur's because I felt like that woman came in and violated me. That was a viewing area, not a participation area. I'm supposed to be safe in there, and I should have told her to stop straight away, but I didn't. I let her do that to me, just like when I was taken. I let him do that to me. It feels the same. I feel like my life is one big fucked up mess all of a sudden and I feel like I'm losing control over it. It's a snowball effect, of everything, and I can't stop it from getting bigger.

I'm by the window having a coffee, and it's a shit, miserable, rainy day. It matches my mood perfectly. I feel terrible, and I can't shake it. The only time I don't feel terrible is when I think about Macen. I've got it so bad for her, and I don't even know her. I knew the minute I saw her — before she even entered Casper's last Monday, that I wanted her. I knew it in my heart. My heart knows it now.

chapter 23

Macen

I WAKE UP TO DIXON JUMPING ON me again. This time, I know I have to get up and take him to school, as I'm on the late shift again today. I remember I won't have to put up with Reid because he will be on the early shift, and I feel such relief at that thought. "Momma, it's time to get dressed. It's raining again. Can I put my rain boots on?" I smile at him; I know he wants to put his rain boots on because he loves splashing in all the puddles. "Yes, of course you can, as long as you don't get your trousers wet for school."

I walk him to school, and I was right, he runs ahead of me splashing in all the puddles. I'm glad I put a clean pair of trousers in my bag because I know he will be soaked when we get there. "Dixon, don't go ahead too far, please. You know the rules. Never leave momma," I tell him as he moves further on ahead of me. A little dog comes out of one of the brownstones I'm passing and starts yapping at me, just as a young girl comes out to collect him, apologizing to me. I crouch down and let the little terrier smell my hand so he feels safe enough that I can pet him then the young girl picks him up, apologizes again, then disappears up the steps to the house.

I look ahead of me and can see Dixon way ahead but stopped at the side of the street — he knows he's not allowed to cross the street without me. I can see him talking, but can't see who he's talking too. As I quicken my pace, Dixon looks my way, and I see him point. Then he turns to whoever he's talking to, and I see a hand pat Dixon on the head. I start sprinting towards him in a panic. He knows not to talk to strangers. I see him wave, and as I get to him, I throw my umbrella to the floor and pull him into me "Who were you talking too?" I ask, looking down the street in the direction he was facing. I just see a male figure in a beanie hat turning a corner, but I don't know who it is. I look at Dixon in a panic, running my hands over his head and coat. He looks fine and relaxed except for the furrow on his brow.

"Dixon, what have I told you about talking to strangers? Do you know who that was?" He shakes his head, no. "What did he say to you?"

"He asked me what my name was. He said he was a friend of my momma, Macen, so I thought it was okay to speak to him. Did I do wrong, Momma?"

I grab him into a hug and just hold him. "He knew you, Momma, he knew your name."

I pull back to look him in the face. "Dixon, I don't know who that was. Have you seen him before?" He shakes his head, no again. "What else did he say to you?"

"He asked me my name, and I told him. Then he asked was I three? I told him no, silly, I'm five and a half. Then I pointed at you and said here's Momma now. He said he had to go and said goodbye to me. I waved goodbye to him as he left."

I hug him again. Who the hell was that? Was it the same guy I saw walking away from school on Friday? Now he's approached Dixon. This is serious and cements my feelings of being watched as being real, not just my imagination. I need to warn school. What if it's a predator picking out his next victim? But he knew my name. How? How does he know me? Was he watching me on Saturday? Did he hear Grandma call me by my name? Did he get close enough? I'm shaking, still holding onto Dixon. I'm terrified. "Was that all he said to you, Dix?"

"He just said goodbye, see you soon, Dixon."

I panic, stand up, snatch the umbrella, and grab Dixon's hand.

I walk us across the street and Dixon tries to let go of my hand, but I'm holding onto him tight. "Momma, can I go, please?" He wants to jump in the puddles.

"No Dix, come on, we'll be late. You can't play in the puddles now." He sulks and starts dragging his feet to make a point. "Hey, Dixon, come on, we're nearly there, and we need to get you cleaned up ready for your day at school. Okay, little man?" he nods, but he's still sulking.

At school, he runs off to his friends once I've cleaned him up, and I speak to his teacher to let her know about the incident with the stranger and Dixon. They are going to look at the CCTV from Friday and talk to the police. It puts my mind at ease a little but not a lot.

I sprint home in the rain, running into the apartment and telling Grandma what just happened. We call the police to report it, and because he's approached Dixon now it's a completely different ball game. I haven't been able to prove that anyone's been following me but now this guy has approached Dixon, and they say I've done the right thing. I'm taking no chances.

I get the tube to work because of the rain. I'm a little early and in hindsight should have stayed back a bit because now I've just run into Reid, outside the back of the restaurant, having a cigarette. He knew I would be coming in any time now — he knew he would see me. He is out here in his normal clothes? Does that mean he's on a late as well?

I don't say anything. I don't even look at him as I reach for the door handle to pull it open, but he puts his foot in front of the door so I can't open it. "Excuse me, please," I say nicely but still don't look at him. He doesn't move. I look up because he's a lot taller than me. He sneers at me, then takes another drag of his cigarette and blows the smoke into my face. That smell: smoke and the cologne. It suddenly takes me back to the time I was attacked. I go rigid. I have never smelt that combination since that day. This is stupid. Hundreds of men who smoke will wear that same cologne. He must see me go rigid and the panicked look on my face because the look on his face is pure evil. "Move, Reid, I won't ask you again." I pull on the door harder, slamming his foot.

Just then, Louis comes around the corner. He sees what's going on and grabs Reid by the neck and shoves him to the side. Reid stumbles and falls back on his ass, but jumps up quickly, not saying a word, and tries to grab Louis. Louis is too quick for him and knocks him down again. The door opens, and Caspian comes out. "Reid, leave now. If I see your ass here again, I will call the police. If you haven't packed up your shit, then it's tough. I gave you the opportunity — now get off my premises," he grits out, snarling at Reid. He looks so angry.

I'm shocked. Does that mean he's fired him? It would explain why he is out here in his normal clothes. I can't help the smile at the thought. No more Reid making me uncomfortable in work. He gets up and still doesn't speak to anyone, just saunters off around the corner. I walk inside with Louis and Caspian close behind me.

"Hey, Mace, you good? Did he say anything or do anything to you?" Louis asks.

I shake my head. "No, Louis, as usual, he didn't speak, and he just blocked me from opening the door with his foot until you came around the corner. Thank you."

"No need to thank me, Mace, he's an asshole." With that, he walks off toward the employee room. "Macen, can I see you for a minute in my office?"

Shit, is it my turn to be fired now? First that scare with Dixon this morning, then this with Reid — could my day get any worse than it already is?

I follow Caspian into his office. "Sit," he says abruptly as he walks around his desk. What's his problem with me? I didn't do anything. "As you have probably gathered, I fired Reid today. He's still insisting that you and he are an item. One of you is bullshitting me."

He's standing up and leaning on his desk, looking me straight in the eye.

He's so angry. I can feel the tension rolling off him. "And you think I'm lying?" I retort. I start to get up to leave. I've had enough bullshit for the day already. I can't handle this from him as well. "Macen, sit, let me finish." He shakes his head. "I didn't say I thought you were bullshitting me. I said one of you is bullshitting me. Now, I saw what went on out back just now on the CCTV. I saw that he blocked your way. It doesn't have sound, but from what I saw, he didn't speak to you. Is that correct?"

I nod my head, yes. "I do…"

"Let me finish, Macen." The ass, why is he being so horrible to me? He's so pissed —why do I think he is hot when he's being an ass? God help me. I hang my head at the thought. He obviously thinks it's because of what he's saying. "Look, Macen, I'm sorry you have encountered this, and I do believe you. Reid's whole demeanor is not right. He has been acting strangely since you started last week. I don't know what his problem is with you if you honestly don't know him."

"I don't know him, Mr. Kade, I thought you said you believed me?"

He holds his hand up to stop me speaking. "Let me finish, Macen, always interrupting. Reid has a problem with you, for whatever reason, and I don't like it. The last thing I want is to lose you."

Wait, what? Did I hear him right? He doesn't want to lose me. "So, you're not going to fire me as well?"

He frowns at me and shakes his head. "Hell, no, I don't want you to quit, and I think if Reid had stayed, that's what would have happened."

"I was going to see how this week went with the shift changes before I quit. Mr. Kade, thi…" "Caspian," he says, correcting me.

"Caspian, I've told you this is my dream job, and I don't want to ruin that. I honestly can't thank you enough for the opportunity, but I couldn't have continued to work here with Reid's harassment." He nods his head. "But I do hate the fact you fired someone because of me, and I'm not sure I can live with that thought, the guilt I already feel is…"

" Macen, let me stop you there, it is not just because of the way he has been treating you. There have been several other reasons to give him warnings before you joined us, this was just the icing on the cake." He smiles at his own joke.

"I see."

"I don't want you feeling guilty about any of this. I believe you when you say you have never met him until working here. That also leads me to another thing. How are you with pastries? Have you had much experience? I'm now short a pastry chef. Do you think you can shadow Tommy tonight and see how you go? I know you can do the sauces with your eyes closed. Louis even admitted you were better than him." He laughs at me. I have never seen him laugh before, and those dimples make me melt.

I'm stunned, both at his beauty and at the thought of being the pastry chef. I've done pastries before and to be honest it's one of my favorites, so learning more will be great. I nod enthusiastically. "Yes, I'm good at pastries and baked goods. I would love to do that. Thank you, Mr. K… Caspian. I won't let you down." He sits in his chair and looks at me. "I know you won't, Macen, which is why I'm asking you to do this. Besides it being a great opportunity for you, it helps me out of a hole."

He's right, but I would also still like to get experience at each station to help me when I get my own restaurant.

I don't realize I'm sat looking into my lap, thinking this, when Caspian speaks and startles me. "Macen, you okay? You look miles away there, deep in thought. Do you want to do this?"

I nod enthusiastically at him "Yes, Caspian, of course I do. I was just thinking that I would also like to go back to commis chef at some point. To be able to learn all the different positions in the kitchen and how they operate and how it all comes together as one. Could I take the pastry chef position now as part of my commis chef duties, then rotate as I would have later on if that's possible, please?"

He leans forward and rests his arms on his desk. "I think we can arrange that, Macen, yes. I love how you want to learn every part of the kitchen and how it runs. I have no doubt you will have your very own successful restaurant one day."

I feel myself blush. He's looking at me with those amazing eyes, but what I see in them is not the hard, arrogant ass he normally is or the angry boss he was only minutes ago. No, this is a softer side to Caspian that I have never seen. His eyes are smiling at me, not his mouth, but his eyes. He's making me blush more with the intensity with which he is staring at me. I cough to break the connection we seem to be having. "Will that be all, Caspian? I would like to get to my new station and see what Tommy is doing if that's okay with you?"

He continues to gaze at me, and I cough again. "Sorry, yes, Macen."

I'm not too sure he knows what he's saying yes to, but I get up and leave his office. I have a spring in my step as I do. This was a good meeting. Reid has gone for good. Caspian doesn't want me to leave. I have a new position, and I think my feelings for Caspian are off the charts. I know he would never go for anyone like me, and he's my boss, but I can't help how I feel.

Caspian

She's beautiful. I can't stop staring at her. I know she's speaking because I see her sensual mouth moving, but I can't register what she's saying. I love those eyes of hers — they're stunning, but it's the first time I've actually seen them sparkle. The aqua green color of them is so bright they stand out. Her cheekbones are prominent, and she doesn't wear make-up, not that she needs it. She licks her lips innocently— and that's it, I'm rock hard.

She coughs to get my attention, and I don't even know what she just said, so I just agree. She's blushing — her cheeks are red but not just her cheeks. When she blushes, it starts on her chest and rises up her neck to her face. Her freckles are more prominent as well.

What is she doing to me? She's getting up from the chair. I don't want her to go, but she has work to do. I watch her backside and those fucking hips as she leaves my office. I'm fucking screwed. I know it. I can't fight this. I know I will have her.

It takes a while for my cock to deflate. It's agony not being able to do anything about it. I get my whites on and head into the kitchen to check on everything in there. Honestly, it's been a couple of hours since I've seen Macen, a couple of hours too long for my liking, and I need to see her again. I head straight to her station and see her watching Tommy closely. He'd better not get too close to her.

I examine some lavender Viennese shortbread closely, not sure who did them, but they are perfect in size. I break one, and the texture is perfect, not too moist and not too crispy. "How's it going here, Tommy, Macen?" She hasn't noticed my approach and jumps when I speak. She was too engrossed in watching Tommy pipe passion fruit cream into the mini chocolate cones, they are part of the trio of desserts they make. It's the signature dessert of the month, lavender Viennese shortbreads with damson filling, passion fruit chocolate cones, and rose petal panna cotta. "Hey, chef, just great. Macen is a blessing to work with and doesn't need much tuition." He winks at her, and she blushes slightly as she looks at me. Fuck, please don't say I screwed up by putting them together?

"Macen, how's it going for you?"

"Great, chef. Tommy is showing me some amazing new techniques."

"Well, she's also shown me one or two I haven't used before." He winks again.

"Who did these shortbreads? They are perfect," I ask, ignoring him.

She blushes more and looks down. "Macen did those, chef, and I agree."

Wow. She is something else.

"These desserts are looking really good, keep it up, you two."

"Thank you, Chef," they both say together as I turn and leave.

The time has flown by today, and there have been quite a few compliments to the chef on the signature desserts, which Macen had a big hand in making. She is very impressive in more ways than one. I had to sort out some more stuff on the L.A restaurant, but it's all going great guns, and hopefully the opening will be on time. This puts me in a good mood. After the weekend I've had, and the nightmares I keep having, nightly now, my mood has not been the best. My life was great until a certain beautiful lady come into it just over a week ago, but now it's gone to shit for many reasons.

One, I want her so badly, and it's getting harder and harder – yeah literally – to stay away from her.

Two, my Poppa suddenly appeared, and I found out about my past and how my life has all really been one lie.

Three, my name isn't my birth name and, what are the chances, I named my restaurant after my real birth name.

Four, I had to fire that dipshit, Reid, but that's a blessing.

Five, I really need to get laid, it's been over a week, and it's killing me. If I call up Darcy to meet me at my place in a bit, maybe it will take away my need to bury myself into Macen. I doubt it, but it's worth a try.

Just then, there's a knock at the door. Most of the staff are finishing up now and leaving. I can hear the chatter outside the office. "Come in," I shout. I don't look up as the door opens as I'm just shutting down my computer ready to leave.

"Sorry to disturb you, Mr. K... Caspian." I look up immediately at the sound of her velvety, shaking voice. She's standing there in front of me in her normal clothes, ready to head home. "Hey, Macen, not a problem. How may I help?"

I gesture for her to sit in the chair. She closes the door and sits down, putting her bag on the floor next to her. "Erm, sorry to interupt you. I just really wanted to thank you for the opportunities you are giving me. I want you to know I really appreciate it."

I hold up my hand to stop her. " Macen, you don't need to thank me. You are bloody brilliant at your job. I am this close—" I say putting my finger and thumb together with a small space between them "—to agreeing with Mrs. Webster, that you are the best chef she's had at the school, but that would make you even better than me." I laugh, and she smiles at me.

She's red again from blushing, and she has dimples when she smiles. I don't see her smile too much, and she's blowing my mind. I wish she were blowing something else. Shit, my cock is rock hard at that thought.

"Oh, I don't think that's true." She smiles again.

"Maybe not the 'better than me' part yet, but you are good at what you do, Macen."

She has so little self-confidence. She needs to know how good she is. I put on my jackass voice to try to get it across to her. "Macen, look at me," I grit it out harshly because she's annoying me now by being embarrassed and having such little confidence. She lifts her head and looks me straight in the eyes. "I have no doubt you will make it big in this industry. I have no doubt you will have your own restaurant. You are very talented, Macen. Don't be embarrassed about it. Accept my compliments because let me tell you, I do not give them out lightly. Ask any of the chefs out there. If I compliment anyone, it's because they made something as good as I did. That doesn't happen very often. I have complimented you a few times, so that tells you that I think you are good, Macen. This is a very hard business to be in — you have to be strong and to be able to take what's thrown at you. You have to learn to be harsh and truthful and if it means your employees think you're a jerk, then so be it because to make it big and to be someone in this industry, that is what you have to do. Do you get what I'm saying, Macen?"

She suddenly sits up straighter in her chair, still looking me in the eyes, "Yes, thank you Caspian for the compliments," she says with more confidence than I have seen from her since she walked into my life. That's my girl. I don't mean to be harsh with her, but she is a little bit too timid sometimes. I would say she's a little scared of people in general. I've noticed how wary she is. She will have to man up to run a kitchen. Maybe that will be my goal. She can certainly do the job, but she needs more balls. She can have mine. Fuck.

I don't hear anyone outside the office, so I get up, and she takes this as her cue to leave. "I just need to check if everyone has left and the cleaners have arrived before I leave. Can you just wait for a couple of minutes, and I will walk you to the front to grab a cab? I don't want you going out there on your own at this time of night, especially if everyone else has left?" She nods and sits back in her chair. I go out and check the kitchen, front of house, and the employee room. All the team have gone, there is just one of the two cleaning managers who come in every night to make sure it's all cleaned properly, and lock up for me.

I head back to my office. Macen is sitting in the chair and has her back to the door I left open. She hasn't heard me approach, so I stand watching her for a few minutes. She's on her phone, and I can just make out a male voice talking. Is she on the phone to someone? I move into the room, "Hey, you ready to leave?" I ask loudly. She jumps at hearing me. When she looks at me, she takes out her ear pods. "Sorry, I didn't hear you there. I was listening to my audiobook." I'm relieved that was the talking I heard. Good, it put my hackles up.

I lock up my office, and we head out the back. I hold the door open for her and guide her out with my hand on the base of her spine. She flinches at my touch; shit I shouldn't have touched her, it was just instinct, , so I quickly move my hand. She looks up at me as she passes, and we both stop and just stare at each other. I nearly lean in and kiss her, but I know I can't do that. I want to so fucking badly though. I lick my lips and watch her eyes follow the movement. She licks her lips, mirroring my movements on instinct, I don't think she realizes she's done it as I watch her tongue on her lips. I sigh out loud and close my eyes.

She must realize what she's done, and she moves ahead of me. We round the corner onto W 57th Street and head to 5th Avenue. She stops suddenly and looks around her, scanning the faces of people close by. "What's wrong, Macen?" She looks worried, and that makes me concerned. It reminds me of seeing her in the park on Saturday when she did this exact same thing. She looks up at me and shrugs. "It's nothing. I'm fine." Well, shit, that tells me she isn't fine. We start to walk again, and we are almost at 5th Avenue when she stops again. "Macen, you want to tell me what's wrong?" I see how pale she's gone — she looks terrified. I gently turn her to look at me. We're standing on the corner of 57th and 5th, I have hold of both her arms in my hands, and I crouch down to look her in the eye. She drops her head so I can't see her eyes, but I tilt her chin up with a finger, so she has no choice. "Do you want to tell me what's got you looking like you've seen a ghost? You look petrified, Macen, and I don't like it."

I see a tear fall from one of her eyes. "Macen, please tell me what's wrong?" She sniffs and wipes away the tear then shakes her head. "I'm sorry, Caspian. It's probably nothing. I feel really stupid."

"Bullshit, Macen. This is not nothing. Now, what is it?"

She shrugs. I still have hold of one of her arms, but she doesn't pull away. To anyone watching, we just look like a normal couple. "I just get these feelings. I feel stupid, and I don't know if it's me being paranoid, but ever since I started working for you, I feel like I'm being watched all the time. The hairs on the back of my neck stand up every time I feel eyes on me. It freaks me out."

I pull back a bit, and I scan the area now as she did. "Have you actually seen anyone watching you?"

She shakes her head, no. "Not when I look around, no. The only times were when I was getting in a cab after work a couple of nights. I would feel it then, and I would turn and look over the other side of 5th and Reid would be stood leaning against the wall between the shops over there, smoking his cigarette and watching me." She points to where she'd seen him.

Fuck. Is he a stalker now? "Have you seen him any other times? Are they the only times you've had the feeling of being watched?"

She shakes her head, no. "It's the only times I've seen him, but it's not the only times I've had the same feelings. I've had it every day. Even over the weekend."

I can't tell her it was me in the park on Saturday.

"Come with me. I only live around the corner. I want you to be safe. I can call my driver to take you home."

She shakes her head. "No, Caspian. I can get a cab. I will be fine, honestly. I don't want to put you to any trouble."

Trouble! Is she fucking kidding me right now? "Come on. I'm not taking no for an answer." I grab her elbow and lead her in the direction of my place.

Chapter 25

Macen

CASPIAN HAS HOLD OF MY ELBOW AND is leading me to his place. Oh, my goodness, he's taking me to his home. I start to panic. I forget the feeling of being watched, and I start to hyperventilate. I can't go to his home. What will people think? What if someone sees us now — him marching me like this. I pull my arm out of his grasp. "No, Caspian, please. I can't go to your home. How will that look if anyone were to see us? You're my boss. I can't go. Just let me hail a cab, and I will be fine getting home."

He stops and turns, then gets right into my space. "Macen, I'm not going to say it again. You are coming to my place. I will make sure you get home safely even if I come with you. Please don't fight me on this. I don't give a fuck if anyone sees us. It's none of their business."

He makes me recoil slightly. I'm not scared of him, but he is forceful. I find I actually like it. I don't argue with him and walk around him in the direction we were heading.

I walk on a bit, but he hasn't followed me. I turn to look at him, and he just stands where we were. He raises his eyebrows at me and has a smirk on his face, thumbing to the left of him. I look at the building, and there are some double doors with a canopy above them. I start to walk back to him, and I notice one of the doors is open. A man in a long grey coat with tails and gold buttons and a grey top hat is standing opening the door for Caspian. Oh, he must live here. I didn't even know there were apartments here. I just presumed he lived in a brownstone over on the Upper West side. As I approach him, I see the twinkle in his eye, and he's trying to hide the smirk on his face. "Is this where you live?"

He nods at me, then puts his hand on my lower back to guide me into the building. I'm reluctant to go at first, but he puts a bit of pressure on me, so I move. I'm not comfortable doing this, and I still have the feeling of being watched. I just don't tell Caspian that.

"Good Evening, Mr. Kade," the doorman greets him.

"Hello, Derek. This is my guest, Ms. Donald. Please add her to the list of people authorized to visit me." "Will do Sir. Ma'am," he says bowing to us.

Caspian steers me to the elevators and pulls out a key card. Once inside, he still doesn't remove his hand from my lower back. The thing is, I like it. I don't want him to remove it. He makes me feel safe.

The doors open to a marble hallway. There is a round table with a floral display on it then behind that are some big wooden double doors. Caspian, still with his hand on my lower back, leads me to the doors and inserts his key card. We enter. I stop dead, and my jaw drops. He bumps into me as I stop. "Sorry." He apologizes even though it's my fault. "Here let me take your coat."

He comes around the front of me, invading my space again, and he starts to take my scarf from around my neck. I let him. Then he starts to unzip my parka, but I halt him by putting my gloved hand over his. "I thought you were going to call your driver to take me home?" He takes my hand and removes my glove, one finger at a time, then repeats with the other one. He's taller than me, and I have to look up into his face. He's staring at me as he's removing my outer clothes. He starts on the zip again, and this time, I let him. He does this very slowly, and I swear he does it on purpose, but as the zip goes over my breasts, his knuckles brush me. My nipples are instantly hard. I gasp and shiver at his touch. Shit, I need to get out of here. This can't happen. I'm so attracted to him, but I have never willingly been with anyone before. I don't know how to act, and he's making me feel all kinds of things I've never felt before. Now I'm scared of him — in the way he is making me feel. I step back as he finishes unzipping me. He tries to pull me to him by my coat, but I step back again. "Caspian, please call your driver."

He moves away from me; looking like he's in turmoil. He's rubbing his hand over the stubble on his face and his hair. "Shit, sorry, Macen, sure. I'll call him now to come and get you." He walks away from me, getting his phone out of his pocket and leaving me standing there with my coat hanging off and my gloves and scarf on the floor. As I bend to pick them up, I can hear him speaking on the phone.

The next thing I know, as I stand to straighten, he's right in my space again. He grabs my face very gently, looking into my eyes as if searching for something. "Macen, tell me you feel this? Tell me I'm not going mad, and it's not just me?"

My heart skips a beat. I have butterflies trying out for the Olympics in my tummy, and I have warm fuzzy feelings all over me from him touching me. He puts his forehead on mine. "Please tell me? I need to know."

I breathe out. "I feel it," I whisper to him.

"Thank fuck for that!" And with that, he closes in on me and kisses me. It stuns me, and I don't move. He tries to coax me, but I've never done this before, and I feel utterly ridiculous, standing here, wondering what to do. I very slightly open my mouth, and that's all he needs. He dips his tongue into the tiny gap, coaxing my mouth open more. His tongue is now inside my mouth, playing with mine, and he's moving his lips. I replicate what he's doing, and before I know it, he has me backed up against the door. My hands are on his waist, and I'm pulling him into me even more without even realizing I'm doing it, and he's holding my cheeks as he deepens the kiss.

He presses his torso against mine. I feel the hardness from down below, and I freeze and go rigid. I think I stop breathing. My eyes are screwed shut, and I must look like I'm in pain.

"Mace, what's wrong? Macen, talk to me. What's wrong? Are you okay? Are you in pain? Did I do something wrong? Shit, I overstepped, didn't I? FUCK" he shouts as he turns away from me and storms off. He's angry with himself, and I feel terrible because he doesn't know what he's done wrong — he hasn't done anything wrong. It's me — it's all on me.

I calm myself down because I'm shaking. I grab my things that I dropped when he kissed me, and I leave. I press the button for the elevator and luckily the doors open. I've left his apartment door open, and just as the elevator doors are closing, I see him running to the door, toward me.

I need to get away fast. I know I have all these feelings for him, but I have never voluntarily been with someone before in my life. I think I'm ruined. I got flashbacks of the attack when he pressed his hardness against me, and I'm not sure I can ever be intimate or have a relationship with a man. I'm crying, trying to put my scarf and gloves on before I reach the lobby. I don't want the doorman to see me upset. The doors open. The doorman is there, and he nods at me. I have my scarf wrapped around my face, and I just nod back at him.

"Do you need me to get you a cab ma'am?"

I shake my head "No, thank you." I leave through the doors before he can reach it to open them for me.

I practically sprint back up to 5th Avenue, all the while looking for a cab. I see one approach just as I hear my name being shouted, but as the cab stops, I jump in the back. Caspian is almost to the cab as we pull away.

"Just drive, please. Don't stop."

I hear a bang. He just managed to reach the trunk of the car and slap his hand on it, trying to get it to stop, but I don't look back. I turn my head to the other side, and that's when I see him. I see the same figure who was talking to Dixon this morning. I can't see his face. He's leaning on the wall, and he's watching me. I cry. I cry for what just happened, and I cry because I'm terrified.

I get home, and Grandma is still up waiting for me. "Oh, Macen, I was worried because you weren't home yet. I didn't wan…" She looks at me — I must look a mess. "Macen, what's happened? Why are you crying? What's wrong? Are you hurt?" I shake my head, no but fall into her arms and hug her while crying. She soothes me. She always does. "Shhh, love, when you're ready, let's sit down, and you can tell me what's happened. As long as you haven't been hurt."

"I haven't," I manage to say.

After another minute, I pull away from her and remove my coat, gloves, and scarf. I head to the living room and sit on the couch. Grandma is next to me.

I tell Grandma everything about the day. She's relieved that I haven't been hurt, but she's worried about me being stalked and also about my state of mind. She thinks I should see a therapist, and I agree. She also gets up to phone the police to report the stalker, especially after this morning with Dixon, which they are aware of.

It's really late before I get to bed. The police came and took my statement, but there isn't much else they can do because we don't know who it is. Once we know, they can get a restraining order, but that's it unless something happens to me. Great, I need to be attacked before anything can be done! I can't sleep. All I can think about is Caspian. He wants me as much as I want him — how can that be? How can he want me? He knows we shouldn't pursue it, yet he couldn't help himself. I want him, I really do, but it will never be. He won't want a damaged person with a child. Once he finds out, then it's game over. Luckily, I'm on a late again tomorrow, so I don't need to get up early. Grandma says she will take Dixon to school, and she will keep a lookout for anyone that looks suspicious. I'm really worried in case this guy is there, waiting again. I'm also worried about going into work, wondering if I should just quit. It's been nothing but trouble since I started and although it's my dream job, I have just been so unhappy — not with the actual job, but with everything that surrounds it.

I'm lying here, thinking about everything, and Reid keeps popping into my head. I didn't realize until just now but the guy watching me tonight was smoking. I remember the orange glow of his cigarette in his mouth. Every time I've seen Reid watching me, he's had a cigarette. Could it be Reid following me? I run into Grandma's room. She's fast asleep, and I startle her by turning the light on. "Grandma, I know who it is?"

She rubs her eyes. "Who, what is?"

"I think its Reid. The guy watching me tonight had a cigarette in his mouth, just like Reid does. I think it's him, Grandma, it has to be, it all makes sense, but how do I prove it's him? He got fired today, I'm sure that's just going to add fuel to the fire, and he's going to blame me. He already hates me. I'm scared of him. He terrifies me."

I fall asleep in Grandma's bed. I don't feel her get up with Dixon and it's almost midday before I wake up. I feel lousy. My face is puffy from crying. I have a banging headache to go with it, and I have to face Caspian in a bit. Great.

chapter
26

Caspian

WHAT THE FUCK HAVE I JUST DONE? I couldn't help myself. I felt the connection between us, and I know she felt it too. I don't know what came over me. I saw her standing in my home, and I just couldn't help myself, but now I've totally screwed it up. I'll probably never see her again. "Fuck!" I shout, running my hand through my hair as the cab gets further away. Not only have I probably lost her, but I've probably lost the best chef Casper's has ever had as well. I'm the biggest dick going.

I'm still in the middle of the street, watching the cab as it rounds the corner onto Broadway. There isn't much traffic or many people around as it's late, but something makes me look across the street. It's dark over there, as it's the wall to Central Park, but I can make out a guy, standing there, and it looks like he's looking this way. Probably watching this play out and wondering what I'm going to do now. I turn and saunter back to my place slowly, hoping she comes back around in the cab, but she doesn't.

Back in my apartment, I pour a whiskey. Even though I'm her boss, her reaction is puzzling me. She was kissing me back and getting into it as she pulled me into her body, and that's when she went rigid in my arms, but why? I've never had a reaction like that in my life. I'm arrogant enough to say women throw themselves at me and always have.

I sit looking at my phone and pondering what to do. It's been thirty minutes since she left, so I text her.

Macen, it's Caspian. I have your number from your paperwork, and I just want to apologize for what I did tonight. Please don't let this ruin your career. Please come to work tomorrow, and I promise I will stay away from you. I thought you were into me like I am you, but I read it all wrong, I got the signals wrong. I'm sorry.

I hit send. I keep checking to see if she's read it, but it remains unread, and I fall asleep after downing a few whiskeys clutching the phone in my hand waiting for it to vibrate with a reply.

I wake, sweating from yet another dream, still on the couch in my living area. I have a wall of floor-to-ceiling windows that look out over the park, and the sun hasn't risen yet. I look at my phone and see it's 3.35 a.m. I haven't been asleep that long, and there are no messages from Macen. I need to get out of these sweat-drenched clothes. It's definitely running into my poppa and reading those articles that have opened up Pandora's box.

I have a quick shower, then get into bed, unsure if I'll sleep now. I lay awake, on my back, staring at the ceiling. What am I going to do? If she quits, I'll have to try to talk her into coming back. Promise her that I'll stay away from her. If I can… I will try, but I figure it will be hard. I'm in too deep, and I know it. That kiss just opened up the floodgates to my cold-as-ice heart. I've never in my life let anyone have a piece of my heart, but she's come along, and I want to hand it all to her on a silver platter, every bit of it. What is it about her? She's gorgeous, yes, but she's quite timid and shy. I think she could probably hold her own — I definitely think she has a feisty streak in her, but I get the feeling something bad has happened to her, especially from her reaction to me earlier.

I just want to hold her and protect her. When she told me about being watched, it freaked me out. I felt this surge of anger, which scared the shit out of me. I felt murderous that someone might want to harm her — over my dead body. I feel so protective of her, and yet I barely know her. What if she has a boyfriend? That might be why she reacted as she did, but I don't believe that. I think there is something more, and I would like to find out.

I must drift back off to sleep, and this time, I don't dream. Fuck, it's 12.15 p.m. Luckily, Francoise is in opening up today. I see that I have two messages from Macen. I cautiously open them, hoping she isn't quitting.

Thank you, Caspian, for reaching out to me. It means a lot. There is no need to apologize. I was as much to blame as you. I am, however, sorry for my reaction. It has nothing to do with you and everything to do with me. I will be at work later, and you don't need to avoid me. We are both adults. Thank you for understanding. x

I read the second message.

P.s. You didn't read the signals wrong. x

She only sent it five minutes ago — maybe it was the ping that woke me up.

No, thank you, Macen. I was imagining all sorts, but the last thing I wanted was for this to ruin your career. I will be professional in work. I promise. I'm on my way into work now, I overslept, probably because I didn't sleep much last night, thinking how I had screwed up. See you later. x

I jump in the shower again, no time for the gym or a run. I decide to go around the back of Casper's, as I don't want to walk the line today, when I stop suddenly. Leaning against the wall at the back door, smoking a cigarette is Reid. "What the fuck are you doing here? I told you not to come back. You have all your stuff, and I'll post your last pay-check to you."

He has the gall to sneer at me as though I've wronged him. He steps away from the wall and takes a couple of steps towards me. Great, this is all I fucking need. I take a couple of steps forward. "What do you want, Reid?"

He throws his cigarette to the floor and stubs it out with his foot, as he squares up to me. "You need to fucking leave her alone."

Who the hell does he think he is? He's got some balls squaring up to me. He's tall, maybe not quite as tall as me, but scrawny. I could knock him out with one blow. "Leave who alone?"

He steps closer again and looks me straight in the eyes. "You fucking know who I'm talking about. I told you — she's mine."

There is no way he's talking to me like that. I get right into his face as I speak. "Who the fuck do you think you're talking to? Get off my fucking property now before I call the police."

I'm not getting into a fight because he's delusional. I've handled enough guys like him since I was in a home, and he doesn't scare me. If he thinks I'm after Macen, then he saw us last night. Which means he's following her, so she was right about being watched. "You need to leave her alone, Reid. You do know stalking is a criminal offense, right? You're not an item, Reid. I believe Macen. She doesn't even know you."

He laughs. The look on his face is sadistic, evil, "Is that right. Well, let's just say I left her a little something from our last encounter."

With that, he walks away, sniggering. What the fuck does that mean? She'll be in soon to start her shift. I know I said I would stay away, but I have to warn her. He's a danger. I can sense it, and there is no way I'm letting him harm her. The thought of him touching her has my blood at boiling point.

Macen

I HAD TO TEXT HIM BACK. I FELT terrible for leaving as I did, and it wasn't his fault. He was sweet in his reply saying that he didn't want to ruin my career. He was right about my feelings as well, and I had to tell him that. I didn't want him to think there was something wrong with him. I still don't understand what he sees in me, though. Maybe it's because he can't have me that gives him the thrill.

The police have just been after I called them again this morning. They said there isn't anything they can do about Reid because I have no proof he's the one that's been watching me or that he was the one that spoke to Dixon. I'm scared because Reid has to do something to me before they will investigate. I don't know what I'm supposed to do. Just hide away and hope he goes away? Why do these shit things keep happening in my life? What did I ever do to deserve any of this? I've always just been quiet, never bothered anyone, and just got on with what I loved to do, which is cook and bake.

As I walk around the corner of Casper's, heading towards the back, I stop dead. Reid is there, leaning on the wall with a cigarette hanging from his mouth like he always does. I'm not around the back of Casper's yet, so he has every right to be there, and I start to shake. I can't control it because he terrifies me. The looks he's giving me now are pure evil like he wants to pounce any minute and kill me. I can't move. I'm frozen to the spot, as he pushes off the wall and steps towards me. I keep looking at him, trying to gauge what he's going to do. I can't read him at all. I finally pluck up the courage to speak, "What do you want with me, Reid? What have I ever done to you? Why are you doing this?" My voice is all quivery from my fear.

He doesn't speak — he rarely speaks, just circling me, eyeing me up and down. He must be able to see me shaking. He circles me a couple of times.

"Reid, what do you want?"

He's behind me, and I feel him close in on me. I feel his breath on the back of my neck where the hairs are standing up with the fear. He moves in close to my ear. "You," he grits out right into my ear before he sniffs my hair and nuzzles into my neck.

I swing around to push him away, but he grabs my wrists in his hands. He pulls me into his chest, tightening his hold on my wrists. He's hurting me. He's so close in my face that he must see my fear. I screw my eyes shut, terrified.

"You have a kid? Does the boss know about that? Is that why you ran out of his place crying last night, whore?"

My eyes fly open searching his face. It was him watching me. He's just confirmed it. "Why are you doing this, Reid? I don't know you. You must have mistaken me for someone else. Please leave me alone. I haven't done anything to you?" I plead with him.

He grips me tighter into his chest, licks my cheek, then suddenly pushes me backward, and I lose my footing, stumble, and fall on my ass. He moves and hovers over me. "You stay away from him. Do you hear me?

You belong to me now that I know. You. Are. Mine. I will be back for you both." He then marches off, leaving me on my ass, shaken and petrified. He just threatened us.

I sit on the freezing floor, my knees pulled up to my chest, my arms wrapped around my legs and my head resting on my knees. I'm shaking with fear. I hear footsteps. I freeze. Has he come back for me? The footsteps stop and then move quickly in my direction. "Macen, Macen, look at me. Macen are you hurt? What are you doing? Did you fall?"

It's Caspian. Of all the people it had to be him. I can't look at him. I feel so ashamed. Ashamed about how I reacted last night and about being on the floor like a pathetic little girl — shit scared. "Macen, look at me."

He's being nice. I can't take it, and I cry. He sits on the floor with me and pulls me onto his lap to get me off the cold floor. He's rubbing my back and has my head cradled in his neck. "Macen, baby, are you hurt? Has someone hurt you? Shhh, I've got you." I feel safe in his arms, here on the floor. I know if Reid were to come back now Caspian would sort him out. I can feel the anger in Caspian as well as the worry.

After a few minutes, I manage to look at him. "I'm okay now, Caspian. Thank you."

He holds my face and searches it, moving his hands over my head and down my body, searching to see if I'm hurt anywhere. He looks at me intensely, trying to figure out why I'm sitting here crying. "Macen, what happened?" I don't know if I should tell him? He will go mad.

"Something happened, Macen, You don't just sit on the freezing cold floor crying for nothing, so what the fuck happened?" He's angry. I know it's not at me — I think it's more to do with him wanting to protect me.

I smile, lift my hand to his face and run it down his cheek. Then I lean in and gently kiss where my hand was. He frowns at me — probably thinking I'm some crazy woman. He's ranting at a crying girl, and she just smiles and kisses him. "I'm okay now you're here. It was Reid."

He tenses under me so much that I feel him go rigid. "FUCK!" he shouts. "What did he do to you? I'll kill the fucker. I told him to stay away."

"He was here just now. I think waiting for me to arrive."

He suddenly pulls me into him and hugs me, kissing the top of my head. He's shaking. I don't know if it's from the cold or the anger. "Macen, he's dangerous."

I nod my head.

"To you, I mean. He was warning me this morning to stay away from you, saying that you belonged to him."

I pull back to look him in the face, and I see the pity there. I don't want pity. I never did, even when it was all I ever got from the people helping me after my attack. I start to get up off his lap, but he holds me to him, not letting me go. "Macen, we need to call the police. What did he do to you? Why were you on the floor?"

I tell Caspian about my suspicions that it has been Reid watching me, and how Reid actually confirmed he was watching me at Caspian's place last night. The only thing I left out were the parts with Dixon in them. I can't go there just yet. I told him about the police visits and that they couldn't do anything without proof.

He looks around us. "No CCTV here. He knew the place to wait so he wouldn't get caught with you. And the CCTV from Casper's has no sound — they will just say he's a disgruntled employee. Shit." He looks at me, and I can see the anger, sorrow, and what looks like awe or adoration on his face. I stroke down his cheek again. "Thank you, Caspian, for helping me."

"Hey, don't ever thank me for looking out for you. If he lays a finger on you again, I'll kill him, Macen. I swear I will kill him."

He means it as well. We get up off the floor and head around the corner to the back of Casper's. He has his arm around me, and I find it comforting. The problem is that there are employees coming and going and they all look at us strangely, some even snigger. Well, Caspian obviously doesn't care, so why should I. I'm still shaking from the ordeal.

It turns out that Caspian had left for the day so he didn't run into me because he didn't want me to feel awkward after last night, but he came back because he forgot some paper's he needed, which is when he saw me on the floor. To be honest, I'm grateful it happened that way as it broke the ice from last night. We'll need to talk about it though, at some point. I get stuck into my work so that I can forget what happened, which is at least a distraction.

The rest of the day goes by quickly. I love being a pastry chef, and I find I thrive in this section, but it's the end of the night, and I'm dreading walking round to 5th Avenue to get a cab. What if Reid's waiting for me? What if he's at my home waiting for me to get out of the cab there? I start to go into a bit of a panic. I know Caspian isn't around, and Tommy left not so long ago because he doesn't know what's been going on and Louis is now on a different shift to me. I brace my hands on my workstation and start to take deep breaths. I can't do it. I can't leave on my own. I'm shaking; my eyes shut tightly as I try to talk myself out of a panic attack. "Breath, Macen, just breath." I'm gripping the worktop so hard that my nails hurt.

"Macen." I look up at Caspian. "Macen, what's wrong? You're shaking and sweating, and you're very pale?"

I try to smile at him, but it's feeble. I feel faint. "Hey, what's wrong? You don't look well? Are you sick? Has something happened?"

I shake my head, no as I try to take in some deep breaths. He rubs my back. I'm still braced against my station. He gently pries my hands from the worktops, standing me up straight, as I take more deep breaths. He gets a towel and wipes my forehead and face. He's very gentle. God, why is life so hard? He pulls me into him and rests my head on his chest — he must feel me shaking. "Hey, it's okay, Mace. I've got you. Do you want to tell me what brought this on?"

I shake my head, no. I feel pathetic. He's going to think I'm so unstable. I wonder why he's here — maybe to close up, or check on the cleaning crew. I'm sure I'm the last to leave.

We stand like that for what feels like ages. I'm taking comfort from him, wrapped in his strong arms, and I'm hugging him back. I look up into his face. He's beautiful. Why am I in his arms? Why does he seem to want me as I want him? He looks down at me and smiles. "You okay now? You've stopped shaking at least. Do you want a drink and to tell me what happened?"

I nod, yes. He pulls away from me, and it's only now I realize he's only in a very tight white t-shirt and jeans. He's got lots of tattoos all up his arms, and I can feel his biceps. He takes hold of my hand and walks me toward his office. We stop in at the employee room to grab a bottle of water each, and he drops the towel he used on my head into the laundry bin. Then he retakes my hand and leads me to his office.

I sit in my usual chair, but Caspian stands in front of me, perched on the edge of his desk and looking down at me. I feel so stupid and humiliated. Twice today, he's found me stressed out. "Hey, Mace, tell me what happened."

I love him calling me Mace, but I feel so stupid right now. I lean back in the chair and hide my face. "I feel embarrassed, Caspian."

"Why?"

I look at him through my open fingers. "I lost it because… because I started thinking about going home." I rush the last words out.

He continues to study me with a furrowed brow. "You don't want to go home? Do you live alone? Are you scared? You can stay at mine anytime you want, Mace. I have a spare room. I could give you your own key card, and you can come and go as you please?"

I shake my head. "No."

His face drops. I didn't mean to say it abruptly.

"No, sorry, Caspian, I don't live alone." His shoulders seem to deflate, and his whole posture changes. Shit. "Oh, sorry, Macen, I didn't realize you had a boyfriend. That makes what happened last night even worse. No wonder you acted the way you did. I'm so sorry that I overstepped the mark. I should have asked you first."

I shake my head and stand up taking his hands in both of mine. "No, Caspian, I don't have a boyfriend. I live with my Grandma and —"

"Phew, I thought I screwed up royally then," he interrupts just as I'm about to tell him about Dixon. "So why did you panic about going home?"

He's now holding both my hands and rubbing his thumb over my thumbs. I watch his movements while I speak.

"I started thinking about walking round to 5th to get a cab and panicked in case Reid was waiting for me, there or at home. My thoughts became out of control, and I guess I just had a panic attack. I bet you're wondering what on earth you've done, hiring a stupid girl like me."

He squeezes my hand to bring my attention back to him. "No, Macen, far from it. Hiring you is the best thing I've ever done. I'm also worried about your situation. I came back here to take you home —to make sure you get home safely, and I will do that every day until Reid is no longer a problem. I have my driver outside waiting for us. I will ride home with you and make sure you get into your place safely. I'm not taking any chances that he can get to you. I want you to phone my driver when you are ready to leave home for your shift, and he will drop you off at the front. And I don't want you using the back entrance on your own." He smiles down at me then brings my hands up to his face and kisses the backs of them.

"Why, Caspian? Why are you doing this for me? The way I was last night should tell you to stay away from me. So why?"

He kisses my hands again. "Because I happen to think you're worth it, Mace, and I want to make sure you're safe. I would never forgive myself if anything happened to you. I don't care about last night. You have your reasons for your reaction, and I hope you will tell me one day. If it's because you don't want me, then that's something I will have to live with, but it won't stop me wanting to protect you. I have feelings for you, Macen. Feelings I have never in my life had for anyone. I just want you to know that as much as I try to fight it, and know it's not good for my business, I'm struggling. My head is saying no but my heart wants you."

I go to speak, but he puts a finger to my lips to stop me.

"Don't say anything. Let's get out of here and make sure you get home safely, okay?"

I just nod. I'm speechless. This guy in front of me is so different from the cocky, arrogant man I've known. He's caring and genuine, and I can see the sincerity in his face and in the way he's looking at me with those beautiful eyes.

I stand on my tiptoes, and I gently kiss him on the lips. "Thank you, Caspian, for everything. Please be patient with me for a little bit, and I promise, I will explain everything to you when I can."

He nods at me, takes my hand, and leads me out to the waiting driver. As soon as we get to the car, I feel it — I'm being watched again. I look around, and Caspian looks with me, but we don't see Reid anywhere. We stand by the car, he takes my face in his hands, and he leans in and kisses me on the mouth. Not a passionate kiss, but a loving, 'I'm here for you,' kiss. He's making a point to Reid. To tell him to fuck off. To tell him he can't chase either of us away.

Caspian

W E'RE IN THE CAR, HEADING TO HER place. I wish it were for other reasons than to just drop her off and make sure she gets in safely, but this will do for now. That fucker, Reid, needs sorting out. I'm holding her hand, stroking the back of it with my thumb. Every now and then I see she's drifted off in thought, so I bring her hand to my mouth and kiss it. She turns to me each time I do and smiles. She never objects to me touching her. Maybe she's coming around to the idea. "Penny for them?"

She smiles at me. "I was just thinking how messed up it is that since I started my dream job, my life has been a nightmare. Wondering how it got to this. I don't even know Reid. I don't know his name or him. I'm so confused and terrified of him, Caspian. I think he's unstable and you never know what an unstable person could do." She looks away out of the window, as we approach her home. Fuck, why does it have to be such a short journey? I want more time with her. Just being with her and being able to protect her is all I want. Well, it is right now anyway.

I give her a kiss on the mouth again. Nothing too passionate, but just enough to give her a taste for me, then I watch her enter the building. I'm not sure if these are apartments or houses. The price of property in this area is high, so maybe her Grandmother owns the place? There's so much I want to know about her. She's an enigma to me. Maybe that's what the attraction is — the mystery of Macen Donald. Or is it because I'm used to women throwing themselves at me, and Macen hasn't done that?

I also know I shouldn't be going there with her. This could jeopardize her career completely, and I find all I want to do is help her with it. She does remind me of me in so many ways, work-wise. She turns and waves to me, and I wave back before she shuts the door.

Back at my apartment, Derek, the doorman, greets me as usual. "Mr. Kade, you had a visitor tonight, sir. I didn't let them up to your apartment."

Strange, I usually know if anyone is coming around. "Who was it, Derek? Did you get a name?"

He shakes his head, no. "Sorry, sir. It was a tall man in jeans and a black biker jacket with a hat on his head. He asked what floor you were on, and I knew straight away that if he knew you, then he would know the answer to that question. I asked for his name to see if he was on the authorized person list, and he mumbled it didn't matter and walked out."

Fuck, now he's trying to get into my place. Thankfully, we have security cameras all over the building. "Can I see the security footage of him please, Derek?"

He takes me to the little office behind his desk and rewinds the footage.

Yes, it's Reid all right. I thank Derek and head up to my apartment.

I must have fallen asleep again on the couch as I wake up in a sweat. These fucking nightmares are starting to take their toll on me. I'm so tired during the day because of them. I think I've decided to contact my poppa as well. Maybe he can give me some more info on my childhood. I feel like I'm lost because my life has been a lie. I need to know more.

I also need to try and find out what we can do about Reid. If the police won't do anything because there is no proof he's doing anything wrong then maybe I need to hire a private investigator to get the evidence we need. I have to do something. The state Macen was in when I got to the restaurant was bad, and that was just because of thinking about getting home safely. I meant it when I said she could stay here.

Macen is on an early shift today, and then she's got Thursday and Friday off because she's in over the weekend. That means we just need to get through today. I'll take Thursday off and sort out the stuff from my childhood and phone my poppa. I have the meeting with my lawyer on Friday about the Vegas proposition, and I have some LA papers to get filed as well, which I need him to sort out for me, then if Vegas goes ahead, I'll put a hold on Canada, for now.

Up to Macen starting work for me, I had my life mapped out. My restaurants opening were my only real worry. Now I feel like my head is in turmoil, not knowing what to tackle next. To be honest, Macen is a priority to me. I never thought I would utter those words, ever — that a woman could be a priority over my restaurants, which are the loves of my life — what a turnaround.

I'm heading to Casper's, and as I round the corner, he's there again, with a cigarette in his mouth.

"Do you have a fucking death wish, Reid?"

He sneers at me but doesn't speak.

"What is your fucking problem?"

He's not on my property so I can't order him to leave. He is where he had Macen on the floor yesterday, and that thought is all it takes. I fly for him, grab him by the neck, and pin him to the wall. He's no match to my height and build. I might be a chef, but I'm built like a tank. I learned a long time ago, when I was in the homes, that being skinny and small was bad for me. Luckily, I grew tall, and I took to working out at a very young age so I could protect myself from ever being bullied again. Now I have muscles any linebacker would be proud of.

He grabs my wrists, trying to get me to release him, but I tighten my grip on him. I've lifted him off the floor without even realizing it. "What is your fucking problem?" I shout into his face. He can't answer because I have him by the throat. I release him, he falls to the floor, and I kick him in the thigh, hard.

I step back. I don't want anyone to come around the corner and see this. Fuck. I turn my back on him, and I hear him move. I turn to look at him as he stands, making sure he doesn't take a run at me. "Reid, you need to stop all this shit. I don't know what your problem is with Macen or me, but it has to stop now before someone gets hurt."

He still doesn't speak. He straightens himself out and just casually saunters past me like he doesn't have a care in the world.

"Oh, and Reid," I say before he disappears. "You lay one more fucking finger on Macen, and I will break every fucking bone in your hands. You will never work in a kitchen again. You get me?"

He just shrugs and walks away, not saying a word. That guy is not right in the head. I hate how I lost it so easily with him. I never do that. Yes, I lose my temper in the kitchen, but that's my domain, where I'm king and I rule, out here in the real world, I never do that.

Everyone's here except Macen. She should have been here a few minutes ago. Panic sets in. Where is she? I'm front of house, just pulling my cell out of my pocket to call her, when she comes rushing to the front doors, out of breath. I rush over to let her in, and I scan her from head to toe. "Macen, are you okay?" I have her head in my hands. This startles her, and she looks around at the employees who are watching us.

She pulls away from me. "Yeah, I'm sorry. I was late getting up because I didn't sleep much last night." She steps closer so she can whisper. "Your driver was amazing getting me here in record time. If it weren't for him, I'd be even later." She smiles, then moves around me, heading for the employee room to get changed. I'm turning into a right pussy. I was in a panic, wondering where she was, and with one smile, she melts my heart.

It's been a long day and one without incident. I see Macen heading to the employee room to get changed, ready to go home. I wait for her near the door so I can see she gets home okay. I smile when she notices me waiting. She smiles back — I love those dimples. "Caspian, you don't have to see me home. Your driver will make sure I get in safely. I don't want to put you to all this trouble. I'm more than grateful for your driver, and I will pay you back for using him, I promise."

I hold up my hand to stop her from talking. "No, Mace, you will not pay me back. I want to make sure you're safe. I feel responsible because all this shit started after I gave you a job here."

She shakes her head and goes to speak, but I cut her off.

"Now, come on. Let's get you home."

I hold out my hand for her to take. She looks around at the staff milling about, then shrugs and takes my hand in hers.

We walk through the restaurant, me nodding and saying hello to the patrons as we go, doing the same outside as we get into the waiting car. I see some paparazzi on the sidewalk, and they snap pictures of me holding Macen's hand and us getting into the car together. Honestly, I don't give a fuck what they write about me anymore.

Macen

I COULDN'T SLEEP LAST NIGHT, THINKING about Reid and wondering why he was doing this, but also thinking about my feelings for Caspian.

I had an instant attraction to him the first time I met him, during my works experience at Casper's, but I was just a young kid to him, and he didn't look twice at me. Then, at my interview, I felt the connection to him and got all those feelings I have never had for anyone before. I still can't fathom out why he seems attracted to me. I've seen him with stunning and famous women and they look nothing like me, in fact, only last week he was snapped in LA on top of a model outside an exclusive club. I'm not ashamed to admit I felt a stab of jealousy.

I've done a few Internet searches on him, well more than a few, and he's usually snapped with different women on his arm, and they are always stunning. I'm not his type at all, so why is he being like this with me? Why is he being so protective? Maybe it's guilt because if he hadn't given me the job, then none of this would be happening…

I'm scared though. I've never had a boyfriend — what if he just wants one thing from me? What if I can't give him, or anyone for that matter, what they want because intimacy freaks me out? When he finds out about Dixon, or that I'm damaged, he probably won't want to deal with all that, and he may bolt anyway.

I knew Caspian would be worried because I wasn't in work, but when he yanked the door open and looked me over to make sure I was okay, I fell even deeper for him. He really cares, and that makes me happy.

The day goes by quickly. I love it. I don't have any worries about being watched, and I learn so much from Tommy. I don't see Caspian much during the day. It's been so busy that I hardly have time to eat, and I haven't had the chance to sample any more of the meals yet to give my opinions on them. At the end of my shift, I go and get ready to leave, and as I walk out of the employee room, Caspian is waiting for me. The nicer he is to me, the more I fall for him. He insists on coming with me, and we walk out the front, holding hands. I'm sure I saw people taking pictures of us. Is that what it would be like to be with him? To be seen out with him— would we always be snapped? He's a celebrity chef after all. I forget that at times.

When we get into the car, Caspian pulls me into his side and puts his arm around me. He's holding my hand, with his other hand resting on his thigh. I've been in my own little bubble in here, cuddling into his side, enjoying the closeness and the contact, and the feelings I've never had before of being loved and wanted. I've only ever had this from my momma and Grandma.

"I had another run-in with Reid this morning," he says, out of the blue. I pull back from him to look him in the face. "What, when? What happened?" He tells me what happened, and there goes the little bubble I was enjoying. I don't know how much more I can take of all this. I put my head in my hands and shake my head. "Mace, I'm sorry I did that to him. I'm not a violent person at all. In fact, I loathe violence, but I snapped thinking about what he did to you yesterday — the fact that he touched you and hurt you."

I look up at him. "Please don't apologize, Caspian. He deserves it. I'm just not sure how much more we can take, and I'm worried in case it escalates to something more. I'm scared, and the police won't do anything until he does something, it's all wrong."

He pulls me back into his side, and we ride in silence, with him kissing the top of my head every now and then, and stroking my arm.

As we get nearer to my apartment, I pray Grandma doesn't come out with Dixon.

The car pulls up outside, and I get out. Caspian gets out with me this time. Shit, I can't invite him up — Dixon will still be up waiting for me. We stand on the sidewalk, facing each other. He rubs both my arms, then pulls me into his chest. I rest my cheek on him, and I wrap my arms around his waist. We stand like that for what seems like ages, not speaking. It's so comforting. I pull away slightly, not letting go, just moving enough so I can see his face. "I'm sorry I can't invite you up, Grandma isn't feeling too good and will no doubt be in her nightdress. I don't think she would appreciate her first meeting with you dressed like that." I smile, trying to make light of the situation but hate lying to him.

He smiles then nuzzles my nose with his. "It's okay, Mace, I wouldn't want to upset Grandma. Look, you're not in for the next couple of days, but if you need me for anything just ring me, okay?"

I nod, yes, but I won't ring him. "Also, if you want to go anywhere and need the driver, here is his card and number. Just call and tell him what time to pick you up. He will be there. Please use him. I don't want you walking around alone until this business with Reid is sorted."

I take the card from him. "Thank you, Caspian. You don't have to do all this. I'm not sure why you keep me around when I'm so much trouble, but thank you from the bottom of my heart."

He widens his stance so he's more my level, and pulls me in slightly by his hands on the base of my spine. I now have both my hands on his chest. He leans down and places his lips on mine, and I start to melt. He makes my scalp and shoulders tingle, I have butterflies in my tummy, and I can't breathe. "Breath, Mace," he mutters on my lips, causing me to smile, which opens my mouth and his tongue darts in. We kiss, and the feelings are now making me tingle everywhere. It's like tiny pinpricks all over, especially my scalp. He pulls me into him more, and I move my arms and wrap them around his waist. The kiss deepens quickly, and we are dueling with our tongues. I've seen films where they do this, but I had no idea this was normal.

We stand, kissing for ages. It's getting a little bit heated, but I love it. We're both pressing our bodies into each other, then I feel him, like I did the other night, he's hard, and I feel it on my tummy. Shit, the images of the night I was attacked run through my head. I can't help it — I freeze, with my eyes and lips screwed closed. I drop my arms to my sides and stand like a statue. I want the images to go, and I want the feelings to go. I'm chanting in my head: it's not real, it's not real. "Macen, Macen." I can feel him rubbing my arms. It's my attacker — go away. I want to scream at him to leave me alone, but my mouth feels full, and I can't see. I smell him, I hear him breathe, and I feel him on top of me. I feel him hard on me. I want to die.

"Macen, baby, look at me, open your eyes, Macen, open your eyes, baby." I hear this voice. My attacker didn't speak — that's not him. "Macen, please look at me, come back to me, baby." This voice is soothing, although it sounds frantic. I feel he's rubbing my arms up and down as if trying to warm me. He's so close to me that I can feel his breath on my face as he repeats my name. "Macen, Macen, come on, baby, come back. Come on, let's sit you in the car."

I don't move, but I slowly open my eyes to look at him. I let out my breath because I feel as though I'm suffocating. Caspian is standing in front of me. I'm with Caspian. I collapse into his chest and cry with relief. He just holds me tight to him. "It's you. Thank you. It's you," I chant, over and over, relieved it's Caspian. He rubs the back of my head and kisses the top of it. "It's okay, baby, I'm here. I've got you. I won't let you go." He has no idea of the trauma I've been through, but he's saying he's got me. Once I tell him about the damage, he won't want me. No man will want me knowing I may never be able to have another child — or be able to carry his child.

We stand there for a while until I calm down. He pushes me back slightly and stoops to be at my level. "Are you okay? I'm not going to pressure you into telling me what happens or where you go, but just know, I'm here for you. I'm not going anywhere, but when you want to tell me, I will listen. It's obvious you have demons. I have them too — believe me. I want you to trust me, okay?"

I nod, yes, and wipe my nose on a tissue. "I'm sorry," I whisper to him. He pulls me back into his chest, cradling my head. "Do not apologize for anything, Mace. You have no need to apologize, baby."

Is this arrogant, cocky man for real? I think I've fallen in love with the loving and caring side of this man. No, who am I kidding? I AM in love with him. Which is why I need to let him go. I can't drag him into my damaged world.

We say goodbye, and he makes sure I shut the front door. I turn to wave and the sight of him there on the sidewalk with his legs apart, and his hands in his trouser pockets floors me. His black curly hair is a mess, and he looks so beautiful as he watches me. He smiles a big smile at me as I wave and shut the door.

I spend time with Dixon. He's like my personal therapy. We laugh and tickle, and then I read him a story in bed.

I sit with Grandma and tell her everything. "Macen, I love you with all my heart. I love seeing these fleeting moments of happiness you are having, but maybe you do need to go and see someone for help. I can see you're head over heels in love with Caspian, but you're scared to start anything, and you want to push him away because you're scared to get intimate."

She's right.

"Don't let your attacker ruin your life, Macen. Don't let him win and take it from you. Maybe do as Caspian asks and talk to him. Maybe he can be the one to guide you, take you on the journey you should have experienced, and maybe that will take away all the negativity surrounding intimacy for you. Let him show you what it's like to be loved. Let him show you what it's like to make love."

I feel myself blush. I want to try, I do, but the fear of it makes me freeze, and I can't do that to him. Then I think of Dixon and huff out, and she looks at me, raising a brow. "I just remembered, he doesn't even know about Dixon. I was trying to tell him, and he interrupted me. He won't want a single momma anyway, so there will be no making love or talking to Caspian."

"Then you make sure you tell him about Dixon, and you will know one way or the other."

I roll my eyes.

I'm taking Dixon to school, as it's my day off today. I can't let Reid rule my life. We're holding hands and swinging our arms singing his favorite song, Baby Shark. He stops every now and then to do the shark mouth action with his hand. "Come on, Dixon, we will never get to school on time at this rate." We round the corner, and I stop dead, halting Dixon with a jerk. Reid is there, leaning against the railings of a house.

"Momma, what's wrong?" I look down at Dixon and smile trying not to look scared. I don't want to alarm him, so I crouch down and straighten his coat. "Nothing, Dix, I just thought of something. Come on, let's cross the street and go down the other road. I'm sure it's a little quicker." I stand up, take his hand and cross the road to head down a different street. I don't look back. I don't want to see if Reid's following us or if he's moved. I quicken our pace a little, still trying not to alarm Dixon. I start our song again to appear normal.

I say goodbye to Dixon in the school, and I start to walk home. I'm looking everywhere to see if Reid is anywhere to be seen, but I don't see him. I walk quickly. Usually, I would put my ear pods in and listen to my audiobook, but I need to be able to hear in case someone comes up behind me. I keep checking just to make sure I'm not being followed. I'm only a street away from home when I get the feeling — the hairs stand up on the back of my neck. He's here. I don't look around, and I start to jog, which turns into a run to get home and to safety. I hear footsteps behind me. Is it him? I can't look. I run up the steps to my door, fumbling with my keys? I'm just about to put the key in when his hand comes around and stops me. He's pressed up against my back. I screw my eyes shut. My arms are in front of me, wedged between my body and the door, so I can't even move them. He sniffs my neck and then licks my ear. I'm frozen to the spot.

His hands start to come around my body to the front. He pulls me into his chest, which releases my hands. I don't have my gloves on, and I dig my nails into his hands, and pull them, leaving deep scratches in both hands. He pulls them away. "Ahh, you fucking bitch," he yells, then he grabs my hair and slams my head into the door. I'm stunned, and my head starts to throb.

"Leave me alone, Reid. What do you want with me?" I scream at him. He's still gripping my hair and pulls it back so he can look down into my face. The evil I see there scares the shit out of me. I fear for my life at this point.

"I told you, you're mine now. Don't go near that dickhead again. If I see you with him, your kid gets it." He grits this out right next to my ear before licking it again and clamping his teeth into it. I scream out. He slams my head hard into the door again. Just then the door opens, and he lets go, sprinting down the steps and running away. I slump to the floor, terrified and shaking, as I curl up into a ball.

"Macen, Macen dear, what happened." It's Mrs. Klamenski, my neighbor. She bends down and tries to help me to my feet. "Oh dear, Macen, did you fall? You've cut your head, and it's bleeding quite a lot. Come on, let's get you up to your place." I get up, I'm wobbly on my feet, and I don't speak, grabbing my keys off the floor. I look both ways down the street to see if Reid is still around. I have the feeling of being watched, and although I can't see him, I know he's there somewhere.

Mrs. Klamenski helps me inside my apartment. I feel dizzy and nauseous. I just want to sit down on the couch and sleep. I don't call out for Grandma, but she must hear Mrs. Klamenski speaking and comes to see what's going on. I fall onto the couch, curl up, and close my eyes. "Macen, Macen? What's happened? Macen, can you hear me." I can hear her, but I don't want to speak. I just mumble. I can hear Mrs. Klamenski speaking, but I don't know what she's saying. I hear Grandma, but again don't know what she's saying. One of them shakes me. I don't want to speak. I just want to sleep.

Caspian

I'M STANDING NEXT TO THE CAR. I haven't moved yet. I'm starting to think that something bad has happened to Macen in her past. She's frozen on me twice now. On both occasions, I have been rock hard, and on both occasions, I know she felt it, and as soon as she did, she froze. She goes into her own little world of panic, and I can see the turmoil and horror on her face each time. Both times, all I've wanted to do is love her and reassure her that everything is okay, but she froze me out.

Did I just say 'love her'? Fuck, I do love her. It's just hit me. I fucking love her. I will do anything to protect her, and all I want to do is take care of her. How the hell did that happen? When did that creep up on me? I have never loved anyone. I run my hand over my face and through my hair. Fuck. Now I want to go in there and tell her I love her. If I do, it will probably freak her out. God knows, I'm freaked out by it.

I want to gain her trust, and I want to help her get over whatever is haunting her. I want to nurture her through it all. Wow, who is this guy and what has happened to the cocky, arrogant asshole, Caspian? Since when have I given a rat's ass about anyone's feelings or wanted to help anyone — erm that would be never. This isn't me at all, but I fucking love Macen Donald.

I blow out a breath. I'm not going to march in there and declare my undying love for her. I turn and get in the car and head home.

I'm running through Central Park after just waking up from another fucking nightmare and soaking wet with sweat. Each one gets more graphic — it's like now I've read about it all, I'm reliving it. I don't know if I remember what happened to me or if it's just because of what I've read happened to me, but the dreams terrify me. I have images of this odd couple, leering and hovering above me, but then I see Reid in the same room, which looks like a child's bedroom, but Macen is on the floor, curled up in a ball. It's like my nightmares are intertwining with each other. This is happening every night now. I'm going to go to my doctor and see if he can prescribe anything for me. I'm not seeing a fucking shrink, that's for sure.

It's still early, and the sun is only just starting to rise. I'm just entering the Willowdell Arch on 67th St when I feel something hit my shoulder. It hurt. I stop, look down and see blood — what the fuck was that — all I see are stones on the path. I'm bent over, looking at the stones when I feel pain.

I'm on the floor, face down in the dirt, my head is hurting, and I can hear someone speaking. I try to get up. "Don't move, sir, you've got a head injury. The paramedics are en-route." What's he talking about? I try to get up but fall back down, my head is killing me, and so is my shoulder. "Sir, they won't be long, just hold on. You have a nasty gash on the back of your head." I stay still. I don't want to move, but I'm also freezing. I remember running and entering the archway when something hit my shoulder and made me bleed, but I don't remember anything after that. I hear sirens getting closer — getting louder, and they're hurting my head. I hear running, then the paramedics are next to me asking me questions: name, date of birth, where am I, what day it is, who is the president?

"Fuck, I'm okay, stop asking me shit, my head is killing."

Two of them tentatively help me get up to a standing position, but I go dizzy, and they sit me on a stretcher, so I don't fall. "Sir, we need to take you to the hospital. We're going to take you to Lennox Hill Hospital on the East side, is that okay, sir?"

I just nod my head, making my head pound.

I think I've been in the hospital for a couple of hours now. The police arrived as I was being put on the stretcher. Apparently, there was a big rock near me with blood on it. They said I was attacked from behind and struck over the head with the rock. They asked if I was missing anything, thinking it was a robbery, but when I'm out running, I only have my phone strapped to my arm, and that's still there. They think that the attacker may have been spooked by another jogger. I told them about Reid, and they said they would pay him a visit. I'm just waiting for the doctor to come and let me know if I can go home yet. They wanted to keep me in for a few hours for observation and to make sure I wasn't concussed, especially with living on my own.

I haven't been to sleep, so I think I should be good to go. If they don't come in soon, I'm discharging myself. I hate these places. I get up to take a walk, and I'm just going down a corridor when the doors open, and the paramedics rush in wheeling in another stretcher. I nearly die when I see it's Macen. Fuck. I run to her. She's holding her side. "Macen, what's happened? Are you okay?"

She looks at me, furrowing her brow, stunned to see me here of all places. I'm walking along holding the side of the stretcher, and she reaches up to run a finger over my head. "What happened to you?" she whispers.

I feel my head — it's bandaged up. "I got attacked while out running. What happened to you, baby?"

"Snap, but not the running bit."

"Reid," we both say at the same time. Maybe now the police will do something about the fucker. I'll kill him if I see him.

"Sir, you need to stay here now while Ms. Donald gets examined."

I'm standing there when an older woman comes rushing in and stands next to me. She looks lost. We glance at each other, and I just know this is Macen's Grandma. They look alike.

"Are you looking for Macen?" I ask her. She looks up at me and nods.

"They just took her through those doors to examine her."

"Oh, thank you. Who are you?"

I reach out my hand to her. "I'm Caspian Kade, Macen's friend and erm boss."

"Oh my," she says as she takes my hand to shake. "I'm Macen's Grandma, Doris. Nice to finally meet you, Mr. Kade. Although I would have preferred different circumstances to this."

I agree. "What happened to her? Why is she in here?"

"Well, you know everything that's been going on. Reid attacked her on our doorstep. He pinned her to the door, smashed her head against it and bit her ear. She told me she scratched his hands badly, so I want them to take the flesh from under her nails. It will be the proof they need that he attacked her."

"FUCK!" I scream out, and punch the wall next to me, making Doris jump. "Sorry," I apologize for scaring her. "I wasn't there to protect her."

She looks at me and raises an eyebrow. "Well, who was there to protect you, Mr. Kade?" Touché.

We sit for a while, waiting to hear about Macen. We talk about Reid and everything that's been happening, and I tell her what happened to me, and how I think it was Reid as well. He must have gone straight from attacking me to attacking her. The bastard.

She's a really nice lady who loves Macen. I don't know much about Macen, but from what Doris is saying, she brought Macen up. There is so much I need to find out about her. Just then, they wheel Macen out to take her to a room. Doris and I get up and walk with them. I hold Macen's hand. She doesn't look too bad, thankfully.

I don't give a shit that the doctor hasn't been to see me, and I haven't been discharged, I'm not leaving her side. The police arrive to question her, and she tells them that we think Reid attacked us both. They take down our statements and request Macen's nails be examined so they can get the DNA from her attacker. They want keep her for a couple of hours observation, but then she can go home with Doris to keep an eye on her. I feel so helpless and guilty. I told her I wouldn't let anything happen to her, yet here she is in the hospital. I heard her telling the police about Reid's threat — that she was his and she had to stop seeing me. He's getting more dangerous.

The doctor comes to see Macen and then examines me while I'm there. He discharges us both, and we walk to the main entrance of the hospital. I phoned my driver to come and take us home. I hold Macen all the time. I have my arm around her, walking down the corridor and waiting for my driver. I'll drop them off first, then go home and rest myself. It's been a hell of a day already, and it's only noon.

We pull up outside their place, and Doris asks if I would like to go in for a drink. I see the startled look on Macen's face. She doesn't want me to go up for some reason. She catches me watching her and smiles. "Sorry, Caspian, it's just a mess that's all. Can we do it another time, please?" I take her hand and kiss her palm. "Yes, of course we can, although I'm reluctant to let you out of my sight. How can I protect you when I'm not with you, Macen?" I feel myself getting angry, not at her, but at myself. I'm livid she got hurt after I told her I had her and wouldn't let anything happen to her.

She holds my cheek. "You can't be with me all the time, Caspian, we barely know each other. Please don't blame yourself for this. We may not know much about each other, but I know you're angry with yourself for this. Don't be. This is all Reid. Not you. He's a psycho, and he needs putting away. Now, at least the police have something to go on. Let's hope they arrest him. They will see the scratches on his hand as I described, and they will have his DNA. Let's hope it's enough."

She leans in and kisses my cheek, where her hand was resting. "I feel bad that you got attacked, Caspian. I feel angry about that, and I think this is all my fault, but I know it isn't anyone's but Reid's. He's the one with the problem. Not us."

I kiss her lips gently. Doris is at the door waiting for Macen. "I'll call you later, Macen, to check on you, is that all right?"

"Yes, I would like that, Caspian. See you soon."

I watch them both enter the building and shut the door before I tell the driver to take me home.

I spend the rest of the day at home. I ring the doctors to make an appointment about getting something to help me sleep. I get an appointment for 4.45 p.m. today. Hopefully, I can start on something tonight. I'm not one for pills, but I need something. I can't go on with these nightmares. I have a meeting tomorrow with my lawyer to find out about the Vegas restaurant, so I spend the next couple of hours going through some paperwork on that. It all looks promising. I have enough finances to start the process, which is great news.

I've just seen the doctor, and he's given me some pills as a temporary measure. If it continues, he wants me to see a shrink — not happening. I'm on my way back home when I run into Darcy coming out of Tiffany's.

"Oh, hey, Darcy, how are you?" She throws her arms around my neck and gives me a big kiss on the lips, typical Darcy fashion.

"Casp, I haven't seen you for a couple of weeks. What are you doing tonight? Do you want to hook up? Hey, what's with the bandage?" Just then I see flashes and look over the street to Casper's, and sure enough, the paps are there, and they've spotted us.

"I fell and banged my head, nothing serious. Sorry, Darcy, no can do. I'm officially off the market," I say with a big grin on my face. As far as I'm concerned, I am.

She pouts. "Oh, Casp, that's my loss for now. When you're back on the market, give me a ring, and we can hook up. You know I love your cock,

Casp." She licks her lips, and her eyes wander down to my crotch. He isn't responding, thankfully.

I lean in and give her a kiss on the cheek. "I don't think it will happen, Darcy. Great to see you though. Take care."

I leave her standing there.

I see the paps over the road with their lenses pointed right at me, snapping away. I know this will be on the Internet within a few hours. Fuck. What's Macen going to think if she sees this?

chapter
31

Macen

I SPEND THE REST OF THE DAY IN the apartment. Grandma picks Dixon up from school and says she didn't see anyone out of the ordinary, but that doesn't mean he wasn't watching — he's good at staying hidden. I'm sitting on the window seat with a cup of coffee, thinking about the last two weeks and how dramatically my life has changed. Seeing Caspian in the hospital today, having been attacked, broke my heart. He's going through all this because of me, and I do feel guilty about it.

Dixon laughs out loud at something he's watching on the TV while Grandma cooks some dinner for us. I had to tell him I tripped up the steps and banged my head when he saw the bandage, and he seemed to buy it. "Hey, Dix, come and give your momma a hug. I need one of my Dixon hugs." He doesn't hesitate and runs over to me, giving me his best hug.

A little later on, I get an alert on my phone, I open it, and it's Google letting me know there's something on Caspian. I open up the alert, and I'm shocked at the pictures. There are two: one of me and Caspian yesterday getting in the car holding hands with the tag line: 'Caspian Kade holding hands with a plain Jane staff member – must be serious.' The next picture is of him with another woman who I have seen him with before. She has her arms around his neck and is kissing him full on the lips. What the hell? The tag line on this one is: 'Caspian Kade — up to his usual tricks with an old flame – Bye, bye, plain Jane.'

I throw my phone down on the couch. He had the bandage on his head so that photo was taken today! The bastard. He's just playing me with all this 'protecting me' crap. Does he just want to play the hero? Well, screw him!

"Hey, what's wrong? Why are you upset?" Grandma sits next to me and hugs me to her. I didn't realize I was crying. I wipe my face on my sweater sleeve.

"I'm confused. Look." I show her the alerts.

"Macen, not every picture tells the true story, love. There may be a perfectly good explanation for the picture. Let me tell you something. Sitting in that hospital today, he was on pins all the time because he couldn't get to you and make sure you were okay. He's in love with you, Macen. I could see it written all over his face. As soon as you came out of that room and he could touch you, the tension, and grief left him. I know love when I see it. Don't be too harsh on him."

I hear her, but I don't believe her. A picture tells you everything.

I've just got out of the shower, and I see I have a missed call on my cell from Caspian. I'm not calling him back. Just then it rings again. I ignore it. I don't want to speak to him. It rings again, ignore, again, ignore. He should get the message. I put it on the bed, then go and brush my teeth. When I come back, I have a text message:

Please tell me you're not ignoring my calls. I thought maybe you were asleep until you kept rejecting them. Macen, can you phone me back and let me know you're all right and safe, please? x

I don't want him to worry.

I'm okay

That's all I put. My phone rings again. I just let it ring off. It rings again.

Please pick up. Please let me hear your voice, so I know you're okay. I just want to hear you. x

It rings again. I press accept.

"Macen, are you there, Macen? Please let me know you're okay. I need to hear your voice." I take a deep breath and close my eyes.

"Macen, please. Why won't you speak to me?"

"I'm here, Caspian and, yes, I'm fine. Thanks for checking in on me. I'll see you at work at the weekend."

I'm about to press end when he speaks again. "Macen, don't hang up. What's wrong? Why won't you speak to me?"

I find the alert I got from Google, open it, and copy the article, then send it in a text to him. "Macen, speak to me."

I sit on the bed until I hear the ping on his end to say he has a text. "The pictures do all the talking I need."

I hang up on him just as I hear him shout: "FUCK!"

I leave the cell in my room and go and sit with Grandma for a bit. I can hear it ringing from here. I need to turn the ringer off before it wakes Dixon, so I go and see he's sent me another text:

I can explain that picture if you'll let me. It's not what it seems, honestly. If you don't let me explain now, I will see you at work. I'm not in on Saturday, and your shift has changed on Sunday to the late shift if that is okay with you? If it's a problem, let me know, and I will sort it out for you. If you're not up to working this weekend after today's events, please let me know. I hope you let me explain the picture. I would never do anything to hurt you, Macen. Goodnight. x

I feel bad. Grandma said there would probably be a good explanation. I text him back:

Sorry, not up to talking right now, had a bad day. Sunday shift is fine for me. See you at some point.

He doesn't respond. I turn my ringer off and take the phone back with me into the living room. I sit cuddling into Grandma's side, watching TV. I see it, but I don't take it in. I couldn't even tell you what the program is. What if he's telling the truth? He sounded sincere, and I know I should listen to Grandma.

"What did he say about the pictures?" I look at her. She's waiting for me to say something. "Just that he can explain, and it's not what it looks like."

There's silence for a few minutes. "Do you believe him? Did he say what it was?"

I shrug. "I told him I'd had a bad day and didn't want to talk. I think I do believe him though, Grandma."

She pats my knee.

"Oh, and my shift on Sunday has changed. So I can take Dixon to Casper's. You coming with us?"

"That's good, and if you can take him, then I will pass. I have Marjorie coming into New York this weekend, and I promised I'd find time to see her, so that works out perfectly."

I don't sleep well. I keep seeing Reid and reliving the attack. I haven't heard anything from the police. I'm going to phone them this morning for an update. I sit down to have breakfast with Dixon while Grandma potters about. He's getting more excited for his party on Sunday. Me, not so much. Caspian will find out about Dixon then without a doubt. It's for the best the truth comes out. It also helps me keep my distance from Caspian. With Reid threatening Dixon, it's another reason to stay away from Caspian. I can't take the chance.

I spend the day relaxing, reading, and catching up on my sleep. I phoned the police, but all they could tell me was that they are still investigating. I don't know if they have him in custody or not. I won't feel comfortable outside until I know for sure, and I want to take Dixon out to get some new clothes for his party on Sunday. Maybe if I call Caspian's driver to take me and pick me up, I will be safe enough. I'm going to text Caspian and apologize. I treated him badly last night for no reason. We aren't a couple, so what he does is his business. I just won't let him get close to me anymore. I can't risk it.

I'm sorry about the way I was last night. I shouldn't have been angry with you. What you do is your business, not mine. I was shocked at seeing myself in the same article. Yep, plain Jane, that's me all right.

He doesn't reply straight away, so I put my phone in my bag and call for the driver to pick me up. Dixon got home a short while ago, and he's excited to get some new party clothes. We're in Macy's on West 34th Street. We've picked out some new clothes, and we are milling around killing time until we can get picked up.

I feel Caspian before I see him. I know he's watching us. Well, it's now or never. I turn around and come face to face with him. "Hi," I say looking down.

"Hi," he says back to me. He looks to Dixon, "Hello there, and what's your name? My name is Caspian, or you can call me Casp." I look, and he's crouched down in front of Dixon, holding his hand out to shake it.

Dixon looks at me for confirmation he's allowed to speak to Caspian. I nod my head yes to him. He smiles and takes Caspian's hand and shakes it. "Hello Casp, my name is Dixon, and I'm five and three quarters, nearly six."

Caspian looks up at me and smiles, still shaking Dixon's hand. "Well, hello, Dixon, who is five and three quarters. It's really nice to meet you. I'm a good friend of your erm…" He looks up at me. Well, this is slightly awkward.

"That's my momma. Do you think she's pretty? I think she's the prettiest Momma in the whole world."

Caspian seems captivated. He smiles and nods his head. "Yes, Dixon, I do, she is also the prettiest friend in the whole world too."

I start to blush. I can feel the heat travel up my neck to my cheeks, and I look away from his gaze. He gets up and faces me. "Hey, how are you feeling?" he says tapping his head to indicate my own.

He doesn't have his bandage on now. I've taken mine off and just have a band-aid over the cut. "I'm okay, thank you. How about you? Is your head okay?"

He nods, yes. "Hey Dixon, how about we go up to the toy department, and you pick out a toy as a gift from me, as long as it's okay with your pretty Mommy?" Dixon looks up to me with a big smile on his face. "Can we momma? Please?"

How can I say no to that? "Yes, of course."

Dixon squeals taking both our hands "Come on then."

We reach the toy department, and Dixon is all excited. He finds where all the dinosaurs are first. We stand back slightly, but I keep my eye on him, never letting him out of my sight for a moment. "I got your text, Macen. You don't have to apologize for last night. I know it looked bad but would you let me explain, please?"

I shake my head. "You don't owe me any explanations, Caspian. What you do is your business, not mine."

"Well, I want to explain. I was on my way back home from the doctors, and Darcy had just come out of Tiffany's. We are old friends, and she is very loud and boisterous. Her way of greeting is hugging and kissing, and that's what she did. It was nothing more. We had a quick chat, she asked if we could hook up, but I told her I was off the market permanently. Then we went our separate ways. I went back home alone. That was all it was. Innocent friends."

He just admitted to being off the market permanently. I feel a fool.

"I'm sorry I didn't tell you about Dixon. I didn't do it intentionally, and I tried to tell you the other day. If you'd asked me at my interview if I had any children, I would have told you." Just then Dixon runs over with a dinosaur, all excited, asking, could he get that one, please? Caspian crouches down to be at his level. "If that's what you want then, yes, of course. What is it?"

Dixon beams because Caspian doesn't know what dinosaur it is. "It's a triceratops."

"Wow, he looks scary. Are you sure you want that one?"

Dixon nods vigorously, yes.

Caspian gets up and ruffles Dixon's head. "Okay, let's go get triceratops for you. Is that okay, Momma?"

I nod, yes.

The driver is waiting outside for us. Something is bothering me, and I turn to Caspian. "How did you know where we were?"

He nods to his driver. "Steve was picking me up from my appointment when you called. I knew it was you he was talking to. I made him bring me here." He shrugs. Dixon climbs into the back of the car, and I get on my tiptoes to kiss Caspian on the cheek. "Thank you, for everything."

He smiles down at me. "Don't thank me, and for the record, you have an amazing kid there. Is his father in the picture?"

I shake my head, no, and it's my turn to beam now.

chapter 32

Caspian

I'M IN HEAVEN — I'M SITTING IN THE back of the car with Macen and her son, Dixon. He is the cutest kid I've ever met. Very intelligent. He looks just like his momma, although his hair isn't red, more a strawberry blonde, but he has her eyes and nose. He's adorable. I do love kids. I always wanted them but never thought it would happen. Who knows now, though? I love this woman, and the more I'm with Dixon, I can see me loving him.

I was going out of my mind with her not talking to me. After she sent me the link with those pictures on, I thought I had lost any chance with her. I know what it looked like. I'm glad she let me explain it to her. I know we're not together in the way I want to be, but I feel reassured at her reaction to the pictures. I loved she was so mad. It shows me how deeply she's into me.

I had my meeting with the lawyer and the research they've done points to a big yes for me going for the Vegas restaurant. I was ecstatic, everything in my gut was telling me I wanted it and to go for it. When I got into the car after my meeting and heard Steve was talking to Macen, I couldn't believe my luck. It's about time I got some luck after all the bad shit that's been happening.

We approach her apartment. I don't want her to go. I want to spend time with her. I haven't held her hand because of Dixon being with us, but she's sitting next to me, and I'm touching the side of her thigh with mine. I nudge her leg, and she looks at me, and I lean in to whisper in her ear. "Are you okay? How's your head?"

She smiles at me then leans in a bit closer, "Much better today, thanks. I am sorry about…"

I put my finger on her lips to shush her and shake my head. "No more apologies, okay?"

She nods. The car comes to a stop, and I sigh, the journey is over too soon.

She looks at me, raising an eyebrow in question at my sigh. I just shrug. "You okay?" She looks worried.

"Yeah, Mace, just too soon." She looks confused. "To say goodbye," I whisper.

She unclips Dixon from his seat, and I get out so that they can slide out this way, onto the sidewalk and not into the street. Dixon runs up the steps. "Come on, Momma, I need to show Grandma my new triceratops, ROAR."

He's funny, running his dinosaur up and down the railings on the steps, making roaring sounds.

I stand in front of Macen, looking down at her. I don't take her hand like I want to, but I lift her chin with a finger so she looks at me. "Hey, Casp, do you want to come in and see all my other dinosaurs? I have a lot, you know. They are my favourite-ist things."

He carries on playing on the steps, as I raise an eyebrow to Macen. "Yes, would you like to come up and have a coffee? Dixon can show you his dinosaurs."

My heart is pounding. She's actually asking me inside this time. Then the penny drops. She didn't invite me in last time because of Dixon, not Doris being sick. She hadn't told me about him. I'm relieved that it wasn't because she wasn't into me. "So, I take it Grandma wasn't sick the other day then?"

She looks at me wide-eyed and shakes her head, grinning. "Come on, Caspian, let's get inside. It's too cold out here, and it will be Dixon's bedtime soon."

I'm shocked at the size of her apartment. Grandma must have some cash to afford this place. "Nice place Doris has here, Macen."

She looks sheepish. "Erm, it's actually my place. Grandma lives in Atlanta, and she's come to help me with Dixon because of the new job. She knows it's what I've always dreamt of doing and wants to help, plus she missed us both so much."

Okay, then this is a really nice place for Macen and being a single mom, it must be hard.

Dixon runs in behind us. "Come on, Casp, let me show you my room with all my dinosaurs." He grabs my hand and pulls me toward his room. I look down in awe — his little hand is so tiny in my big one. I look at Macen, making sure she's good with this, and she's smiling from ear to ear. She nods, letting me know it's fine.

"I'll just put the coffee on for us. Then, Dix, once you've shown Caspian your dinosaurs, it's ready for bed."

"Aww, but, Momma, there's no school tomorrow. You said it's weekend. Casp, I'm at a party on Sunday." He looks up at me. I'm huge compared to him so I crouch down, as he's still holding my hand.

"Oh, wow, where's your party at?"

He puts a finger on his lip and tries to think. "It's for burgers I think, at some fancy place, but I don't care about that because after it's watching live dinosaurs, and I can't wait for that." Macen looks at me. "The party is at Casper's. I didn't know we did kid's parties?"

Ah, yes, I have a private party in the restaurant on Sunday for one of my regular customers who is a friend as well. He's a very wealthy businessman, and he's paying me a fortune to put on his kid's party. I don't do private parties, let alone kids' parties, but the money he is paying was too good to turn down. The fact that I'm open to the public an hour later than usual will quadruple the amount I would have taken.

Dixon tries to yank me to his room and nearly pulls me over. I get up, and he drags me along. I hear Macen laughing, and I turn and wink at her. "So, these live dinosaurs — won't that be scary, Dixon?"

He stops and looks up at me. "Silly, Casp, they're robots. Momma told me we don't have real-life dinosaurs anymore because they all be extinct-ed."

I smile down at him and ruffle his hair. "You mean extinct?"

"Yes, that's the one. Come on, Casp." He drags me to his room. I look back again, and Macen is still watching us, leaning on the wall and smiling from ear to ear. I wink again, and she blushes, then I disappear.

I sense Macen standing at the door to Dixon's bedroom. We're sitting on the floor, and I'm surrounded by dinosaurs. We've been playing dinosaurs for ages, both of us roaring at each other. I turn to look at Macen, and I wink at her again. She's smiling. I love seeing her this happy. "Right, Dixon, come on let's get you into the bathroom and ready for bed. I'm sure poor Caspian is ready for a coffee after all this roaring."

"Aww, Momma just a few more minutes, pleassssss?"

"Nope, come on. It's late. You need your milk and supper, then I can read you a story before Caspian has to go."

He looks sad now, and I've loved playing with him, he's such a great kid. "Come on, Dixon, lets tidy the dinosaurs up and then get some supper, sounds good to me, what do you think?"

He shrugs, gathering up the dinosaurs except for the new triceratops I bought him, which gets placed on his nightstand. Macen comes in to help, and as the three of us are tidying, it feels so right.

I sit in the living room, waiting as Macen gets Dixon ready for bed. I feel a bit lost, not knowing what to do. I would make the supper if I knew what he was having and where the stuff was. She has a lovely place here, full of pictures of Dixon, Doris, and her. You can see the love they all have as a family. It makes me a little sad not knowing what that's like, but also happy because I can see how happy Macen is.

Dixon comes back into the room in his T-Rex PJ's. He has a book in his hand, and he sits next to me on the couch and hands me the book. "Wow, this looks interesting. Is this what your momma reads to you? Is this how you know so much about dinosaurs?" The book is nearly as big as him. I open it, and he starts telling me about the dinosaurs on the pages. It's a great book with a lot of details.

We're still reading when Macen comes in with Dixon's milk and two cookies. "Come on, Dix. I'll let you sit at the coffee table to have these if you want instead of the kitchen table?"

He nods and goes to kneel on the floor, eating his cookies and drinking his milk.

"Hmm, they look nice, Dixon."

He looks at me while eating a cookie. "Momma makes me special cookies. She makes different ones all the time but says they are special healthy ones. I love Momma's baking."

I raise an eyebrow to Macen as she hands me a plate with a couple of mixed cookies on them. "I make my own, that way, I know what goes in them, and I know what Dixon gets is healthy and not full of sugar." She shrugs, taking a cookie and sitting next to me on the couch.

I take a bite of a cookie and, wow, they are amazing. "Well, Dixon, I have to agree with you, buddy, these are the best cookies I've ever tasted. Your momma is a great baker." I turn and wink at her again, and I see the blush rising up her chest, neck, and face. I smile at her.

"Casp, how do you know my momma?"

I'm still looking at Macen when he asks. I raise an eyebrow, but Macen answers for me. "You know Momma got a new job in the fancy restaurant? Well, Caspian here is Momma's boss. He owns the fancy restaurant where you will be going to the party on Sunday."

Dixon looks puzzled for a minute as if trying to work something out. "So, you are Casper that owns the fancy Casper's, and that's where Momma works?" He shrugs, I nod, and Macen tells him yes. "In a way, but my name is Caspian, not Casper."

"Okay, but you are friends as well?"

"Yes, we are," I tell him, smiling at him, then Macen.

He finishes his supper, then says goodnight as Macen takes him to bed.

"I won't be too long if you want to stay for a little bit?"

Of course I want to stay. "Yes, I'll be right here."

I finish the cookies, then decide to take the dishes into the kitchen and clean up a little. I sense Macen behind me, and I turn my head as she approaches me. "Hey, you didn't need to do the dishes."

I shrug. "I was just waiting for you and thought I'd make myself useful." I finish the last dish and turn to face her. She's still standing behind me, and I pull her to me. She puts her arms up in front so I can't pull her into my chest tightly, trying to keep a bit of distance. "Is this okay, Mace? Are we okay?" She smiles and nods. "How have you really been, Mace? I mean with the Reid stuff? Anything else happened? Is your head okay, now?"

She nods and looks up at me. "To be honest, the shopping trip was my first time out since coming back from the hospital, and I only did that because of your driver. If I'd had to walk or get the subway, I wouldn't have gone. Thank you for that."

I frown at her. "What about taking Dixon to school and picking him up?"

"Grandma has been doing it," she replies as she moves out of my grasp and goes to make us more coffee.

She tells me about the incidents on the way to school, and I'm so mad. Mad because she couldn't tell me before because I didn't know about Dixon, and livid that he would even speak to a kid and then threaten him if we continued. "I'm fuming, Macen. We need to see if the police have got him yet. I don't feel like it's safe for any of us with him still out there. Fuck, how could I not see how unstable he was when he started working at Casper's?"

We're sitting on the couch, next to each other. She puts her coffee on the table and holds my hand. "Please don't be angry. I'm sorry I didn't tell you about Dixon. I would have told you if you asked me, but I just wasn't forthcoming with the information because, well, because I wanted to prove I could still do the job even as a single mom. We single moms get a bad rep sometimes, Caspian. People think we cant do a job because we are parents. I needed to prove to you I could still do the job."

She hangs her head as though in shame, and I lift her chin with my finger so she looks me in the eyes. "You're right, Macen. I probably wouldn't have given you the job, and I know that is terrible. I need people who are committed, and I wouldn't have thought you could be committed with a kid. You've proven me wrong so far, and I'm ashamed for being one of those people."

She smiles at me. "I can commit Caspian, but Dixon comes first and always will. People assume single moms got pregnant on purpose or we are whores, but no one ever stops to think it could be something completely different."

I get the feeling this is bad and that this is why she has frozen on me? I lean in and kiss her on the lips. "I'm sorry that's how you are categorized, Macen, and I'm sorry I'm one of those people that has pigeonholed single mommas. I feel ashamed."

I kiss her again, and deepen it this time, she opens up a little, and I take the plunge and insert my tongue. I love the taste of her. I pull her further into me, and she responds, but I'm wary of taking it too far. We do this for a while, just enjoying each other. I have butterflies, and yes, I'm rock hard again, but she hasn't felt that. The last couple of times she did, that's when she froze. We break apart and talk a little. She was fine with the kissing, and I want to test my theory. I lean in again and kiss her, and this time I really go to town, deepening it. She responds with no problems. I then turn more into her, lean her back on the couch and press myself into her side, still kissing. She feels my cock, and that's it, she freezes. I was right. This is something much deeper. She's into me as much as I'm into her, but she has a deep fear. I stop, pull her upright, and cuddle her into my side, waiting for her to come back to me. She can't bolt this time. All she can do is kick me out. I hope she doesn't. I would like her to confide in me.

Macen

I'M ON MY COUCH WITH CASPIAN when I freeze again at feeling his hardness against my ribs. He knew as soon as it happened, and he pulled me up and into his side. The flashback was more vivid than the last one. This time it was as though he was there on top of me again, then the words, 'Leave, bitch,' ricocheted through my memory. I've blocked that out for all these years, but now I remember he was close to my ear when he gritted out those words. "Leave, bitch," I whisper to myself. Why is that now bothering me, and why is it familiar?

Caspian moves slightly so he can look at me. I don't think he's realized I'm not still in my memory. He furrows his brows at me. "Do you want me to leave?" he asks me quietly. He wipes my cheeks as I have tears streaming down my face. I shake my head, no. If he's still here, it's because he wants to be. He's seen me do this a few times now, and he's never bolted. He knows there is something wrong, and he's said he will always be there to listen.

Grandma said I should talk to him — that it would help him

understand that he isn't the problem — and decide if this is what he wants, so I need to tell him. I take a deep breath, and I tell him everything about that night, including the end result — Dixon.

He doesn't speak for a minute. He just gently takes hold of me and places me on his lap. I go rigid in case I feel him hard, but I don't, so I relax. He just holds me tight to him, resting my cheek on his chest. I have a hand on his pec, and I rub gently — he's mirroring the action on my back. "Caspian, I understand if this is too much for you. I already don't understand the attraction you say you have to me, but please, don't pursue this if you can't handle it."

He leans back to look me in the face. "Oh, god, Macen. I'm not going anywhere, baby. I'm just trying to process everything you've just told me."

He kisses the top of my head. "You know, as bad and as traumatic as the whole thing was, I got Dixon out of it. I got my chance to be a momma, and he is the most amazing little boy." Caspian nods his head at me and smiles in agreement. I haven't told him yet that the chances of me having any more children are almost impossible, but I have to tell him now. He needs to know.

Caspian lifts me off his lap and places me back on the couch. He kisses the top of my head then heads to the bathroom. He hasn't spoken since I told him about maybe not being able to have children. He went white as a ghost, then got up. I think I may have just ruined everything, but I had to be honest. If he desperately wants children of his own, then he needs a woman who can give them to him. Not one that may never be able to do that. I'm not sorry I've told him any of it. I love him, the way he is with me, and the way he was with Dixon earlier, and he will make a great poppa to someone one day. I stay where I am, but curl up into a ball on the couch, silently crying to myself. He's been a while now, but I want to give him time to process. This has been one of the hardest days. I don't know if I'm glad Grandma is staying with her friend Marjorie tonight or if I wish she were here to comfort me after Caspian leaves. I know I will be a mess once he's gone. I just hope this hasn't jeopardized my job at Casper's.

I must have fallen asleep while waiting for Caspian. I don't remember coming to bed, yet I'm in bed, still in my clothes. I look at the time. It's 2.15 a.m. The only person who could have put me to bed is Caspian, although how he managed to carry me, I have no idea. I feel a little lost and upset. He left, and I wonder if that says it all. My throat is dry. I need some water.

I pad down the hallway to the kitchen, and I jump out of my skin and squeal when I see Caspian sat at the island with a coffee cup in his hands. "Oh my god, you scared the crap out of me," I say, trying to be quiet so I don't wake Dixon.

He turns to me and gives me a weak smile. "Sorry."

I can't believe he's still here at this time and he's wide-awake. I get a glass and get some cold water out of the fridge, and I sit opposite him. "Thank you for putting me into bed…" He nods but doesn't look at me. This isn't good. He won't look at me. He's sullen. This is it. He's going to tell me he's leaving. He can't do this. I try to make a joke. "How on earth did you manage to lift me?" But it doesn't work.

He finally looks up at me, but he doesn't smile. He just stares at me. Funnily, it isn't making me uncomfortable. It's like he's trying to read me — trying to gage me. "How are you so damn strong, Macen? How do you go on? I mean, with all the shit that's happened to you and now all this shit with Reid? It's so fucking unfair all this crap is landing on you. You don't deserve any of it. It makes me so fucking angry."

He looks really hurt, and it looks like he might have been crying. "Caspian, hey, are you okay?"

He looks at me and huffs out a shallow laugh. "You're asking me if I'm okay — as though I'm the one that's had all this shit for years? You fucking amaze me, baby. I'm in awe of you." I thought he was going to leave me. "Come here," he says.

I get up and go around to his side of the island. He lifts me very easily and puts me on his knee. "See, that's how I put you to bed — you're very light." He's trying to lighten the situation. He put's his forehead on mine and just stares into my eyes.

I lean back and scowl at him. "Yeah, right, have you seen my ass?"

He laughs a proper laugh now. "Oh yes, baby. I most certainly have, and it's a mighty fine ass may I add."

I blush, and we sit there in silence for a while just comforting each other.

I look him in the face. "So now you know all my demons and secrets. I wouldn't blame you for walking away, you know. It's a lot to handle. I'm damaged, Caspian."

He scowls at me. "Are you fucking kidding me right now?" I lean back to examine his face. He's angry and serious. "Macen, I'm not going anywhere."

"But do you want to be with someone that may never have your children? Someone who is terrified of being intimate? Someone with so many demons?"

He sighs. "Come on, let's go to the couch. You told me your demons — I need to tell you mine."

It's 4.30 a.m., and we're still on the couch. He's told me all about his childhood, about meeting his poppa and the revelations about his momma. I crawl onto his lap, and I hug his head to my chest. We're a pair together with our issues. Although he doesn't remember his assault, as he was so young, it's no less devastating.

The dreams he's been having recently since finding out have been getting more and more vivid and he thinks he's remembering the attack. We sit and just hold each other for a while until I lean back. "Caspian, you need to think about what I have told you. If having a family is something you've always dreamed of, then you need to find someone that can make that dream come true for you."

He scowls at me, and then he kisses my lips. "I already have, Mace."

I shake my head, no. "I can't give you a family, Caspian?" I hang my head.

He tilts my chin up to face him. "You already have. You are a ready-made family. I already adore Dixon, and Doris for that matter. There's still a small chance you could have a baby, or there is always adoption. Dixon is the cutest kid I have ever known. I would adopt him in a heartbeat if you agreed. I lived it, Mace. I lived, waiting every day for would-be parents to come in and just pick me. I know what it's like for those kids in homes. I would adopt anyway, even if you could have babies."

I smile at him. "We're not even dating, but we're talking about having babies and adoption. I think we're jumping the gun a bit here, Caspian, don't you?"

He shakes his head, no, and leans in to kiss me. "When you know — you know. It's like a light bulb goes off in your head, and it says 'she's the one.'"

I smile and cuddle into him.

We must have fallen asleep on the couch together, and I wake with the feeling of someone watching me. I bolt upright in fright, which in turn wakes Caspian up, and he shoots up. "Momma, how come you were asleep on the couch with Casp?"

Dixon, God he gave me a fright. "Oh, hey, sweetie, I guess we must have fallen asleep. We were up late, talking."

He shrugs. "Hey, Casp," he says as though it's normal to see him here. "Can we have breakfast now, Momma, I'm starving. Can we have pancakes? It's the weekend, and we have pancakes at the weekend?"

I nod and smile at him. "Yes, we can. Do you want pancakes, Caspian?"

He's rubbing his eyes and yawning. He looks from Dixon to me. "I would love some pancakes. Yes, please."

I show Caspian to my bedroom so he can use the shower to freshen up. "I'll go and make pancakes, be ready in about ten minutes, that okay?"

He nods, but just as I start to walk away after giving him fresh towels, he grabs me by the wrist and pulls me to him. "Since coming back from Vegas last week, there hasn't been a night that I didn't have a bad dream and wake up in a sweat until last night with you in my arms. Thank you."

He kisses my nose, and then my lips. I smile at him, then turn him to the bathroom.

"Ten minutes," I tell him with a smile.

"Momma, it's not raining today. Can we go to the park, pleeease? Can Casp come too?" He chokes on his coffee, not expecting that. I don't think he will want to come, so I make up the excuse for him. "Oh, I don't know if Caspian can come. He's very busy with his restaurant, and he might not have time for the park, but we can go?"

He beams at me, then looks at Caspian, who is wiping the dribbled coffee from his mouth.

I, on the other hand, go on an internal panic. How do I go to the park just the two of us and not go into a panic that Reid might be around?

Caspian is studying my face. He sees it. He sees the turmoil I'm in. "I can go to the park with you, Dixon. I'm not in work until tonight. Do you have a football or a baseball and glove?"

I let out my breath. He side-eyes me as he's talking to Dix, and sees as I put my hand on my chest with relief.

He looks concerned, but I nod to say I'm good. "Come on, Dixon, let's get you dressed then we can head to the park. Momma is working later on, then it's party time tomorrow, and going to see all those dinosaurs. Roar." I chase him out of the room looking like a T-Rex roaring at him. This is one of our games. I turn to glance at Caspian, and he's laughing as he clears up the dishes. He catches me looking and winks at me. If only he knew what that wink did to me. I melt every time.

chapter 34

Caspian

I CAN'T BELIEVE I'M WALKING TO A park to play with Dixon and spend more time with Macen. It's like we are in a feel-good movie — parents, walking along with their kid, both holding his hand.

Dixon took my hand at the same time as he took Macen's, and I just looked down in awe at him. He's taken to me as though he's known me all his life —not like he just met me yesterday. It's a dry, crisp day — great for playing in the park. I have never done this before, and I feel like a five-year-old, all giddy about it.

Macen stops on the spot. I see the terror on her face, and I know that look by now. I scan the area around us, looking for him, as I pull out my cell, rotating on my heels, looking for any sign of him. I need to call the police and see what's going on. I need to know if they have hauled him in yet and if so, why is he here now.

Although I can't see him, I know from Macen's reaction that he's close by, watching us. If I see him, I swear to god I will go for him. I walk away slightly so Dixon can't hear me on the phone. I ask for an update on the case, but as I suspected, they won't speak to me because I have nothing to do with it. It was Macen he attacked. My attacker is unknown with no witnesses.

"Mace, can you please speak on the cell and ask for an update on Reid? They won't tell me, as it's not my case?" I shrug and hand the cell to her, and then I take Dixon's hand and walk on a few paces so he doesn't hear the conversation. I watch her carefully while trying to distract Dixon and scan the area around us.

I see her nodding, then speaking, but I don't know what she's saying. She finishes up, and we are just about to enter the park when I spot him. I take off, running in his direction. The look on his face is one of pure evil as he sees me, and takes off, running in the opposite direction. I almost don't want to catch him because I'm scared to death that if I start on him, I won't be able to stop, and that won't do Macen or Dixon any good.

Reid runs and darts between cars as he runs across 5th Avenue then down E 71st Street. I don't cross 5th Avenue, and I stop opposite E 71st, but I don't see him anymore. He's gone. I hope he stays gone.

Back with Macen, I take her in my arms, and she clings to me. Dixon looks at us. "Are you my momma's boyfriend, Casp?" I laugh down at him and ruffle his hair, looking at Macen and seeing that she's smiling, and in my happiness, I completely forget to ask Macen what the police said.

"Come on. Dixon, race you," I say, starting to sprint into the park. I don't leave Macen behind. I make sure she's holding my hand, running with us. We have a great morning, playing, getting ice cream for Dixon and coffee for us, going to see the ducks on the lake and watching turtles coming to the surface for the bread some older kids are throwing in. This kid is so infectious. He makes me so happy.

We head back to Macen's. I carry Dixon part of the way — he's worn out and sleeps on my shoulder. Macen is linking me as we stroll home. Home: God, I wish this were my life. I've had a snippet of what my life could be like, and I want it. I want it desperately with Macen. I know we have stuff to sort through first, but I have to let her know how I feel. I don't care about how it could impact Casper's at this point — screw the head versus heart decision, I want both, and I want Macen at my side doing both.

"I haven't told you why I was in Vegas, have I?"

She looks at me and shakes her head, no. "You don't have to tell me your business, Caspian."

"I know I don't, Mace, but I want to." She gives me a great big smile.

"I'm buying a restaurant there, instead of Canada?"

That gets her attention. "Seriously? Wow, that's amazing. You will do so well in Vegas. Where will it be? Will you move there? What about LA? What about England and…" "Macen, I will tell you it all. I will tell you everything about my business." I stop and turn to her, still with Dixon asleep in my arms. "Macen, I want this. I want you. I want Dixon. I want you in my life. I know two weeks is nothing, but I knew the moment I laid eyes on you again that I was in trouble. Macen, I'm in love with you."

She gasps and puts her hand to her mouth. I see tears fall out of the corner of her eyes. "You okay, Mace? I'm sorry to just blurt it out, but I've never been one to hold what I think inside as you may have gathered."

She smiles at me, and nods, wiping at her eyes. "I've fallen hard for you, Caspian. I just never ever imagined someone like you would even look at a plain Jane like me."

I scowl at her. Plain is not how I see her. We need words about this but not right now. We need to get home.

I leave Mace and Dixon and head back to my place to get changed and then into work. She will be in later, and to make sure she gets here safely, my driver is picking her up and bringing her to work. I'm in such a good mood that my employees are going to think I'm sick or something. I can't believe the way my life has changed since she came into it.

I also need to talk to my poppa. Macen suggested calling him and asking him to come and visit. She thinks it would be good for me and she said she understood that he had to sort his life out. She said he tried to give me the chance to have a better life rather than being dragged up with a homeless alcoholic and drug user, and what she says makes sense, so I leave a message on my poppa's phone to ask him to ring me back so we can talk.

I'm in my office, doing paperwork and catching up from not being in yesterday when my door flies open, and Reid comes storming in. Is he out of his fucking mind?

"Get the fuck out of my restaurant. I told you never to set foot in it again."

He comes towards my desk, and I stand up tall to intimidate him, staying on my side of the desk. If I walk around to meet him, I'm likely to lay into him and not stop. I want to kill this bastard so badly but and I'm trying to think of Macen and Dixon and not get into trouble myself.

"You have three seconds to leave, Reid." I pick up my cell and dial 911. "Can you send a car to Casper's on 5th Avenue? I have an intruder in the kitchen by the name of Reid Hughes who refuses to leave. I believe Mr. Hughes attacked me yesterday in Central Park, and I fear for my life. He is also stalking my girlfriend, Macen Donald, and you have a warrant out for his arrest."

He raises an eyebrow at me and smirks. "By the time they get here, I could do plenty of damage and be long gone," he sneers at me.

"What do you want, Reid? Don't you think you've done enough? You attacked me. I know it was you. I can't prove it yet although an eyewitness has come forward, so you're on borrowed time, and you attacked Macen too. That can be proven from the scratches I see on your hands and the DNA they took from her nails."

He glares at me. "I told you to stay away from her. That's why I did it — you both need to know I'm serious. We have something together, and you're not having her. Leave her the fuck alone, or you will both regret it," he spits at me before turning to leave.

Two minutes later, the police arrive, and I show them the CCTV footage and tell them what he's said. He's threatened both Macen and my lives. They told me, yes, there is a warrant for his arrest, but each time they have gone to his address, he hasn't been home.

Great, Macen is going to freak at this.

A little while later, there's a knock on my door. I'd asked Tobias to send Macen to me once she arrived.

"Come in," I shout. Macen comes in, smiling at me. I get up and walk around the desk to greet her. She shuts the door, and I take her mouth with mine, deepening the kiss before we both realize what's happening and where we are, and she breaks away from me. "Sorry, I needed that and couldn't help myself."

She smiles. "Yes, but at work, we need boundaries. We still have a lot to discuss, Caspian. There isn't just me in this relationship. As you know, I'm a package."

I beam at her. "I'm fully aware of that now, thank you, and I want the whole package. Doris as well." She smiles. "Wait, does that mean I'm now your boyfriend?"

She laughs at me and swats my chest.

I take her hand and lead her to the chair to sit. I stand in front of her, resting on the desk. "Okay, there's no easy way to say this, but Reid came storming in here earlier."

She looks shocked and panicked, scanning me for injuries. "What did he do? What did he say? What did he want?"

I take her face and kiss her gently. "He was warning me away from you again. He didn't do anything, and I didn't touch him, although I wanted to fucking kill him."

I tell her what he said and about the police arriving, and she nods in agreement when I say they couldn't find him. She looks worried. "Why does he keep saying I'm his and we have something together? I've never met him before, Caspian."

I kiss her again. "Hey, don't worry. They will get him sooner or later. He will slip up, and they will get him, baby. In the meantime, I'm not going to leave your side. When you want to go anywhere, tell me, and I will be there. Even taking Dixon to school, I will be there. In fact, I think I should just move in with you, Dixon, and Doris." I wink at her to let her know I'm semi-joking, although I would move in with them in a heartbeat.

She laughs at me. "Don't be silly, Caspian, you do more than enough now." I raise my eyebrows at her. She gives me a quick kiss then leaves to get ready for her shift.

I've been on the phone with the LA restaurant, and we should be opening up, on time, in a couple of months, when my cell goes, with my poppa's number flashing up. "Hey, old man, how's it going?" We chat for a while. He's pleased I phoned, and he said he would love to come to New York to see me and to visit Casper's. He's been researching me and says he doesn't like all the women I'm pictured with — that it makes me look like a man whore — turns out my poppa has family values after all.

"Hey, don't worry, I have a girlfriend now. She's it for me. I love her. In fact, it was her that talked me through our situation and got me to see it from a different angle. Hence the call to you."

"Sounds like you've got a good one there, son."

I'm nodding and grinning from ear to ear, even though he can't see me. "I have, old man. I sure have."

He's going to see what his schedule is like and try to come in the next week or two.

There's a knock at the door. "Come in."

Macen comes in. "I'm just finishing up. Be about five minutes. You nearly ready?" She looks sheepish as though she feels awkward asking me, but there is no way she's leaving without me, and I'm so happy she came and told me it was time.

In the car on the way to hers, I tell her about the call with my pops. She's happy for me. We arrive at hers, and I get out with her and take her in my arms to say goodnight.

"Do you want to come up for a coffee and say hi to Grandma?"

I beam from ear to ear, again, until she goes still. I don't know how she knows, but she senses danger whenever he's near. In one respect, it's a good thing because she gets the warning, but then in another, it's fucking shit knowing you're being watched. "Don't look, baby. Just hug me and act normally. Don't let him know you're aware he's around?"

I speak to my driver and tell him to leave once we are inside. As soon as we shut the door, I call 911 to report him. I hope they come quickly and catch the fucker this time.

Macen

I KNOW CASPIAN TOLD ME NOT TO GIVE it away when I knew Reid was there, but I start to panic every time, and I want to scream. We're standing behind the door, just holding each other, and I'm shaking with fear. Caspian is trying to sooth me, but I'm terrified at what Reid might do next? Is he going to take me, kill me, or even…

No, not going there.

Why does he keep saying I'm his, and why does he say we have something together?

I take so much comfort being in Caspian's arms. He's a big strong man who can look after himself, that's for sure. I know this is eating him up inside, and I feel terrible because he has his own demons and worries. He doesn't need mine.

I pull away and look up at him, and I feel a tear fall from the corner of my eye. He notices and bends to kiss it away. Who knew the man from last week, who was an arrogant ass to me, could be so gentle, caring, and protective of me? And not just me. He's taken to Dixon in a big way. What are the chances I would meet someone like that?

"Hey, it's going to be okay. I've got you, Mace."

Just then we hear sirens outside. "What the hell! Why use sirens — that tells Reid they are on the way, and he will just bolt?" I shake my head in despair.

There's a knock at the door, and I jump out of my skin again. Caspian still has hold of me. "Who is it?" he shouts.

"NYPD sir."

He opens the door, and they come in, and we all go up to my apartment. They take yet another statement, but until they take Reid in for questioning, nothing can happen. It's all a waste of time even though he's stalking us.

Grandma's so worried something bad is going to happen, and I can't say I blame her. The three of us talk for a while, then Grandma excuses herself and says goodnight. I think she's trying to give us some time alone.

The thing is, I need to break this off with Caspian before it gets really started. I know we love each other, but I can't get in too deeply and cause him all this worry, and it's not fair to Dixon to get used to seeing him around. I just don't know how to tell him.

I get us some wine, then sit on the chair when I return to the living room. He scowls at me because I've not sat next to him as I was before. I can't look at him, so I twiddle with my wine glass for a distraction and try to think how to start this. "Oh no. Don't you even think about it, Ms. Donald."

Oh, he's a mind reader as well, it appears, and I smile to myself.

"What's that for?" he asks, noticing my small smile.

"Just smiling because you always seem to know what I'm thinking. You're a mind reader." He smiles back. "We'd make a great circus act. You can sense danger, and I can read minds." He shrugs. "Come here, Mace. I don't want you sitting over there." He pats the seat next to him on the couch, but I shake my head, no. He raises his eyebrow to me. "You're saying NO to ME?" he says emphasizing the no and me. I nod, smiling. I love the playful look on his face. "It's like that, is it?" he says, trying to look very serious but failing. I like playful Caspian. I've never met him before.

Before I know it, Caspian is off the couch and over the table and standing right in front of me. He lifts me as though I weigh nothing and slings me over his shoulder. I squeal and put my hand over my mouth, trying not to wake Dixon or Grandma, but it's hard. He swats my backside gently. "I'll teach you not to defy me, milady," he says in a peculiar accent — it's a cross between Australian, Italian, and Irish.

I crack up — I can't help it. "What was that accent you just tried?"

He slides me down the front of his body until my feet touch the floor and he looks down at me and scowls. "What do you mean? That, milady is me bestest Game of Thrones accent, don't you know, milady?"

I can't help it. I fall back onto the chair and curl up, laughing, but bite the cushion, trying not to make too much noise. He lunges for me and starts to tickle me. He's on his knees in front of the chair, speaking in the strange accent. "So, milady, you want to laugh at my British accent, do you?"

I try to tell him it's more Australian/Italian/Irish but can barely get my words out. "Stop, Caspian. Please stop, we're going to wake Grandma and Dixon up." I'm laughing so hard that I don't think he can understand what I'm saying.

He suddenly stops, and I pull the cushion away from my face. I look at him and see the love and adoration written all over him. "God, I love you, Macen. To hear you laugh like that makes my heart swell so much that I think it's about to burst from my chest. I love it when you smile, and now, I want to make you laugh all the time." He swipes at his eye just as I spot a tear escaping.

I lean forward, take his head in my hands, and I gently kiss his lips. "Thank you." He pulls back, looking at me questioningly, and I smile. "For making me laugh, Caspian. I can't remember the last time I had a good laugh like that. All my life, everything has been so serious. I laugh with Dixon and Grandma, but I don't ever remember experiencing anything like this. I feel all fuzzy, and euphoric – is that the right word? You make me happy. I have never felt this in my life."

I still have hold of his face, and I see his eyes well up. "Me neither, Macen. I've never had or felt anything like this in my life."

I decide that it's my turn to see if he's ticklish. I push him back. He thinks I'm about to get frisky by the look in his face, but I straddle his legs near his knees, then I go to town on him and try to find his ticklish spot. I find it on his hips. He's laughing hard, but he's bucking me as well. I'm going to fly off if he's not careful.

He's still laughing hard when I lean forward to put my hand over his mouth to try to muffle the sounds. He freezes under me and has a panicked look on his face. I remove my hand quickly. "Caspian, you okay? You look terrified. You okay, baby?"

He doesn't say anything, but his breathing is labored, and his eyes are screwed tightly shut. "Fuck!" he shouts out as he bolts upright knocking me to the floor with a thud.

I wince in shock at the outburst. "I'm sorry, Mace. God, I don't know what happened there. It was you putting your hand over my mouth. I got images as a little boy and a man doing that to me to stop me from screaming out when we heard my poppa calling me. I remembered being in so much pain while he had his hand over my mouth. I'm so sorry that I startled you."

I move back onto his lap and hug his head to my chest, kissing the top of his head and just holding and loving him. To think, not fifteen minutes earlier, I wanted to end this with him. How can I when I love him so much that it makes my heart ache to see this man who is a big force of nature, a natural protector, so broken and so vulnerable? We stay like this until his breathing evens out. "You okay now?" I ask, kissing the top of his head.

He nods, "Yeah, I think so."

We hold each other for a little while before he looks at me and gives me a quick kiss. He lowers me to the floor, leans down and kisses my mouth gently at first until he deepens the kiss. He then moves so he hovers over me and lowers his body partly onto mine, I freeze. He must feel me go rigid because he stops and looks at me. "You okay, Mace?" he says looking concerned. I know I'm going to panic. I'm trying my hardest not to ruin the moment, trying to calm myself and not panic but feeling some of the weight of his body on top of me is starting to bring back images. I screw my eyes shut trying to get rid of them. It's not working. I shake my head, No. "GO away!" I shout. The next thing I know, I'm being hauled off the floor, and I'm sat on his lap on the couch while he hugs me and rubs my back, comforting me, telling me it's all going to be fine. I calm down, holding onto him. I start to move off him. If he hurts like I did watching him go into a meltdown then how can I put him through that hurt over and over again and never know if I will ever be able to be with him intimately?

He shakes his head. "No Macen, don't bolt — talk to me. Tell me what's going on in that gorgeous head of yours?"

I look at him, holding me, desperate for me to stay and not leave him. "How can we both be so traumatized? How can be both be damaged and get through it? Caspian, I don't think we can do this. If we're both damaged, how can we help each other heal? If you hurt as much as I just did watching you, then I can't put you through that every time it happens. I may never be able to be intimate with you and to put you through that pain every time you try... I can't do it Caspian. I can't hurt you like that."

He scowls at me. "Don't you get it, Macen. Don't you see that we're meant for each other? Because we are damaged, we can help each other. We can nurture each other, and we can hold each other when the other is in meltdown — we can support each other, baby. I don't think you could find a more perfect match than us. We share the same passions and ideas. We are as compatible as good old mac & cheese, baby."

I bury my head back in his chest and laugh out loud, pulling at his shirt. He starts to laugh with me. "What's so funny?" I look up with tears in my eyes, happy but conflicted tears. "You, comparing us to mac & cheese. Only a celebrity chef would compare us to food!"

He shrugs and laughs. "I make the meanest mac & cheese — even you would be impressed. It's Dixon's favorite, and he won't eat it from anywhere else because it's not like Momma's. I have secret ingredients, you see." I wink at him, and he grins.

"Does this mean we have to have a mac & cheese off?"

"I'd win, so it's pointless." I shrug. I'm that confident.

He pulls my face to his, and he kisses me hard. I don't even hesitate, and I kiss him right back. In fact, it's me that gently pushes my tongue into his mouth this time. We do this for a while. He doesn't move us. I think he knows what my triggers are and he's avoiding setting them off. I can do this — I need to do this. I need to expand my boundaries, and I need to push through as much as I can. I know I'm going to have meltdowns and flashbacks, without a doubt, but if he's there to hold me every time, then I'm feeling confident that we will get there and knock each boundary down.

It never takes long for it to get heated once we start kissing, and I get wet down below, which is new to me. I need to learn to treat this as a new experience. One of those boundaries is to let him love me. I hope to god we get to make love. I do want to make love to Caspian. He is the only person I have ever thought about it with. "God I love you Caspian."

Just like that, meltdown averted.

Caspian

IT MELTS MY FUCKING HEART THE MINUTE the words are out of her mouth. She's never actually said that before, and I feel like crying, but I don't want to make it into a big deal. We make out for a while on the couch. She's on my knee, and I'm learning to make sure she can't feel how hard I am.

We cuddle into each other, not saying anything. I haven't even looked at the time, and I should probably head back home, but in all honesty, I don't want to. I know as soon as she falls asleep on me because her breathing becomes shallow and her body, limp. I stay still, not wanting to disturb her until I know she's in a deep slumber.

I think about earlier and me, of all fucking people, having a meltdown. As soon as she put her hand over my mouth to stifle the laughing my mind went black, and all I could see was the image of him hovering over me, and the feeling of him lying down behind me. I heard my poppa screaming my name outside, and I shouted and cried. The man put his hand over my mouth to stop me, and the next thing I remembered was being in so much pain from him entering my ass. I feel sick thinking about it — not just thinking it, remembering it. God, what must Macen be like, remembering her attack? She was a teenager for God's sake. From what she told me, it was a vicious attack.

I have to help heal her. I have to let her know that what happened was not normal and making love is completely different. It's going to take time, but it's time I'm willing to surrender, for her. I'd surrender my life for her. I know it's going to kill me, not being able to get intimate for however long it takes, but I'll take what I can, very slowly. I need to coax her to open her mind. I need to make her forget the bad and only think of the good that comes with sex.

If I can show her how good foreplay can be and let her explore me as much as she wants too, and let her feel the joy, excitement, and love, then I think that's the way forward. To replace the bad feelings with only the good feelings that come from making love.

I know she was going to call it off between us earlier because I could see it on her face, but there was no fucking way I was letting that happen.

I know she loves me. Not only did she actually tell me, but I feel it in her touch, and see it on her face and in her eyes.

I fucking love her so much, and she's right, every time I see her freeze and start to panic, it tears my heart apart, thinking of the pain she's feeling and the memories of that night. It's why, more than ever, I think we are now perfect. Not just the passion we both have for cooking, but because we have both been rap… violated.

I can't even say that word.

I move us slightly, so we are on the couch, face to face, and I watch her beautiful face as she sleeps. I'm mesmerized by her. She thinks she's a plain Jane, but to me, she is the most beautiful, natural woman I know. She is slender but has curves in all the right places. Her hair is a lovely color of red, and as for her eyes, I could stare at them all day if she let me, the color reminds me of the Indian Ocean — aqua green like I've never seen before.

I move some hair from her forehead, and she moves slightly, but it's to cuddle right into my chest. This feels right — it feels like home.

"Momma, why is Casp here again? Did you fall asleep again?" I hear him, but it takes me a little bit to realize who it is and where I am. Shit. I fell asleep. I peel my eyes open one at a time, and I stare straight into those pools of aqua green, smiling at me.

"Good morning," she says, smiling.

"Good morning." I kiss her nose then she rolls over to face Dixon. I look up, and I see her Grandma standing next to Dixon, smiling down at us.

"Oh, hey, good morning, Doris." I smile at her.

Macen goes to get off the couch, but I pull her back. "Just a minute or two," I whisper into her ear. I don't say it, but I have morning wood, and he's rock hard. Thankfully, she isn't aware.

"Wow, I guess we fell asleep again, huh, Caspian? All this talking is wearing us out."

"Huh huh, and the laughing, I guess," Grandma says, still smiling at us.

"Come on, Dixon. Lets you and me start on breakfast for these two, and we'll let them go and sort themselves out. Then we can get you ready for your party."

"Yay," he shouts. "Momma, it's party day. Casp, are you coming with us?" He looks at me expectantly. "Well, I will certainly be at the restaurant when you're there, that's for sure, buddy."

He goes off with Doris to the kitchen, all excited. I turn Macen toward me, but I don't let my now semi-deflated cock touch her as I go in for a kiss. "We did it again, huh? Fell asleep in each other's arms. But, Mace, I didn't have a dream again. You are most definitely the tonic I need." I smile down at her, and she beams at me, grabbing my head and pulling it down to give me another kiss. Who gives a fuck about morning breath?

We meet in the kitchen after Macen and I both shower — separately, unfortunately. Dixon is chatting away excitedly about seeing the live robot dinosaurs today. I'm in another world, thinking about Macen. I don't want to be away from her. I want to stay with her all the time, which means staying overnight. I don't know how it will work with Dixon and Doris living here. Will they accept me? I think they already have, but maybe they're just being nice. "Casp?" Dixon says, bringing me from my thoughts.

"What buddy, sorry, I was miles away there?"

"Are you going to come and see the dinosaurs with us?"

Shit, that's not my call. I look to Macen for help.

"Let's see how it goes at Casper's first, Dixon. Caspian may have to work this afternoon, but if Mr. Williams says it's okay for parents to see these dinosaurs, then who knows, maybe he can come along as well? Grandma's going out today with Marjorie before she goes back to Atlanta." She smiles at me, letting me know it's fine for me to tag along. Thank fuck for that. How am I going to leave her? I start to panic, thinking about it — what if that dipshit, Reid gets to her, and I'm not around. I've been with her twice now when he's been watching her. Fuck.

We're in the car heading back to my place so I can get changed into clean clothes.

"I think you better leave some clothes at my place if this is going to be a regular occurrence…"

I stare at her. Did she just say that? Did she just suggest I stay at hers?

She leans over and pushes my jaw up. I didn't realize my mouth had dropped open. She smiles at me, then leans in and kisses my cheek. We hear Dixon giggle because he saw us. "Momma and Casp, sitting in a tree, K.I.S.S.I.N.G."

We burst out laughing. "How on earth do you know that rhyme, Dixon?"

He shrugs his shoulders. "Lucas Williams sings it to me when Stacy kisses my cheek."

Macen starts tickling him and teasing him for having a girlfriend, and he's laughing hard now, as is Macen.

I love this. I love this whole family vibe. I love them. "Come here, you two. I think it's time for the tickle monster," I say in a pretend voice and reach over to tickle them both.

We're just stepping out of the elevator to my place when I stop dead, causing Macen to walk into the back of me. Reid is there, leaning against my door. How the fuck did he get up here without a card key or Derek seeing him? I don't let Macen and Dixon out of the elevator. Instead, I lean in and press the ground floor button, giving Macen a 'don't argue with me' look. I see the moment she sees Reid stood there as the elevator door is closing, and I mouth for her to call the police and I hope she does.

"What the fuck are you doing here? Do you have a death wish, Reid, or are you just not right in the head?"

He glares at me, and if looks could kill, I would be dead. I don't move — there's a table with a floral display between us. I can't believe the guts this guy has got. He shoves from the door and starts towards me. I can hold my own, but I want the police to handle him, and although he's here, it's outside of my property, so I can't say he's an intruder in my home. I watch him warily, in case he makes a move for me. He's walking slowly, sneering at me as he does. He's starting to move around the table towards me, and it's then I see a switchblade in his hands.

Fuck. He's a head case.

I move in the opposite direction, keeping the table between us.

I hope the police, or Derek the doorman, come up, just to distract Reid.

"What's up, you cocky bastard, cat got your tongue now? Not got much to say, have you?" He's goading me. He wants me to go for him so he can attempt to stab me. I don't speak. I just watch every move he makes, ready for him to pounce. I can disarm him, no problem, and render him unconscious with one strike because I took Krav-Maga as soon as I could afford it, to protect myself.

He's coming for me slowly. If he lunges for me, then I will just take him out. That way, the police will finally have him. I know it's being recorded because we have CCTV all over the building. All of a sudden, he lunges over the table, sending the vase of flowers flying in my direction. That was his plan. I sidestep him, then take his arm with the switchblade and block it with one of mine so he can't make any stabbing motions. I take the back of his neck, and with his knife arm behind him, I push him to the floor and kneel on his back. He can't move now, but he's still conscious. Well, that was easy enough, the stupid cocksucker. I make him drop the knife by bending his wrist, and I move to put a knee between his shoulder blades, still holding his arm rigid behind him.

"You fucker, get off me. You can't have her. If I can't have her, no one will. She's mine, you ass-wipe. Her and the kid are mine. You will never have them." He's going on and on, repeating himself.

The elevator doors open and two cops come rushing out, with their weapons drawn and aimed at me. "Whoa, wait, he attacked me. I'm Caspian Kade, and I live here." I nod with my head to my door. "This is Reid Hughes. You have a warrant out for his arrest." I slowly get up, releasing Reid's arm and hold my hands up. Reid starts to get up, but the two cops charge for him and kneel on him like I did, while they get the cuffs on his wrists.

I let out a breath and bend over, putting my hands on my knees. I feel sick. I feel a hand on my arm, "Hey, you okay, sir?" It's one of the cops. I stand up and nod. "Yeah, just a bit shaken. He had that switchblade and came at me?" I nod to the knife on the floor.

The cop gets a plastic bag from his pocket and picks the knife up with it, then seals it inside. He looks around, seeing the cameras. "I'll get whatever footage there is so it helps you out, in case he makes up some cock and bull story."

I nod.

Macen comes running out of the elevator just as I'm coming back out of my apartment. "You fucking whore. You're mine. No one will have you ever if I can't have you. You and the kid are mine. We're a family, you stupid bitch."

The cops haul him into the elevator, telling him to be quiet and that everything is being recorded on their body cams. I run over to Macen, who is standing back from the elevators, holding Dixon's face to her tummy, and hiding his ears so he doesn't hear Reid ranting and raving. I pull them both into me, and we just stand, hugging.

Dixon squirms out of his momma's hold. "Can we go now, Momma? It's nearly time for the party to start."

"Come into my place for a few minutes while I get changed. We still have time before the party starts?" He walks past Macen and me and straight into my place. I hear him running around. "Wow, Momma, have you seen it in here. It's really big — so much room, and I can see all of the park. Momma, come and look." She looks at me, and I shrug. We walk into my place, hand in hand.

I watch as she too walks around in awe at all the space. It is huge, and has the best view over Central Park. I move up behind her, wrap my arms around her waist, and rest my chin on the top of her head. "It's beautiful up here, Caspian. That view is to die for."

Don't say that. It could have happened, I think to myself.

Dixon is standing with both hands on the glass and his nose resting on it, breathing on it then drawing in his breath — the little tyke.

We walk round to Casper's with ten minutes to spare. Some of the party guests have started to arrive already. We go in, and I take Dixon with me to my office, then I put a chef's hat on him, and we head into the kitchen, with Macen following. I show him where his momma works, and then show him the food some of the other chefs are preparing. "Oh, I'm going to be a chef like Momma when I grows up big, Casp. What do you do?"

I laugh at him. "Well, I'm a chef too, just like your momma, but this is also my restaurant, so I am the boss and the head chef."

He's thinking. I can see the cogs turning. "Oh, well then, I'm going to be what you are. The boss and the head chef."

I ruffle his hair "That's my boy," I say without realizing what I've just said until I see a tear slip from Macen's eyes and the beam she has on her face.

Macen

I CAN'T HELP IT. MY HEART JUST MELTS when I hear him say that to Dixon. My knees turn to jelly, and my heart beats so fast with all the love for those two bonding.

I know what just happened was traumatic, but I feel such a sense of relief that the police finally have Reid in custody. I don't know what will happen now or how long they will have him, but for now, I feel I can breathe.

I sit at the bar, watching Dixon enjoying his party, with Caspian and Mr. Williams, whose son is having the party, and when we leave to go and watch the dinosaurs, Caspian's with us, and I love it. It's just like having a proper family.

The show's great and watching Dixon get so animated with each dinosaur that comes out is just the best. Caspian sits with me the whole time, holding my hand, at the back, away from the kids, although I swear Caspian wants to join them. He's just as excited as they are. The show's just finished, and I take my cell out, just in case Grandma has tried to contact me, and see that I have a missed call from an unknown number. If it's important, they will phone back, I'm sure. Grandma should be waiting outside to take Dixon home, as Caspian and I are on the late shift.

"Hey, Macen, what do you say to us taking Dixon to the T-Rex crazy golf next weekend. Has he ever been? What do you think?"

I beam at him for thinking of Dixon and nod in agreement. "He would love that, and no, we've never been. It sounds like a fun day out though. I will just have to check my shifts next weekend and let you know."

He smiles down at me. "I'm sure your boss will be kind enough to make sure you have a day off next weekend."

He winks at me, and I melt.

Grandma takes Dixon home, and Caspian and I decide to walk back to Casper's as we have time before our shift starts. It feels so normal walking through Central Park, just the two of us holding hands, and I feel quite emotional. I've never had this with anyone before.

Caspian catches me smiling and bends to gently kiss my lips. "What are you smiling at?"

I shrug then stop and face him. "I feel normal, like a real normal person, doing this," I gesture between us, "I've never had this or done anything like this. I've never been part of a couple. Does that sound stupid? Are we a couple?"

He takes my face in both of his hands, so we're stopped in the middle of the path, and a biker comes past ringing his bell at us, but we ignore him. We just stare into each other's eyes. He leans down, lifting my head slightly, and he takes my mouth gently. I automatically respond, my hands rest on his hips, and I melt. The feelings coursing through me are like none I've ever had before, even all the other times he's kissed me. I feel like he's pouring all his feelings and love into this one kiss. Showing me that we are a couple. Someone on roller blades goes past us shouting, "Get a room," but we ignore them.

He pulls back and looks me in the eyes, still holding my face. "Yes, yes, we are a couple, Macen. In one respect, I'm grateful you have never had this with anyone else, but in another, I'm sad you have never experienced any of it. I'm delirious that it's me who gets to love you and show you what it's all about. I'm a good teacher, you know?" He wiggles his eyebrows at me, and I laugh. "I love it when you smile, Macen. I see those dimples of yours, and I fucking love it even more, when you laugh, knowing it's me making you smile and laugh. You have no idea what you do to me."

I move into his chest and hug him, wrapping my arms around him tightly. "I love you, Caspian. I have so many feelings that I have never experienced before, and it scares the crap out of me."

He pulls back, looking at me, and there is a tear rolling down his cheek. I wipe it away and then reach up to kiss where it was trickling down. "Hey, you okay?"

He nods and holds my face again. "I love you, Macen. I have never loved anyone in my life. You've come along, in the space of a week, and my world has changed. Everything I thought was important before, like Casper's, is all second place to you. You are important: you and Dixon. I love you both. Oh, and for the record, you are my first as well?"

I scowl at him. I know he's slept around. "I mean I have never had this, the walking in the park as a couple. I have never been in a proper relationship." He shrugs.

As we approach Casper's and are about to head around the back, I feel it. I feel the hairs stand up. "He's here!"

Caspian stops with me and rotates, searching for him. "Why the fuck have they let him out? Why would they do that when they have the DNA and the evidence of the scratches, not to mention the video evidence of him attacking me?" Caspian is rigid beside me. The anger is rolling off him.

I fear that if Reid is here, Caspian will do something he'll regret. "We need to get inside, Caspian. Let's ignore him." I look at him fleetingly, and he's pulling his cell out. He hits 911 and speaks quietly into the cell. I start to walk towards the back door to Casper's, holding onto his other hand and watching all around me.

"Fuck!"

I stop and look at him. "What is it?"

I look to where his gaze is — on Reid.

"You fucking pussy. Yes, they let me go. They believed me and her were just having a lover's tiff." He gestures between himself and me. "That we had an argument, and she fell and banged her head, but as she fell, I tried to catch her, and that's when she caught me with her nails." He smirks and shrugs. "There is no proof of me stalking her, and as for attacking you, well there was no CCTV footage either — apparently, it had just stopped working. I would get your building to check it out if I were you." He glares at us, smirking.

"I have personal CCTV footage?" Caspian says.

Reid shrugs, "Maybe, but then they have to catch me again. In fact, I think the cops will be coming for you any time now. It was you they saw attacking me. You had me pinned down. The sooner they come for you, the better. Macen and I can then get on with what we started." He raises his eyebrow at me.

Caspian starts to move towards Reid, and I have to pull him back, "No, Caspian, don't. You will make it worse. He will end up looking like the innocent one in all this. God knows what bullshit he's been telling the police. Come on. Let's get inside."

I start pulling him towards the back of Casper's, but Reid moves at the same time as we do, trying to block our way. "Move, Reid," I grit out at him. "Don't you think you've caused enough trouble? Why are you doing this? What have I ever done to you?" I'm looking at him, pleading.

He cocks his head to one side. "You still have no idea, do you?"

I shake my head, no. "I don't know what it is, Reid, you have me mixed up with someone else or something, but I have never met you before in my life."

He laughs out loud, a real belly laugh. He scares me, and even with Caspian here, I'm terrified. He's dangerous and who knows what he will do next? "You and that fucking kid of yours are mine, Macen. We will be a proper family. Like we should have been, you dumb fucking whore?"

Caspian lunges at him and sends him flying to the ground. He sits on his chest, pinning his arms to his side so he can't do anything, before grabbing him by the neck and lifting his head towards his own. I see the spittle coming out of his mouth with the anger. "You ever fucking come near her, or me, again, and I will kill you. You ever speak to her again, and I will kill you, do you hear me, you crazy mother-fucker? Leave us alone. She has never been and never will be yours. Get that through to your fucking tiny pea brain," he says, tapping the side of Reid's head.

Reid is just smiling, goading him, wanting him to punch him or mark him in some way. I move closer. "Caspian, come on, he isn't worth it. Let's get inside."

I pull on his arm. He looks at me. I see the confusion on his face: should he stay and fight or should he come with me? He releases Reid, shoving his head back, which bangs on the floor, then gets up off him. He takes my hand, and we both walk into Casper's.

Inside, in his office, he is visibly shaking. "The cops said they released him as there was no real evidence, and they couldn't hold him. They did say they needed to speak to me again, though. It was me they saw pinning him down after all."

I move to him, I sit on his knee, and we hold each other. He's still shaking with anger, as he rests his head on my chest. I know something else is bothering him. "What is it, Caspian? What else has got you so worked up?"

He looks at me, and I see his eyes are glazed with unshed tears.

"Tell me what's wrong?"

He looks into my eyes. "I just feel so hopeless and helpless, Mace. He's doing this to you, to us, and I can't stop him. I can take anyone down. I learned how to protect myself when I was a teenager because I was bullied in the homes. I could kill someone with my bare hands, yet I can't protect you and Dixon from this dipshit, and it scares the fuck out of me what he's going to do next?"

"I don't understand it. How has he managed to get away with it — attacking you twice and me once? He has all the luck. I don't understand how they bought his story, that he and I were a couple having a row and I fell. It doesn't make sense, Caspian. What will it take?"

He rubs my back because I'm starting to get a bit hysterical, and he's trying to calm me down.

"I have CCTV footage. I have my own security, so they should be able to charge him with something. I need to get it to them — the sooner the better, but then, as he said, they have to catch him again. Macen…" He pulls my face to look at him. I see the anguish. "He's not stable. He's convinced you and him will be together as a family with Dixon. That scares the fuck out of me. Maybe I should hire a PI to look into him and his background? See if we can find out where this obsession with you came from. In fact…" He lifts me off his knee and unlocks his filing cabinet, searches through the papers. "Here we are. His employee records."

He's quiet for a bit, reading the records. "Nothing really, just that he was at NYCS, passed top of his year, had a few jobs with smaller restaurants for a few years, then started here for me. I have an address, but he's probably moved on from there?"

I wonder when he was at NYCS. He looks older than me, but then when I first went to school, I was the youngest there. "How old is he, Caspian?"

He looks at the papers. "Twenty-seven."

Okay, so that makes him two years older than me. There's still a possibility. "What years was he at NYCS?"

He looks again. "2009 for three years."

I do the math in my head. I started at the school in 2009 and left in

2011 after my attack. "Mace, hey, look at me? What's wrong? You look like death. What is it, baby?"

He looks at me worriedly.

"He was there the same time as me! We went to school together. I don't know him or remember him." My heart is racing. He must know me from school. He must remember me. Had he changed in looks or changed his name?

"Macen, why are you looking like that?"

I look at him. "I need to find a picture of him at school and see if I recognize him at all?"

Caspian

She looks like death, and she's scaring me right now. She looks like she might pass out. I do a search for yearbooks at NYCS and look for 2012, which would be the year he finished school. I bring up his picture and turn the computer so Macen can see his image. He looks like he does now, but younger. He's certainly aged a lot since then.

She shakes her head. "No, I don't recognize him from this either. Are there any more images?"

I search his name, and it only brings up his Facebook account. I click on that and see if there's anything on there. I search for his photos, but there aren't that many. He doesn't have many friends either — eleven friends. Weird, even for someone like Reid you would expect more friends. He doesn't post much on Facebook, but I spot an article about some exceptional new students from his first year at NYCS. One of those students being Reid Hughes. I scan the article. It doesn't give much away, but there is a picture underneath with his name under the picture. I turn the computer back to Macen.

"Oh, my god. He looks so different. Is that him? With blonde hair, it makes a big difference. He looks familiar. I think I saw him a few times when I was there, but I didn't know him as such. There were always parties at my shared house, but I just kept myself to myself. I didn't interact with anyone much." She's nodding her head. Well, shit, we may be getting closer to what his problem is. We leave it at that for now, and Macen goes to start her work. I need to go and get the CCTV footage from my apartment and take it to the cops before they come looking for me.

At my apartment building, I ask Derek about the CCTV not working, and how Reid got up to my apartment without having a key card for the elevator? The only thing he can think of is that Reid must have waited for him to use the bathroom and then come in and disconnected the security. The only way he could have gotten up to the top floor without a key is through the stairwell, and it's forty-eight flights of stairs up to my apartment. It's a killer, I've done it a few times.

I'm fucking fuming at the fact it was so easy for Reid to gain access. I'm lucky he didn't break into my apartment. In my security closet, I find the footage I need, and I make a copy of it and load it onto a USB stick. I make another copy and put it in my safe. I don't want to take any chances. I head to the Mid-Town north precinct on West 54th street to hand in the USB to them and hopefully get them off my back, and after Reid again. I give them my details and the USB. They will pass it to whoever is dealing with the case.

Back at Casper's, I work the kitchen to pass the time. I also go in front of house to greet the customers. I'm standing at one of the window tables talking when out of the corner of my eye, I see Reid standing over the other side of 5th Avenue, leaning against the wall. I don't turn to look at him. I don't want him to know I've spotted him, so I carry on talking, then make my way back to my office and call the cops to let them know he's out there. I go back out front and work the room but keep my eye on him to see if they get him. It's almost an hour later when I see a cop car pull up, but Reid bolts. He looks straight into the restaurant and sees me watching as they pull up curbside, then he runs. They don't get him. They don't even give chase. Fuck.

The shift is over, and I wait for Macen. I motion her to come into my office, and I tell her what happened earlier. "Macen, what do you say to staying at my place tonight? Will Doris be okay with sorting Dixon in the morning?" She looks at me, horrified, I just suggested it. I hold up my hand to stop her going into panic mode. "Wait, it's not for what you're thinking. I just think we can get to my place nice and quickly, and Reid won't be expecting it. He may be near your place waiting for you to get home. I don't know, but it may be safer if you come to mine. You can have your own room, nothing to worry about. And you're on an early tomorrow, so you will be just around the corner. We can get up early and go to yours if you need to see Dixon before school?"

She's thinking about it. I know when she's in turmoil because she bites the inside of her lip. "It's your choice, Mace." She nods her head. "I need to phone Grandma and let her know before it gets too late." She pulls out her cell and calls Doris. I get up and leave her to it. I check the cleaners have started and that everywhere is locked up.

We head out. I have her wrapped under my arm and tight into my side. I scan everywhere, checking the shadows, around corners, making sure he's not about to jump out at us. We walk fast, and we make it to my building in record time and head straight up to my place. I leave the elevators first, making sure he's not got in again so I can push Macen back in if need be. This fucking dick is making us both nervous wrecks.

I lead her inside, with my hand at the bottom of her back. Once in the foyer, I'm standing behind her, and I remove her coat, hat, and scarf. I lean down and kiss her neck and her exposed shoulder. She shudders from my touch and leans back into my chest. I drop her coat and wrap my arms around her, splaying my hands across her tummy. "You okay, Mace? I mean, okay being here with me? If it freaks you out at all, just let me know."

She nods her head and tilts it back to look up at me. I lean down, place a kiss on her forehead, and smile down at her. I better move before she feels how hard my cock is getting. I step back and pick her coat up, taking mine off and hanging them both up. I take her hand and lead her to the seating area, and then I sit her down, which is the wrong thing to do, as I'm in front of her, and my fucking rock-hard cock is now at eye level. She looks up at me, startled. I smile down at her and shrug. "I'm sorry, kind off, but I can't control him. You do that to me."

I walk away so she doesn't feel too embarrassed. I can tell by the look on her face she's going to panic if I stay in front of her too long. "Do you want a drink, baby? I can make a coffee, or I have wine, or whiskey?"

"Wine, please," she says it too quickly. Maybe she needs to calm her nerves.

We sit on the couch, cuddling and drinking wine. I tell her I took the USB to the police, so hopefully, they will get him soon, and we talk a lot about Dixon.

"Have you thought any more about if you remember Reid from NYCS?"

She shakes her head, no. "Can we not speak about him right now, Caspian? I'm just enjoying being here with you and getting to know you. Although, I still have a hard time believing you want me here with you." She snorts, and we both burst out laughing. I take her glass before she spills it and place it on the table with mine. I turn and take her head in my hands, looking her straight in the beautiful eyes of hers.

"Macen, you have no idea how beautiful you are to me. I can tell you until I'm blue in the face, but you are gorgeous, and I fucking love you more and more. I can't tell you enough. I have never had feelings like this for anyone."

I kiss her lips gently, making sure I don't let my cock rub on her anywhere. She breaks the kiss and leans back, looking at me. "I just don't get it, Caspian. I know I keep repeating myself, but I'm a plain Jane, a curvy one at that. I'm nothing like any of the models you date." She hangs her head.

I tilt it up. "And I keep telling you: I didn't date. I fucked — simple as. I never had feelings for any of them. You turn up and knock me for six. I was waiting for you all along. I don't care that we are broken, Mace, we will fix each other, baby. Piece by piece, we will mend, okay?" She nods, and I lean in and kiss her again. This time it deepens and gets heated.

A few minutes later, I break away. If I don't, I know my hands will start to wander, and I don't know if she's ready for any exploration yet. I look at her. I have my arm at the back of the couch, propping me up, and I hold her hand with my other hand in her lap. "You okay with this, Mace?" She smiles at me, showing those fucking dimples that get me every time. She grabs the back of my neck and pulls me into her for another kiss. I start to stroke her thigh with my hand. I feel her stiffen slightly, but she carries on kissing me. My hand wanders to her hip, then her waist. We're still kissing, and she hasn't moved my hand. I start to make circular movements on her waist. She's ticklish there, and I smile on her lips as she starts to squirm, smiling but still kissing me. I break the kiss to look at her. "You okay with this. Mace?"

She's embarrassed, and she's blushing, but she smiles and nods, yes. I lean in, and I kiss her exposed shoulder. I feel the goosebumps on her arms from my touch. She's very responsive to me. She strokes my arms, and then puts her hand on my waist, mimicking my movements. She finds the bottom of my tee and slowly puts her hand under the hem to find my naked waist. I feel the electricity from her touching my flesh coursing through my body, all the way from the top of my head to my toes. I shudder as she strokes my waist and hips, my tummy muscles concave, and I take in a sharp breath. Fucking hell. I've never felt anything like it. She looks at me shyly. "S-sorry, did I do that wrong? Don't you like that?" God, if only she could feel what I feel right now. I smile at her. "Your touch is heaven, Mace. I could die happy right now." She looks down. She can see what effect she's having on me because I can't exactly hide the massive bulge in my slacks. "Hey, tell me if you get uncomfortable with anything? If you don't want me to touch you, then just say so. We take this as slowly as you need, Mace. Okay, baby?"

She nods.

We start to kiss again, and she gets a little braver, moving her hand up my chest. She's stroking me so gently, and it's making me all tingly as though I have little pinpricks all over. She rubs gently over my nipples, which are nearly as hard as my cock, before feeling all the ridges of my pecs. I'm trying my fucking hardest not to rip her clothes off and bury myself deep inside her. I decide to see how far I can push her, making sure she is comfortable with everything. I start to edge under the hem of her Tee, resting my hand on the bare flesh of her waist. She stops kissing me for a second, not losing connection, but testing how she feels, I think. I slowly move my hand round her back, stroking very gently, pulling her into me more, but still trying to keep my cock from touching her. I'm at an awkward angle, but I don't want her to freak.

She pulls at my t-shirt, lifting it because she wants it off. That's a good sign. I break the kiss and help her remove the tee. She stares at my chest. "Wow, Caspian. I never knew you had so many tattoos." She starts to trace my artwork, all over my chest and arms. "Can I see your back?" I move away from her and stand up. She moves with me and explores my back with her hands. I'm now full of goosebumps from her fingertips sweeping over my flesh, sending tiny waves of electricity coursing all through my body, and I start to breathe heavily. It's driving me mad but in a good way. This is so sensual. I'm not sure she knows what she's doing to me. I turn to face her. She rests her hands on my pecs. "Caspian, you are a work of art. Not just your tattoos, but your body. You're so defined in every way. You're beautiful." She blushes as she says it.

I take her face in my hands, and I kiss her. I kiss her like there is no tomorrow, and she responds the same. Her hands wander again, feeling all over, so I move to grab the bottom of her t-shirt and start to raise it, but she freezes. Shit, too much, but she breaks the kiss and nods at me to carry on. "You sure, Mace?"

"Yes," she breathes out. I lift it, then step back. "Fucking hell," I say taking her in. She is stunning. She tries to cover herself up with her arms, so I take her hands one at a time and hold them. "Please don't cover up, baby. You are the most perfect woman I have ever laid eyes on. In fact, you should never cover up around me."

I smile down at her. We're still standing up and taking each other in. This, right here, is perfect. She's putting her complete faith and trust in me. I feel like crying at that thought. Knowing the trauma she's been through and that she's never willingly given herself to any man before, is making me delirious. I start to run my fingertips down each of her arms, and she shudders at my gentle touch. I smile at her. She runs her fingertips along my hips, and I move to her hips and do the same, making circular motions, then I move them upwards to her ribs and then under her tits. Fuck, If I take these in my hands now, I think I will explode. I lean down, kissing her neck, which she exposes to me, then down to her shoulder. I move her bra strap down her arm and continue to kiss, crouching down slightly, and I kiss along her collarbone, feather-light kisses, then use my tongue.

Her breathing quivers as I go lower over the swell of her breast. I'm still stroking gently with my thumb, and I move slightly and gently brush her nipple, still kissing and sucking the swell of her breasts.

She inhales sharply as I stroke over her nipple. "Caspian," she breathes out, She hasn't stopped me, and she hasn't frozen or gone into a panic. She starts to circle both my nipples with her fingertips and thumbs, and I mimic her with both hands. I kiss her lips. "Is this okay, baby?" She looks me in the eyes, smiling, and nods the biggest yes at me.

I slowly pull down the other bra strap, kissing her shoulder as I do and moving my hands around the back to undo the clasp. She slows, so I stop and look her in the eye. "Too much? Just tell me, and I'll stop? I will not force you or think any less of you. We take this one step at a time, Mace, no more. Baby steps." I smile at her.

She hesitates, but then she relaxes, and takes the bra off herself. "Fuck," I say. She looks up at me and I smile and kiss her lips. "Perfection."

I start to kiss her again and move my hands to her tits to take hold of them. They are a perfect fit for my big hands. I move them around in circles, squeezing very gently, being as tender as I can. Her hands are on my back — she's caressing me, and I love it. I lean down to kiss her tits, and I suck and lick as I move towards her nipples. She's breathing heavy and pushing out her chest to me. I take one into my mouth, sucking and circling it with my tongue, and I nip gently, but she goes rigid. Fuck. I look at her. She isn't moving — she's gone. Fucking dipshit. Too much.

"Macen, baby, come back to me. It's okay. I won't hurt you. You're safe here, baby."

I've sat her back on the couch, and I'm hugging her to my side, with her head to my chest, trying to make her come back from the terror she's reliving. I feel her shaking badly as I hold her to my bare chest. I feel the wetness of her tears streaming down my chest. "Shhh, come back, Mace, come back to me, baby." She slowly starts breathing normally, and the shaking starts to subside. I just keep her to me, trying to reassure her she is safe. I take the blanket I have over the back of the couch, and I put it over her shoulders.

She moves to look up at me. "I think maybe I should go home."

WHAT! Is she serious? No way is she leaving. I'm not letting her bolt. I shake my head, no.

"Caspian, I'm damaged, too much. I don't think you can fix me. I think it's best if I go and you find someone who's not damaged, someone you don't have to be gentle with for fear they may break again. It's too much to ask of anyone, Caspian. I know you have needs, and I don't know if I will ever be able to fulfill your needs. What if I ne..."

I stop her talking with my lips. I kiss her hard. Maybe it's not what she needs right now, but I need it. She is not talking herself into this. I will not lose her because she has no hope.

I break the kiss and look her in the eyes. "You are not going anywhere. You may be broken, like me, Mace, but we can fix each other. Do you hear me? WE FIX EACH OTHER."

The tears are streaming down her cheeks, but I wipe them away with my thumbs. "I love you, Mace. I'm not going anywhere, and neither are you. Look how far you've come tonight. Look at this." I point between us, both semi-naked on the couch. "This would never have happened if you didn't trust me. This was fucking amazing, Macen. You made me feel fucking amazing, and I'm hoping I made you feel the same. You are fucking amazing. We can do this. Once I know your triggers, we will work around them. Then we work on them until you never have a trigger and you only associate this with the love I have for you. Do you hear me, Macen? Let me know you understand, and you're not going anywhere."

chapter 39

Macen

I NOD AT HIM. I HAVE TEARS coursing down my face, but I nod before I lean up and kiss him. "Yes, Caspian. I hear you. If you have this much faith in us, then who am I to argue? I'm with you. You're right. I would never have done this with anyone." I motion between us. I can't believe I've gone this far in the first place. I cuddle into his chest and hold him tight. Who would ever believe I just did what I did? Seeing him with no shirt on is something I read about in books, not something I thought would ever happen to me. He is stunning —beautiful. I sigh.

"Hey, look at me."

I do as he asks. "We can do this together. One baby step at a time." I smile and nod, wrapping my arms around him and staying cuddled into him. I can't believe I let him touch my breasts. The feelings I felt from his fingers stroking my body were like nothing I've felt before. It made my scalp tingle like the first time he kissed me. I wanted more. I wanted him to explore more. His fingertips making gentle, sweeping touches over my body sent shivers down my spine, and my panties are wet from all the sensations. I feel myself blushing — my chest and shoulders getting hot as it travels up my neck to my cheeks. Luckily, I'm buried in his side, and he can't see me.

We sit like this for a while. I know exactly what triggered my panic. He bit my nipple. It was very gentle, but it was enough to bring back the memories of that night and what my attacker did to me. I'm scarred from him biting my nipple so hard. The doctor thought it might do some permanent damage to me, and that I may lose the sensations there altogether. Well, it's clear that I haven't lost the sensations. When he was sucking my nipples and licking them, I wanted to tell him to make love to me quickly. I felt the urge. I felt the need. I felt wanted and loved by his touches. I know it's nothing like my attack. This is completely different. He told me the other day that making love and having all those feelings would wipe out the bad from that night. That remembering all the good feelings would become normal, and he's right. Just remembering those feelings is getting me going again. It's not fair on him though.

We sit in silence, and I feel his breathing become labored. He must be exhausted. He's fallen asleep, and I don't want to move and wake him. I look into his lap as it's not far from my face and he's still hard. I can see his cock tenting in his slacks. I wonder what it feels like. I have never had the desire to look before, but I want to see Caspian's. I feel embarrassed having these thoughts, but each time I've felt him, it's felt like stone. How can something like that be so hard? It's all flesh. I feel sorry for him being hard all the time and me not being able to help him out or do anything about it. I wonder though. What if I touched it? Would that help? Maybe if I stroke it — that's what happens in the books I read. The woman strokes it or blows on it. I don't think I can put it in my mouth. Maybe if I touched it though.

I slowly move my hand to his thigh. He doesn't move, so I edge it up slightly towards his cock. He sighs, and I see it grow bigger — is that even possible? My hand is gently moving up until I brush it with my fingers. He moves. I look at him, but he hasn't opened his eyes. His breathing is slightly more uneven now. I move again and brush again, a little firmer than the first time. Then I move my fingers back and forth at his crotch, catching him with each stroke. He wiggles his behind on the couch, and slightly jutting his hips upwards. I think he wants more.

I creep my fingers onto his bulge, very gently. Wow, it's hard. It's like stone. I want to rub it with my full hand and not just my fingers so I can get a good feel of it. I gently palm it and massage, and he starts jutting upwards, a little firmer this time, trying to get more traction from my hand. I press harder and palm harder, up and down. Suddenly, he grabs my hand and stops me. "Macen?" he questions. I look up at him, sheepishly. He's looking down at me with hooded eyes, looking gorgeous in a sleepy daze. I smile gingerly at him, embarrassed he's caught me. I go to move my hand away, but he clamps down, making me press harder on his cock. "Macen, look at me, baby. Do you want to do this? Is this something you want to try, to explore? You're not just doing this because you think you have an obligation?"

I shake my head and stare at him. "I wanted to feel it?" My voice is shaky.

He smiles down at me, a great big smile. "Baby, if you want to, then I will not argue with you. But you don't have to. I can take care of myself in the shower like I usually do, thinking about my fucking hot-as-hell girlfriend."

My face drops — his hot girlfriend. He lifts my chin, "Macen. You, you are my fucking hot-as-hell girlfriend."

He laughs, and I do too because he knew exactly where my mind went.

"I would like to feel it, Caspian. Only by hand," I add hastily. He laughs again. He is wide-awake now. "Do you want to just feel like this?" He still has hold of my hand, and he starts to move it up and down, pressing harder on himself. I shake my head, no. He furrows his brows. "You tell me what YOU want, Mace. We only do what you want?"

I bite my lip inside. I feel stupid, nervous, and embarrassed all at once. I look at him, rubbing himself using my hand, and I clear my throat. "In the flesh," I whisper.

I hear his sharp intake of breath, and I look up at him through my eyelashes as he leans forward, tilts my chin up and kisses me hard. He lies back, then he unbuttons his slacks, lifts his ass, and pulls them down with his Calvin's. His cock springs free. It reminds me of the Jack-in-the-box toy that Dixon used to have, and I laugh. He looks at me, a bit concerned; I hold my hand over my mouth to stifle the laugh, but it doesn't work. He scowls at me. "What's so funny?" I laugh harder because he's so offended that I'm laughing at his cock. I can't help it, and I go into hysterics at the look on his face. He's not amused, which makes me laugh more. I end up on the floor, curled up, laughing into a cushion that he hits me with playfully.

I calm myself down and peep out from under the cushion. He's stark naked on the couch. He's sitting on the edge, looking down at me on the floor. "Have you quite finished with your little laughing fit at the expense of my cock?" He raises his eyebrows at me, and it sets me off again. "Right, that's it."

Uh oh, I watch from behind my cushion as he gets up off the couch. He's towering above me, and his cock is stuck out rigid. That stops me in my tracks. He's a sight to behold that's for sure. I need to keep this memory. He stands with his hands on his hips, looking down at me, smiling that cocky smile of his that I love. It's assertive Caspian standing above me right now.

He takes one of my hands and starts to help me up. He then lifts me up over his shoulder. "I think I need to show you to your room now, young lady. Laughing at my cock is a serious crime. I need to think of a suitable punishment for you."

I swat his naked backside as it's right in my view, then I grab his ass cheeks in both my hands and start kneading them. He swats my ass.

"Take me to your room, Caspian," I whisper. He stops walking.

"You sure?" I swat his ass again.

"Yep."

He moves, almost running with me. He kicks open a door, and before I know it, he lowers me very slowly to my feet then sits me down on the edge of his bed.

He's standing right in front of me, naked. His cock is eye level, and I can't stop staring at it. If I just reach out, I can take it. I don't even realize my hand is doing what I was thinking, as I wrap my fingers around his cock. It's huge. I start to feel it properly, and I gasp. "Wow, it feels like velvet. It's so smooth to the touch."

I hear his breathing getting more and more ragged as I feel and squeeze his cock. It's wet at the tip where the hole is. I rub my finger over it and smear the liquid over the top of his cock. I look up and see his eyes are screwed shut. I stop moving. "Am I hurting you, Caspian?" Oh shit, what have I done? Does this hurt him? He shakes his head, no, then slowly opens his eyes. I see the love and adoration all over his face. He reaches out and strokes down my cheek. "I love you, Macen. I don't care if you do any of this. I love you so fucking much." He leans down and takes my mouth gently. I still have his cock in my hand, and I start to stroke him. He takes my hand, and he shows me what to do, gripping my fingers around it as much as I can, adding pressure, then moving it up and down. He lets go once I have the rhythm, and he continues kissing me as I continue rubbing his cock.

He breaks off, standing up straight, and jutting his hips harder into my hand. He grabs my shoulders, but not tightly. I think he just needs something to hold while he thrusts. I start moving faster with his thrusts, and I watch his face closely. I see mixed emotions cross it fleetingly, sometimes he looks in pain, then it changes to adoration, then pain again, then love, and he never takes his eyes off mine. I'm getting faster and faster, and it's wet with all the cum seeping out slowly, then, "Oh, fucking hell, Macen, I'm coming. FUCK!" he screams that last word out as he thrusts.

Cum is shooting out of the end like a fire hose and its squirting all over my chest. I don't stop pumping him — I love it. I love I can do this to him and for him, and the feelings I have watching his ecstasy is making me feel brave, and I have this urge to taste his cum. I lean down, and I lick the top of his cock. "FUCKING HELL," he screams, and it squirts out more, right into my face. I look up at him, licking my lips, as he wipes the cum off with his thumb, then he takes my face, and he smothers me with kisses. I let go of his cock, and I fall back on the bed. He falls on top of me, but panics, trying to lift himself up quickly before I go into meltdown. I hold him to me tightly. "No, stay. I want to feel you. I want you to feel me, and I want you to touch me — show me how it should feel, Caspian, show me?" I say into his ear as I hold his head close to mine. I don't let him look at me or ask if I'm sure. I take his hand and place it between my legs. I want him to touch me. I want to feel love.

He starts to move his hand, rubbing me gently. I start to move with his hand, wanting the friction. "Show me, feel me?" I say to him. He lifts, and I undo the button and zip on my slacks. I raise my hips and pull them down with my panties. I see the look on his face, asking me with his eyes if I'm sure, and I just nod and smile. He gets up off me, and kneels on the floor, removing my slacks and panties completely, taking his time as he does, before he spreads my legs wider so he's between them. He looks at my most private parts and then into my eyes. I nod. I feel brave and powerful — like I have power here, and I'm in control. The feelings are so overwhelming. He leans forward and kisses my pelvis, then peppers downwards with kisses. He's going to kiss me there. I've read about this in my books, and the women in those books can't get enough of it. I want to try this. I want to have new feelings.

I lay my head back and wait. But am I waiting for the panic to set in or something else? He blows on me gently. He must be able to see how wet I am? I feel embarrassed. I look at him one more time, just as he bends his head and licks me from bottom to top, keeping his eyes on me at all time, trying to gauge my reaction. I can't take my eyes off him as he repeats the action a few times. It is so erotic, watching him watching me as he licks me there. He sucks my clit, then licks, then sucks again, and I start to squirm. I have never felt anything like this in my life. I want to scream. I grab his head, and I pull on his hair, yanking him further into me. I want more. I want to feel him. I want him to lick inside.

Just then, he puts his tongue at my entrance and pushes inside me slowly. I shudder, then he sucks my clit again, but this time I feel his fingers playing at my entrance. I'm pulling his hair hard; squashing his nose into me. I'm not sure he can breathe, but I don't care. I love how it feels, and I want more. Then he does it — he inserts his finger into me and starts gently pumping in and out, still sucking and flicking my clit. "More!" I shout, so he pumps faster, deeper, and harder. Then it's two fingers. I hear how wet I am. I need to let him up for air, but I don't want him to stop, I don't want him to break off. Then it hits me. The explosion in my body like someone lit a firecracker inside me. I scream out so loud I think I've deafened him as well. "Caspian, Casp, don't stop, oh, fuck, fuck, fuck. I fucking love you." I can't see because there are lights going off in my head, and my body is tingling all over. I feel like I'm convulsing. I feel euphoric, elated, ecstatic, and emotional all at the same time. I cry, big sobbing cries, and I don't know why.

Before I know it, he's got me in his arms, hugging me to him tightly, comforting me. "Shhh, baby, it's okay. I'm so sorry. I knew it was too much, too soon. Shhh, Mace, I'm sorry." He keeps repeating how sorry he is. I look up into his worried face, and I stroke his cheek.

His stubble is soaking wet from my cum, but he looks so adorable. "You didn't do anything wrong, Caspian. I can't explain how I'm feeling right now, except to say, I probably feel how you felt when I was making you cum. I don't know why I'm crying. I have never felt anything like that in my life. It felt out of this world, literally." I smile from ear to ear at him, and the relief on his face makes my heart melt. He hugs me, rocking us on the bed.

"I thought I'd made it worse, Mace. I thought you hated me when you cried so hard."

I shake my head. "I love you, Caspian. I just can't put into words how much. You just gave me my first ever orgasm."

I laugh, and he laughs with me.

We go into his bathroom to clean up, and I grab a towel to cover up. I feel strange being naked, I've never been naked in front of anyone voluntarily. He stands in front of me, unfolds the towel, and lets it drop to the floor. He pulls me to him by my hips and looks down at his hands. "I fucking love these hips. They are made for me, Mace. No one else, just me."

I look down and go to cover my chest. "No, don't," he says. "Please don't feel uncomfortable with me. You are perfect. I want to see all of you. Come on, let's have a shower, then if you want, I will show you your room."

My face falls. My room! That hurt. A tear falls down my cheek, and he sees it and wipes it away, then lifts my face to his. "Hey, what's wrong? What did I say? We don't have to have a shower together if it's that traumatic for you."

I move from his hold and grab the towel off the floor to cover up and head back to his room to get my slacks.

He has no idea, does he?

chapter 40

Caspian

OH FUCK, WHAT HAVE I DONE? She's angry with me, and I don't know why. I follow her into the bedroom where she's picking her clothes up off the floor and is heading for the door. I move quickly and take her hand. "Hey, what's wrong? Is it the shower, Mace? You can have one in your room if you want?"

She glares at me, then moves to leave the room again, so I pull on her hand. "Macen, talk to me, baby, please, what did I say?"

She stops, then turns to me. "So, you get what you want, then it's off you go, little girl, to your own room?"

Oh fuck. I roll my eyes and look up to the ceiling, letting go of her hand and rubbing my stubble. She bolts out of the door, and I follow and watch her open each door, looking for a spare room, then I move behind her and pull her into my chest. She tries to wriggle free. "Macen, please stop. That is not what I meant. I didn't want to presume you would sleep with me. I would rather you did sleep with me in my bed than be in another room, driving me mad because I want to be next to you, but you've come so far tonight, further than I could ever have imagined, and I didn't want to jeopardize that. I'm so fucking proud of you, and I fucking love you. Please, if you don't think I'm after just one thing, I would love for you to sleep in my arms. Please, baby."

She tilts her head to look up at me. I release her, turn her in my arms, and I crouch down to be at eye level. "Macen, please stay with me tonight in my bed?"

She nods yes, and I sigh out in relief. "Can we take a shower now? It means scrubbing your scent off me, but I will rectify that later." I wink at her, and she slaps my shoulder.

We shower, cleaning and exploring each other, and I notice a scar around her left nipple, the one I nibbled on when she froze. I suspect this is from her attack, but that's a question for another day. She then puts one of my t-shirts on to sleep in. I would prefer her naked, but if she feels more comfortable in that, then one step at a time.

I'm still in awe of her. I can't believe we've come so far. I know the feelings we have for each other are deep, and I can only put it down to that. She trusts me, and that is massive for me. I trust her too — when I have never trusted or loved anyone in my life. She is it; she is mine, and I will do whatever it takes to protect her. We snuggle in bed. I hope to God I don't have a bad dream tonight. I don't want to scare her. "Baby, I know one of your triggers is my hard cock touching you. I have to warn you; he will be rock hard throughout the night and especially in the morning with you being in my arms. I don't want you to freak. I want you to try and remember how he felt in your hands. He's not your enemy — you need to think that. Come on, lets chant, 'Caspian's cock is heaven. It is not my enemy, Caspian's cock—"

She slaps my chest playfully and laughs hard. "You weirdo."

I wake suddenly. It's not from me dreaming this time, but Macen is thrashing about next to me. She's shouting 'no, no,' and crying. Fuck. I kneel up and take her in my arms, holding her to my chest to comfort her. She's still asleep as I rock her in my arms. "Shhh, baby. Macen, Macen. Wake up, baby, look at me."

She slowly opens her eyes, and I look down into her terrified face. Realization dawns where she is and who with. She wriggles free from my arms and scrambles out of bed.

"Macen, look at me."

She walks to the bathroom, ignoring me. "MACEN!" I say firmly. She stops, "Look at me!" She doesn't. I get off the bed and walk up behind her, putting my hands on her arms. She flinches. "Macen, it's okay, look at me?" I turn her slowly and gently into my arms, pulling her to my chest.

She wraps her arms around me tightly, pulling me to her, and she cries into my chest. "I can't do this to you, Caspian. It's not fair to you. It's best if I just leave." Not this again. I move back and tilt her head up to me. "Baby, we did this dance a few hours ago. I'm not going anywhere. Screw this being fair to me. If you're not with me, then that isn't fair to me. How is that going to help? I'm here for you, just as you would be if it were me that had been thrashing about in a nightmare. Let's clean your face, and then I want you to tell me what happened, okay?"

I get us some water, and we get back into bed. I sit upright, and she lays her head on my chest. "Do you get a lot of nightmares, Mace?" She shakes her head, no. "Not many, no. It only usually happens when something triggers it." I think what it could be. Maybe it's the intimacy we shared earlier? Then I remember my cock was hard when I woke up. "I wonder if you felt my cock on your backside, and that triggered it?" She looks up at me, smiles, and shrugs. "I don't remember, but it's possible, I suppose."

"What about the dream. Do you remember what it was about?"

She thinks for a minute. She sighs. I know she finds this hard. "Yes, it was him rubbing his cock on me, down there." She nods downwards. "He was rubbing it on me before ramming into me, hurting me. It was that."

"Then I definitely think you felt my cock in your sleep, and it triggered it."

We're silent for a while. I think she's gone to sleep until she murmurs, "Caspian, I want to be able to stay with you in your bed. It will get better, won't it?"

I rub her arm. "I'm sure it will, Mace. I'm sure it will." We're silent again. "In fact, once you worship my cock. I don't think you will have a problem."

She slaps my chest playfully again and laughs. I laugh with her.

"I think for the time being I either get a protective cup or jockstrap to cover him up like some pro footballers wear or we have a barrier of pillows between us. Actually, no barrier. I need to cuddle you. Jockstrap it is."

We both laugh. I cuddle her to me, and she falls asleep on my chest. "I love you, Macen Donald, and I swear to god, I will do everything in my power to protect you and help you heal."

41

Macen

I WAKE UP SLOWLY, TRYING TO GAUGE where I am. *Caspian.* I fell asleep resting my head on his chest, and that's how I've woken up now. We haven't moved. "Good morning, sleepy head. How are you feeling after last night?" He's awake. He must have been waiting for me to wake up so he didn't disturb me. I roll onto my side and stretch out beside him. He looks down and cocks his brow without looking at me — his eyes are fixed lower. "Macen, that's not a good thing to do, baby. We don't have much time if you want to see Dixon before school."

I know what he means, but I stay with my arms stretched over my head and turn it to him. "Why's that, baby, what's wrong?" I know I'm playing with fire, as I sit up and see my t-shirt is up around my waist. I look at his lap and see the tent in the sheet that is over his lower half. I lick my lips, seductively. It works — he pounces.

Before I know it, he's on his back, with me straddling his upper chest. He's careful, making sure I don't feel his cock in the position I'm in. He reaches under my tee, and he starts to play with my breasts, rolling and kneading them, then he pulls me forward so my breasts are in his face and he sucks and licks my nipples. He doesn't use his teeth. He's caught on so quickly what my triggers are. I start to move on his chest, rubbing myself on him. He kneads my ass with both hands, and I start to moan at his touch. He lets go of my nipple, then he pulls the tee over my head so I'm naked on his chest. He smiles at me, then he edges me forward towards his face.

"Lift up on your knees, baby." I do as he asks. He slides down the bed farther until his face is under my private parts. He lowers me down onto his face, and he strokes me with his tongue. He sucks and flicks my clit before inserting his tongue inside. I gyrate on his face, holding onto the headboard, and I rock backward and forward. He manages to move a hand, and he places his fingers right in the place I need them.

On my next push down, he sticks two fingers into me. I push down harder, and then I'm up and down on his face. "Oh, God, Caspian. Oh My God." I explode into my second orgasm.

In the shower, I play with his cock while washing him. I jerk him off, making him cum all over me again, and I rub his cock in the cum on my chest. I'm getting braver that's for sure.

We arrive at my place just in time to see Dixon. I've missed him so much, and we promise to take him out for Pizza tonight after school. I get changed, and we head to work. We're both on the early shift today. "I was working on some new ideas if you're interested in looking at them. It's okay if you don't. It's just you said in my interview, you would love to see them." I don't want to push my luck because I'm now sleeping with the boss.

"I would love to see any ideas you have, Mace. Never be ashamed to ask or show me." He smiles at me. He's holding my hand in the back of the car, and I love how he always has to touch me. I'm not sure if it's for his assurance or he's trying to reassure me.

We arrive at Casper's, and as soon as the car pulls up, I look over the street, and he's there. He's watching us. Does he know I stayed at Caspian's last night? I start to breathe heavily, and I don't realize, but I'm squeezing Caspian's hand, hard. He looks at me, and then to where I'm staring out of the window.

"Fuck, when will he leave us alone?" He gets his cell out and dials the police. "It will probably take them an hour to get here like yesterday. Come on, Mace, let's get inside the restaurant. We have to ignore him. He can't be arrested for being on the street."

We get out and into Casper's quickly. I go and get ready and then head to my station to start prepping for the day.

I haven't stopped once. Caspian has been in here most of the morning working — I think because he wants to keep an eye on me. I head to the employee room to get some lunch while there is a lull. I get my cell out and see I have another missed call with no caller ID. Just then it rings in my hand, and I answer.

"Hello, Ms. Donald, is that you?"

"Who's calling, please?"

"This is Captain Colber. We haven't met, but I have some information and wondered could you come down to the precinct, please?"

"Can I ask what information?"

"I need to speak to you in person. Can you bring some ID with you, please? When is convenient for you?"

Oh God, is this about Reid? "Hmm. I finish my shift at 4 p.m. I can be there for 4.30 p.m. Is that any good?"

"Yes, that's fine. I will see you then."

She hangs up, and I just stand there with the cell in my hand. Caspian walks in and sees me staring at the cell. "Mace, what's wrong?" He rushes over to me, stands in front of me and takes my face in his hands. He looks concerned, which means I must look worried.

I tell him about the call. "Well, the dipshit isn't out front anymore because I checked before coming in here. Maybe they did pick him up? Don't worry about it, Mace. I'll be with you."

I look at him. "Will you come with me?"

He scowls. "Of course, I will. You're not alone in this, baby. It's you and me, remember?" Caspian lets go of my face and moves towards the fridge to get a bottle of water. "Do you want one, Macen?" he asks, and I nod my head before I ring Grandma to explain why we might be late.

I get back to work, but my mind isn't on the prep, and I make a couple of mistakes. Luckily, they are caught before they leave the kitchen. Caspian comes over to me. "Can you come to my office, Macen?

When we get to his office, I start to apologize. "I'm so sorry fo—"

He holds up his hand to stop me speaking. "I haven't brought you in here because you're in trouble. I'm just concerned for you. I know it's playing on your mind. Francoise is on his way in to cover for me, and then we can go straight to the precinct and find out what this is about. Okay?" I nod yes, I'm so grateful to him.

We're in the car, and I'm gripping his hand tightly. "You're biting the inside of your lip, Mace. I know you're really nervous." He kisses the back of my hand, and I smile at him. "Try not to worry, Mace. I know that's easier said than done."

We are shown to an interview room and wait for Captain Colber. She comes in with a big file in hand and a tablet. "Ms. Donald," she greets me, shaking my hand then reaching for Caspian, "And?" She takes his hand. "Mr. Kade. I'm Macen's boyfriend and also the person Reid Hughes attacked. Please tell us you now have him locked up." She frowns at us, then looks at Caspian.

"Mr. Kade, I don't think you should be in for this meeting. This is not about Mr. Hughes attacking you?"

"But he attacked me as well," I say pointedly. I don't like the way she's speaking to Caspian. "And I want Caspian to stay in with me. He knows everything that has happened, in fact, Reid used to work for Caspian until last week." She looks at us both, then starts tapping away on her tablet. "I think there's some confusion here, Ms. Donald. I haven't asked you here today about any recent attacks. I didn't realize there was an issue with Mr. Hughes until just now. I'm sorry for the confusion."

She looks at me, then at Caspian, as if trying to think what to say next. She coughs. "This is about an incident some years back in a shared house while you were at NYCS."

I have hold of Caspian's hand, and I grip it so tight my knuckles are turning white. I freeze. She's talking about the attack. What's that got to do with anything that's happening now? I feel Caspian rubbing the back of my hand. I slowly look down at our joined hands and realize I've probably cut off the circulation to his fingers. He kisses the back of my hand.

"It's okay, baby, I'm here with you. We've got this."

He turns to the captain. "I know all about the attack on Macen, Ma'am. What is this about?" She looks at me. "Ms. Donald are you okay with Mr. Kade being present? I need your permission before I can continue?"

"Yes, of course, I want him with me." I feel Caspian go slightly rigid — he's getting annoyed with the captain. "Please tell me you have a reason you're looking into a cold case?" he snaps at her. She scowls at us, then continues. "Some DNA has been flagged as being connected to Ms. Donald's attack nearly seven years ago."

Caspian looks at me. "Mace, are you, okay, baby? You look very pale."

I just nod. "Are you telling me this new DNA is connected to my attacker?"

She nods, yes. I look at Caspian, who is looking as confused as I feel. I explain to him.

"After my attack, they took DNA from all the known males from the house and the party. Then, when Dixon was born, they took his DNA to see if it matched any of the samples they took. It didn't, which is why no one has ever been caught."

The captain is watching us both, and she nods. "Because of the severity of the attack, it remained an open case — a cold case. But some DNA was taken recently, and it came up as a match to your son, Dixon. This could only mean one thing. That the owner of the DNA is Dixon's biological father — your attacker."

I feel the tears running down my face. I go to swipe them away but miss because I'm shaking so much. Oh my God. I can't believe this.

"Do you know whose DNA it is?" Caspian asks the captain. She nods, yes. "Do you have him locked up? Are you going to tell us who it is?"

It's a good job he's here with me. I wouldn't know what to ask.

"Yes, we know who it is, but unfortunately, we don't have him yet. He's proving difficult to find."

The penny finally drops. I sit rigidly, and I think I'm going to throw up. I start to heave. Caspian is quick to react — he jumps up, rubbing my back and crouching beside me. "Mace, what is it? Are you okay, baby? Captain, I need a wastebasket or something." He's panicking, I can hear it in his voice. I stop heaving and I turn to him.

"I know who it is, Caspian. I know it's him." He looks confused until it hits him, and I see the rage slowly entering his face as it turns red and his eyes get dark.

"It's Reid Hughes? It all makes sense now."

Caspian

I'M DUMBSTRUCK. REID! COULD IT BE? I look at Macen, and she faces me, her face so pale.

"It all makes sense: the recent DNA they took that from my nails, him stalking me and saying how we are a family. He knows, Caspian, he knows Dixon is his. Why else would he keep saying that? Last week, when he was talking to Dixon, he asked him how old he was. He put it together then. Oh God, it's him. The smell. When he attacked me all those years ago, I smelt his cologne mixed with cigarette smoke and again when he got into my space in the employee room last week. It's the only thing I knew about my attacker, and it's the same smell. I know hundreds of men who smoke will use that same cologne but it's him, I know it. He barely speaks to me. I bet that's so I don't recognize his voice. The only words he said that night he attacked me were, 'Leave, bitch,' so I don't remember much about his voice. But it's him. I know it is."

She turns to the captain as do I. "Is she right. Is it him?"

The captain is watching us piece this together. "Before we go jumping to conclusions and accusing anyone, we need to get Mr. Hughes's DNA."

"But you have his DNA from under my nails?" Macen snaps back.

"Yes, the DNA under your nails matches the DNA to Dixon, but we can't prove it's Mr. Hughes's DNA until we bring him in and take DNA of our own. The DNA under your nails could quite easily be Dixon's DNA, and that would be argued if it were taken to court."

Macen gasps and puts her hand to her mouth. The tears are streaming down her face. "I would never hurt Dixon. I wouldn't scratch him."

The captain holds up her hand. "I'm not saying you did for one minute, but it could have been an accident. The results have come back at a 93% match. Mixed with your DNA, that could be Dixon's, and if it went to court, as it stands, it would be thrown out. We need to bring him in, and do our own DNA, to get an accurate and positive match that can't be thrown out of court."

Macen puts her head in her hands, and she cries. I pull her into me and comfort her. I'm shaking. She can probably feel it. I'm fucking breaking inside for her, and I want to kill him. He damaged her — he's traumatized her for the rest of her life. He needs castrating, and I'd be first in line to do it. "What if he's done this again? What if he's attacked other women after Macen?" The captain doesn't answer me. She shuts her file and looks at us. "I'm sorry, Ms. Donalds, but let's hope we can finally close your case."

I'm comforting Macen. "Is there anything else, Ma'am, can I take Macen home?"

She's still curled into my side.

"Just one thing. We need to catch Mr. Hughes. Reading through these notes, you've both reported him stalking you several times in the last few days alone. Have you seen him?"

"Yes, he's at the restaurant most days, just watching us. He's attacked us both, although there is no proof, I know it was him. He's waited for both of us behind my restaurant, at the employee entrance. He's attacked Macen there more than once, but because there is no evidence, there is nothing the cops can do about it."

She's thinking and taking notes. "I bet he'll be there tomorrow or watching my apartment tonight. He always seems to know where we are."

Macen hasn't looked up. I'm worried she's blocking it all out.

"Where does he wait exactly?"

I tell her the exact spots both front and back, and what time we will be there tomorrow for our shifts.

"Okay, I'm going to put some of my detectives on 5th Avenue, and down West 57th. Catching him is a priority now. I have no doubt we will catch him, Ms. Donald."

Macen doesn't acknowledge her — she's gone still in my arms, but she's stopped crying. She's just listening to the captain.

"Please, can I ask that you both act as normally as possible tomorrow or even if you see him tonight? Mr. Kade, I know how difficult this is for you both, and I also know you probably want your own revenge and to take matters into your own hands. To help the case, please, please, don't do anything rash. Let us do our job, and we will get him, now we know who he is. If the DNA is a match, I can assure you he will spend the rest of his life on Rikers Island. Let's just say, between us, there are a lot of cold cases that will get closed when we catch him."

I nod. She's right to ask because I want to kill the fucking bastard. Just one hit in the right place, and I could finish him, but then, I know, I'd never see Macen or Dixon again.

She gets up and shakes my hand, but Macen doesn't look at her. "I'm truly sorry it's taken this long and that you've gone through all this in the last weeks. Please take some consolation that these recent events are what's lead to him hopefully being caught."

She leaves the room. I'm still cuddling Macen into my side, and I rest my chin on the top of her head. "Mace, baby, look at me."

She slowly lifts her head up. I smile a tentative smile at her and kiss her lips. "God, I'm sick of all this crying." She says wiping at some tears. She looks like she's in so much pain. "I can't believe it will be over after all these years, Caspian. To finally know who did it — which bastard ruined my life. Why did he do it? He said, 'leave, bitch' that night, and I did. I left the school and didn't go back until after having Dixon. I couldn't finish my course. He wanted me gone, but why? Was I a threat to him? He purposely attacked me, wanting me gone. He did it to get rid of me. Oh God, did he do that to me, then get a taste for it and attack other women? Fuck, it's my fault if he did. It's all on me. He attacked them because of m—"

She's getting hysterical. I pull her onto my lap, hold her tight, and stop her tirade. "You listen to me, Macen Donald. NONE OF THIS IS YOUR FAULT. Do you hear me? This is not on you. This is all him. HE attacked you. HE did this to you and maybe others. HIM, Macen, do you hear me? HIM!" I emphasize my words, trying to get it through to her that it wasn't her fault.

We sit there for a few more minutes until she calms down. "You know it's not your fault, don't you?"

She nods and shrugs at the same time. "Come on. Let's get out of here."

Back at Macen's, Dixon is just the tonic we both need. He is so excited to be going out for pizza. I play dinosaurs with Dixon in his room until we're ready to leave. I want to give Macen time to sit and talk with Doris, so I keep him distracted. I love this kid already. He makes me smile so much. Knowing who his father is, has only made me love him more. I couldn't give a shit that Reid is his biological father. As far as I'm concerned, his father died, and when he starts asking questions, we should tell him that. I don't think he should know how he came to be or what his father did, but then that's up to Macen to decide. It's a conversation we will have though. I honestly don't think she would disagree. Why ruin Dixon's life, knowing his father was a rapist. I think it would destroy him.

I feel Macen in the doorway, and I lean into Dixon, "I take it your beautiful momma is watching us play?"

He looks up and smiles. "How did you know Momma was there? Are you magical, Casp?"

I laugh and ruffle his hair. "Yep, but only where your momma is concerned."

He gets up and runs over to Macen, hugging her legs. "Can we go for pizza now, momma? I'm hungry — starving. I waited a long time."

She bends down to be at his level and straightens the hair I just ruffled. "Yes, ready when you two have finished playing dinosaurs. Grandma and I have been waiting for ages."

She smiles and kisses his cheek. He runs to get his coat and shoes on, and I get up and move to Macen, taking her into my arms. "You okay, baby?"

She nods and reaches up to kiss me on the lips. "Yes, and thank you for today, Caspian. Thank you for being there. I couldn't have gotten through that on my own. I don't know what I would have done if yo—" I stop her with a kiss.

"You don't ever need to thank me. I'm here for you and with you. The three of us are one, now and always, Mace. Always."

chapter 43

Macen

WE ATE PIZZA AND LAUGHED WITH Dixon and Grandma, but I couldn't take my mind off the new information we'd been given. I found myself looking at Dixon more, really looking at my son, and seeing if I could see Reid in him. His hair color is similar to Reid's in the one picture we found earlier, but other than that, no there is nothing that screams out that he's Reid's son. He's me: 100%. He's mine, and from what Caspian said earlier, he's his as well.

How on earth did I get lucky with Caspian? I'm a single momma — he's a hot celebrity, and he wants Dixon and me — he wants us both. I struck gold with Caspian. I've watched him interact with Dixon in the restaurant while I was speaking with Grandma and you would think he was already his poppa. They get on so well.

We're on the couch in my living area. Dixon is in bed, and Grandma went to bed to give us some space. We have some wine, but we haven't spoken much. "You okay, Mace? You're very quiet tonight. In fact, you were very quiet when we were out to dinner?"

I nod and sip my wine. "I was thinking at dinner about how I've struck gold with you, Caspian? How are you so enamored with Dixon and me? The way you are with him, anyone would think you were his poppa. He really looks up to you, and I see the admiration on his face because you talk to him and play with him."

He kisses the top of my head. "Macen, I love him like he's mine. It's like I've always known him. It's so weird to explain, but we just click. We understand each other as a poppa and son."

I smile up at him. "I didn't think I could love you any more than I do, Caspian, but you just melted my heart. I love you so much."

He kisses me.

We sit, not speaking for a while longer. "You're quiet again?"

I am because I haven't stopped thinking about Reid. "I'm sorry. I'm not the best company tonight. I'm enjoying being here with you, but I can't stop thinking about tomorrow and Reid." I sit forward, put my glass on the table, then turn to him. "I have never felt so much hate for a person. I mean, yes, I hated my attacker, but it's difficult to hate someone you don't even know. I want to kill him, Caspian. That's how I feel, even though I know that's bad, but I don't want him alive, I don't want to breathe the same air as him and there's no way on this earth Dixon will ever know his biological poppa. He's dead to him."

He takes my face and kisses my lips. "Thank fuck for that. I was having the same battle in my head earlier when I was playing in Dixon's room, but I had to talk myself down because it's your decision at the end of the day, not mine. I have no right to say anything. We're new together, and Dixon isn't mine. As much as I wish he was."

He's looking me straight in the eyes.

"I want to hear your opinions. You are part of our lives now, and yes, I know it's only been a week but..." I look down. I feel embarrassed.

"But what?"

"I feel utterly stupid, Caspian but... I can't imagine you not being in our lives." I blow out a breath. "There, I said it, and now I feel pathetic. Like you say, it's only been a week, and the trauma we've both been through could be why I feel like this now. Who knows, you may feel differently, especially once the Reid business is sorted?" I shrug and then lean into his chest so he can't see the tear escaping my eyes.

"Macen."

I can't. I shake my head, and he pushes me away slightly so he can look at me as he wipes the tears away. "God, the shit we've gone through this last week is bad enough, but what you've gone through for years is enough to send anyone over the edge. I get that we've become close really fast, but I couldn't imagine either of you not being in my life now. It just feels so right, so normal. We're going to have ups and downs, but we're here to pick each other up. I love you, Mace. I've told you, I never had anyone to love before. It's always been just me. But with you… Macen, I want you, Dixon, and Doris in my life for good. You will be mine, Macen. You will be my wife one day, and I will adopt Dixon to make him mine."

I go to speak, but he stops me. "No, Mace, no, you're not saying anything. It will happen. Not just yet, but it will. We just need to get rid of all this Reid shit first. Then start a normal life together, drama free. Do you hear me?" I'm sobbing now. I can't speak because I'm so choked up. How, in just a few days, can it be like this? I love him with all my heart.

It's late. "Caspian? Do you want to stay over?"

He looks down at me, "What about Dixon and Doris?"

I shrug. "Grandma knows how I feel about you; she'll be fine. I can put a note under her door not to let Dixon in my room in the morning. I would rather he didn't see us in bed together right now. I can lock the door as well." I feel really embarrassed. I don't want him to think I'm being forward. I just want to sleep in his arms. "Mace, I would love nothing more than to stay and sleep with you in my arms." I'm waiting for the 'but.' "But, if we do, I will set an alarm to wake up early, and come out here and sleep on the couch. If that's okay with you?"

I beam at him, nodding my head. I get up, take his hand then lead him into my room.

I close the door and head to my bathroom, but he grabs my wrist and pulls me into him. He kisses me hard. It deepens quickly, and both of us have wandering hands, but I pull away. "Can we just cuddle? I would prefer when we're here, to just sleep, I mean no, erm, you know." I feel myself blushing.

"It's okay, Mace, we can just hold each other. We don't have to do anything. Just one problem, though." He looks down at his cock that is now tenting in his slacks and smiles at me. "I need to sleep with a cushion or pillow against my crotch. We can't have you freaking out here. Dixon or Doris might hear and come in to see what's wrong. Is that okay?"

I laugh at him. "Yeah, in fact, I have just the thing." I rush into my closet, and I find a little cushion I've had for many years. It's only small and should just fit inside his Calvin's. I smile to myself when I find it, and I walk back into my room, with the cushion behind my back. I reach him and pull him by the waistband towards me, then I undo his slacks, and I put the little cushion into his Calvin's.

He flinches and sucks in his breath. "Sorry, did I squash him?"

He laughs at me. "No, Mace, it's just you touched him, and you know what that does to me, baby."

He takes his slacks off, folds them up, and places the cushion where it's comfortable for him. I can't help but stare as he adjusts himself. If we were at his place right now, I would be exploring more. "Don't, Macen." I look up to his face and see the anguish there.

"What?"

He pulls me into him. "The way you're looking at me, licking your lips like that, makes me want to do naughty things to you. I would love nothing more than to be speaking to my friend right now."

I have no idea what he's talking about and frown at him.

He laughs, then he cups my private parts with his hand. "This is my friend, Mace, and we had a few good chats last night. I would love to continue my conversation right now."

I move away from him and laugh as I head into my bathroom to get ready for bed.

I hear an alarm and feel Caspian get out of bed, but I don't wake up. I just turn over and go back to sleep.

"Momma, Momma, Casp stayed over last night. Momma, he's on our couch. Did you know he stayed over?" I'm being shaken by a little hand as I'm buried under the comforter. "Momma, wake up. Can Casp take me to school today? Please, Momma."

I slowly move the comforter to peek at Dixon. I smile at his adorable face. He has dimples in his cheeks. In fact, Caspian has dimples as well. He jumps on the bed and gets under the comforter with me to give me a cuddle. "Can he take me, Momma? I want him to take me, please."

"Well, if Caspian is okay taking you, then I don't see why not. Did you ask him?"

He shakes his head. "No, he was still asleep on the couch. Grandma told me to leave him and not to wake him."

"Oh, so it's okay to wake your poor momma who needs some sleep, is it?" I start to tickle him, and he giggles and starts to wrestle in the comforter. I hear a knock on the door, then the comforter is pulled back slightly, and there is a gorgeous face staring down and smiling at me. He's smiling like he's never seen me before. Oh crap, I'll have bed head and look a right mess. "Morning," I say quietly.

"Good morning to you, beautiful. I heard Dixon laughing and thought I would come and see what he was up to?"

"It's Momma, she was tickling me, 'cause I waked her up and not you. Casp, will you take me to school today, please?"

He looks at him with adorable puppy eyes. I think even Caspian would have a hard time saying no to him. He looks at me to see if it's okay, and I nod at him. "Of course I will, Dixon, but only if we leave your momma to go back to sleep. How about we go see Grandma and get you some breakfast? Then we can get you ready for school, and you can show me where it is. How does that sound?"

He squeals gets up and starts jumping on my bed. I laugh and so does Caspian. "Come on then, Dixon. Let's go. Give your momma a kiss."

Dixon throws himself on me and hugs and kisses me. Caspian holds out his hand, and Dixon takes it. "See you soon, Mace." He winks at me then leans down and gives me a kiss on the cheek, then leaves with Dixon. I melt.

I must have fallen asleep again because the next thing I know, Caspian is crawling into bed with me and taking me into his arms. "Hey. Is Dixon getting ready?"

He laughs. "Dixon is in school and has been for the last two hours."

"Oh, oh, I must have fallen back to sleep."

I'm up against his chest, and it's bare. I lift up the comforter and look down his body. He's naked, and I raise my eyebrows at him. "Well, I thought I would get a shower, and I saw how comfortable you looked, then thought I would join you"

"What, naked?" He shrugs. "Why not? Now, if my beautiful girlfriend were to get naked as well, that would make this pit stop to the bathroom worthwhile, wouldn't you agree? Besides, I have a conversation that needs to be resumed." He raises his eyebrows at me and wiggles them. I laugh. "Where's Grandma?"

"Well, she apparently had some errands to run. She made it quite clear she would be out for a couple of hours."

I lay back, trying to catch my breath. He'd wanted to have a conversation with his friend, and who was I to deny him? I've just had two more orgasms — each one getting more intense. I'm just coming down from my second orgasm, and Caspian is still between my legs. "You know what?" I manage to say. He looks up at me from kissing the insides of my thighs and raises an eyebrow, waiting for me to continue. "I think I'm addicted, and it's your fault." I breathe out.

"Addicted to what?"

"Well, you for one, but orgasms. I love orgasms — they are my new favorite thing. I would even say better than chocolate."

He laughs out loud, then he crawls up my body, holding himself above me. "Come on, Mace, time for a shower before Doris comes back."

I look at the time. It's almost lunchtime. "Wow, I can't remember the last time I stayed in bed until this time."

He gets up and takes my hand, leading me into the bathroom. In the shower, I decide to be brave and step further outside my comfort zone. I want to talk to my friend. I've not done this before, but I want to try it. I gingerly lick his cock, licking the pre cum from the tip, then I put it into my mouth. The noises he makes encourage me more. He's grabbing my hair and gently gyrating, "Baby, I fucking love your mouth around my cock, but why are you blowing?" I look up at him with his cock in my mouth. I let it pop out. "It's a blowjob? I'm blowing. Don't you like it? Am I doing it wrong?"

He pulls me up to standing and takes my mouth, hard. I break the kiss. "Caspian. Didn't you like what I was doing? If it's wrong, then tell me. I've never done this before." I feel offended. I thought he would love having his cock in my mouth. I get a little frustrated and start to leave the shower. I feel so stupid.

He pulls me back to him and bends to look me in the eyes. "God, I fucking love you, baby. I loved you putting my cock in your mouth — it was the best feeling ever. Don't be offended because I pulled out. He's going back in very soon." He wiggles his eyebrows at me. I pout and he takes my pouty lip in his teeth, gently biting. I slap his chest. "Baby, It's called a blowjob, but you don't actually blow. You suck and lick and suck and stroke. You put him in as far as you can and use your fist to help at the base. Then, if you feel like it, because I fucking love it, you can take my balls in your hand and caress them. Do you want to try again?" I nod, yes, but I'm embarrassed. I lower to my knees, and I take hold of the base, and I put him in my mouth. This time I suck him like a popsicle. I lick and suck as he said, and then I take his balls and fondle them. He starts gyrating harder, and he's deep in my throat. I find, once I get into it, I really start to enjoy it. I even like the taste of him. He's very salty, but it's nice. "Baby, Macen. I'm going to cum. If you are not ready to swallow, then please stop now, baby. I can't wait. Ahhhhh, fucking hell." I feel it all squirt down my throat, and I swallow as fast as I can without choking.

"Oh, fucking hell, Macen. That was fucking amazing. Did you like it, baby?" I nod yes, but I'm embarrassed. He lifts me and kisses me hard, and we can taste each other on our lips.

"You, my love, can talk to your friend any fucking time you want to. I will never stop you."

It's time to head to Casper's. I've been dreading leaving to go to work. In fact, I'm terrified. "Macen, I need to go to my place to change first. Do you want me to see you into the restaurant, or do you want to come with me?"

"With you," I say quickly, not wanting to leave his side.

"Hey, it will be all right. I won't leave you, okay?"

I nod, yes. He can see I'm scared.

We're in the car, heading to Casper's. I have hold of his hand in my lap, and I'm squeezing hard. I don't know how I will react if I see Reid. I don't know if I can hold back. I hope to God the police get him before we arrive.

Caspian

THE GRIP SHE HAS ON MY HAND is a killer — it's going numb. I place my free hand over hers and start to rub, hoping she eases up a little. I feel her shaking. She's terrified. I just want this over with. If we see him, what will she do? What will I do? I want to kill the fucker for what he's done to Mace. We approach my building, and I'm scanning the street, but I don't see him. "Come on, Mace, let's get up to my apartment quickly." I open the door and hold my hand out to help her out of the car.

I've just pressed the button to call the elevator when I hear him. "You fucking pair of pussies. You think you can get one over on me? You think you can avoid me forever? Well, think again?"

I have hold of Macen, and I feel her freeze. She doesn't look round to where he is, and she doesn't look at me. I have my back to him, but I turn my head. I need to see where he is, and I need to make sure he doesn't come for us. "Don't fucking ignore me, you fuckers," he shouts at us. I turn my body to fully face him, keeping Macen tucked behind me. She's right at my back and gripping my coat with one of her hands. I have my key card out ready for the elevator, and I slip it into her hand, ready for when the doors open. When they do, I'm going to push her into it and make sure he doesn't get in it. He's not getting near her. Over my fucking dead body.

"Got a problem, Reid?" I say gritting out the words. I want to kill him. Thinking about what he did to Macen is making my blood boil. I'm not sure I can hold back. I notice Derek behind Reid, and I nod slightly, hoping he takes it as a sign to move away quietly and call the cops. I hear the doors of the elevator open, and I turn my head slightly and motion for Macen to get in it. She shakes her head, no. I move back slightly and push her into the elevator, still keeping my eyes on Reid.

He moves towards us. "Go up, Macen. NOW. Fucking go." I shout at her, and I lean in and press the penthouse button. I hope to God she knows to put the card in so it starts to move to my floor.

He charges at us, but I stop him dead in his tracks with one hit to the stomach. He keels over, trying to catch his breath. I've winded him, which was my intention. The doors have closed, and I check to make sure she didn't get back out. I need her safe. I need her to call the cops. As long as she isn't here, she's safe. I hope she doesn't come back down. Derek disappeared as Reid charged, and I hope he's calling the cops as well. I just need to hold him off until they arrive and try not to kill the fucker in the process.

He stands up straight. "You fucking cunt. You can't have her. How many times do I have to tell you?"

I sneer at him. "She will never be yours, Reid. You think after what you did, you will ever go near her again? You will have to go through me first, you fucking dick." With that, he comes for me again, charging me and sending me flying.

I grab his neck and put him in a headlock. He's weak and pathetic, and he's got nothing on my build. "Do you have a fucking death wish, Reid? You know I can ta…"

I stop mid-sentence. I feel a strange sensation in my side. It hurt, but it didn't. That makes no fucking sense. I'm starting to shake slightly, must be the adrenalin. I'm starting to feel cold, but I'm also sweating. He punches me on the other side, not that I feel it much from the angle he's at. It's just a tap really, but for some reason, it really hurts.

I tighten my hold on his head, at least I thought I had tightened my hold on him, but I haven't. I start to feel a little lightheaded and weak. He's gotten loose from me. I look at him, furrowing my brow. How did he get out of my hold? I'm stronger than he is. I look at my hands, my vision is blurry, but they feel weird, but I don't know why. Why am I feeling like I want to be sick? Fuck, my side hurts. I look at him and see the smug look on his face. It's then I notice the knife in his hand. It's covered in blood. I see blood on his hand, and then I see droplets on the floor. I follow the blood trail, which gets heavier, the closer it gets to me. Fuck, I grab my side, and it's soaking wet. I lift my hand and see it's covered in blood. He got me — the bastard fucking got me. He must have had the knife up his sleeve, and he fucking got me.

"What's up, chef, got nothing to say now, huh? You fucking pussy. I told you, she's mine. One way or another, she's mine."

I stumble back onto the elevator doors, gripping my side tightly, trying to staunch the flow of blood, but it's no good, I feel faint, and I feel sick. I want to lie down. I feel the doors open behind me, and I start to fall back. "You fuc..."

45

Macen

I'VE BEEN STUCK IN THIS BOX FOR WHAT seems like ages. I have the card in my hand that Caspian gave me, ready to get into his apartment, but the elevator won't move. I press the penthouse button, but nothing. I try my cell to call the police, but there's no service in here. What do I do? If I go back out there, who knows what will happen, but I can't leave Caspian to fight Reid alone. I know he wants to keep me safe, but I need to help him. I feel so helpless stuck in here. My hands are shaking so badly. I can hear noises on the other side of the doors, I press the button to open them. I've pressed it so many times and they won't open god damn it, fucking open. Suddenly there's a loud thump on the doors. I jump back, then panic. "Caspian!" I shout. I need to open the doors, I look at the panel and it's then I realise I've been pressing the close doors button and not the open doors button. I press the correct one and they start to slide open.

I scream as the doors open, and Caspian falls backward into the elevator. He lands with a thud to the floor, covered in blood. So much blood. I fall to my knees next to his head and lift it onto my lap. I'm cradling his head. "Caspian, baby, wake up, Caspian," I whimper out to him. He won't wake up. His breaths are very shallow — I can see the trail of blood out of the door, and I meet feet with my eyes. I follow up the body to his face. Reid is standing there, smiling down at me, with his head cocked to the side. He has a mad look on his face, and he's holding a knife smothered in blood in his hand. "What did you do?" I whisper, holding Caspian's head, I look down at him then back to Reid, "WHAT DID YOU DO!" I scream at him. "You crazy fucking bastard. He's dying. Why, Reid? Why?"

He stands there, cockily wiping his bottom lip with his thumb. He slowly moves his arm and points the knife in my direction. "I fucking told you, Macen. I told you that you were mine, and no one could have you. I told you we would be a family."

I cradle Caspian's head, stroking his hair. "Caspian, come on, wake up for me, come on," I whisper into his ear between sobs. I move his hair from his face. He's so cold now, and his lips are getting blue. I have tears streaming down my face. I try to get my cell out of my pocket, but just as I get it out, it's snatched from my hand and thrown across the marble floor. "Leave us alone, Reid," I scream. "I need to call for an ambulance. He's dying. He needs help," I shout at him.

"No, you're coming with me, you're mine now." He tries to grab my hand to pull me up. He's stronger than I am, and I try to bat his hand away, but he grabs my wrist. He starts to pull, and I can't fight him, I need to move Caspian's head so it doesn't fall hard onto the floor. I manage to lower it with my other hand as gently as I can, all the while being dragged away by my wrist. He's hurting me.

He manages to pull me out of the elevator. I knocked Caspian, and I swear I heard him murmur something. I try to watch his lips, his chest — anything for movement.

Reid drags me across the marble floor by the hair, away from Caspian. I scream, "Stop, Reid, leave me alone. I need to help him. STOP."

He ignores me until I'm thrown against the wall near the outer doors. He punches me in the side of the face, then he gets right up into my face, sneering, before slamming my head into the wall hard. I feel dizzy, and my eyes roll back as he slams my head again, then again, laughing as he does it. I start to fall to the side, he lets go of me, and I go with a thud. "You're coming with me. We'll go home and get Dixon. Then we'll leave this fucking city once and for all and start a new life, just the three of us. We can go anywhere we want to. How about Houston or Chicago? We can make a great life, maybe open our own restaurant together — you and me as it's meant to be." He's looking at me like all this is normal. Like stabbing someone and leaving them to die is normal. Like dragging me across the floor by my hair and slamming my head into a wall is normal. He looks almost happy. He's crazy.

I try to shake my head at him, but it won't move. "I'm not…"

I feel like my face is swollen, and my head is splitting. I'm slurring, or it feels like I am, and my tongue feels like it's enormous in my mouth. I try again. "I'm not going anywhere with y… y…ou. Look what you've do… done? You're fucking crazzz…y… You hurt people, and you don't give a shit." I take a breath, struggling to get my words out. Why do I feel like this? "You're not gett… getting anywhere near my s-son. Over my de..dead body," I manage to get out.

I feel the tears streaming down my face. I move my head slightly to look at where Caspian is. I can't tell if he's breathing. Just then I get kicked in the stomach, then I'm grabbed by the hair, and my head is yanked back hard, and he punches me in the side of the face again.

"Now, look what you made me do to you, stupid bitch. Don't call me crazy. You hear me? Yes, we will go and get OUR son. Do you hear me, bitch? You will come with me now, and then once we get to yours, you tell the old lady we are friends, and we'll go and get OUR son. If you don't, she gets it like him." He points over to Caspian with his knife, then looks back at me. He strokes my cheek with edge of the cold blade. I take in a sharp breath. He's going to cut me. He pulls the knife back and sneers at me before he lets go of my head, and it falls with a thud to the floor again.

I hear a noise and open my eyes — suddenly Reid is crumpling to the floor next to me. He's looking at me as he goes down, and he lands right beside me. I can't work out what's happening. I'm confused until I look up and see Derek, with a fire extinguisher in his hands.

I need to get to Caspian. "Call the po..police and the ambu…" I think I shout to Derek. "Already on the way."

I try to crawl over to Caspian. I need to get to him. He's not far away, but it's taking everything I have to move. My head feels like it's going to explode. I can't see clearly. I wipe at my eyes, and my hands come up wet, and I see blood on them. I don't care, and I crawl to him, dragging myself along the floor with my hands. He's cold — his hands are cold as I grasp one of them, and I stroke his face and it's colder than it was. I can't see him breathing as I watch his chest. I scream out, trying to get close enough to pull his head to me. "Caspian, ple…please don't di…die, please co…come back to me. Ple…please don't lea…leave me. I lov…love you, b.b.baby."

I can barely keep my head up as I collapse next to him, my head hitting the floor yet again. I'm facing him, trying to see him breathe, and watching as he turns blue. I try to keep my eyes open, but I lose that battle. The last thing I see is Caspian, dead next to me.

I feel myself being moved. I'm with Caspian one minute, then the next, I'm on a stretcher. I look around, and I see lots of people: police, paramedics, other men and women. I don't know how much time has passed. I look at the floor where Caspian is and see him being lifted and put on a stretcher. He's so limp. They strap him in, but I'm having trouble seeing clearly. My vision is all blurry. I don't care. I close my eyes. He's gone. He's dead. I don't know what I will do without him. I've only been with him for a week, but he's already become my rock, my life, along with Dixon. He's made me feel so special these last few days. I have Dixon, I know my life won't end now he's gone, but I will never love again.

There is just so much going on around me. I hear so much noise, but it's distant like white noise in my head. I need to just rest. I close my eyes again.

Macen

I WAKE UP, WITH MY HEAD POUNDING. I try to look around to figure out where I am, but I can barely move my eyes. "Oh, Macen, love, thank goodness you're awake. How are you feeling? I'm so glad you're awake. I've been so worried about you — we all have." It's Grandma. Why can't I see clearly? One cheek hurts, and I raise my hand to feel my face.

"Where am I, Grandma?" God my mouth is so dry, and my throat hurts.

She takes my hand, "You're in the hospital, love. Do you remember what happened?"

I try to think. I gasp. Caspian. I feel the tears start to roll out of my eyes and pool at my ears. "Shhh, it's okay love. You're safe, and you're going to be fine now you're awake. You still have some swelling, and your cheekbone was fractured, but they got him, Macen. They took him away. He will be locked up for a long time. He can't hurt you anymore."

I take a deep breath. I remember Caspian wasn't breathing, just lying on the floor, dead. My head hurts badly, and crying is torture.

I must have fallen asleep again. When I wake, I remember I'm in the hospital. Grandma has hold of my hand. She's rubbing the back with her thumb, and it's comforting, but reminds me of Caspian.

Caspian, oh God, he's gone. I don't look towards Grandma. I close my eyes again and think back to him. It hurts. I know she said Reid would be locked up for a long time, but it's all my fault. If I hadn't have taken the job, then none of this would have happened. I can't keep the sobs in. I need to leave. I need to be at home with Dixon. Grandma strokes my head.

"Hey, Mace, baby. It's okay. You will be fine."

My good eye flies open, and I turn my head slightly to face Caspian. He's sitting there, stroking my head. But how? I must be dreaming. I must still be asleep. "How, how are you here. I saw you on the floor. You weren't breathing, Caspian, you were dead."

He smiles at me and shakes his head, no. "I'm here, baby. I'm here for you, I will always be here for you."

He's stroking my forehead. It's soothing, and the tears are streaming down to my ears again.

I wake with a start, déjà vu, and turn my head to the side to see who's there. It's Grandma. I sigh. I must have been dreaming that Caspian was here with me.

"Hey, love, you keep falling asleep. The doctors say that's normal after being in a coma."

I frown at her. What is she talking about? "A coma?"

She nods. "Yes, love. You've been in a coma for a week. You had us all terrified, Macen, but now you're awake, and the doctors say there'll be no permanent damage. You're going to be just fine, my sweet girl." I can't speak. I've been in a coma for a week! I wasn't that badly hurt, was I? I was still awake next to Caspian in the elevator. Grandma starts to stroke my forehead. It must have been her last time I woke up — not Caspian. A feeling of loss comes over me. I know he's gone.

"Grandma, how have I been asleep for so long? What happened?"

She tells me that I had a bleed on the brain, and they had to relieve that. They didn't know if I had sustained any kind of brain damage until I actually woke up. I've lost a week of my life. I can't comprehend that, and Dixon must be going out of his mind wondering where I am. Who has him now?

"Where's Dixon?"

"He's at school. I'll be leaving soon to pick him up. I want to bring him to see you if you feel up to it?"

"Yes, yes, please, Grandma."

I don't ask about Caspian. I don't want to know that I've missed his funeral. It hurts, and my heart feels shattered. I need Dixon. I need him close.

I'm woken up sometime later, by the door being pushed open and it banging against the wall. I look, and I see Dixon running into the room, closely followed by Grandma, who is out of breath. He climbs up onto the bed, throws his arms around my neck, and he lands on me with a thud and winds me. "Dixon, Dixon, I told you, sweetie, you have to be very gentle with your momma. She's been very poorly, and she needs us to look after her. Can you do that?"

He nods, smiling right into my face. "Momma, don't cry. I missed you so much. Grandma said you were very poorly, and you were sleeping a really long time. Did you miss me, Momma?"

I'm crying. It's all I seem to do. I nod my head, which is painful, but I don't care. I wrap my arms around him and hug him tightly to me. I pour all my love into this little human of mine lying on my chest. I would never survive if I didn't have him and Grandma. She strokes my hand, looking at me in sympathy. She must see the sadness I feel for the loss of Caspian. She squeezes my hand, then sits in the chair next to the bed.

They stay for a little while, but I struggle to stay awake, as much as I want to for Dixon. He is so excited, telling me all about school and what has been happening. I say goodbye to them. They'll come to see me tomorrow. I lay awake for a little while, and all I can think about is that day and what Reid did to Caspian. I cry myself to sleep again.

I feel my forehead being stroked again, and my hand being held. I slowly come around from my sleep and turn my head. Caspian is there, and he smiles at me. I close my eyes tightly. I'm dreaming again. I can't take this, and the tears squeeze out of my scrunched-up eyelids. I feel the tears being wiped away. It's all so real. Is it Grandma back? Is it the next day and Dixon is at school? I don't know. I only know I don't want the feeling to stop. I want to feel his touch so badly, but I know I will never feel it again. "Mace, baby, open your eyes. Look at me."

I shake my head, no. It's so real. Why is this happening? "Baby, look at me."

"It's not real, and it hurts. I love you Caspian. I don't know how to survive without you in my life. I want this to be real, but I know it's not. I love you."

"Baby, please look at me." I open my eyes, and I turn my face. I lift a hand and run it down his cheek. He grabs it and kisses my palm; he has tears streaming down his cheeks now. This is real — this is happening. Surely this can't be a dream, is it my mind playing tricks on me? I had a bleed on the brain — maybe it's something from that. I close my eyes, and I chant, "This is not real, this is not real, this is not real," out loud.

"Baby, it is real, it's me. You scared the fucking crap out of me though. I thought I'd lost you, Mace, I thought you would never wake up. Baby, look at me? It's me, I'm here — because of you and Derek. I'm here."

I suddenly sit bolt upright, ignoring the pain in my head and face. I turn and grab him, and I hug his head. I can't believe it's him. I lean back. "But how? You're dead, Caspian. You weren't breathing. I watched you turn blue. You died in front of me. I can't do this. Am I in a coma again? Am I dreaming? Are you really here, maybe I do have brain damage?"

He takes my face very gently in his hands. He leans in and kisses me on the lips, where he lingers, and our tears mingle on our lips. I sob. I can't believe he's here. We pull back, and I look him over. It's then I realize he's in PJ's, and he's in a wheelchair. I gasp. "Caspian, how are you? Are you okay?"

He nods. "Yes, I am now you're awake. I will be fine. It was touch and go apparently. I lost so much blood. Thankfully, he didn't hit any vital organs, although the surgeon said a fraction of an inch to the side and he would have pierced my liver. He hit an artery, which is why there was so much blood loss. He also damaged a nerve, which has left me struggling to walk a little. I'll be fine with a bit more rehab. I'm getting there now, the nurses just insist on wheeling me in here every day for now. They're ready to discharge me. I'm going home tomorrow. I wasn't going to leave until I knew you were on the mend. You scared the life out of me, Mace. If you hadn't come round, I wouldn't be able to live without you." He kisses my hand and squeezes.

I smile even though I'm still crying. I'm so happy right now. Not because he's going home but because he's here — he's alive. "What are you smiling at?"

"Life, Caspian, life. I can't believe you're here. I woke up and saw you. You were stroking my hair and holding my hand, but then I fell asleep, and I was convinced I dreamt it. But you're here, Caspian — you're actually here. I thought I had lost you. I thought that was it. I thought…"

He stops me by kissing me. "Never, baby. I'm here, and now I've found you, I'm not going anywhere anytime soon. I love you, Macen. You have me for as long as you want me." "Forever," I whisper, kissing him.

epilogue

Macen

I CAN'T BELIEVE WE ARE HERE. I'M STANDING with Grandma, just about to walk down the aisle to marry Caspian. Grandma is giving me away. Dixon is there, waiting with Caspian. He's Caspian's best man and has the important job of holding the rings. He's almost nine now. Time has flown since Reid attacked us.

I was discharged from the hospital three days after Caspian. Reid was in the hospital for a day with a concussion then arrested and transferred for questioning. The DA filed charges against him, and he was arraigned in court by a grand jury. There was no bail, the evidence against him was too strong — mainly thanks to Derek who had witnessed the whole attack and managed to phone the police without Reid noticing him — and he pleaded guilty in front of the Grand Jury. He pleaded guilty to raping me and nine other women and also the attempted murder of Caspian and the two attacks on me.

He knew going to trial was futile with the DNA match, Derek's testimony, and the video evidence. He was sent to Riker's until a date was set for sentencing.

For my rape alone, which was a Class B Violent felony, he got fifteen years, for the other rapes, the total years were forty-nine, and the attempted murder was twenty years. He wouldn't be getting out of prison in this lifetime. No parole would be granted.

Caspian didn't leave my side. He moved in with Grandma, Dixon, and me. Over time, I progressed in the kitchen at Casper's, and it had nothing to do with me dating the boss. He stayed out of all my promotions and left everything to Francoise. I practically run the place now, and we've introduced a lot of my dishes onto the menu over the years. Caspian travels a bit, and I go with him as often as I can.

Grandma decided she wanted to stay in New York with us. We moved out of the city and bought a beautiful house with a big garden and Grandma has her own annex. She loves it. She gets the best of both worlds. She loves Caspian too, which helps.

I have a surprise for Caspian after the wedding ceremony, and I can't wait to see his face.

My life has turned around completely. I never did try to find my father, who knows, maybe one day, but the time isn't right now. Dixon loves Caspian and calls him Poppa. The first time he did it, Caspian cried, as did I, and Dixon thought we were soft. Caspian loves playing in the garden with Dixon. They play soccer or football. Caspian even takes him out fishing on his boat, just the two of them. They love their boys' time. We've been talking about adoption. Caspian wants a big family, Dixon also wants brothers and sisters, so that's going to be on the horizon soon.

I turn to Grandma, and she smiles at me. I'm so glad she's giving me away. "I love you, Grandma. Thank you for always being there for me. At one time, I thought my life was over, and I thought about ending it. I'm so glad I never did. I'm so glad I was brave enough to carry on, but I couldn't have done it without you." I lean in and kiss her cheek.

She has tears in her eyes. "Come on, love, let's get you married to that gorgeous man of yours before I whisk him off for myself."

We both laugh just as the doors open for me to walk towards the love of my life. My Chef.

Caspian

THE MUSIC STARTS, and I hear the doors open. Dixon stands in front of me — we're dressed in the same suits, and he looks handsome. I turn, and I gasp when I see her standing at the doors. She looks absolutely stunning. I don't have the words to describe how I feel right now. I'm the luckiest man alive, that's for sure. I have my hands resting on Dixon's shoulders, and I'm trying not to shake, but it's not helping. He looks up to me. "She looks beautiful, Poppa. Momma looks so beautiful and happy."

I nod down at him, smiling from ear to ear. "Yes, she does, son, she's the most beautiful woman ever."

I look up and meet her eyes. I see the love and adoration mirrored from my own face. She smiles at me, and I mouth, 'I love you,' to her, and she beams. She starts her walk to us. I can't wait to make her Mrs. Kade. She will officially be mine.

We've come such a long way after she was released from the hospital. It didn't take long for me to move in with them. I stayed with her from the day she was released and never left. I will never forget the first time we made love. I thought it wouldn't happen for such a long time, and when it did, it was beautiful.

It was the night Reid was sentenced. We celebrated, knowing he would never do anything to us again, and we knew Dixon would never have to know about him. We were both very relaxed after a nice night out, and once in bed, we started kissing and touching. I was on top of her, my cock was at her clit, and I was rubbing gently up and down. I was at her entrance. We stopped kissing, and she gave me a look I will never forget. She grabbed my ass, and she pushed me into her while lifting her hips to take him in. We both froze. I thought she was going to bolt, and she closed her eyes as I entered her. When she opened them, I was holding my breath, waiting for her to tell me to get up, but she didn't. Instead, she grabbed both my ass cheeks and started moving up and down on the bed, pulling me into her. I let out my breath and asked if she was okay with this, and she smiled the biggest smile at me and nodded. I started to move, very gently at first. Finally being inside her and feeling her tightly squeezing my cock was exquisite. Feeling the love for her tenfold. I cried as we both climaxed together. She cried, holding on tightly to my shoulders.

I opened the restaurant in LA and having Macen and Dixon by my side made it the most perfect day. Following that were Vegas, London, and Paris. Macen and Dixon were with me at each opening and Macen helped me with all the restaurants: setting them up, running them, and the menu selections. We discussed her opening her own restaurant as it was her dream, but she was more than happy at my side and being part of the management of the Casper's chain. I have a surprise for her after the wedding ceremony.

I look over to my poppa sitting in the aisle. We've got to know each other, and I've forgiven him. Macen made me realize he was not to blame. He lost the love of his life, and he couldn't cope with it. I felt the same when I almost lost Macen. I know if she hadn't made it from her head injury, I would have struggled to cope.

He came to see me in New York, and we talked a lot about our feelings, trying to understand each other. He still calls me Casper. He said I will never be anything else to him.

We started to bond, and now we have a good relationship. When he can, he comes to New York and comes out fishing with Dixon and me. Macen, Dixon, and I have been to Florida a few times to stay with him and his wife, Rosy. She is a nice lady, and we all get on well. Once Dixon started calling me Poppa, he started calling my poppa and Rosy, Grandpa and Grandma. He loved being spoiled with two new grandparents.

Now, here I am, about to marry the love of my life. As we both say our vows, we cry. I'm not ashamed to cry in public because this tells the world I am officially off the market. Thank fuck for that.

I've closed Casper's for the day because we're hosting our reception here. Of course we are, only the finest food for us. We don't have a lot of guests, as neither of us has many relatives and not that many close friends, so we kept it intimate. My team have dressed Casper's up with white flowers, and there are flower arches over our table and at the entrance, with a red carpet to greet us. It looks amazing. "Baby, can we just go into the back office, I have something for you?" I say as I raise my eyebrow at the look of lust on her face. "Mrs. Kade, where is your mind wandering too, right now?" I laugh and lean in to kiss her, which immediately gets heated until we get lots of whistles, catcalls and shouts to wait for the honeymoon.

I lead her out the back, holding her hand, and in my office, I go to my drawer and pull out some papers. "I just need a signature on these from you, my beautiful wife."

She looks at me, quizzically. "What is it? Why do I need to sign?"

I hand her the documents and let her read them.

She looks up at me. "You're making me your partner in business? Caspian, I can't do that. The restaurants are yours. You've worked hard to get where you are. They are your babies!" She puts the papers down on the desk and shoves them towards me.

I move around and take her in my arms. "Baby, the new restaurants are as much yours as mine. You had as much to do getting them up and running as I did. In fact, without your input, I don't think they would have succeeded. You are my partner now, baby, every decision about work or life is ours to make, not just mine and not just yours. Please sign them. Please don't fight me on this. I love you my, beautiful chef wife, and what a force we are together. The two best chefs there are."

She signs the papers. Now I take out the other envelope and hand it to her. She takes it from me gingerly and gasps. "Oh my god, Caspian, when did this happen? I'm now a Michelin Star chef. I'm a one star. I can't believe it." She jumps into my arms, kissing me. I can't tell what she's more excited about, the partnership and her now owning half of all my restaurants or the Michelin Star. I don't give a shit — she's happy. That is all that matters to me.

"Wait there," she says, leaving me in the office. She returns two minutes later, and she hands me an envelope. "My turn. Happy wedding day, baby!" I open it and pull out the papers. "It's official. You're Dixon's Poppa. It arrived yesterday — the adoption has been finalized. Congratulations, Poppa."

I beam from ear to ear. "We're officially a family. I have a family? I can't wait to tell Dixon I'm officially his Poppa."

She nods at me. "Turn it over." It's just one piece of paper — there's nothing attached. I turn it, trying to comprehend what I'm looking at. It's a black box like a photograph that is all grainy. I don't know what it's supposed to be. I must look really confused. She moves towards me and takes the paper from me.

"Well, as this was your official notification of being a poppa to Dixon, I thought it best you had both of your babies on the one form."

I have no fucking clue what she is talking about.

She rolls her eyes at me. "This is a peanut. Our peanut. Mine and yours. One we made together. Do you see?"

Holy fucking shit. I see it. I see the peanut. I notice the name and date. "It's a scan, Caspian. It's our baby."

I grab her, lifting her into my arms and twirling her around. "We're having a baby? Me and you? How? How, Macen, When?"

"Well, Caspian, when a man and a woman make lo…"

I kiss her hard. "Smart ass. I know how they are made. I just mean… I thought you couldn't get pregnant?"

She laughs at me and at how startled I must look. "Well, they said the chances were very slim, almost impossible, but as we know, the impossible happens with us, my husband."

I slide her down my body, and we kiss until we are breathless. "I love you so much, Mrs. Michelin Star Kade. I can't wait to spend the rest of my life worshipping you and making you happy. My beautiful wife." We stand, hugging and crying together for a little while. This is the best day of my life.

We join the rest of the wedding party and break the news to everyone. This is my life, and I will take it over any Michelin Star any day.

The End

REVIEWS

I really hope that you enjoyed this story. Reviews are lovely! Honestly, they are! And they also help other people to make an informed decision before buying this book.

I would really appreciate it if you took a few seconds to do just that.

Thank you!

Amazon

Goodreads

Bookbub

Lynda Throsby Xx

ALSO BY LYNDA THROSBY

Catfish
The Best Day Of My Life

Read on for a free sample of my
debut novel Catfish.
Catfish is a dark, gripping, romantic thriller.
and
The prologue and first couple of chapters
of The Best Day of My Life.
This is a sweet but sad single dad story

CATFISH

ONLINE DATING MEANINGS

Stashing – When you start seeing someone, but they keep you a secret and stash you away–usually because they are married or seeing other people. You are their secret.

Ghosting – When you start seeing someone, and they just disappear and vanish without a trace. They don't return your messages and even block you from social media and dating sites. This is so they don't have to tell you they are breaking up with you verbally.

Zombieing – If you have been ghosted the culprit may resurface back on the sites. This is usually a fair bit of time after they ghosted you. They try to make contact, only to probably ghost you again.

Benching – This is before you discuss exclusivity, and they bench you like in a football game while they look for someone better. You are their backup option. They may come back to you if no one better comes along.

Catch and release – Where someone persistently pursues you as they love the chase, but as soon as you agree to a date they release you, as you're not a conquest any more.

Breadcrumbing – This is where someone seems to be pursuing you, but really, they have no intention of being in a relationship with you. It could just be the chase they like, or it's a game as they are already in a relationship. They message and chase, leaving you breadcrumbs with no outcome.

Cushioning – When you're dating, but they know it's not going anywhere or will not end well so instead of cutting you loose they prepare you for the break up by chatting and flirting with others online to cushion the blow to you.

<u>Kittenfishing</u> – Someone who has out-dated images of themselves and lies about their age, height, job, hair etc. If you were to meet you would know they were lying.

<u>Catfishing</u> – The pinnacle of online dating deception. Where someone pretends to be someone else. They use fake images to lure you in and use false information to make them seem more interesting. This can be dangerous if you decide to meet up, although you would never know until you decided to go that far and by that time it could be too late for you.

catfish

LYNDA THROSBY

GEORGE

IT HAS TAKEN ME A LONG TIME TO reel this one in and get her to finally agree to meet me for a date. It's been too long now since my last catch, just over a year ago now. This one is going to suffer because i've waited for wait so long, I've missed out on others while I've been chasing her, and my need is growing more and more. It's getting harder each day—both figuratively and literally. The things I'm going to do to this bitch now… I can't wait, and boy will she regret making me. I am a very impatient man.

The minute I laid eyes on her profile picture while scanning the hordes of whores for my next catch, I knew I had to have her. It was the long mousey brown hair and the hazel eyes, although the others had looked similar, this whore was the spitting image of my fucking bitch of a mother.

My brow is wet from sweat, and I'm shaking, knowing I will finally have her tomorrow. I'm so fucking hard right now just looking at her picture. God help me when I get my hands on her. She will regret ever responding to my messages and playing with me, stringing me along. Why the fuck I get hard for these whores that look like my mother is a mystery to me. They should repulse me, but I can't help myself, and it makes me hate myself even more. I feel sick to the stomach. Now I need to take care of my fucking cock. That bitch, Katherine has done this to me yet again.

KATHERINE

WHAT HAVE I DONE? I SAID I WOULDN'T date for a long time, so why have I just agreed to meet this Lewis guy. Why am I doing this? Why do I put myself through this? It's not like I need someone. I have my own business, right here in the city, which takes up most of my time. But still… it's lonely, and his pictures are hot. I mean, those abs and biceps and the tattoos… Oh, god, they make me drool. But it's the bright, mesmerising, light brown eyes with long eyelashes and black curly short hair that made me succumb. He is just so pretty in a masculine way. I still think this is too good to be true. Why would someone that looks like him be on a dating site? Surely, he can get any woman he wants.

I've had such bad experiences with men in my life, going back to my family. I had no father to speak of. He left mum, my brother Brad, and me when I was two, so I never knew him. Brad is three years older than me, and although he did look out for me in school and was very protective as most big brothers are, he's an arsehole.

He has a wife now, Cindy, and he is mean to her like he used to be mean to me. Not the hitting, but he does have some serious anger issues, and I'm sure it stems from him being so young when our dad left.

Brad used to get angry a lot and hit me, and if I ventured into his room, all hell broke loose. He even broke my arm one time when I was eleven. He had a girl in his room; mum was at work as usual. He was on top of her, grunting away, and all I saw was his arse, but he jumped off that bed so quickly, grabbed me and threw me hard on the floor of the landing that my arm snapped. He was sorry, of course, and persuaded me to tell mum I'd fallen. That was just one of the times in my childhood that I ended up at the hospital, being told how clumsy I was.

Mum worked two jobs. She was the only one bringing money in for the three of us. She was a room cleaner in a hotel in London during the day, starting at 6.30 a.m., she finished that job at 3 p.m. just in time for me to get home from school and see her for half an hour before she had to work the evening shift from 5 p.m. to midnight down at the local petrol station.

She trusted Brad to look after me, being my big older brother, but it was best I stayed away from him as much as possible, or I ended up with bruises. I never told mum he did that to me. She had enough to worry about.

So yeah, men! Dad left—arsehole, and Brad hit me—another arsehole.

THERE WAS MY first boyfriend at fourteen. Luke Jones. At first, he was really nice and made me feel special, but it became clear that was only because of what he wanted from me.

We were going steady for about three months and we'd only ever kissed, that was a trauma in itself the first time. I had no experience, and when he stuck his tongue in my mouth and tried to push it down my throat, I almost puked in his mouth, much to his dismay. Having never had a boyfriend before; I didn't want to go any further than kissing, although he did try to put his hand under my skirt or up my top a few times.

He even tried to put my hand on his erection over his trousers, but I was scared and naive, so in the end, he got fed up and called me a cock-tease because I wouldn't have sex with him or let him feel my boobs.

He told all the boys in school not to waste their time with me because they would get nowhere, and he told everyone who would listen that I was a frigid bitch. The girls in school picked on me anyway. I thought it was because I was quiet and kept to myself, but both Brad and Luke told me they were all jealous of me because I was pretty, and I had a good figure for my age, that the other girls felt threatened by me. When Luke dumped me, it just got worse with the mean girls. They had more ammunition to throw at me just because I wasn't a slut like them.

I really think I should cancel on Lewis. It's just he is so sweet in our messages, saying how beautiful I am and asking if I've ever considered modelling. He wants to meet to talk and get to know me. Nothing more, he said he has no expectations as he respects me. I mean who does that these days? It's usually 'wham bam thank you, ma'am.'

I just can't see someone like him wanting to get to know someone like me. I don't think I'm ugly. I'm curvy in all the right places and in some not-so-right places, but I'm not a size zero by any means. I'm more a comfortable fourteen to sixteen in clothes.

I'm successful in my business, and it takes up most of my time, I've worked hard to get it where it is today. Porter Properties is one of the top property investor/developers in the city, and I'm proud of that. It's so hard being a woman at the top in a man's world, but I have this knack of knowing a good deal when I see one. I own several commercial buildings and apartment blocks.

I have a penthouse apartment in Knightsbridge, not far from my office, which I use during the week, and at the weekends I head to my five-bedroomed house in a lovely area of Chelmsford. I bought a big house because I was hoping mum would move in with me and quit her jobs, but it wasn't meant to be. It's very quiet where I live. I love the peace and tranquillity, and I know mum would have loved it too.

GEORGE

Just one more night and I will have that bitch. My thirteenth catch. I may prolong it. Make her suffer like that bitch has made me suffer for weeks. I've checked her out on social media, and from what I can tell, she doesn't socialise much. There are some work references and a few pictures with work colleagues, that's it. After digging, I found she owns the company, but other than that, there is not much about family or friends. I just hope, as I suspect, she lives alone. They nearly always do or why would they be looking for love on these shitty dating sites?

In our messages on the dating site: LookingforLove.com, she never gave much away about herself. She was always quite vague and guarded, and I suspect she's had bad experiences with tossers who go on these dating sites purely to get free sex with no intentions of dating. I can't blame the wankers really. Why get tied down with some whore permanently when you can have pussy on tap? Looking for love, what a load of bollocks. I know why I go on the dating sites. It's to rid the world of anyone who looks like my useless mother. They don't belong here—don't deserve to live, just like she didn't. She used to say she loved me, yeah right, like fuck she did. What mother would let her waste of a husband do the things he did to me, do nothing about it, even joining in herself? Sick fuckers—both of them were.

Who needs love and all that crap when you can just take what you want and then do away with them? Love: what is it anyway? Is it what my father showed me when he used to punch and burn me while stubbing out his cigarettes on me when he couldn't be bothered getting off his lazy fat arse to find an ashtray?

He would make me sit in the room with him while he jerked off to his porn. I would have to sit on the floor next to his chair and get him anything he needed. I was his personal slave. 'Boy get me a beer.' 'Boy get me something to eat.' 'Boy get me my playboy magazine.' 'Boy, light me a cigarette.' The only thing I didn't do was shit and piss for him. I had to have tissues ready for him jerking off, or it would be my hands used to clean him up. He even made me suck him clean sometimes, telling me to lick every drop or he would beat me. He used to make me lift my t-shirt up, if I was wearing one that is, so he could pinch and twist my body when he was about to shoot his load. If I cried from the pain, he would kick me so hard that I would fall over and end up bruised, knocked out, or with broken bones. Once, he kicked me so hard, I sailed across the room, knocking the T.V. over. He flew out of his chair to make sure I hadn't broken it. I had never seen him move so fast, and for that, I got punched in the stomach and kidneys, a black eye and bloody lip. He never once looked or asked me if I was okay. Never. He didn't care what he did to me.

I never went to school. No one knew I existed. No one ever came to our house, and I was never allowed to leave except on the rare occasion I was allowed out to help mum with shopping when he'd severely beaten her and she couldn't move properly. When the man at the shop asked who I was, she just said I was a visiting nephew. I didn't know if we had any other family or not.

My mother used to work all day at a café in town to keep the money coming in for my dad's booze. God forbid if there was no beer or whiskey in the house for him, then he would lay into her with his fists—always on her body, never visible because she needed to go back to work. He couldn't have her staying off work and not bringing in the money. I would go days without food, and when they finally gave me something, it was only something basic like rice or porridge oats. Even though she sometimes brought leftovers from the café, I never got any. He got everything, and she was just as bad. She let him treat me like shit.

He wanted to watch me with my mother. I didn't know that what he had us doing was wrong. I had no idea. I thought all kids did it with their parents. He used to jerk off, watching me go down on my mother or with my cock in her mouth. He liked to join in sometimes and make her suck me while he ploughed into her backside. The bastard was sick. I know that now. I hated them both so much and the older I got, the worse it got. Being a teenager was a nightmare, but I was plotting in my head. Plotting to rid the world of the vile pair. I was plotting to fight back.

Available on kindle
BUY LINKS FOR CATFISH
Amazon UK https://amzn.to/2OmLYWc
Amazon US https://amzn.to/2zpwI5L
Also on Kindle Unlimited - KU

The Best Day Of My Life

LYNDA THROSBY

PROLOGUE
10 YEARS EARLIER

S HE'S GONE.

My life is gone with her.

This was supposed to be the best fucking day of my life.

It's turned into the worst nightmare of my life.

This can't be real.

I have to wake up.

I'll find her sprawled out beside me like she is every morning. Me cursing as I'm hanging off the bed because she's taking up all the room. She says it's because of the size she is now, that she needs to spread out but it's not, she's always done it.

I love her.

Time to wake up.

Except I can't.

I'm standing here in the emergency room. I can hear babies crying, but she's just lying there. They haven't covered her up — I wouldn't let them.

I remember screaming at them when they called time on her.

I scream when they try to cover her.

"What the fuck are you doing? Why are you covering her?"

The doctor tries to put a hand on my arm, but I shrug him off.

"Fix her!" I cry

"Just fix her…" I fall to my knees on the floor, my head in my hands. Trying to wake up from this nightmare.

My wife is gone.

I can't fathom what happened. It was a birth. They do this day in and day out, multiple times a day, so why did my wife die?

"What happened? Why is she gone? She was giving birth. You do this all the time. WHAT THE FUCK HAPPENED?" I scream at them.

The doctor crouches down to be eye level with me.

"I'm sorry, Mr. Tourney. Your wife had eclampsia and went into cardiac arrest. We did all we could for her, but, unfortunately, we couldn't save her. It's not common to have deaths in childbirth these days, but especially with twins, eclampsia can be a complication." I stare at him, not quite understanding

"She had a heart attack? She's only 27. How the fuck could she have a heart attack?"

He winces slightly at my outburst. "Mr. Tourney. I'm so sorry. I know this is hard for you, but you have two healthy babies over there." He nods his head in the direction of the crying babies

"They could probably do with meeting their daddy. Being born is stressful enough, but they've lost their mother. I believe they'll know that they've lost a connection. Would you like to meet your son and daughter?"

Would I?

Do I want to?

Did they kill her?

What the fuck do I do now?

I can't look after two babies on my own. They need their mother.

"Bring her back, doctor. Just bring her the fuck back. They need their Mommy. I need her. She's my life."

I break, collapsing backward on the floor. I'm curled up tight, tucking my legs into my chest as tight as I can get them. I start rocking and wailing. How pathetic must I look? A grown man curled up on a delivery room floor …

Not something they see every day.

CHAPTER 1
10 YEARS LATER

Present

"Evelina, Evander, come to daddy, please. No more hiding. It's school, and we need to finish getting ready," I shout to the terrible twosome.

They do this most mornings. Have breakfast then disappear to play instead of getting ready for school.

My mother in law, Sonia has made the lunches for them. She comes over every day and waits for them to get back from school and looks after them for me. She makes dinner just in time for me getting home from work. I insist on having dinner with them every night. They have baths and are ready for bed, and Sonia does their lunches for the following day. It's quite a well-oiled machine now. To be honest, I couldn't have done any of the last ten years without the help of Sonia and Arnold, Evelyn's parents.

The school bus will be here for them in thirty minutes. If they don't get ready now and get to the end of the driveway, they will miss the bus, which means I will end up taking them to school yet again, which in turn will make me late for work.

"Evelina, Evander! I won't tell you two again. I'm getting really annoyed now. Get your little butts down here now for school." I can hear the murmurs from them upstairs somewhere, Evelina muttering, "It's dad, not daddy. We're ten, not two." Cheeky madam. She calls me Daddy when she's creeping for something like dolls or ice cream.

Why do I have such an enormous house? It's easy to lose them in this place. Maybe I need a smaller one. I just want them to have a good life and everything I can give them without spoiling them. Raising twins on your own is hard work. Evelyn had a good upbringing with everything she needed, and she turned out to be amazing. I'm just hoping the Evs — as I call them — turn out as good as she did.

Evelina is sassy already. God love her, she drives me crazy with her smart mouth. She is the spitting image of Evelyn in looks, but I'm not sure where her little spitfire personality comes from. I sometimes put it down to not having a Mom. Evander is like me both in looks and personality. He will be and, in fact, is a nerd. Takes after his dad — 100%.

I haven't dated since the twins were born. I couldn't. I love Evelyn and always will. She was my college sweetheart. I've had sex since I lost her, but that's all it ever was. I never had feelings for anyone. Even having sex with other women felt like I was cheating. Plus, I don't have the time for a relationship. I have work and the kids. That's my life, and it's all I have time for.

"Ok, you two. Down the stairs, now. It's a good job I don't have a boss to moan at me when I'm late for work."

"That's because you are the boss, Dad," Evelina shouts at me from over the galley at the top of the stairs.

She's right. I am the boss, but it doesn't mean I like being late. We started the company together, Evelyn and I, back in college. I fell for the hot nerd, and she said she fell for the hottest guy in the school.

CHAPTER 2
18 YEARS EARLIER

WE STARTED DATING IN COLLEGE — both of us majors in computing.

Evelyn was gorgeous. She was my crush.

I wasn't a jock. I was a typical nerd, so she wouldn't be interested in me.

I admired her from afar because she was way out of my league. I'll never forget the day she walked into the lecture hall. I felt sure she was in the wrong room. This class was full geeks and nerds; she didn't belong here, but wow, was I wrong …

There are lots of empty seats, but she chooses a place just one away from me on my row. I start to sweat and try not to look at her. It's hard concentrating, that's for sure. I'm lucky I excel in computer programming and gaming. Let's face it, what else does a nerd have to do every night? It's not like we're out partying with the popular kids.

About two months into the semester, our tutor pairs us up for a gaming project. I'm stunned and start to panic. I can't believe my luck, but when I look over to Evelyn to acknowledge her, she looks as shocked as me. Just trying to speak to her has my heart racing and sweat beading my brow. I do it somehow but make a fool of myself stuttering out the words. We arrange to meet in the library at lunch to discuss how to go about this and see what ideas we have.

I'M NERVOUS, TO say the least. I get to the Library early so that when she walks in, I can watch her, only I don't get the chance. It's like she had a radar or something because as soon as she comes into sight, she looks straight at me.

I nod my head up in a kind of hello gesture and watch her walk towards my table and put her laptop and bag down. She mesmerizes me.

"Hi, Theon." She looks as embarrassed as I feel, and I wonder if she doesn't want her friends seeing us together, looking around I don't see any of her friends so we should be good for now.

She's a popular girl, and I've seen all the jocks hanging around her. I did notice however she didn't like all the attention that much.

"Hi, Evelyn." I'm a little uncomfortable. I blush. I can feel my cheeks burning. I grab my bottle of water from my bag and quickly gulp some down, trying to hide my awkwardness. The problem is, I gulp too fast and start choking, drawing attention to myself. Oh god, kill me now. I'm going to die of embarrassment. Evelyn rushes behind me and starts patting and rubbing my back. I stop choking, I think from the shock of her touching me

"Thanks, Evelyn," I manage to choke out. My throat is burning.

"Call me Eve if you want, Theon. Everyone else does."

"I like Evelyn." I shrug, and she smiles at me.

We start to discuss the project, and how we are going to work on it.

Evelyn says we can work at her house — only if I wanted to. She explains her parents are hardly home, mainly just the housekeeper, and she has her own office set up in her bedroom. She seems a little shy when she suggests it.

I'm seriously out of my league here. Housekeeper and her own office! Her parents must be mega rich.

I'm glad she offers her house though. I would be too ashamed to take her to my place. I live in a trailer. It's just my grandma and me. She brought me up. My mom got pregnant at sixteen, and my dad didn't want to know her or the baby. She didn't want me either. She was seventeen and wanted to party. I never knew her — she died when I was two from a drug overdose. My grandma is my hero. I love her to bits. She works hard to keep me.

I got a scholarship to college. Otherwise, I would have been working somewhere to help her out. I feel bad as it is, so I make some extra money by tutoring in the evenings and weekends. I make good money this way.

We plan to go to Evelyn's after college to brainstorm and put our ideas down. I already know what I want to do. I've been working on creating games for a while now.

I wait for Evelyn on the steps as soon as college finishes. She arrives just seconds after me.

"Hi, Theon. We can walk to mine from here, it's not that far, if that's okay with you, unless you drive?"

"Hi, Evelyn, no, I don't drive, so walking is good with me." We start walking, and I'm surprised at how easily the conversation flows. I can't believe I'm actually here with her, talking about games and nerdy stuff. She is unexpectedly easy to talk to, and my embarrassment seems to be subsiding. It turns out Evelyn has been creating her own games as well. I tell her what I'm currently working on, and she seems impressed. We have so much in common. I'm in awe of her — beautiful and a nerd.

We reach her house, and I have to pick my jaw up off the floor.

"You live here?" I ask, just gawking at this huge house in front of me. It's set back from the road with a sweeping semi-circle drive up to it and lots of garden to the front.

"Fucking hell," I whisper to myself but judging by the look on Evelyn's face she hears, and she looks down in embarrassment.

"Oh god, sorry, Evelyn. I didn't mean to say that out loud. It's just ... well ... I've never been to a house like this. It looks like a mansion."

"I've never brought anyone here before, Theon. I never wanted people to judge me based on my parents' wealth."

I feel terrible and look away wondering if I should leave. We could have done this in the library at school.

"Maybe I should just ... erm ... go, Evelyn. I'm really sorry if I offended you." I look everywhere but at her. I feel like a real ass now,

"No, I don't want you to leave. I know you didn't mean anything by it. Come on." She links my arm like we are best friends, and we head up the drive. I try to keep my mouth shut because the closer we get, the bigger it gets — it's huge. I feel her glance at me a couple of times, but now, it isn't the mansion in front of me making me gawk, but rather the girl at my side who thought nothing of linking me as though it's something we do all the time, even though this is the first time we've spent any time together. She's touching me, and that alone is doing things to me. Things I like but don't have much control over. I'm going to embarrass myself. I just know it.

I look in awe at our linked arms and smile. She suddenly drops her arm from mine.

"Sorry, I didn't mean to be so forward. I just automatically did it. It's what I do with my friends."

"No, please don't be embarrassed. I, erm, I like it," I said shyly not looking at her. I hadn't realized we'd stopped walking.

"Come on, let's go round the back and through the kitchen. I don't think my parents will be home yet. Not that it's a problem if they are. On the rare occasion they are home at this time they like us to have dinner together, but it's not often they get home early."

"Can I ask what your parents do?"

"They are both plastic surgeons. They have their own practice in the city and well, this being L.A., you can imagine how busy they are."

"Oh," is all I manage as she links my arm again and we head around the massive house. We pass another building to the right. I glance over at it, and Evelyn must notice.

"That's the garage." She shrugs.

"Wow, that's bigger than most houses."

"They have a lot of cars. Daddy is a bit of a petrol head."

We carry on walking, and out the back is the biggest swimming pool I've ever seen, complete with built-in cave and slide. I gasp and quickly try to cover it with a little cough, but I'm not sure I pull it off. Over behind the pool is another building.

"That's the pool house." Again she shrugs but looks a little embarrassed. We walk past the pool, and there's a lanai at the back of the house with an outdoor kitchen and stunning outdoor furniture. This is a completely new world to me. I feel out of place. I feel uncomfortable. I want to leave, but then that's me judging her. She doesn't act like she's spoilt, and I would never have thought it if I hadn't come here. She doesn't drive a flashy car that I've seen. In, fact, I've never seen her drive.

"Do you have a car, Evelyn?"

She looks at me trying to gauge where this is going.

"No. Well, yes. I can drive, and my parents bought me a car, but it just sits in the garage. I didn't want it, and they didn't ask me first. I like walking places," she says on another shrug. She's not stuck up or spoilt, which makes me fall for even more.

We enter the kitchen where there is a lady pottering about and cooking.

"Hey, Maggie, this is my friend, Theon. We have a computer project to do together, which counts towards our final marks. I'll just grab some drinks and cookies."

"Hello, Eve. Hello, Theon. Nice to meet you. Don't have too many cookies, Eve, your parents just phoned. They are on their way home, so you're having dinner with them tonight."

"Ok, thank you. Did they say when they would be home?" She turns to me as she opens the huge fridge. "Theon, would you like to stay for dinner?"

Shit, no, I can't. I need to get back to Grandma.

"Sorry Evelyn, I can't stay too long. My grandma will have my dinner ready."

"They said they would be home for six," Maggie says.

"Oh okay, Theon, no worries. What time do you need to be home for dinner?"

"I said I'd be back for six thirty."

We head through her house up the stairs to her room. I try hard not to let it show just how much in awe I am. Her room is huge. It's at the top of the house in the attic. We move through it, I notice there are lots of sea turtle ornaments on some shelves, and posters on her wall of them, her bed is big but looks small in this room, which also has its own sitting area, we head to the back where she opens the door to a very large office with desks and computers. Not just one computer, oh no, she has two computers that I can see and four screens set up. We move to the biggest desk, and she wheels a chair over so we can sit side by side.

"Evelyn, this place is amazing. You look like you have everything you need right here. I envy you," I say looking down as I start getting my laptop and notebook out of my bag.

"I know how lucky I am, believe me, I do. I just don't like to flaunt it, which is why I never bring anyone home." I look up at her in admiration yet again. She amazes me. She is the most beautiful girl I know, with her short auburn hair, her sparkly green eyes, and pixie-like features. She has a stunning figure, not too skinny like those cheerleader girls who I think barely eat. She is just amazing, but if I carry on thinking like this I may need to use the bathroom.

"Will your parents mind you bringing me up here? Just not many parents would allow their teenage daughter to bring a boy up to their room to study." Way to change the subject, Theon.

"I've never brought anyone home before, but I don't think it will be a problem. They are easy-going, and they trust me. I'll check with them later when they're home."

We brainstorm for the rest of the time. We have some amazing ideas working together, we bounce off each other perfectly, and I can't believe how relaxed we are in each other's company. But, it's almost six, and it will take me a good half hour to walk home from here.

"I best make a move, Evelyn, before your parents get home. I need to get home in time for my dinner." I really don't want to go. I don't want to leave her.

"Yeah sure, Theon. That was a great couple of hours. My head is full of so many ideas. I think we made a great start. You're amazing with all this, and your ideas are truly remarkable."

"Ditto, you really know your stuff too. You amazed me. When you walked into the lecture theatre, I thought you had the wrong class."

"Why do you say that?"

"Well, you're not exactly a nerdy type, are you, Evelyn?" I can feel myself getting very red again, as I pack my stuff up and rush to the door without looking at her before she can question my comment

"Right, I'll see you tomorrow in class." I rush for the stairs. I hope I can remember my way out of here, it's like a maze it's so big, and I didn't exactly pay attention walking up here. With following behind Evelyn, my mind was elsewhere.

"Hey, I'll show you out. You look like you're in a rush?"

"Yeah, thanks, just need to get home."

"Do you want me to take you?"

"No, it's okay. I can run home, thanks anyway. I need my run, I didn't get it in today, I was distracted," I say with a small, shy grin.

She distracted me.

I would have run home from school like I usually do. I may not be a big muscled Jock, but my physique is pretty good for a nerd. I lift weights in the college gym then run home, but it looks like I won't be doing that for a while. I'll have to run in the morning, go to the gym, shower, then let my school day begin.

We pad quietly down the stairs, not speaking. When we get to the bottom into the vast hallway, Evelyn overtakes me and heads to the front door.

"Here, this way is quicker. I can't hear any talking, so I take it my parents aren't home yet."

We stand on the steps, and I'm just about to turn to say goodbye when a car rolls into the drive. Shit, I didn't want to meet her parents, not yet anyway.

The car is a Maserati, not that I know much about cars but the Maserati emblem of the trident on the front grill gives it away, I have no idea of the model. I hardly know anything about Fords or Chryslers never mind these expensive types of cars. It is a beauty.

"Too late, Theon, you didn't escape my parents, sorry." She has a great smile, and it's aimed right at me as I turn to her.

"Hello, darling, what a nice surprise, having you here to greet us when we get home. I usually have to tear you away from your computer. Hello there, I'm Sonia, Eve's mother and you are?" She reaches her hand out to shake mine — shit I'm sweating. I wipe my palm on my top before shaking her hand,

"H-h-hello Mrs. Westcott, I'm Evelyn's friend Theon. Theon Tourney." I'm so nervous my voice is shaking. Just then her dad comes around to us. He eyes me suspiciously. I'm still holding Mrs. Westcott's hand. I drop it.

"Hello, darling." He leans in for a hug and kisses Evelyn on the cheek.

"I miss you, darling. I'm just glad we were able to get away to have dinner with you tonight. I want to hear all about your week." He puts his arm over her shoulder facing me.

"And who might this be?" he asks Evelyn looking directly into my eyes.

"This is Theon, my friend from school. We've been paired to do a project together. We were having a brainstorming session." Mr. Westcott puts his hand out to shake mine. I take his hand, stuttering again, "Nice to meet you s-s-sir." Shit, I feel stupid.

"Good to meet you too, Theon."

"Sweetie, would you like to join us for dinner?" Mrs. Westcott asks me

"He has to get back home, mother. He's having dinner with his grandma. I'll be inside in a couple of minutes. I'm just saying goodbye to Theon." I think that's Evelyn politely telling them to leave us. Thank god. She's good at reading me. She can see how nervous I am.

"Nice to have met you, Theon," Mrs. Westcott says as she heads inside.

"You too, ma'am. Sir." Mr. Wescott just nods, appraising me for a second, kisses Evelyn's temple then puts his hand on the bottom of Mrs. Westcott's back, directing her gently inside. I let out a breath I didn't realize I was holding.

"Tense huh?" Evelyn says to me. I run my hand through my black mass of curly hair that needs a cut.

"You could say that." I laugh.

"I must get going, Evelyn. Thanks for this. I had a great time. We seemed to get a lot done today, I'll see you tomorrow."

"I agree. I love sharing my ideas with someone who understands and is as enthusiastic as me. Bye, Theon. See you tomorrow."

I turn and walk down the steps and out of the drive heading home. I have a definite spring in my step. As soon as I turn the corner at the end of the road I set off running. I can't stop smiling when thinking about Evelyn as I run along the streets home. You would never know she comes from money, she doesn't act like she does and that puts me at ease. I'm pretty sure she won't judge me based on where I live, but it's not info I will freely share yet.

That was by far the best couple of hours of my life, and I'd say the best day of my life so far. There is no doubt I've fallen for this beautiful, unassuming girl. I can't wait for tomorrow.

Available on kindle
BUY LINKS FOR The Best Day of My Life
Amazon UK UK – https://amzn.to/2VfQqKy
Amazon US US – https://amzn.to/2GWVteT
Amazon Australia Au – https://amzn.to/2E3sH9l
Amazon Canada Ca - https://amzn.to/2IxudWH
Also on Kindle Unlimited - KU

MORE ABOUT LYNDA

Lynda lives in Cheshire in the UK with her husband Peter and cat Bailey also with two grown up daughters and an 11-year-old granddaughter.

She runs a successful financial business with her husband. As a young teenager Lynda used to read horror books with a love for everything Stephen King and James Herbert. She has always wanted to write and even wrote horror stories at age 13.

A little later she started reading Jackie Collins and Jilly Cooper and has always had a love of books. This then exploded with Twilight and Fifty Shades of Grey as it did with most people, oh, and the introduction of E-Readers.

In her spare time, she has a season ticket for Manchester City Football Club and goes to all the home games. Loves going to concerts and the theatre. She goes to the cinema at least once a week. Then when the weather is nice you can see her gliding down the road on her Harley Davidson 1200T motorbike. Travelling is also high on the agenda and her dream is to visit every state in the USA.

ACKNOWLEDGEMENTS

I wouldn't have done this without the help and support I got from friends and family.

First to my Husband who made time for me to write by running our business and the continued support he gives me, encouraging me to carry on.

My family and friends who read the book and gave me feedback.

My Editor Claire Allmendinger for guiding me through and being patient with me, as always.

Sybil Wilson from Pop Kitty for the amazing cover.

Stuart Reardon again for being on my cover and to him and Peter for the cover picture.

Cassy Roop from Pink Ink Designs for the fantastic formatting and making my words look pretty.

Thank you to everyone who supports me and reads my words.